IKIRI B

KEPT FROM CAGES

PHIL WILLIAMS

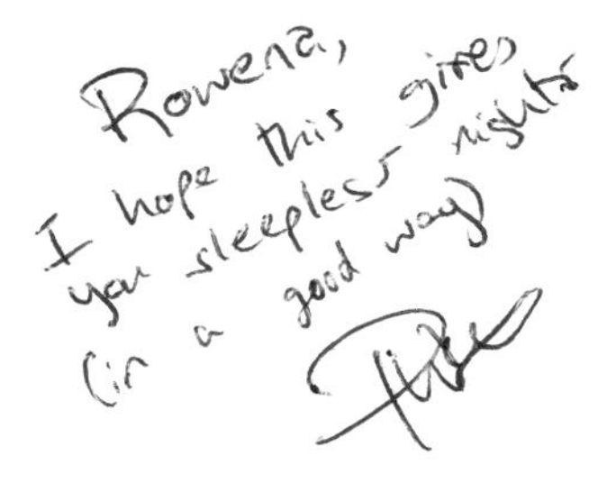

MMXX

ISBN-13: 978-1-913468-09-5

Cover design by P. Williams

Published by Rumian Publishing

Visit **www.phil-williams.co.uk** online for more information and regular news regarding the writing of Phil Williams.
Join the newsletter to be the first to hear about new projects.

1

"Don't blame yourself," Reece said, hefting Stomatt's unconscious bulk up the dirt track. "None of us guessed he lost that much blood."

"Even still," Caleb replied, stooping to help. "Shoulda been me behind the wheel. Always shoulda been me behind the wheel."

"He insisted, didn't he? What were you gonna do, two maniacs shooting at us?"

"Insist back!" Caleb's eyes shone in the dark. "Coulda said, 'No, listen, Sto, I'm driving.' Coulda got us clear with no hassle."

"We *got* clear, and you did *good*." Reece grinned. A grin that could charm the devil's horns off his head, Leigh-Ann liked to say. Even in a thick boiler suit, torn and dirtied from a day's fighting and fleeing, his hair dyed a murky green. They might be filthy and stinking and hurt in places they were yet to check, stranded on some unlit path to the middle of nowhere, but they were damn alive after taking on a billion-dollar company of thugs. Yeah, their car had flipped and they were still a long way from the safety of Stilt Town, let alone home, and Stomatt might be seriously injured – but they'd done what Reece said they would do and *won*. That's what the smile said, and Caleb smiled back.

"Sure," he said. "But we maybe shoulda switched driver. Made for the main roads after all?"

Reece checked the wood-panel house ahead again. A little further and they'd hit its two-step porch, knock and see who, exactly, lived in the empty fields halfway between Waco and Shreveport. Only an occasional tree on the black horizon told them they were anything short of stumbling through limbo itself. But lights shone yellow in the cross-barred windows, behind curtains – beacons to salvation.

"Reckon they cannibals?" Caleb said.

Reece traded his it's-all-good smile for his that'd-be-a-laugh one. Even if this wasn't the home of good honest farmhands, there wasn't much the Cutjaw Kids couldn't handle. They dragged Stomatt across a shingle drive, the scrape of boots on stone announcing their approach. Caleb grumbled, "Don't like leaving Leigh-Ann alone back there neither."

"She's better than fine," Reece said. "You wanna worry? Worry about how we're gonna spend all that money once we get back to Cutjaw."

The floorboards creaked as they climbed the steps. The only sound besides them breathing. All those lights on and nothing happening inside: no talking, no TV, no movement.

"Think they're not in?" Caleb said.

"Find out, won't we? Lower him here, easy."

With Stomatt propped against the wall, Reece straightened out the boiler suit and patted down his legs, then twisted his gun belt round so the pistol was hidden to his rear. Caleb caught his eye like he wanted to suggest something worrisome, and Reece smiled it off before it was said. Because everyone liked Reece once he got talking. He rapped a knuckle on the door. "Excuse me, good people! I know it's late but we're in bad need of assistance." No reply. "Had ourselves an accident back up the road. Damnedest thing, you wouldn't believe – car on its roof, and we got a man down."

Nothing. Caleb worried, "Think they heard us coming, hid away?"

"Why'd anyone hide from a couple harmless musicians?" Reece said. Caleb's eye tracked down to the gun belt. Reece curled his nose: even if they did see La Belle Riposte holstered there, it was an instrument as exquisite as his trumpet. And they were in Texas – who *didn't* have a gun? He knocked again. "Hate to be a burden, but my friend here lost a lot of blood – can't even stand right now." Still nothing. "We're decent people, like yourselves – just trying to get back home."

Caleb shifted. "We could try another one?"

"Another house?" Reece raised an eyebrow to indicate the hundred miles of nothing surrounding them. He called out, "We don't need to stay long, just got to patch up my friend – get him some water, fresh bandages. I gotta insist on that much at least." One last pause. "We'll make our own entrance if we have to."

"Better y'all go on your way!" a gruff voice finally answered – a big man.

"Gladly, with the barest assistance!" Reece answered amiably.

"Get on! What you're looking for's not here."

"All the same, if you could open up, it'd save –"

The door swung in on a man with a double-barrelled shotgun. "I said –"

Reece spoke over him fast: "No need for that, sir, we didn't come looking for trouble. Name's Reece Coburn, horn-maestro, as reviewed in *Two Shoots Magazine*, and this here's my associate Caleb 'Low Bone' Gray – heard of him?"

The man's mouth hung open in surprise, his threat trapped there. He was large with over-indulgence, someone that could knock you down with a swat if it didn't give him a heart attack. His ruddy face was partly hidden by a tangled beard, and he had on a faded check shirt, leather suspenders clipped to mud-caked jeans. Over his shoulder, in a doorway down the hall, was another man, as lean as the first was wide, snub-nosed, warty-faced, with shirt and jeans as tatty as a scarecrow's. Unarmed and nervous.

"What?" The shotgun farmer recovered slowly from Reece's friendliness, eyes darting to the green hair and back. "No, listen here – get on back down that road or I'll –"

"We would *kindly* get on," Reece said, "but see, Caleb and me with our tender frames, we're not up to carrying this burden far." Reece scuffed a foot to draw attention to Stomatt. The farmer looked at the bleached-blond oaf splattered black with dry blood.

"The hell –"

Reece stepped into the kitchen, pushed the shotgun down with one hand and drew his pistol with the other. Stunned the farmer with his speed, as his companion exclaimed, "Jesus!"

"Stay put, friend, and relax," Reece said, grip tight on the shotgun. "I got no intention of hurting you, I mean it. Water, medicine, shelter, that's all we want. Our priority's keeping him alive. Anything else is a bonus we won't assume." Moving around the farmer, Reece sped on, "You *can't* have heard of us – two parts of the Cutjaw Kids – otherwise you'd know we're decent people, only ever hurt them that deserve it." The slim man threw an instinctive glance back, into the next room. Blocking that doorway for a reason. Reece slowed down. "We interrupt something?"

The farmer went rigid on his shotgun, for a second seeming like he might pull the trigger just to shake Reece off. Reece warned him against it with a casual wave of the pistol.

"Caleb, you haul Sto in here?"

"I'll try," Caleb answered honestly, and gave the farmer an apologetic look as he started to manoeuvre Stomatt's bulk through the doorway.

"Listen," Reece said. "We got problems enough of our own not to interfere with yours. But I think you oughta let go of this gun now."

The farmer didn't shift. Caleb huffed upright from struggling with Stomatt. "Want I should cover him, Reece?"

"Wish you didn't have to."

"Go to hell," the farmer said.

"That'll be a yes."

Caleb drew a pistol from inside his boiler suit. "Got him."

The farmer gave him a sceptical glance. People tended to go one of two ways with Caleb; kind-faced, softly-spoken, hunched with self-consciousness, he struck people as either slow enough to take advantage of or too quietly calm to trust. After a moment, the farmer settled on the latter, and finally loosened his grip on the shotgun. Reece took it. "Now what's the fuss?"

The slim one straightened up. "You ain't coming through here, no way –"

The man flattened himself against a wall as Reece pushed past into the next room. The farmer called out, an explanation or a dismissal. Reece didn't hear it. A woman on the far side of the room gasped, but she wasn't his concern. Dead centre, with the other furniture cleared to the sides, was a girl no older than seven, sat on a wooden chair. Her arms, legs and chest were bound by thick leather belts. Her black hair hung in locks over hazel skin, the white of her eyes haloing big dark irises that fixed on Reece.

Reece glanced at the woman for an explanation; young but built big, in the same farming slacks as the men. Likely the farmer's daughter. She cringed at the pistol, too scared to speak. Reece turned back to Slim, who raised his hands.

"Ain't what it looks like! She's the devil, I swear!"

"What is it, Reece?" Caleb asked.

"Like y'all ain't involved?" the farmer snarled.

"What in hell kind of –" Reece spun back to the girl. "They hurt you? Jesus – what'd they do –"

He crouched, about to grab her bindings, when Slim pleaded,

"No, don't!" He flinched at Reece's pistol but continued, "Look at her eyes!"

Holding his gun steady, Reece checked the girl again. Her gently dark skin was marred around the extremities: grubby at her neck, dark under the eyes and nose, scratched. She had on a white t-shirt and denim dungarees, all stained – fallen in mud a few times. Her gaze hadn't left him since he entered. Eyes massive in her face. The irises, now he looked, were red as blood.

"You see it, don't you?" Slim said.

"Don't bother, Donny," the farmer growled from the hallway. "Think they come rolling in here by chance? With all that thing's been saying?"

"Dammit," Caleb said, "let's see."

Reece frowned as Caleb pushed the farmer into the room. "That *thing*?"

"Ho-*ly* hell," Caleb gasped, over the farmer's shoulder.

"She ain't right." The farmer's daughter found her voice, a squeak. Terrified as slim Donny, getting busted like this.

"We wanted to *help* her, man!" Donny insisted. "But she says things –"

"Get yourself up against that wall," Reece said. "The pair of you. And you" – to the woman – "untie this goddamn child."

"I ain't staying." Donny made a move. "Not if she's loose."

"Please," the girl said, weakly. Donny winced. "Help me …"

Reece said, "None of y'all are leaving. Didn't I ask you to untie her?"

"Don't you dare," the farmer rumbled, before his daughter could budge.

"You miss the part where we got guns on you?" Caleb asked. "Shit, I'll do it –" He stepped forward and the farmer lunged for the gun. The pair of them twisted over it, the farmer's weight bearing them to the ground. Donny sprang for the door and tripped, the stumble making Reece's shot hit the wall where his head should've been. The farmer shouted murderously, grappling with Caleb, and the daughter screamed, as Donny dived out the room and Reece's second shot hit the doorframe.

A third shot sounded, muffled by Caleb's scuffle. The farmer's angry shout spiked and Caleb yelled, "Get this fat bastard off me!" But Reece was running through the hallway, as Donny sprawled spider-like out across the drive. Reece aimed as he reached the door, but hit a patch of Stomatt's blood and slid, landing on his rear. He scrambled upright and saw a last slither of Donny's angular joints slipping into shadow. Man moved like a damn greyhound.

Caleb grunted around the farmer's bulk and the daughter's screams turned to fierce curses. Caleb insisted, "Ma'am, you saw him attack me! Woulda killed me!"

Reece trotted back to the living room to find the farmer inert on the carpet, blood pooling under his chest. His daughter was shuddering in a crouch as Caleb stood over her, gun at his side. "Stop screaming, please – I didn't want to have to do it!"

And in the middle of the chaos sat the red-eyed girl, eyes locked on Reece again. Afraid. Reece holstered his gun and took a knee. "It's gonna be alright, cher. We've got you." The farmer's daughter kept whimpering, *no no no*.

Rapid footsteps came over the entrance boards and both Reece and Caleb spun with pistols raised. It was Leigh-Ann, running in with a MAC-10 submachine gun and a deadly look on her face. Reece yelled, "Dammit Leigh there's a kid in here!"

She shouted, "What in hell are y'all doing?"

The shrieked question stilled the room, even the farmer's daughter going quiet. The trio of gun-toting criminals looked at each other, the dead farmer and tied-up girl. Reece stood, in silent admission that this had got well out of hand.

Leigh-Ann laughed. "Shit, boys, this your idea of getting help?"

2

The closer he got, the more Agent Sean Tasker, Ministry of Environmental Energy, hoped something was actually wrong in the fishing village of Laukstad. He'd been sceptical flying from Tokyo to Norway, and for the three-hour drive from Tromsø, and occupied his mind trying to focus on the snow-blanketed mountains that he could describe to his daughter Rebecca, rather than consider how he was travelling especially far for this latest dead-end lead. His driver and escort, Police Inspector Akre, refused to believe there was anything worth investigating. Red-faced and cheery, he had explained that Laukstad had sporadic phone connections at the best of times, so two days without hearing from the village was nothing. Three days, by the time Tasker arrived, was slightly unusual, but not enough to raise alarm. Snowstorms might have cut them off, but the villagers would be taking care of themselves.

Tasker imagined some slick-suited bastards in corporate offices laughing at him, redirecting MEE resources to the strangest possible places, to find nothing amiss. This "lead" had come from Duvcorp, after all, a corporation known for making their own rules. Some bored Duvcorp researcher had told a newbie MEE director that they'd picked up unusual energy readings out here, so why not have an agent travel all the way from Japan to check it out? Well. It was about time he came home to debrief anyway, and he hadn't seen Helen and Rebecca in three months, but even so – the deputy director had lapped it up, insisting this contact was going behind Duvcorp's back, giving the Ministry a unique chance to subvert them. Tasker knew better than to trust that crap. Most likely, it was revenge for him hounding Duvcorp's mates in Tokyo, Mogami Industries. Some vindictive Duvcorp strategist figured exactly how to position this so that it'd be him making this hopeless journey.

But as Tasker watched the roads getting narrower, winding and remote, he found *some* hope creeping in that this might be an exception, at last, and he could actually take one of these companies down a peg and make a difference.

Duvcorp had exploded into the American automobile industry in the late 1970s and reinvested huge profits into electronics, to become world-leaders in computing technology in the '90s. Their components quickly became ubiquitous: whether you settled on a Mac or a PC, you still got a Duvcorp sticker somewhere. Making all the right connections in business and government, they soon became one of a handful of corporations who wielded as much power as the governments who might hold them accountable. And, somewhere along the way, they got wind of the technology the Ministry tried to keep out of the public eye. Unexplained phenomena, dangerous curiosities. It was simple enough to keep a lid on individuals and smaller entities, but Duvcorp were too powerful to regulate. Putting untold lives at risk.

Every four or five months, Tasker found some way to humble a big corporation, when their latest (classified) technology was revealed to be dangerously esoteric. Ferociously catastrophic events were averted and mid-level fall-guys were imprisoned (or conveniently disappeared), and Tasker could go back to his wife and daughter proud that he was Making a Difference. He had to be, to justify staying away from home for so long, missing Rebecca growing up, leaving Helen alone, even if she always managed words of support when they spoke. He wanted to be with them both, badly, but more than that he wanted to come home knowing it was safe. These corporations were stretching their grubby claws into every corner of the world; it was only a matter of time before one of them accidentally unleashed some unholy force in their own backyard.

He'd travelled to Tokyo for that; seeing that Mogami now had connections in Ordshaw, UK, he needed to know exactly what they were up to. But Mogami's Japanese prosthetics project had been swept under the rug before Tasker had uncovered exactly what untold horrors they'd been experimenting with. They'd probably resurface in two years, building clones or engineering war spiders or something.

Everything about Laukstad felt like an opportunity to double his losses. The snow cover was thick on the roads, no one had been in or out of this area in days – all he was going to find was a town whose phone-lines had gone down. They probably had Duvcorp hardware up here, that was how the informer had known . . .

After a final turn, the village sat ominously below, at the bottom of a steep slope, by the harshly churning sea, in the eerie mid-afternoon dark. Akre grunted at the wheel to say he felt something was off. Tasker felt it too, tensing at the too-quiet scene.

They drove closer and the officer slowed right down. He whispered a Norwegian curse. Tasker leant into the windscreen to see why. Laukstad was a tiny community, not more than a dozen timber houses, a jetty and swaying boats. All unlit. Its single road was scattered with bumps of snow, like a mess of randomly placed speed bumps. The length and height of prone bodies. The closest one had a smaller bump out to the side – like an outstretched arm. Bodies was right, buried under snow.

Akre stopped, cursing again in whole sentences Tasker didn't need to translate to understand. Disbelief and fear and outrage. The officer turned a questioning face to Tasker, like he would know what was going on here. Tasker did not, but the Duvcorp lead had contacted his Ministry for a reason. Whatever this was – and it *looked* like a lot of people dead – then it must border on the unnatural. A test gone wrong, a substance spilt, or worse? A creature set loose?

"Have your gun ready," Tasker advised, drawing his own pistol from under the heavy winter coat. Akre nodded, doing the same but clutching his weapon tightly. They hopefully wouldn't need them. Whatever happened here happened days ago. When Duvcorp's leak said so.

They each took a torch and exited the 4x4 into a biting gust of wind. It passed in a second, having taken the top dusting off one of the nearest mounds, revealing boots underneath. Akre rushed ahead to brush handfuls of snow away, uncovering a man with taut clutching fingers, eyes open under a shimmer of ice, blood frozen around his neck and chest and mouth. His throat had been torn out as though by a wild animal or a jagged tool. Fishing hook or wolves, who could tell the difference now? Tasker's gut hinted worse. What lurked in the Arctic circle? The ice jackals of Archangel had been culled years ago, but it wasn't unthinkable.

Akre shook all over with horror, so Tasker patted his shoulder to indicate they move on.

There wasn't enough left of the next body's smashed face to preserve the pain and terror.

Tasker stepped away as Akre radioed back to Tromsø in stuttering starts. He noticed other mounds in the snow, now – smaller ones. Bits of debris and household items partly covered. A long pole stuck out of one buried body like a grave marker. Harpoon? Windows in the buildings were shattered. A door rocked against its hinges. Another had been broken off entirely, jammed across its entrance. Walking between the bodies, looking into the dark recesses of the houses, Tasker saw how the people had fallen, chased out of their own homes? There was blood around a door jamb. Smashed crockery in one entrance. He moved closer. Another body in there, feet pointing out, opposite direction to those that died fleeing. He crouched and gasped at the likeness. It could easily be Rebecca – a girl no older than ten with frozen blonde hair, stubby nose, and a death-mask of terror, neck raked by four claw marks and a chunk bitten from her cheek. How could this happen – what manner of monster left marks like this, a bite that size and shape? He moved from the girl to the next nearest body, a woman fallen while fleeing from the building. A horrible gash ripped from her throat. He brushed the snow away from her hand, revealing nails cracked and bloody. Whatever this was, these people had fought against it, coming and going.

"What happened?" Akre demanded, torch-hand shaking. "I don't see any animal tracks."

Tasker cleared his throat, swallowed, making like he was giving the massacred village another careful look while trying to stop his voice coming out in a frightened squeak. He tried not to picture the worst, that this was Rebecca and Helen, that this was so close to home. "Cut off out here, four hours of sunlight a day, must've been people not right in the head. Junkies on a spiked batch of drugs or outsiders with a bad religion?"

Akre wore a horrified expression Tasker was all too familiar with. The policeman could scarcely believe such a thing possible, *knowing* things like this didn't just happen, but forcing himself to take this mysterious expert's explanation seriously. Akre couldn't know there was only one reason for the Ministry to have been alerted to this. This wasn't a random attack. Someone or something had made this happen, with means that would be anything but natural.

*

"No weapons used that weren't the basic tools they had lying around," Tasker confirmed to Caffery, his handler, over the phone. "Teeth marks, clawing from fingernails, lot of blunt force, but no signs of unusual tracks in or out of the village."

"Not ice jackals, then," Caffery said.

"My instinct says there's a human element, or something close to it," Tasker admitted. Were there reports of yeti in Norway? He doubted it; this felt messier. "There was a fight, or at least the start of one. These people *thought* they could defend themselves. But so far they've not identified anyone who shouldn't have been there, and it doesn't look like anything was taken. It's like some gang of killers swept in from the mountains or off the sea and disappeared in the mist."

"A cult?" Caffery replied hopefully. "Or a particularly effective mass-murderer. Unthinkable, sure, but perfectly human."

"Except someone in Duvcorp knew it was happening."

A couple of hours of surveying with extra hands flown in from Tromsø turned up little more they could go on. Back in the main station, the officers milled about in stages between vengefully angry and utterly devastated. They insisted it never happened – people were *used* to these conditions – but he insisted back, it *could* happen. A mass psychosis brought on by isolation and dark. There was one glaring discrepancy, though: how had an Englishman happened to check on it?

For the locals' sake, Tasker settled on his usual ground somewhere between the truth and a cover. He explained that they monitored for unusual energy readings, this one being a particularly dramatic change in atmospheric pressure. Something *like* atmospheric pressure, he corrected – in case their meteorological offices disagreed. Chances were the weather had been affected by whatever Duvcorp picked up on, anyway. Could this anomaly have driven a group of people to brutal murder for no good reason? Sure, possibly.

Besides the chill mystery of exactly what had happened – and how the killers had left no traces of their retreat – Tasker found himself most concerned with what in hell it had to do with Duvcorp. Their mole must have been aware that something was going down. Concerned to the degree that they would go behind their employer's back. Tasker told Caffery, "I recommend sending a Support team up, take energy readings on the ground, see if anything unusual was left on the bodies."

"Done," Caffery replied. "You staying on the ground to ease them in?"

"I've seen all I need to," Tasker said. "I want to talk to the mole myself, as soon as possible. It was the Ordshaw Ministry that put us onto this, right? Have them pick him up."

"I can put in a request to Duvcorp's management –"

"Pick him up, Caffery, as soon as possible."

Caffery went quiet. He was technically Tasker's superior, but as Tasker was the one physically wading through these messes, it was rare that London didn't accede to his demands. "The Commission won't have us provoking a company like Duvcorp."

"Yeah, not without an airtight case, which we won't get without provocation."

"What *case*, Tasker? Duvcorp picked up on this, but it doesn't mean they're involved."

"Please, everything that company touches stinks. You don't want to pick up their mole, at least put a man on him until I get there. Which will be how long?"

Caffery sighed deeply, like Tasker was the bane of his existence. Eighteen people dead, and he had the gall to sound put out by Tasker's travel demands and willingness to cross a big company. "I'll look into it. Meantime, you keep a lid on things there."

"Already done," Tasker said. Unlike some people, he didn't need telling to do his job. But saying that, he saw more looks coming his way across the station. Upset cops, wanting to blame him, suspecting he knew more than he was letting on. Well, it couldn't be a rabid doppler; they stayed mostly hidden, and the massacre clearly wasn't the work of one creature. The venom of the *tremer vesper* might induce madness, if Duvcorp had poured that into the village's water supply. But why would they? And if they had done this deliberately, where was the clear-up? The only thing he did know was that the answers weren't here in Norway.

3

"Here, rest here, cher," Reece said, lowering the girl onto a squeaky bed. She weighed nothing but he had to prise her fingers off him. Her unusual eyes glowed with desperation. *Don't let go.* "Sorry you had to see that, but you're safe now, understand? How you end up here – with them?"

Her lower lip trembled.

"You're *safe* – it's over." Reece stepped back and smiled to show it, triggering tears. She pressed her face into her small hands. He glanced to the empty doorway, half-expecting Stomatt to jump in laughing at her for crying. But Stomatt was unconscious downstairs, with Leigh-Ann tending to him, while Caleb hunted after Donny. The kid was Reece's responsibility alone.

She whimpered, almost too quiet to hear, "I want to go home."

"Sure," Reece said. "Where's home, cher? How you get here?"

Sniffing in her last sobs, the girl knotted her brow against the question.

"How about a name? I'm Reece" – he put a hand on his chest – "and you?"

She braced herself, then said, "Zip."

"Your name's Zip?"

She nodded.

"Weird, but I *like* it." He wore a goofy grin. Zip watched his teeth suspiciously. "Zip's a real pretty name. These people, Zip, they take you from your family? Your school?" She shook her head. "So where you live? My friends and me, we come outta Cutjaw, Louisiana – you ever heard of a place like that?"

Another head shake, getting curious.

"Long way from here, right now. Cutjaw's like nowhere you've been, we got swamp and a river nearby, every family a different trailer. You ever slept in a trailer? No? Well, we live in them.

People in Cutjaw work wood, mechanics, all good with our hands – decent, family folk."

Zip watched him warily, and her eyes ran up to the green hair.

Reece ran a hand through it, laughing. Seemed a good idea at the time – confuse anyone looking for him once he washed it back to black. "Ah, this – *not* my natural colour. Part of this shabby costume, see." He picked at the boiler suit. "We do *not* normally look like this. The Cutjaw Kids are usually the most best dressed crewe you ever saw. That's *crewe* with an *e* – making us like family. I got no brothers but Caleb and Sto are my kin. Leigh's got no dad but mine treats her like a daughter, see? You got brothers, sisters? Mama, a daddy?"

Zip considered it carefully. "Dad."

"Just a dad?"

She nodded apologetically.

"Well, stick with us and we'll be your family. Cutjaw moms raise us to take care of strangers. Talk proper round kids and ladies. Respect elders and all that. We even came into Texas to do some good." Reece pointed vaguely, probably in the direction they'd come. Maybe not. "Working with Caleb's uncle, against people that would take advantage of us in Cutjaw or elsewhere. We're good people, see?"

"You've got guns," Zip whispered.

Reece paused, then twisted his gun belt forward. "This? This isn't any old *gun*. You looking at La Belle Riposte. A work of art. Wanna hold it?"

Zip blinked disbelief. Yes, he was offering a child a gun.

"Maybe later, huh? We armed because of people like them downstairs, Zip. We been into Waco to tell some bad men *No*. Same as we told them *no* downstairs, understand?" She didn't entirely. But the kid didn't need all the details of how Steer Trust had been forcibly expanding their "Gold Star" network into Louisiana. How the gang had valiantly combined sending a message that Louisiana didn't want them with stealing a lot of money. He diverted: "Speak funny, don't I? That's Cutjaw – ain't no one talk like us, no one play music like us, no one play *cards* like us. Like that where you're from? Your home special?"

Zip remained silent. She did *not* want to talk about home.

"You local, at least? Don't look like a Texan."

Her face crumpled guiltily. "No."

Reece laughed, lightly. "Then how you get all the way out here? Cher, please. Tell me something, I'm dying here."

"I . . ." Zip searched the carpet for an answer. "I wanted to help. My daddy. He didn't know – he never let me – said I *always* should stay home –" Speaking quicker, upset. "Never follow, never talk to strangers, never *think* about it –"

"Slow down," Reece said. "Your daddy ain't gonna blame you, okay?" Her accent was a clue, at least. Cracked from dryness and crying, but refined, almost British. Fancy folk in country estates adopted accents like that. "You got a big house?"

She shook her head, then stopped rigid, realising she was giving something away.

"All right. I'll have to earn that trust, won't I? So you were supposed to stay home but followed your daddy to work, that's how it went? But these folk picked you up along the way?"

Zip swallowed, then nodded.

"So forget home a second – where might Daddy be?"

She considered this carefully. "There was a big river. A blue pyramid. Grithin."

"A griffin?"

"Gri*th*in," Zip accentuated the sound, tongue against her teeth. Definitely moneyed.

"Forgive my ignorance. Gri*th*in it is. Well I don't know that for dirt, nor a blue pyramid, but I know rivers. Gushing like the Mississippi or piddling like a creek?"

"Mississippi." Zip liked that word. "Mississippi. Yes. Mississippi. That's a very big river?"

"The biggest. But that's three hundred miles away."

She went quiet again, like she'd done something wrong.

"Hey, I'm not saying that's not it," Reece said. "Only that's a long way for a kid. Your daddy had business there, did he?"

Her lip trembled again, eyes worried. Tired, stressed.

"Tell you what, let's have a break. Important thing is we're friends now, ain't we? I'll get you a hot drink. Have Caleb put on a Cutjaw stew. You talk when you're ready, doesn't have to be a second before."

He moved towards the door and fear at being left crept into those big eyes. She voiced it in a simple, bleated word: "Reece?"

Reece grinned back in at her. "We'll take care of you. That's a promise."

Leigh-Ann perched on the chair-back with a foot where the girl had been bound, staring hard, wondering what the fuck these yokels were up to. The living room was heady with the stench of stale blood and sweat. The farmer lay against one wall, rolled in a rug, and Stomatt was hanging half off the three-seat sofa. He was even paler than usual, and his bleached-blond hair was patterned like a hyena's hide with blood and dirt. Leigh-Ann had removed his jacket and wound a clean bandage round his neck, while the farmer's daughter cowered in an armchair.

Mostly, Leigh-Ann was marvelling at how they'd managed to make a shitty day this much worse. The gunshots from the farmhouse had come right when her nerves were finally calming from the car crash, and the crash had come only when her nerves started to calm after escaping Waco. They'd started the day prepared for a fight but hoping there wouldn't be one. Only Stomatt had been overjoyed at finding more Steers in the warehouse than they expected. Now at least three of Dustin Fallon's men were injured or dead and Stomatt was shot. Leigh-Ann didn't think she'd hit anyone herself, laying down covering fire, but who knew? And now they'd offed a random farmer and had a distraught daughter hostage – a woman even younger than them.

Leigh-Ann moved to a counter and found some mail. Mr Hexley, that'd be the farmer. One addressed to Ms N. She asked, "That you? *N*?"

The daughter didn't look up.

"*N* Hexley. What were you up to here, *N*? Why you couldn't leave that kid alone? *N*, you gonna talk to me?" Leigh-Ann tapped the MAC-10 against her thigh. The daughter saw that. "Come on, *N*."

"Nina," the woman said. "My name's *Nina*."

"There's a girl. And why's *Nina* Hexley kidnapping kids?"

Nina stared back boiling hatred.

Leigh-Ann smiled. Reece entered to interrupt their clash of intellects, so she fixed on him instead. "Here's a quote, Reece Coburn, circa eighteen minutes ago: 'What's the worst that can happen?' Didn't I warn you never say shit like that? And another one, 'They're probably decent folk.'"

"I'll admit on this occasion I was wrong," Reece said, scanning Stomatt.

"Don't he look peaceful? Not running his filthy mouth nor snoring up a storm. Oughta get shot in the throat more often."

"He gonna be okay?" Reece asked. "He said it only clipped him."

"He also claims he met Kid Ory – you believed that, too?" Leigh-Ann blew air out her teeth. "Bullet took a chunk of flesh with it, but he's okay. Just bled more than a little. He'll get back to pissing us all off once he wakes, mark my words. More than can be said for some." She nodded to the farmer's body.

Caleb came in the other door, grumbling. "Had no choice. You saw, didn't you Reece? He went for my gun. He woulda shot *me*."

"No sign of our friend Donny?" Reece asked.

Caleb shook his head. "Got as far as the fence and lost his tracks. Figure he cut across a field on foot, but there's no houses for miles. His truck's out front, I reckon – three vehicles, total. I took out the spark plug cables. Can we get going, Reece? This place gives me the creeps."

There was a question. Half-hour ago they were making good time, now they had a kidnapped child and a house of horrors to deal with. Leigh-Ann said, "That kid okay?"

"Near as I can see," Reece said. "She's not saying much. But I figure she's an awful long way from wherever she's supposed to be."

"So are we."

"We got time. Donny's not going to the cops, is he? Worst case, he comes back with some friends, and if they're involved in this I'd happily give them a piece of my mind. But my bet is he's halfway to Alaska." He indicated the daughter. "She spoken?"

"Name's *Nina*," Leigh-Ann said. "That's as far as we got."

"Nina?" Reece echoed. There were those hate-eyes again. "We're all sorry about your old man. Even if maybe we shouldn't be. Wanna explain your side?"

"Go to hell," Nina said. "Murderers – animals, bastard pigs –"

Leigh-Ann snorted laughter and clapped a hand over her mouth. "Sorry – this bitch is moralising at us? Like, we're gonna be judged by child molesters?"

"Cut it out, Leigh." Reece said. "She mightn't have had a choice. Did you?"

Nina had another insult waiting, but held it in.

"Not so sure it was molesting anyway," Reece said. "That kid's well-spoken. Dirty but not hurt. Maybe your old man wanted to lean on her rich parents, Nina?"

"He was a good man!" Nina spat at him. "You came in with guns!"

"What choice we have?" Caleb said, too loudly. "Answered that door with a shotgun, he did. Then snatches at my weapon? A guy tying up *kids*? I'm putting that bastard down eight days in a week."

"She needed binding!" Nina's voice rose too, veins popping up on her neck. "Promising we're all gonna die! Screaming murder in her sleep! She's got a devil in her, look in her damn eyes!" She went to stand, but Leigh-Ann took a step towards her and she dropped back.

"Nina," Reece said, "you gotta do better than that. Where the kid come from?"

"You tell me!" Nina snorted. "You're the ones came for her, exactly as promised!"

The gang exchanged looks. No one could've been expecting them – only got into Texas last night, hit the Steers dressed in masks, switched cars, and only diverted up these lanes on Reece's snap decision. Shit, they'd even left their phones back in Stilt Town so no one could ever track them.

"Nothing to do with us," Reece said. "We're here by happy chance. Lucky for her."

"Plenty places we'd rather be," Leigh-Ann added.

Nina faltered, but shook her head. "No. You're the same wickedness. Why else you come and kill – kill –" She choked on the word. Tears in her eyes. "That kid turned up on *our* land. We tried to *help*. Spiteful little monster. She came in making threats – said trouble was coming."

"She's out of her mind," Leigh-Ann decided, then told Nina, "If any of that's true, this *ain't* a rational way to deal with a kid making threats."

"And she sure didn't summon us," Caleb said.

"Then who in hell are you?" Nina snapped. "How *dare* you! You animals! Get out of my house! Get out!" She sprang up and shoved Reece with both hands. He took a step and pushed back on instinct, sending Nina over the armchair. She fell near her dead dad and froze on her hands and knees; the sight of him rolled up in carpet made her slide lower, blubbering, the fight all knocked out of her.

Caleb took a step forward to pick her up, comfort her, but Leigh-Ann caught his arm. He shook her off with annoyance, but stopped where he was.

"Caleb," Reece said, a little strained for once, "do me good and take Nina here to her room? Secure her. We'll have a chat once she's calmed down."

"What –" The woman turned with panic.

Caleb closed on her quickly, showing his pistol but saying politely, "If you'd be so kind. I don't want to do nothing we'll all regret."

"And you come with me, Leigh. Let's get our shit out the car."

Leigh-Ann held down the urge to resist for the hell of it, didn't need telling what to do now. But with Nina bucking against Caleb she figured she had the better job.

She headed outside, scuffing her boots, Reece just behind her. Back down the long dirt road to their overturned car, both of them watching shadows along the way, in case Donny was waiting after all. They reached the car and admired Stomatt's handiwork – the thing lying dead and crumpled on its roof. A miracle they all made it out unscathed. Together, they squeezed the big black duffel bags out past bent metal and broken glass. Damn heavy; one filled with guns and the other stuffed with more cash than any of them had ever seen. Leigh-Ann unzipped it just to look at it. Reece grinned, too.

The gang were now richer in their twenties than most Cutjaw trash got their whole lives. Alban Gray in Stilt Town still had to clean the cash, but they were as good as free. Reece had delivered exactly as he said he would. His easy smile as they hefted the bags up promised he'd figure this latest setback out, too. Leigh-Ann's bag clanked as they walked; somehow she'd ended up with the one full of guns. Definitely the heavier of the two.

"Prefer to swap?" Reece offered.

Leigh-Ann kept on walking. "I'd prefer you found us a place where the locals welcomed us with apple pie. Didn't think we'd have to kill anyone else today."

"Well," Reece said. "Imagine if we didn't come out here when we did. That kid."

"Yeah," Leigh-Ann said. "Assuming we're any better for her than them. It wasn't all good, what we did today, Reece."

"No." He didn't deny it. Didn't remind her everyone on Fallon's payroll knew who they were working for. Steers had gone into gas stops busting up displays, broken a guy's wrist near Shreveport. Spread slander online about anyone not paying premiums to join their loyalty network. That didn't exactly forgive killing them, so all Reece said was, "Saving a child's a step in the right direction, though."

"What're we gonna do with her? Stilt Town's no place for kids."

"They got families there."

"You know what I mean."

Reece hummed concession.

Yeah. They needed Stilt Town for shelter, to process the cash they'd stolen, and all of that, but Alban Gray and his progeny were not Leigh-Ann's favourite commune of God-bothering loons. She pointed out, "They think I'm unholy for being Black with tits – what's a kid with red eyes to them? Might find they agree with Nina."

"They think you're unholy for living a life of vice," Reece reminded her. "Gray's not gonna have a problem with her. Trust me, Leigh. It's a *good* thing we found her. We get to be heroes twice in one day."

She could believe he'd convinced himself of that already. The world didn't hold Reece Coburn back. "Only you could come out of a shitty day smellin' of roses."

But he smiled again and it was infectious.

"So we taking one of their rides, then? It's late as hell."

"No," Reece said. "The kid's shook up, Sto's down and we got no idea where we are. It's time for a break, I say. Food, sleep, get out of here come dawn. No one's finding us here, are they?"

Leigh-Ann wanted to argue. Sensible thing was to plough right on. Like any of them had the momentum to keep going all night long. But hell, the invitation was there now and she wasn't batting it away. She wasn't ever turning down food and sleep. They came back into the farmhouse and she tossed the bag down in the kitchen, calling out to Caleb to rustle up dinner. Meantime, she prowled back through the house looking for the master bedroom. A big room upstairs, where a couple photos of the dead farmer and his presumably gone wife scowled at the bed. This would do. And damn if she didn't need to get out of this boiler suit. Made her look even more like an overgrown Popsicle than usual, with her skinny neck and massive ball of hair sticking out the top of formless drab blue. She wrestled at it, got it down to her ankles when Caleb entered. He recoiled – spent their whole lives together and the idiot still got bashful at a bit of flesh. Leigh-Ann breezed over it. "Food ready?"

Caleb nodded, lingering in the door. "But first we gonna move the . . . out to the barn." Didn't wanna call a corpse a corpse. The guilt hunched his shoulders up. And it left him falling back on old instincts, gravitating her way for comfort. Never mind Leigh-Ann wasn't ever thinking of him as more than a brother.

With the day they'd had, she threw him a bone. "When we're done, you crash here with me. Plenty room in the fat man's bed. You keep your hands to yourself."

His face screwed up – not expecting that. "There's floorspace in the office, or I could be watching over Sto." Yet he lingered.

Leigh-Ann put her hands on her hips. He wanted to talk, or for her to talk to him, to let him know he was still good people, the way Reece did for her. But she wasn't Reece and didn't want to be. She said, "If you're gonna sleep on any floor, might as well be here so you can keep watch over me. Now show me what the hell you cooked up."

4

"Agent Tasker?" As he left the arrivals terminal, a woman in a dark suit approached. Short and mousy with the uncertainty of an intern. "Deputy Director Ward. Is that all your baggage?"

Tasker stopped. He was aware that Ordshaw's new deputy director was young, but at least expected a go-getter arranging power meetings in central offices, not someone who'd pick up subordinates from the airport herself. How understaffed were they? She was keenly waiting for a response, making him look at the bag. "Yeah. I don't need much more than a spare suit and toiletries."

"Then we can get moving. I thought it best I come personally. I've got some bad news." She turned her back on him and started marching before he could confront that bombshell. Ward led Tasker through scattered crowds and out into a car park, with occasional tosses of small talk: how was your flight? How was Tokyo? Did you have any problems with the Norwegian police? He dismissed it all with growing irritation that she had let him stew on the *bad news*.

"We've put you up in the Grand Hotel, in Central, I hope you'll like it," Ward said. Then added, a little graver, "The least we can do."

He slowed down, now they were alone in a quiet alley of parked cars. "What's happened?"

Ward scanned their surroundings, no one around. Over her shoulder, through the gap between floors, was the steel sky of cloudy England. Drab, disappointing England. She said, "Someone reached Parris before us."

"Piss and hell," Tasker huffed, looking away from her disappointed face. She didn't comment, so he went on: "I've just come from a damn open graveyard. We had one lead. One *pissing* lead." He took a breath, closed his eyes, and remembered this was *not* just another hapless escort. Even if she was ten or fifteen years younger than him. "Apologies, Deputy Director, I mean no disrespect."

"I'm the one who should apologise, Agent Tasker. I sent an agent as soon as I got word from London, but it was already too late."

"How bad?"

"Bad," Ward admitted, then continued towards a little Honda Civic. Not a director's car. "I've got a file for you."

Tasker got in and checked the glove box as Ward started the engine. He took out a manila folder which would no doubt contain details of the featureless, traceless death of a corporation target. Duvcorp and the like were rumoured to have "fixers" on their payrolls, so good at hiding their crimes you'd never know they were there. It was why Tasker spent half his life checking surfaces for poisons and worrying about unattended vehicles, and he'd had more than a few arguments with Helen by shifting those fears onto her. But the photos inside were not what he expected.

Duvcorp's researcher, Simon Parris, was captured slumped in a bathtub, one jaggedly cut arm hanging over the edge. Blood all around him, across the porcelain, sprayed up his face and across the tile floor. Tasker turned over one photo then another while Ward, eyes averted, started the car and pulled them out. As staged suicides went, it was crude.

"Don't suppose he left a note?" Tasker asked dryly.

Wards took it seriously. "No. And it's stranger than it looks."

"He was pregnant?" That got a frown. "Sorry, gallows humour."

Ward hummed, preferring to brood on it. Hell, they just lost a crucial contact, wasn't he allowed some deflection. As Ward studied the traffic with exaggerated care, Tasker sat back and mused, "Someone got to him after he leaked information. Suggesting he wasn't on their radar before he talked to us."

That got an even more uncomfortable look from Ward. She put it off a second, pulling out into the flow of the motorway, and finally said, "I've considered that. The information passed through a lot of hands between me, you and Norway. There was discussion in London about it. Half a dozen people with all their assistants could've tipped someone off."

"Great," Tasker said. He tapped the folder. "So how'd this go down?"

"Our agent was the first on the scene," Ward said. "He found the door open, with signs of a struggle in the living room. Take a look."

The next photos showed a modern lounge, a blood smear by one door, a smashed glass. Parris had been forced into the bath but the attacker had fled without clearing up. "They leave anything to go on?"

"The security feed for the building was cut," Ward said. "The neighbours haven't reported anyone coming or going, but one heard shouts, something smashing. She thought it was the TV, at the time."

"Of course she did."

"We found fingerprints in the blood. No matches in the database. The police are taking over now, treating it as a home invasion."

Tasker found a picture of a fingerprint. Part of a handprint, in the blood smear on the wall. If there were no matches, it was either someone with zero record or someone who'd been erased from the system. The former unlikely to be trusted with something like this, the latter unlikely to leave traces. What was the third option? "They sent in a pro to arrange a suicide, but they got interrupted."

"Or wanted to send a message?" Ward suggested. "To show they didn't care enough to pretend it wasn't murder?"

Tasker gave her a look. "How's your relationship with Duvcorp in Ordshaw?"

"Tenuous," Ward admitted. "As far as rank and file are concerned, it doesn't exist. But we're on sharing terms in a needs-must situation. This isn't the first time Simon Parris has been in touch, and last time it happened, Tycho Duvalier himself tried to have strong words with me."

Tasker appreciated her use of *tried to*, imagining this small woman standing up to one of the world's most powerful moguls. "What happened?"

"We borrowed some measuring equipment. Parris wanted to help, being ex-Ministry. You were aware of that? And of how their research intersects with ours?"

"Yeah." It wasn't commonly known, but Duvcorp's studies into a life energy the Ministry called novisan were always troubling Tasker. They had their own scanners and were definitely researching ways to exploit it. Possibly to weaponise it. He wasn't aware it was being done right here in Ordshaw, but he could've assumed. With Rebecca just two hours down the road. "And Parris just handed over their tech?"

"Under some pressure," Ward admitted. "This might have been his attempt to call in the favour. But all he sent me was the suggestion that was forwarded to you. 'Investigate Laukstad.' No explanation, no extra details. And the reality is, if they were sending a message, it's received. My people aren't used to tackling corporations, Agent Tasker."

Tasker nodded, no surprise. Most local Ministry offices were in place to contain what trouble already existed. State secrets. Monsters. They weren't homicide detectives, and hadn't signed on to tackle mass murderers or corrupt companies. Likewise, they weren't necessarily the most professional or trustworthy colleagues he could hope for. Not everyone had the training and experience of an international agent, that was simple fact.

Tasker checked the photos again. He realised none of the pictures of Parris showed any injury beside that wrecked arm and the splattered blood. In fact, going by Parris's pose, and the shower curtain hanging neat, it didn't look like he had struggled. Might've been drugged. No, the method and the mess didn't add up to a message. Tasker said, "Let's assume the attacker was interrupted. But not by someone looking to help Parris. Was anything taken?"

"Apparently not," Ward said. "His laptop was left behind, his phone too. Duvcorp's lawyers are already on us to hand them over. It's all strange, isn't it?"

Her tone was hopeful, because *strange* might mean the big bad corporation *weren't* in control. Yet.

As for Parris's devices, well. Tasker had got his hands on electronic devices that promised untold secrets before. Between corporate encryptions, lawyers and Ministry bureaucracy, there was often nothing to be gained from them. Still, he said, "You have the devices, but haven't accessed the laptop?"

"We'd risk a lawsuit."

"If Duvcorp found out about it."

Ward cleared her throat uncomfortably, but without looking at him gave a slight nod. Enough to say yes, they might sneak a peek. Good, she got it. Considering how dirty this whole situation was, they'd get nowhere playing by the rules. An entire village wiped out, a man with some clue as to why, and his killer driven off by an unfriendly third party. He couldn't let the Ministry itself get in the way. Tasker said, "Presumably you have some idea of how I can be of use?"

"Right now, I thought you'd appreciate the chance to freshen up in the hotel, get some rest," Ward said. "But I've set up a meeting with Parris's manager for this afternoon."

Tasker nodded appreciation. She got it alright. Thrown into a situation like this, you brought in a man like him and let him do what was necessary, even if it was just grilling office workers. He'd at least help her look tough while Duvcorp flat denied everything.

The motorway slanted up, to a raised ring-road that gave a view towards Ordshaw Central's skyline. An expanding, prosperous city a world apart from the isolated hovel of death Tasker had visited last night. Exactly the sort of place to harbour people who could get away with the murder of distant foreigners. At the least, Tasker could look them in the eye.

Left alone in his room, Tasker took a long, hot shower, trying to ignore reality whispering at him that this was already over. The more time he took, the more doubts crept back in. He'd posture and make them look good, sure, but Ward's meeting would be a bust and might mark them as future targets themselves. Duvcorp's connections to something terrible would go unproved, and next time it might be Ordshaw with a score of savage murders. Hell, why not Bracknell. Helen would be expecting a call later, and what would he say? *Hey, I've made it back to the UK, but guess what? I failed to stop these bastards, so keep the doors locked.*

Or. Or he could end the Duvcorp meeting with his gun. Storm the offices, up to the top floor where he'd take Hank Duvalier by the lapels, fuck the rules and evidence, throw him off the roof. His son, too, if Tycho was around. Two lives for eighteen fishermen, that was a start. Assuming Duvalier himself ever touched this city with a barge pole. He was off on some American ranch or in a New York penthouse, wasn't he?

Tasker came out the shower and stared at himself in the mirror, plush white towel around his waist, darkness dragging his eyes down and a taint of grey misery misting his chest. He had time to hit the hotel gym before the meeting. That was something he *could* control. He put his glasses back on and scratched his stubble, knowing he would be neither shooting up offices nor relaxing on beaches. He'd do everything he could for Ward and Laukstad over two or three days, finally return to Bracknell and spend three days off unable to explain to Helen exactly what he was worried about, then take guidance from London as to what pointless stepping stone to take next. Smugglers dealing in monster parts in rainy Eastern Europe or weird lights in the sky outside a sewage plant or something.

He exited the bathroom with a gust of steam and stiffened. His eyes shot from his pistol, holstered on the desk, back to the woman standing in front of it.

"I ordered room service," she said, brightly. "You want something for yourself?"

She had a gun of her own, and blood all over her clothes and face.

5

Bare feet padded against hard-packed ground, a warning beat as she reached the village. "Help! Someone!" Charlene shouted outside her neighbours' huts. Why weren't they answering? They couldn't have all disappeared too . . .

A door opened – Ade! Big-chested, bearded Ade, strongest in Igota. He wore the same confusion at the stillness, and her shouts further flustered him. Charlene told him, "Quick, Ade – to the crossing – I was walking with Marie –"

"Slow down," Ade said, moving into the open, watching the other huts. As troubled by the quiet as by Charlene's fear. Where were the boys? The talking, the laughter? Had more people disappeared? "What's happened?"

"Here?" Charlene swallowed.

The outsiders were responsible. It had all begun the night before they arrived. Men missing in the night, and now this. Everyone else. She listened, and finally heard goats, braying fearfully. Snapped out of it, she locked on Ade again. "Marie – she's been attacked. Richard – I don't know what came over him. Please hurry!"

She started away, but after a few steps skidded to a stop. Ade almost bumped into her. Both looked to the side, between shacks. There were the children. Ade said, loudly, "What are you doing, boys? You didn't answer this woman shouting!"

They said nothing.

Charlene moved closer to Ade. He stepped towards the skinny boys, half-naked in the afternoon sun. They stood still as stalks. "This is some kind of game? Ezra, come here right now!"

"Ade –" Charlene warned. He was a stride away, already, and the children pounced. Their shrill cries were met by noises from every hut.

*

Reece imagined a composition. It started super simple, two perfect D fifths an octave apart – maybe two octaves – and a five-step descent. Repeat. Again. You keep doing it, until you break free and go wild – chase the sound up, weave around inside the fifth . . . but keep coming back to that bold refrain. It wasn't jazz, he had a sense of that. A march? Another new Cutjaw sound. Creeping in his mind – he couldn't wait to test it out in Stilt Town, where the instruments were stashed. But this wasn't trumpet material. Wanted a piano at least. Might work on their little pipe organ, if Gray's people let him touch it.

Either way it had him happy. Had to keep happy, not thinking about all them people they hurt. Remember what it was for. Freedom of expression, freedom from oppression. That's what the tunes would speak of, without words. Different ways to get themselves heard and seen. He ran a hand through his hair, rocking on a little wooden chair on the porch while the others slept. That was another way to be seen, damn smeared green hair that hadn't come out in a wash like he intended. Then, they should've been back in Stilt Town already, where he had other dyes or bleach to deal with it. Instead of here, where none of them had imagined sleeping, as much Reece's fault as Stomatt's. The back roads seemed a good idea at the time – it was a wild ride that'd brought them here.

A squeaking floorboard made him sit up in the chair. Light footsteps on the porch. His hand slipped to his pistol but it was only Zip, looking worried out the door. Reece rubbed his eyes and said, "Come see, cher. You sleep well?"

Zip considered the question carefully. Her skin and clothes looked grubbier in the low light of dawn, from tiny mud-caked tennis shoes up to hair hanging in disarray over her shoulders, but there was class and intelligence in those eyes, same as he'd heard in her voice. She said, "I had a funny dream."

"Make you laugh?" Reece suggested.

Her expression suggested no. "There were poor people, far away. Goats crying."

"Ah. Just a dream, huh? No goats here. The others up?"

Zip must've passed Stomatt on the sofa to get here, but she ignored the question. "They died. The goats knew, but they weren't ready. *Igota.*" She lowered her voice, experimenting with her dream memories. "A village in the rainforest."

Morbid, but her dreams could've been plenty worse after what she'd been through. Now she'd rested, her voice was even clearer – might actually be British. A bright foreign kid dreaming of exotic places. Reece said, "You been to a rainforest before?"

She shook her head, then her attention lingered on his pistol. Reece took it out and her worry shifted to wonder. The sun peeked between the clouds to catch its mirrored shine.

"I told you this was art," Reece said, and spun the gun round his finger. He turned it back and forth at speed. "Platinum and gold plated, etchings designed by Blanc Tweedman himself. Le Belle Riposte is the finest sidearm in the States, count on it."

Zip's nose wrinkled. "How did you get it?"

"I wouldn't settle for anything less, that's how." Reece stood. He stretched and fought down a yawn, scanning the horizon. Open corn fields, dotted with trees. To the right, beyond the parked trucks and farm machinery, was the wooden barn where they'd stowed the farmer's body. Need to bury him before they go. And then there was the daughter . . . Reece smiled at the kid. "We're artists, Zip. Try to be in all we do, but we especially like making music. Me on the horn, Caleb's on the bass, Sto on the drums. You bring us anything that can make music, we'll give it life." He held up the gun again. "This another instrument I try to play my best."

Zip looked sceptical. "You can't play a *horn*."

"Trumpet," he explained. "And you better believe I play. No one expects it, bunch of white boys outta trailers with some kinda swamp jazz. But we live our best lives. They played us on the radio, you know? Whispers Phan, he called us *revolutionary*. You like jazz?"

Her scepticism shifted to positively pitying, as though his entire life philosophy, laid out before her, was misguided. Reece laughed. "Right. You don't play music where you from?"

Zip considered it carefully. "We have a piano. But I don't know if it works. Daddy doesn't like me to touch it."

"That's sour," Reece said. "He play himself?"

"No," Zip said, then focused on the gun. "He has a sword hand."

"That so?" Reece said. "And what's he need a sword hand for?"

"Killing monsters." She turned thoughtfully, towards the barn, like she knew the body was there. Serious enough to make Reece pause.

"What kind of monsters?" he said. "Big old bears? Criminals, maybe – the police? In England? You don't have guns so he has to use a sword?"

"A sword *hand*," Zip said, but he'd made her smile, like he was teasing. "Because guns aren't enough. And because he has to *always* be ready. The monsters used to be people – he gets them before they can get us."

Well hell. It sounded like she was being literal, and her father genuinely had a blade instead of a hand or something. Which didn't gel; a kid this well-spoken coming from some mutilated sword-fighter? Must've been some tale he told her, or she told herself, to make sense of something else. Reece asked, "Was that what he was doing on the Mississippi? Hunting monsters?"

She nodded. "Just one. Grithin. *Slippery scum*." She accented it like quoting a rough-talking thug. So yeah, she might be cut from different cloth to Dad. "He was looking for Grithin for *years*. And he was worried. That's why I followed. I wanted to help. I didn't mean to . . ." She trailed off.

Reece cocked his head to one side. "This Grithin dangerous?"

"Yes," Zip whispered. "But my dad's not scared of anyone. Only, I . . . I got a bad feeling. I told Daddy not to go and he told me off. Because I was listening to my feelings. I'm never supposed to listen to those feelings." She picked up speed, as Reece floundered on that messed-up detail. "I followed him – I even got on a plane – so busy and noisy and long, but I came here – not here – the river – and it *was* bad, but not because of Grithin – a real monster, one Daddy never stopped – two monsters – coming for *me* –"

"Hey, *hey*." Reece crouched. "Those men are gone, hear me? You don't got to worry about it, not now you're with us. We'll get you home, sure enough. Meantime, we're headed to the safest place in all Louisiana. Ever heard of Stilt Town?"

Zip shook her head.

"Caleb in there – you like Caleb? He's nice, isn't he? – his uncle owns this place, Stilt Town. Grew up in Cutjaw himself but left to start a church, and that church became a whole town, but not like any town you've seen. Because Alban Gray – that's Caleb's uncle – he still got some Cutjaw in him. Never lived in brick houses with concrete streets and that. *He* made houses all lifted up in the air. A church, a school, floating so you can run underneath. High enough that no flood can take them. And they got animals – you like animals? Pigs, cows, chickens."

"Rabbits?"

"Yeah, they got rabbits. You like rabbits?"

She jumped forward and wrapped her arms tight around Reece's neck. He went rigid with surprise before relaxing. He patted her head and she whispered, "Thank you, Reece." Then she pushed back. "Can we go there now?"

"Soon. Once we're all up and figured out what to –"

"We should go now," she said, seriously. "Before they find us."

"Who?" Reece frowned. She didn't get to answer, as a yell shook the farmhouse and Zip jumped with surprise. "What in *damn* hell is going on here?"

Reece stood, putting a hand on her shoulder. "Sto! Get your ass out here!"

"Reece!" Stomatt shouted. He sounded like a bull charging through the house. "Where the fuck are we? You motherfu –" Stomatt skidded to a halt on seeing Zip. Her eyes screwed shut in fear. The big guy's face went from angry confusion to delight. "Did we take hostages?"

"It's okay, cher, he's one of us," Reece assured. "For what it's worth."

Stomatt was bigger than most, thick around the middle, and not a handsome man. His top lip and nose curled slightly up and his mouth was always open, like he was forever mildly perturbed. He looked especially unhinged this morning with the bandage loose round his neck and his tatty, unbuttoned boiler suit all covered in blood. He looked up from Zip. "We make Louisiana, Reece? Don't look like Stilt Town."

"You don't remember? We weren't halfway there when you passed out."

"Passed out –"

"At the *wheel*. You flipped the damn car. Fortunately we –"

"Because you took us on this fuc –" Stomatt caught himself, eyes on the kid. "On this *frigging* detour, didn't you? Unlit damn dirt roads."

"Just as well you crashed out here, with no one to notice the wreckage."

"That don't look like no one."

Before Reece could fill him in, Leigh-Ann burst out onto the porch. "Stomatt you motherfu –" she spotted Zip and expertly redirected "– ungus. You're up and uglying up the place!" Dressed in just an enormous (stolen) flannel shirt, with her big ball of curly hair a tangle, she cut a balance between sultry and dishevelled.

"Woke on a damn sofa by some leather straps like some kinda bondage chamber," Stomatt said, moving off the porch to check the view. He noted the house's second storey. "Took all the beds for yourselves, huh?"

"You want hauling upstairs next time you get shot," Leigh-Ann said, "*weigh* less."

"Hey fu – urget you." Stomatt stumbled over the words, frowning at Zip again. He gave up on minding his language: "Why the shit is there a kid out here, Reece, come on!"

"Things got strange," Reece said.

"Sicko farmers had her tied up," Leigh-Ann said. "Now she's our new lucky charm."

"You want to take a *kid* –" Stomatt started, but Caleb lumbered outside to interrupt.

"Sto, you're loud enough to wake a rock."

"Interrupt your beauty sleep?" Stomatt only got louder as he plodded on the shingle. "Someone fill me in! Did we or did we not hand it to those shitbergs yesterday, and are we or are we not now rich and clear?"

"Rich but we ain't clear," Leigh-Ann said. "Not by a few hundred miles yet."

"Then why the hell we stop?"

"Because you wrecked our car!" Caleb cried. "And then – this!" He gestured wildly to Zip, who cringed closer to Reece. Their volumes had escalated loud enough to hit bursting point, but they all quietened on seeing how Reece watched them.

"So where we at?" Stomatt asked.

"Ready to keep going," Reece said. "Soon as someone gets a grill on. Barring one loose end here – got a girl upstairs."

"Another girl?" Stomatt cocked an eyebrow. "She older?"

"She's a *pederast,*" Leigh-Ann said. "Or at least mixed up with them."

"So she needs taking care of," Stomatt said. "Yes?"

"Ain't no *way* you leave it to him," Caleb said.

They all went quiet again, looking to Reece. He'd been telling himself they could just up and leave Nina. She wouldn't want the police out here, so what was the harm? But however seedy those men might have been, it was hard to accept that young lady's involvement. Was that him being hopeful, naive, sexist or what? He looked at Zip. "Cher, that woman? She as bad as the men?"

Zip hesitated under the attention. "She didn't touch me. She didn't want to come close."

Everyone kept waiting for Reece's guidance. He said, "I'll talk with her while y'all get ready to go. Zip, Leigh'll take good care of you. Once she gets some pants on."

Neither Zip nor Leigh-Ann looked happy about this, and Stomatt made it worse by whispering, really loud, "And just what the hell is *up* with her eyes?"

But Reece winked off the worry. "It's gonna be a good day, guys, wait and see."

Leigh-Ann could've thrown something at him, plain enough. Damn if she didn't hate optimism.

There was a scuffle of movement when Reece entered the bedroom, as Nina kicked up over the bed and against the wall. As far as she could manage with one wrist cuffed to the metal frame. Sat on the pillow, she stared fire and held her free hand up taut like she might gouge his eyes out if he came close enough. Reece stayed in the doorway.

"You've rubbed your wrist raw," he said. There was also a boot on the desk and another near the door, evidently tossed to help her escape. He couldn't guess how.

"I gotta pee," she said with her mouth closed.

"All right." Reece held the key up. "I'm trusting you're smarter than to try anything. Right?"

That wasn't getting an answer, but he approached anyway. She breathed heavier and recoiled when he unlocked the cuff. Quickly nursing her wrist. He stepped back to give her space and she slunk into the hall, never taking her eyes off him. Over to the john where he waited outside trying not to listen. After the flush, she stayed inside. The gang were arguing below.

"You never do it right, that's not enough mayo," Stomatt was complaining.

"You want a sandwich or a soup?" Leigh-Ann snapped.

The restroom door opened and Nina looked out with a resigned huff. Admitting that whatever new escape plan she had concocted had come up bunk. Reece flashed her a smile and gestured back to the bedroom. She considered making a break for it and he let her think it through, as Leigh-Ann's voice bounced up the stairs, "I swear to God you're the only man I know asshole enough to be able to sleep off a damn gunshot so he can irritate the hell out of everyone!"

Realising there were more people here than she could outrun, Nina moved back into the bedroom. Reece followed and closed the door behind them. He said, "Now we're rested, why don't I start? We've got a kid taken from her family, tied up and –"

"Eyes red as the devil," Nina said viciously.

"Lemme finish," Reece told her. "We've got a guy drew a gun to hide her away; would've shot us rather than let us get near her. His pal, I guess, was helping, and here's you – young, frightened? Forced into your old man's sick hobby? I pray that's true – it'd mean we did you a favour. The alternative, though . . . you your dad's daughter or what?"

"My *dad* was a good man – you have no idea."

"So fill me in."

Nina crossed her arms tight. "I told all. That little bitch showed up on our doorstep and we took her in. Fed her. She was mute as a plank except she started raving and screaming when she went to bed. Freaking the hell out. Talking prophecy of doom shit."

"A scared kid starts talking and you tie her up?"

"Wasn't just talk! There's more'n red in her eyes! It's a demon in her! Donny almost chopped a finger off under her witch words!"

"She distracted him from cutting carrots?"

"Cursed him, more like! She was talking ghosts and – and apes! Coming for her, here, gonna kill us all." Nina snorted. "And look what happened. You blame my dad? The kid *warned* us you was coming – he was defending his home."

"Forgive me," Reece said, "but tying her up and waving guns about still ain't a reasonable response to an upset child, even if she did get lucky predicting someone might come save her. Someone ties you up, you're not gonna make threats?"

Nina's eyes bored into him, not caring to hear his reason. "You gonna kill me, too?"

Reece saw fear, more than anything, gripping her. He said, "I guess we've –" A noise tore through the farm like the low war cry of some nightmarish animal. The windows shuddered as Reece froze. Nina's terrified eyes went to the window.

Reece asked, "What the fuck was that?"

As if in answer, Zip shrieked from below, "They're here!"

6

Tasker sat on the hotel bed as the woman ran her free hand over his gun holster on the desk. His was government issue, modern, sleek; her gun was faded around the edges like something salvaged from a grandparent's loft. It fit her vagrant look: medium height with a brown leather jacket worn bald, loose jeans ripped not by design and once-white trainers breaking at the seams. Bloodspray patterned her shaved head and face like warpaint. The door was closed, but the lock-chain lay on the floor amid shards of snapped wood. The fact that he hadn't heard her kicking her way in warned him she was likely more capable than she looked.

Why hadn't he taken the gun into the shower room?

Her eyes probed the armchair, heavy green curtains, bed and mirror. When she spotted her reflection, her cracked lips stretched to a grin. "This place is too fancy for me." The accent was a breezy Eastern European. "You do not say much. What's your name? I'm Katryzna."

Matching her conversational tone, Tasker said, "You broke in and don't know who I am?"

"I know *what* you are. Government spook. Yes?"

"Sure. If that's me, then what are you – a corporate contractor?"

"Can you imagine? I could have business cards. What was your interest in Parry?"

"Parris?" Tasker corrected.

"Potato potato." She pronounced both words the same. "You are some kind of specialist, isn't it? They paused everything to pick you up from the airport, I was watching. What's your name?"

When he didn't answer straight away, she frowned at her left shoulder.

"I didn't kill him. The opposite." Her eyes rolled up. "No, I didn't give birth. Or keep him alive. Yes, some of this *is* his blood. What's your name? Are the UK government investigating Duvcorp?"

Tasker stared, a little stunned at her random chatter.

"Please." Katryzna sniffed hard. "I can practically smell government on you. What's your *name*?" She glared and waited this time.

"Agent Sean Tasker."

"Working for?"

"The Ministry of Environmental Energy." Tasker nodded to his wallet, near the gun. "ID's in there."

Katryzna rummaged through the cards – not just his warrant card but the bank issues and Frequent Flyer memberships. She cooed at the Platinum. "This is to use those fancy lounges?"

"Some."

"Your Ministry treats you well. Putting you up in a place like this. And you travel with your gun? I like that. You were already on the way when Parry died? I guess they wanted him dead because of you? Why did he call you? What does your Ministry *do*?"

Tasker gave the flurry of questions a moment, before answering the final one, by rote: "The Ministry are concerned with environmental concerns. Those outside typically human factors. Parris suspected Duvcorp were involved in something that might interest us. We didn't get to ask him what. Now maybe you can explain your part in this?"

Katryzna stepped closer to him. Her clothing smelt of decay. "Sean. I'm likely to do bad things –" She twitched and hissed something foreign. Polish? Was it some kind of tick? She put on a friendly face again. "You obviously know something, otherwise why fly you in? We can be friends, but if you are sneaky around me, you might get hurt."

Tasker gave her a flat smile. "Friends don't point guns at each other."

"I am not *pointing* it at you. It's just ready in case I need to shoot you." Katryzna looked sharply aside again. She had to be hearing voices. "That's not the point. But okay." She placed the gun on the desk, within reach. Her jacket fell open to reveal the hilt of a large Bowie knife sheathed at her hip. "Now. You may continue."

Tasker quickly made assessments. She was part of their system – one of the corporate hired guns, even if she didn't look the part.

But not Duvcorp's hire; she was suggesting she was the one who interrupted the murder. If she was lying about that, he was dead anyway, so he might as well make the most of this. He said, "You're not familiar with the Ministry?" She shook her head. "We monitor unusual energy patterns, amongst other things. Parris was ex-Ministry himself, and went on to do similar work for Duvcorp. He tipped us off to something their research picked up in Norway, four days ago. A lot of people dead. For some reason, Duvcorp didn't want anything to do with it themselves."

"Four days ago," Katryzna echoed, a little disappointed. "I got a call *yesterday*."

"Sorry," Tasker said. "Parris called you himself?"

"Oh no." Katryzna took an old Nokia handset out of a pocket. The sort only good for calls and texts. "He tried to message a friend of mine. What kind of *unusual* energy readings do you chase? Are you ghost hunters? Is your UK government that advanced?" Her expression became eager like a child's.

Tasker said, "You think that's likely?"

"What did I say about being sneaky? I want –" A knock on the door interrupted her. She narrowed her eyes. "Who's that?"

"Room service," a young man called.

In a flash, Katryzna had both her pistol and Tasker's in hand. "If you used some kind of alarm –"

"You said you ordered food," he reminded her.

The knock came again, and Katryzna said, with a testiness that didn't seem directed at him, "I *know* – I appreciate that *now*." She gestured. "Open the door."

Tasker tightened his towel and did as she said. He blocked the busboy from seeing into the room while he accepted the covered plastic tray, and the moment the door clicked shut Katryzna tore it from Tasker's hands. She piled an entire limp burger into her mouth. Both pistols were back on the desk. Tasker made no move, aware of how fast she had snatched them up before. She paused, cheeks bulging, and spoke messily around the mouthful, "Wampth thome?"

"No," Tasker said.

"Fine. Talk. Whaph waph Parrith doing?"

"Didn't say. There must have been an unnatural force involved in these deaths in Norway. Duvcorp either recorded it and didn't want anyone to know they could – or they caused it themselves.

You weren't sent to silence him?"

She shook her head as she struggled to work her jaw around the burger.

"But you met the killer?"

Katryzna nodded as she swallowed with a series of impossible gulps that could've been retches.

"My word, woman," Tasker said, "were you raised by pelicans?"

She raised a finger for silence, finished swallowing, then said, "I was not. But you will want to have my babies. I have your *unnatural*. This message from Parry was my first clue in forever for what happened to Eyes. He was *swimming* in unnatural."

"Eyes?" Tasker questioned carefully.

Katryzna nodded, starting to shovel greasy chips into her mouth. "My only friend I ever had." A pause to chew, giving Tasker a moment to unwrap her diction. "He disappeared. Or died. Eight years ago?" More chips. "Eyes was Duvcorp's best secret weapon. He made things seem like they didn't happen." She finished her rapid feast and choked back a small belch. Tasker could barely focus on her words. "I have meant to kill Hank Duvalier for a long time. He never appreciated Eyes enough. Definitely to blame for whatever happened to him."

"Forgive me for being slow," Tasker said, "but what was the unnatural element?"

"Oh," Katryzna said. "Hank had Eyes chasing ghosts and ghouls and silly legends. He complained about it all the time, how ridiculous it was. Except the last assignment, that worried him. We met just before he left – he helped me chop up a Libyan." Her eyes glazed over as she sank into the grim memory. "He didn't need to come, he just wanted to see me, and turned up uninvited, smoking against a wall like I should expect him. He asked to talk. Sure, I said, once we kill Fahid – *and* feed him to crocodiles. But no, he said, talk and work, and started to explain while we dragged the body off a balcony. It landed on a car." This didn't sound like the high-grade contract killing Tasker had assumed the big corporations capable of, and his expression must have showed it, because she quickly added, "It made Eyes laugh until he coughed and almost fell over. He never let things like that happen, he was always so *specific* – he only laughed around me. But what were we talking about?"

Tasker gave a shrug, letting her flow.

"Ah. So he reminded me about these ghost stories. He said this one felt different and he gave me his phone, in case things went wrong. I never got a call and he never came back, so, great plan, Eyes. No contacts or anything on the phone. All I knew was that he flew to Africa."

"But you were already in Libya?"

"We killed the Libyan in Madrid, try to keep up, Sean. Do your Ministry know anything about Africa?"

Considering it was a whole continent of activity, yes, Tasker could imagine there were a thousand cases of note to the Ministry across Africa. But the woolliness aside, she was talking about Duvcorp setting contractors onto investigating the supernatural. The origins of the company crossing over into Ministry territory. He said, "Was Parris involved this Africa trip?"

Katryzna shrugged. "Eyes wouldn't give that number to just anyone, so *probably*. Duvalier had him looking into strange things. Bigfoot and haunted houses. So." She took a step forward and prodded a finger into Tasker's chest. "Does that fit your idea of unnatural?"

Her poke left a chip-grease sheen on his clean flesh. He said, "We might, conceivably, investigate haunted houses. To disprove them."

Katryzna backed off with a smile. "Then you will want to work together with me. Take Duvcorp down." She punched her opposite palm.

Tasker paused, unsure of what she even was, let alone what aligning himself with her meant. But here was a promise of results, nonetheless. He said, "Are you alone?"

"Well. I am with you? And –" She pointed to her left shoulder, which had distracted her before. Indicating an earpiece he couldn't see? "There's Rurik? Listen, Eyes was the only person that ever treated me right –" Her mouth tightened with irritation, then she spoke sideways. "You do *not*, you do nothing but *annoy*." No, there was no earpiece, just voices in her head. She collected herself. "We have the same interests, isn't it?"

"Maybe," Tasker replied slowly. "But I don't take partners outside the Ministry."

"That's good," Katryzna only smiled wider. Strangely healthy teeth. If you ignored the food stuck between them. "Me neither.

You can help us move around. Legally, so I don't have to keep leaving weapons behind. Less people get hurt this way, that should make you happy." A bitter twist towards her shoulder suggested that wasn't meant for him. She smiled again. "Sean. I see you're overthinking this. I am here to help. You are making a face – be honest, remember?"

"I make a career of discretion," Tasker said. "You look like roadkill."

Katryzna put her hands on her hips. "And I got into your super-cool hotel without any alarm going off, yes? You want to cross Duvcorp, you need me. Stuffy suits and government regulations don't work against them."

Well, that was true. Tasker could see himself wrapped up in the same red tape and complications that surrounded Parris's electronics. Conversations that amounted to no more than warnings to back off. Questions unanswered, guilty forever free. With eighteen senselessly dead – probably more to come. That poor girl, a Norwegian Rebecca, her face ripped apart. Tasker said, "I'm interested, but you need to give me more than that. Your friend died eight years ago? What've you learnt since then?"

"Ah." Her face went blank a second. "I thought you might ask. Now, when I say we were friends – we did not see each other often – and, life is hard – actually Eyes used to get me out of trouble, a bit, so without him around –" She stopped herself, took a collecting breath and rushed out the explanation. "Long story short, I was out of circulation and a bad friend but I am compensating now."

Tasker eyed her. He could believe this erratic, unwashed woman could be the sort to leave the disappearance of her friend unanswered for years. "But you are connected to these people," he said, "the corporations and the –"

"I work occasionally." She rolled a dismissive hand. "Not right now. This is personal. Lucky I was nearby when I got this message." She clicked her fingers, then took up the phone again, thumbing through. "Just yesterday."

Tasker read off the two-tone screen: *It's Parris. Not sure you remember me. You said contact you if things got bad. Please come to Ordshaw ASAP.*

They had a past agreement Parris was cashing in on from eight years ago?

"I had people trace the message," Katryzna said, "and found this guy who was all muscle bending over Parris in the bath. Not perfect timing. I cracked his skull with my gun, so I could question him, but he didn't stop. He made a lucky punch and ran, while Parry was gargling his last words."

"You got a good look at the killer?"

"For what's it's worth. Big, like a thug, with a tattoo" – she gestured vaguely around her neck – "military insignia? Short dark hair, flat nose. Stupid eyes. Average ex-army goon. Ring any bells?"

It was about as useless as descriptions of thugs went. Tasker said, "I'll run it by my people. What'd Parris say to you?"

"Well, he spat two names. *Ikiri* and *Miguel Lopaz*. From how his face looked, they're *really* important. That's where I need you. With all your Ministry resources, with those two names, you can tell me where in Africa we need to go, isn't it? More importantly, you can get us there. With our guns." What she lacked in a plan, she made up for in enthusiasm.

"I'm visiting Duvcorp," said Tasker, evading the point. "I'll ask them about it, shall I?"

Katryzna raised an eyebrow. "If you want them to kill you? I'd better come with you."

"Absolutely not. If you knew this Eyes, I assume they know you?" She didn't deny it. "I'll get my people on this. You can . . . lay low here for now."

"I relax while you do the boring work?" Her face shone at the offer, and she took in the room anew. Her hand was suddenly in front of Tasker, dirty skin cracked. "Deal."

"I just washed," he reminded her.

Katryzna wiped the hand quickly on her jacket and held it out again. Possibly dirtier. But it was earnest enough. Tasker shook and she squeezed hard before backing off with a wink. "Great, this is going to be *fun*."

It would be something, he was sure enough of that. His best bet was probably to get a couple of local agents to watch her in the meantime, run background –

"Oh!" She raised a finger. "Don't tell anyone you met me. Even your friends. *Especially* your friends. That's for your safety, more than mine."

7

When she was done needling Stomatt, Leigh-Ann moved from the kitchen to crouch in front of Zip, whose little legs dangled over the edge of a stool. "Well, little miss, how you hanging in here?"

"I'm fine," Zip said, going still at Leigh-Ann's proximity.

"You don't gotta be scared, okay? Get past Sto's loudness and everything else about us is pure charm. I, for one, am glad to have another woman on the team."

"Are you Reece's girlfriend?" Zip asked, so blunt it made Leigh-Ann back off and laugh. The kid looked hurt, not sure what was funny.

"No, nope, never," Leigh-Ann said, summarising a complicated relationship in three simple words. Not all true; they'd had a fling when they were, what, fourteen? Awkward, fumbling shit – on account of they knew each other too well. All the girls loved Reece, but it didn't click for either of them – and that was the start of Leigh-Ann having all sorts of Doubts she wasn't entirely resolved on yet. But she gave Zip the simplest explanation: "We like family, okay? All of us. Now, do I hear a tinge of the English in that accent? I've got some British in me – *Leigh's* spelt all funny with the *g* and the *h* – my dad wanted me to have an old country name."

"It's pretty," Zip replied. "Zip's from the Bible. Zipporah."

Leigh-Ann snickered. "Wow. And your God-loving sadistic-child-naming mommy, where's she right now?"

That flummoxed the poor kid.

"Your mom, Zip? She home with Daddy?"

Zip chewed her lower lip.

"Don't you wanna go home?" The child nodded vigorously. "Then what's this hang-up? You can trust us, we're your *crewe* now. Even though Sto smells like garbage and Caleb would give up a kidney for magic beans, we stick tog –"

A roar shook the room and Leigh-Ann shot upright. A great raw sound, not machinery but something alive, something massive. Zip's eyes got bigger as Stomatt stumbled in – then the kid shrieked, so loud Leigh-Ann had to cover her ears: "They're here!"

"Damn hell!" Stomatt shouted, and the noise outside came again.

Leigh-Ann turned towards it, about to run for the door, but Zip latched onto her, crying, "Don't let him get me don't let him get me!"

"What in hell, kid?" Leigh-Ann barked, pushing back at her. "What is that?"

"Who's coming?" Stomatt demanded, as though they'd been keeping something from him. "Sounds like a damn dragon!"

"Please please please!"

Leigh-Ann struggled to disentangle Zip's clawing grip. Every time she got a couple fingers free the others snapped back into place. The roar came again, closer, a battle cry. Leigh-Ann shoved, hard, and Zip stumbled with a gasp.

"Leigh!" Reece's voice cut through the room. Suddenly staring from the door. Hell of a time to walk in.

"She wouldn't let go!" Leigh-Ann snapped, not about to apologise with some devil beast out there. She followed Stomatt's example, going for the weapons bag, and pulled the big guy out of the way. He dragged his stumpy shotgun with him as Leigh-Ann got a hand on the old familiar MAC-10.

"What is it?" Reece said. "Anyone see –"

"It's them, Reece, it's them!" Zip said, running terrified to embrace him.

"What's she talking about *them*?" Stomatt yelled. "That's something inhuman!"

"Something in the field!" Caleb skidded into the room. "Think it's Steers? Sto?"

Stomatt ran out the door, pounding for the back porch. Slipping free of Zip, Reece moved right behind him, pistol twirling out the holster. Leigh-Ann and Caleb exchanged a dumb look – the child trembled worriedly in the middle of the room. Leigh-Ann said, "You got those trucks going?"

"Was just –"

The roar came again, undulating as whatever made the sound

moved up and down, quickly approaching. Stomatt shouted back at it, loud and harsh and without meaning. Leigh-Ann said, "Fuck it, load up! Grab the kid!"

Caleb swooped to lift Zip, as Leigh-Ann hoisted the weapons duffel over a shoulder and snatched the other bag. Weighed down like her knees might buckle, she charged through the living room away from that awful sound.

A gunshot boomed, Stomatt's shotgun shaking the windows.

"Go go go!" Leigh-Ann screamed and Caleb raced ahead. She burst into daylight and skidded over the porch, twisting to see Stomatt and Reece running to the side of the building. "What in damn hell is it?"

"Damned if I know!" Reece shouted. "Ran right past – quick as a snake, big as a bull!"

"I'm getting it!" Stomatt disappeared around the corner. He fired again.

"We're leaving!" Leigh-Ann shouted, and Reece backed up, nodding. Caleb was already halfway to the trucks. Leigh-Ann moved on, throwing a look back at the door as Nina emerged, pale and uncomprehending. "What kind of animals you got on this fucked-up farm?"

Nina's mouth moved wordlessly, shocked as the rest of them.

"More messed up by the second," Leigh-Ann muttered, then shouted to Reece's back, "What's the worst that can happen! What's the worst, he says!"

A huge crash of metal and snapping wood came on the other side of the farmhouse, spurring them all to move faster. Caleb threw the first truck's door open and gently, for all the urgency, lifted Zip in.

"Whoa!" Reece warned and Leigh-Ann twisted to see the beast tear into view, breaking through the far corner of the house and ripping chunks of wall with it.

"Holy hell," Caleb gasped, stepping back from the truck.

"The fuck . . ." Leigh-Ann added.

It was a creature of size and ferocity to match the noise that carried it here. Its skin was black as pitch where it wasn't patterned by clumps of grey fur, and its eyes shone mad, murky yellow, within a flat face of wrinkled flesh and bared fangs. Though hunched, with its hind legs doubled and back arched, its shoulders stood tall as the truck and the front-arms that supported it were wide as pillars, ripped with muscle and jointed in more places than looked natural. Breath came out its big nostrils in steam as it reared up.

In hushed, fear-filled awe, Zip gave it a name: "Giza."

Leigh-Ann swung her gun round, pulling the trigger before she'd got close to aiming. The gun bucked and bullets spat all over the ground in a stream up to the monster, giving it enough time to lurch sideways before her spray rioted past it. In one great stride it closed half the distance to them, dipping around the vehicle so Reece couldn't get a clear shot past Caleb. Its second stride brought it up in the air, knuckles punching the ground away, and both fists windmilled above it – cut off mid-jump by a booming shot to the side. It twisted with a high roar, both arms flapping as its momentum carried it on into the truck. Caleb pulled Zip clear with a split-second to spare, the beast smacking the windscreen with such force it folded the roof in.

Stomatt ran into the open, pumping the shotgun, yelling incoherently. Reece and Caleb dived for cover as he fired again, shot sparking off the closest truck chassis. The beast rolled off the other side, the vehicle banking under its weight.

"Other truck, other truck!" Reece pushed Caleb and Zip ahead of him. Leigh-Ann hiked up the duffel bags to follow. Stomatt pumped and fired, bullets pinging off the crumpled truck, and the shadow of animal mass rolled out of view. Onto the ground and then suddenly away. Off the lot with unbelievable speed, out through the fence and into the long grass, before disappearing around the barn.

Stomatt chased after it, passing the wrecked vehicle.

Reece shouted: "Here, Sto! In! Leigh!"

Leigh-Ann nodded, breathlessly following under the bags' weight. Caleb dropped behind the wheel of the next pick-up, Zip in the back, as Reece waited by an open door.

"I hurt it!" Stomatt backed towards the truck. "Didn't you see I –"

Another gunshot cut him off, bullets pinging into the vehicles around Stomatt as he dropped for cover. Leigh-Ann's gaze darted from him back to the farmhouse, to the porch where Nina stood with her father's double-barrelled shotgun in shaking hands, swinging it from their direction to out over the field, then back again. Torn between protecting the farm from that creature and revenging herself on them. The gun fixed on Leigh-Ann, the girl making a decision, and Leigh-Ann froze. There was another shape moving beyond Nina, a shadow stalking up through the fields. Smaller than the monster.

"Behind you," Leigh-Ann uttered, unable to say it louder. "Behind you."

Nina stepped out off the porch. Wanting to look Leigh-Ann in the eye.

"Leigh, move!" Reece shouted, from behind the truck.

The huge beast roared on the other side of the barn, no quieter for having been shot. Leigh-Ann held up a defensive hand. "Sweetie – I swear –"

Nina made a noise little more human than the monster attacking them, taking another step closer. Reece peeked up again, and, seeing the situation, raised his pistol. "Nina you drop that now!"

A loud scrape on the shingle announced Stomatt stumbling, trying to get up but slipping, and Nina threw the gun his way and fired on nerves. Leigh-Ann flinched her eyes shut and needed a second to check she was still there. A hand locked on her arm and dragged her back. One of the bags was lifted off her shoulder and Reece shouted by her ear, "She's empty, move!"

But Leigh-Ann was looking back as she stumbled after him, trying to spot that shape she'd seen before. Nina fumbled in a pocket for another shell, breaking open the gun. "Reece –"

He wasn't listening, dragging her to the truck. Stomatt moved parallel in a crouch as Caleb got the engine going, calling, "Come on guys!"

"You bastards!" Nina screamed, jamming the barrel flush again. "You –"

Leigh-Ann snapped a look back just before Reece bowled her into the truck, seeing the shadow reappear behind the farmer's daughter. A man, dark as a silhouette, so quick he barely seemed to move. Metal glinted in the sunlight and Nina's expression flicked with surprise – on to off in a second. The girl split into two parts as she fell to the ground. Leigh-Ann shrieked, "Reece!"

Zip shrieked louder, "Giza!"

With another tremendous roar, the first beast tore out the front of the barn, beating its huge chest. Half in the truck, Reece slapped the truck roof for Caleb to drive, then straightened his pistol-arm over the roof and fired three times. Leigh-Ann rolled over the back seat, watching through the windscreen as the beast fell back into the barn wall, arms smashing through the wood. The truck wheels spun and the tail swung out as Caleb hit the accelerator. With a massive eruption of dirt and shingle they sheared forward. Reece was thrown to the side, almost falling out, and Leigh-Ann caught him by the belt. She tugged him in, down on top of her, and they both fell onto the scrambling kid.

In the bed out back, Stomatt rose and slammed his beefy hands into the rear window, laughing madly. "Did it! We fucking did it!"

Leigh-Ann struggled upright to look back. The creature was out of sight, but the other figure was calmly walking through the dust cloud. A short, slender man, with a sword down at his side. She whispered, "What in hell just happened?" She turned the question to Reece. He wasn't looking back, but down, at Zip, like she was the one to ask.

The child was curled up against the far door, head buried in her arms, making little sobs.

"Reece," Leigh-Ann said, because damned if she was going to ask that child. "What in hell just happened?"

8

Leaving Katryzna to enjoy the shower, Tasker met Ward outside the hotel. He didn't mention his bloody guest as Ward drove through the city, instead silently ruminating on what she had told him. He wasn't sure if it was a threat or simple fact that mentioning Katryzna's name was dangerous: he suspected both. After all, if she had stumbled upon Parris's murder, someone was likely to be out to silence her next. Provided, of course, everything she'd told Tasker was true. A quick online search had turned up a small mountain in the heart of the Democratic Republic of the Congo called Ikiri, but identifying Miguel Lopaz required more nuance than Google could offer – a job he delegated to Caffery with a brief call. The only thing he could really be sure of was that Katryzna had *some* connection to the dark side of the big companies, and if the Ministry found that out, they would want to Do the Right Thing and capture her. Interrogate her. At the very least hire her.

He should probably want to Do the Right Thing, himself, but was hesitant. She was youthful, vibrant in her own degenerate way. Repellent but also fascinating – she kept her weapons close and heard voices, and was likely highly dangerous. He couldn't help wondering what if . . . What if this potentially weaponised woman really was looking to turn against Duvcorp? It was a different kind of insurance, a promise of meeting these people on their own terms for once, instead of with the limp impotence mandated by the Ministry's restrictions. The image of the dead child in Laukstad came back to him, her blonde hair stiff and brittle in the ice. Didn't she deserve that justice?

Ward took Tasker's silent contemplation as an invitation to fill him in on her own developments. They could all but confirm Parris showed no signs of struggle – something about his posture or the blood splatter indicated he had been calm when the wounds were inflicted. And the blood in the living room did not belong to him. Ward said, "Looks like your theory was right. But were there two intruders there separately, or did two hitmen disagree in the middle of a job?"

Tasker leant heavily towards the former. Somehow, he believed Katryzna's claim that she worked alone.

Ward also explained, quietly, that her people had scanned Parris's laptop for the most recently accessed files. One file stood out for its ambiguity: a spreadsheet of thousands of rows containing five columns of numbers that seemed to show energy readings with dates, co-ordinates and what appeared to be angles, with numbers ranging from 1 to 360. They were already trying to see if any of the co-ordinates pointed towards Laukstad. Meanwhile, Ministry people testing on the ground there were reporting novisan fluctuations standard for a coastal village. Reports that were useless: they needed readings from four days ago, but Norway didn't have their own MEE, so no one was watching then. Except, apparently, Duvcorp.

Tasker's initial perception was so far validated, though; the investigators had turned up a variety of wounds on the bodies, caused by knives or blunt instruments, but the claw and bite marks could well have been from human teeth and nails. Ward went on to say her Support team had run historical checks, for similar unexplained mass murders, with no apparent motive or specific suspect. There was a village in Estonia, Silna, in 2009. Sixteen people killed in some kind of mob attack. It was during a heatwave and got passed off as caused by unusual atmospheric gas – one of the Ministry's favourite fallbacks. There was also an unresolved group murder in the Brixton riots, in the early '80s, and an Arctic expedition who all died violently in the '60s. Nothing flagged more recently, not concerning the Ministry. But then, they might not have flagged Laukstad without being tipped off to it.

They took a great stone bridge across Ordshaw's river and the skyline opened up to the right of the car. Duvcorp's HQ stood out: a trio of cylindrical towers at staggered heights, reflecting light even on this dull day. The opposite of subtle.

"The lady we're meeting," Ward said, "is Ms Marge Cosgrove. Head of their Renewable Energy European division. In company structure, she's not far below the upper executives. London advise that we don't bring up their novisan research, though."

"I'm sure they do," Tasker murmured. There wasn't much they could discuss, was there? This was just an opportunity for Duvcorp to confess, if they'd be so kind.

Ward parked in a large drop-off zone and a stiff-legged man led them through a cathedral-scale lobby to a gilded lift. That took them onto an expansive roof terrace, atop one of the building's lesser towers. A dozen tables sat opposite a café bar, overlooking an expansive view of Ordshaw's South Bank. Marge Cosgrove was the café's sole occupant, waiting in a crisp grey suit. She had the hard-lined face and straight posture of someone who strategised her life down to the most efficient way to breathe. She put on a welcoming smile, about as genuine as the ones Tasker used.

Cosgrove invited them to sit and said, "Naturally, we were all devastated to hear about Simon." You could almost believe it. "It's shocking anyone would want to hurt him. He was quiet, kept to himself. Hard working. But I expect you know all that, given his history with the Ministry."

Ward gave Tasker a deferring look and he started, "He fit in at work?"

"I never saw a problem," Cosgrove said. "He was a senior researcher, promoted multiple times. Simon was pioneering new solar energy solutions."

"Did it somehow concern activity in Norway?" Tasker dived straight in.

The smile tightened, the rest of Cosgrove's body motionless. "Why do you ask?"

"Parris specifically requested me," Tasker lied. "That is, an agent based in Norway. Did your work involve surveying irregular energy readings?"

She looked at Ward as though asking if such topics were really fair game, and Ward didn't meet her eye. Cosgrove said, "In Norway? Do they even have sunlight at this time of year?"

Tasker waited for a proper answer.

Cosgrove calculated him carefully. "Agent Tasker, we have no concerns in Norway. If you're alluding to that tragic village massacre, I can emphatically insist there is no connection. But . . . Simon brought such concerns to you? He had ideas of his own, separate to his research here. Perhaps he couldn't leave his

Ministry work behind? When we have access to his computer again, we might check exactly what he was up to."

Sure – check, delete and/or replace.

"He didn't bring any concerns to you?" Ward proffered. "Before he came to us?"

Cosgrove put on the act of trying to recall. Then evaded the question. "He was a private man, he didn't like to cause a fuss or draw attention."

"Well he got someone's attention, didn't he?" Tasker bristled.

"After talking to your people, you mean?"

"Do you mind me asking," Tasker moved straight on, "where Parris's work *was* concentrated? Geographically. Do you have overseas production centres? Research labs? Elsewhere in Scandinavia, or Europe? Maybe south, to study solar energy research – Africa? I don't know – the Congo?"

For a second, Cosgrove was surprised. Then the wall returned. "I don't follow."

"No? Parris never got assigned work in Africa, I suppose? What about his coworkers? A Miguel Lopaz, for example?"

Cosgrove's mouth twitched, just a little. "Agent Tasker, I have no idea what you're referring to." Ward frowned, looking more confused than their host.

Tasker said, "Just a name we've an interest in."

"One he told you?" Cosgrove said, making a show of checking her watch. "Something to do with the Congo?"

Tasker held her eyes, waiting for more, and her mouth curled tightly.

"Very well, let's be frank – from one illicit research body to another. Yes, Simon was involved in research that might overlap your own. No, it had nothing to do with anywhere in Africa, nor Norway. That he spoke to you about it, and not me, suggests a throwback to a project from his past which he clearly never let go. I couldn't begin to suggest why he would do that, unless . . ." She indicated Ward with a knowing look.

Ward frowned. "He wasn't working for us."

"Interesting." Snideness crept into Cosgrove's tone. "It would seem he wasn't entirely working for *us* either." She stood. "Now, without meaning to be rude, if it's only a name you have to ask about, I'll have someone from HR talk to you."

"Wait." Ward rose, too. "We'd like to discuss Parris's job –"

"Ha" – Cosgrove dropped the friendly act – "but you are clearly better informed than me, Ms Ward. And I'm sure you're well enough informed to know how complicated pushing your point could make things, for everyone. Good day to you both."

Ward looked to Tasker, chilled by the audacity of that tone. He gave her the slightest shake of his head and Cosgrove indicated for their stiff-legged escort to take them away. They rode the lift in silence and were taken back to the lobby, where Tasker noticed two burly men emerge from some double doors, looking their way with all the appearance of nightclub bouncers. Tasker couldn't make out a neck tattoo.

Ward asked, "Who's Miguel Lopaz?"

"I don't know," Tasker admitted. "And I'm not sure she did, either."

"And *Africa*?" Ward prompted. "Where'd you get these ideas?"

"We should get moving." As they walked, heading down wide steps towards the car, he said, "I've got a contact. Someone who spoke to Parris."

"You've –" Ward started incredulously.

"I'm sorry, but considering his fate I'm being cautious about who I share with. Those details in there probably marked us already, but I'll go through my handler to follow up, keep it out of your office. You should make a show of releasing Parris's case to the police."

"Releasing the case? Hold on –"

"You said there's nothing left to involve us in Laukstad," Tasker said. "Better they believe there's nothing tying us to Parris, either. I'll leave town, continue alone."

"Tasker," Ward said firmly. "The MEE is not afraid of corporations like Duvcorp."

"We don't know who we're supposed to be afraid of yet," Tasker replied. "Right now, the best thing we can do is get to Lopaz before they do, and I can do that best without people thinking it's what I'm doing."

Ward didn't like it, but left it at that. They got back in the car and as she drove he called Caffery again. Yes, Duvcorp had an office in the Democratic Republic of the Congo's capital city, Kinshasa, and there was a Miguel Lopaz who worked there. Their own contact out there was Special Intelligence Service, not someone to be trusted with Ministry business. But the way

Cosgrove had given them the brush-off was enough to convince Tasker that Katryzna was on the money, so he had a new destination. He could do with the African sun. He immediately demanded a flight out there – with two seat bookings, the second anonymous, to protect his contact – but Caffery postured and complained and said it was a big ask with or without a travelling companion. The DRC was a war zone and they couldn't even be sure this was a Ministry case.

Wait and see, the bastard said. Enjoy the hotel, check in with your family.

It caught him off guard for a second. Helen and Rebecca were almost close enough to touch, but to let them know that he was here and leaving again would be crueller than them not knowing at all. He curtly ended the call, asking that Caffery merely do as he was asked.

Ward said, "Time's a factor, isn't it?"

"Yeah," Tasker said.

"My people could help," Ward continued, carefully.

Tasker raised an eyebrow.

"Agent Tasker. It's my job to enable people like you to do yours; that can include expedited travel arrangements. I'm not . . . always convinced Management run things smoothly out of London. We can have you on a plane in a couple of hours, I'm sure."

A manager offering him the support he actually needed? Here was a marvel. "I'd appreciate that."

"And I'd like to drive you to the airport myself, to be safe."

Ah. There was the choice – between introducing Ward to Katryzna and waiting on damn Caffery. Well, it was her funeral. He said, "All right. But fair warning, I just met this woman and I'm not sure how safe she is."

Ward looked happy enough just to be trusted, though, and after they pulled up to the hotel he left her waiting by the car to go get his errant guest.

Katryzna greeted him, gun in hand. She had changed into fresh clothes sent up by the hotel lobby, and looked almost presentable in too-big khaki trousers and a pale blouse – more like she had escaped from a penal colony than just murdered someone. Though she had failed to get her shaved head completely clean, and her knife-belt remained strapped around her waist. Tasker pointed to her neck, still flecked with blood. "You missed a spot."

She stuck out her tongue to show how little she cared. As he gathered his things, and packed away her weapons, he explained about the meeting and the next step taking him to Africa. Katryzna smiled at his drive and said she knew he'd deliver – eager to keep moving herself, right away.

Despite her shower and new clothes, Katryzna's appearance at the car still startled Ward. Katryzna gave her name then jumped forward for a hug. She aborted at the last second and backed off, abashed. Ward did a bad job of hiding her confusion. Tasker settled into the passenger seat and watched Katryzna in the mirror. She flashed him a cheeky smile but kept quiet as they started driving.

Ward confirmed she'd arranged things in the time it had taken Tasker to round up his vagrant travelling companion. Then she put her effort into avoiding the urge to stare, while Katryzna flicked little looks at her. Studying her body as well as her face. Tasker wondered if she might bite out Ward's throat mid-journey, and his concerns mounted when Katryzna snapped little whispers at her invisible companion. Ward shot Tasker a sideways look.

"Do you get cute little assistants everywhere you go?" Katryzna asked Tasker, face suddenly appearing between the seats. Ward almost swerved into the next lane.

"This is the Deputy Director of Ordshaw's MEE offices," Tasker told her, levelly, and Katryzna fell back with an impressed whistle.

"You're important, Sean. Can we take her with us?"

"I'm sorry," Ward said. "Who exactly *is* she, Agent Tasker?"

"I kill people."

The car got a few degrees colder as Katryzna's grin stretched wider. Tasker could hear Ward's cogs turning. "What's your connection to Parris?"

"Eyes," Katryzna answered with a cheery shrug. Ward mouthed it back.

"A friend of hers," Tasker explained. "He worked for Duvcorp. Parris tried to contact him, same as us, and got her instead."

"I bit his *face*."

Tasker didn't have a response for that, and Ward's frown intensified.

Katryzna continued, "First time I met Eyes. Near London,

actually. He was sent to kill me and I bit him to get away. A few months later, we met in Budapest. Bucharest? I get them confused. Anyway, we had dinner in Belarus when he helped me out of prison." Her jumbled thoughts got more tangled. "You didn't fear Eyes, because if he was out to get you, you were already dead. Well, except me. Because I'm *me*."

"Sounds . . . romantic," Ward commented weakly.

Katryzna bolted forward again. "Oh, it wasn't like that. Men? Yuck." Her hand was on Ward's shoulder and the deputy director looked very afraid. When Katryzna looked to Tasker to press her point, he nodded for her to back off. Her brow creased and she carried on. "He was sad, *never* stopped smoking. He only wanted someone to talk to – about how bored he was, unfulfilled. People like talking to me, I'm a good listener."

Hard to believe. She sat back, at last. Ward checked where she'd touched her shoulder like it might catch fire.

"We worked together sometimes, and met up when we were nearby. It's important to keep social. And he *needed* to vent about the ghosts and things Hank Duvalier made him hunt. He hated not knowing things, and he couldn't find explanations for everything. He described something to me once that sounded" – she barked a laugh – "like a floating woman, half-invisible. Dead. He did not understand it at all, so he blamed himself. Overtired, low on oxygen, whatever. Eyes was so *dry*, he saw everything as a logic problem, and this one did not add up. I told him he should pack it in. Retire. Except to retire from our work, usually someone retires *you*. He should have killed them first." Katryzna scowled at her shoulder again and hissed something Polish, then said, "Yes I did. How would you know?" Ward's expression got more concerned and Katryzna smiled like a kid caught misbehaving. "Sorry. My conscience."

Tasker came in to clear that up: "Rurik?"

"Don't worry." Katryzna patted Ward's arm again, more interested in convincing her than him. "You can't see Rurik. He is no problem. Though . . ." She considered something carefully. "I shouldn't have told you *my* name, isn't it? Forget it, okay?"

Ward gave a very uncomfortable nod. When they reached the airport, she shook hands and wished Tasker good luck, keeping her distance from Katryzna, who looked like she might try that hug again. Rurik apparently advised her against it and she stalked aside, snarling at him. Ward gave Tasker a parting look that said now she'd met the contact she was happy to keep clear of this. Rather him than her. Story of his damn career.

9

Reece revisited the action at the farm in drumbeats, trumpet blasts. The gunshots and shouts were punctuation in a score. A powerful piece, full of force, fear, triumph. He tapped his fingers against the pistol on his lap, picking out the sound. That's how you made sense of it. Because it made shit-all sense otherwise.

"Almost outta gas," Caleb said quietly, drawing him back into the moment.

"How's that?" Reece said. He was sat in back with Zip huddled down between him and Leigh-Ann. Caleb and Stomatt were in front, both staring ahead like they each had something they were burning to say, not sure it was wise to say it.

"Why I chose that other truck," Caleb muttered. "Had more gas. This one's dry."

"You're telling us now?" Leigh-Ann said, hotly, and Reece gave her a look. They were all on edge. Not a time to take it out on each other. She thumped back into her seat.

"Haven't seen a stop since the farm," Caleb continued. He'd hoped a solution would turn up along the way. But they must've done an hour now, without a break nor barely a word shared between them. It was a bad way to break the silence. Hitting this long, empty highway had been a mixed blessing, a straight line to Louisiana but one likely to be patrolled. Stopping for gas was a sure way to get back on the Steer Trust's radar. The rest stations, the stores along the roads, even some of the roads themselves were their domain.

That's why it made sense to get off the beaten track, Reece recalled now. Why they'd deviated and ended up on that farm. Because he had that feeling they were gonna run into trouble. Same feeling he got now.

"How far till the state line?" Reece asked.

"Not far," Caleb said. "I wanna say twenty minutes?"

"Got enough to last us that long?"

Caleb didn't answer, rather than lie or offer news none of them wanted to hear. The Steers had had time, now, to lock down the state. They were a glorified protection racket, for Christ's sake, they'd be keeping an eye on anyplace Caleb might pull up, and probably had all sorts of people set to inform on a likely crew of miscreants racing by.

"Keep going, it's all we can do," Reece said, because they needed to hear him calm, even if he hardly felt it. "Get as far as we can, then we take it from there."

Caleb nodded, rolling his shoulders with relief at getting his bombshell out the way. But now it was Stomatt's turn, the little bit of chat triggering him into twisting in his seat. The big guy was grinning in an unfriendly way, focused on Zip. He said, "What do you think, that gorilla knew which vehicle to trash? Make sure we didn't get away." He moved restlessly. "It was a gorilla, right? Big, ugly, hard to put down, but a gorilla all the same. You got it between the eyes, right, Reece?"

"Looked like," Reece said. "But I wouldn't like to go back and check."

"I didn't like leaving her there with it," Caleb said uneasily. "That farm girl –"

"Took a fucking shot at me! Psycho!" Stomatt half laughed. "What was it – what are we into here? This kid? That thing?"

Reece shifted an arm over Zip's shoulders, seeing her tensing. "Calm it, Sto. Kid's got more poise than you right now."

"More poise, more fu–" Stomatt almost stood out his seat. His bandages had come loose in the fight, fresh blood had dried on his shirt and coveralls. "I ran that thing off. You wake me up in some land of dead farmers and freaky kids and mutant gorillas, and you're talking about my *poise*?"

"*You* trapped us out there, dammit," Leigh-Ann snapped, her own bottled feelings at breaking point. "We'd be in Louisiana already if you'd given over the wheel!"

"I was good for it till Reece directed us to the ass-crack of nowhere –"

"And what'd become of her?" Reece said. "Might've been a mistake heading out there – definitely a mistake letting you drive – but if it hadn't gone down like that, no one else was rescuing Zip. She'd be living them horrors alone."

"Last I checked," Stomatt said, "we set out to make money, not run a fu" – he leered, under Leigh-Ann's scolding look – "a *frigging* charity."

"Last I checked we were musicians holding them Steer bastards to account," Reece shot back. "Not cold-as-coal assholes. You can take your share and hike – any one of you can – but I'm not leaving a *child* behind."

"Yeah me either," Caleb grumbled. Leigh-Ann let her expression say the same.

Stomatt looked from one to the other, his mocking grin returning. Pissed off and refusing to admit it. "Think I'm some kind of lunatic?" he laughed. "Of course we're not leaving her. But maybe – here's a thought – maybe *she* can tell us what kind of mess she got us into? What do you say, princess? Time to share that with us, now?"

Zip cowered, tiny in the middle of the seat, and looked up pleadingly to Reece.

"She can talk when she's ready," he said.

"That before or after we're all dead?"

"Sto –"

"I'm sorry," Zip interrupted quietly. "I'm sorry."

"You got nothing to apologise for, sugar –" Leigh-Ann started.

"They came for me," she said. "They came for me before and they'll keep coming. It's why – it's why I didn't get to Daddy. They couldn't find me at home, but I left the safety and now, they'll keep coming, they'll find me *anywhere*."

Stomatt gave that a beat before demanding, "The hell's she talking about? Kid, what are you on?"

Before Reece could tell him to pack it in again, Leigh-Ann came in with a softer question. "You named it. That gorilla? You knew it from somewhere?"

Zip bit her lip. "Giza. I didn't know it before, no, I ..."

"The hell does that mean?" Stomatt started up again. "How the –"

"I felt it," Zip rushed out. "Sometimes I feel things. Feelings. Names. I know I'm not supposed – it's not allowed – it's dangerous, but I can't help it!" She stared at the big guy imploringly, full of apology. That confused him enough to stay quiet for a second.

"You felt that gorilla's name?" Reece clarified, gently, and Zip nodded guiltily. "And that's something you're . . . not allowed to do?"

"That's why they're *here*," Zip said.

"You told me your daddy hunts monsters . . ."

Zip confirmed it with a serious look, and the group were quiet. Even Stomatt kept it down, now he saw Reece was getting onto it. He asked, quietly, "How'd you get here, cher?"

Zip swallowed. "Followed Daddy. On the plane. And when he took a car, I got a bus. I walked. And . . . I couldn't find him so I looked . . . in here." She tapped her head, eyes full of apology. "I looked in here. And I was trying to catch up when they came. So I ran. I found a train – I ran more – until – until those men at the farm found me."

"How long you been at this?"

"*Days*," Zip insisted, "at least four – five days." Like that was the worst thing about it, like it was all the time in the world and not even stranger that she could've made those crazy journeys so quickly. Her eyes swelled with tears. "And I tried to warn them. I *told* them they would come."

But the farmer didn't want to hear it, and figured she was possessed. Thinking something like that monster was after her, and was probably gonna kill them all. Reece imagined her freaking out, making them freak out in turn. They might've been innocent after all.

"Who *are* they?" Leigh-Ann asked. "That gorilla and – the other one? With a sword?"

"Vile," Zip said, with a focus that said it just occurred to her. "He's called Vile."

Stomatt boomed, "*Vile* ain't a name. She's talking shit, guys, why you listening to this? Kiddy fantasies. Runaway from home on planes and trains, as if. Making up names –"

"You're Stomatt. Max Stomatt, but everyone calls you Sto," Zip interrupted, with new firmness now he was pushing her. That got his attention, but she kept going. "You're angry about your mum. I mean, not right now, but actually kind of. Under the other anger. I get angry about my mum, too. The same way. But I don't remember her, not like you remember yours."

Stomatt froze solid and Caleb stiffened on the wheel. Zip looked to Reece, questioning eyes asking if she was right. He stared back. Damn hell she had Stomatt's measure. His drunk mom had beaten her husband, a thick-skulled brute himself, and Stomatt was the only soul in Cutjaw that regretted her leaving without a word. He got especially belligerent during family holidays.

Stomatt said, "You bastards put her up to this?"

"There's power in all of us, my daddy says," Zip said. "Only *he* knows how to control it. Anyone else would be dangerous with it. That's why he has to track the others down. And why I'm not allowed. I . . ." She threw Reece an apologetic look. "I didn't mean to just now. Or before, to get the monsters' names, but it just –"

"Easy," Reece said, and added, "You done nothing wrong." Less sure of that by the second.

"What *is* this?" Stomatt demanded. "Genetic experiments all out the same lab? Red-eyed psychic kids? Damn gorillas with metal skin, freaks with sword fetishes?"

Zip was afraid to answer, or didn't have one, and suddenly everyone was looking to Reece like he was somehow gonna explain this. He didn't have a clue. She looked like any other kid, if a bit grubby and weird about the eyes. But her sensing that thing was after her, reading emotions out the air, what could he make of that? He said, "Where you come from, Zip? You gotta tell us about your home."

"I . . ." She hesitated. "Daddy said it isn't safe. He said don't even *think* about it. They'd find us."

"But we need to know, to help."

Zip swallowed. "It's just where we live, though. The really dangerous place – that's what you want to know. Where the power is?"

Reece frowned. A lab or something, like Stomatt was suggesting?

"I call it the Eye Key." Zip said. "I don't remember it. But I know I was there. It kind of . . . *hurts*? To think about it. I can't ever go back there. *No one* can."

"Sounds like Sto's trailer," Leigh-Ann tried to joke, but it came out flat.

"Daddy gets upset about it," Zip continued, voice almost a whisper. "It makes monsters, he says. And now I've made things worse." She sniffed, hard. "I should've stayed home."

"Hey, if your daddy kept things from you," Reece told her, "how can it be your fault? Way I see it, Zip, probably he thought you weren't ready for all this yet. Look at us, Zip – people call *us* dangerous, being that we know how to shoot guns. But we use them right – ain't *never* hurt someone that didn't deserve it. Your gifts ain't dangerous, it's how you use them." She gave him a flash of hope and he smiled.

Caleb hit the brakes hard. They all flew forward in their seats, Reece shooting a hand out to hold Zip back, and Stomatt cursed Caleb before the driver hissed, "Company, up ahead!"

The road had curved to look onto a stretch that ran past a gas station, where a burgundy Cadillac was parked blocking both lanes. Close enough to see it was flying the Steers' eagle-skull flag – two little ones, in fact, one above each headlamp – as if that needed signalling. A tall guy in a ten-gallon hat leant against the hood while another with a bolo tie and panelled jeans loitered near the rest stop entrance. Both had pistols in shoulder-holsters out on display over their check shirts.

Ten-gallon stood up straighter, looking their way. Fifty, a hundred yards off, and they'd skidded to a conspicuous halt. Stomatt rumbled, "I can take them down."

"We ain't out looking for a trail of blood," Reece hissed, but his fingers were closed tight on his own gun. "We can pull back, find a side road, find some place to syphon gas."

"I didn't see no side roads, Reece," Caleb warned.

"He's already seen us," Leigh-Ann said. "How far we gonna get if word gets out about our route?"

"I can help," Zip said quietly.

"You all stay put, keep your heads down," Reece decided. "I'll handle it." The gang went quiet. The Steer by the car moved to the side, calling at his friend, so they were both looking up the road. Gripping the door handle, Reece took a breath. He'd talk to them, that was all. Charm the horns off the devil.

Zip watched him with fear. Her eyes went to the gun in his hand. He smiled, like this was nothing, and winked, then opened the door and stepped out. Bolo tie had moved to linger near the driver's seat as Hat stepped away, hand ready to draw. In the truck, Zip whispered something and Leigh-Ann whispered back assurances.

With the door for cover, gun down behind it, Reece called out, "Excuse me, boys, but you appear to be –"

Zip jumped out of the truck as Leigh-Ann grabbed at her. Too fast to stop, she was on the asphalt in an instant, running towards the men. Reece came out of cover after her, shouting, "Zip!"

Hat fumbled at his shoulder holster, flustered at seeing the threat was a waist-high child. Bolo stiffened with confusion. Reece brought his own pistol up. “You boys even think of moving, I’ll –”

“Stop!” Zip shouted and Reece skidded to a halt himself. She had both hands up like a preacher as she came in front of the Steers, and the men stared at her raptly. Her voice was different somehow, bigger, impossible to ignore. “We don’t want trouble.”

10

Tasker and Katryzna were picked up at the airport by a uniformed man with a luxurious van, who drove them wordlessly through the dusty, plaster-cracked streets of Kinshasa. Hotel Memling was a welcome oasis against the hot, arid and deafeningly busy outdoors; the sort of opulent satellite haven Tasker was accustomed to the world over. Katryzna had been subdued since the flight, but entering Le Cockpit Bar, a classy room of distressed brown leather sofas and high stools, she whooped and commented, "Colonialism's still going strong, I see."

There was a lot Tasker had wanted to ask her about Duvcorp and their cohorts' shady dealings but she had been oddly quiet on the way, glued to in-flight movies. He instead drafted messages for Helen, explaining the diversion from Japan had been extended, and that he would call later. He loved them, he missed them. He couldn't stop picturing that dead girl's face. When he tried to sleep, the memory was more vivid than ever, and he had finally ordered rounds of whisky to help. Entering the hotel bar, he could happily resume that drinking.

Charles Smail, the Secret Intelligence Service representative for the Democratic Republic of the Congo left his table with a beer in hand to greet them. He was tall, at just over six foot, but gravity pooled his weight around his waist, his tucked-in linen shirt drawing attention to that uneven body shape. He had on brown shorts, sandals, and a too-small sun hat that barely concealed his tangle of straw-like hair. Smail had clearly given up professional appearances long ago. He cheerily invited them to join him, offering local beers. Tasker suggested that whisky, but Katryzna merely requested water. Smail swayed to the bar like a bowling pin ready to topple.

"He's a British spy?" Katryzna asked.

"I guess so."

"Not exactly James Bond."

"Part of the disguise, I suppose," Tasker said.

Smail was posing as a mining official – who was to say what passed for smart when studying holes in the ground amid oppressive heat. He returned with loud comments about the weather, pumping his shirt to fan himself. Never mind the room was air-conditioned. He slid onto his stool and assessed the pair anew. His eyes lingered particularly on Katryzna. "So, all this way to meet our man Lopaz? I must admit I'm keen to exchange notes on him. The chap is shifty as they come, which is saying something in this city. Is he really still with Duvcorp?"

"He give an impression he's not?" Tasker asked.

Smail laughed. "Well, he's been here as long as me, but never talks shop. Never seems to do any work for them. They have no actual interests in this part of the country – Duvcorp's mining reps are in Kananga. I always pegged their office here down to administrative error. Set a man up on some idle idea they never followed through, but forgot to cancel his pay cheque. Have a seat, won't you?"

Katryzna did so reluctantly, watching him.

"My personal profile?" Smail continued. "Lopaz is ex-military, from a long time ago. He dabbles in underground fighting and tries to stay off the grid. Left whatever his old life was far behind, or at least wants to. I've put word out that you're after setting up a meet, under the guise of investors, but doubt he'll have much interest in it."

"Can we go to him?" Tasker asked.

"Yes." Smail nodded. "He'll be around Club Clash. You know what Clash is?" He turned the question to Katryzna, to include her.

She told him matter-of-factly, "I do not even know what *you* are."

Smail tapped the side of his nose in appreciation of her discretion, not admitting confusion. "Clash is a gym. Some of us keep sane with chess and reading classics by the river; Lopaz manages fighters. Bets big on them. He hangs out at the fight bars, too. Misses the machismo from whatever military he served in, would be my guess."

"Club Clash it is, then," Tasker said.

Smail took a long swig of beer, noting the cabin bag by their feet. "You don't want to check in first? Wait long enough and Lopaz will surface here. All the expats do, eventually."

"I'd rather not wait," Tasker said. "People have a habit of disappearing on me."

"Or dying," Katryzna added helpfully. If it surprised Smail, he didn't let it show.

"Well, so you know, Lopaz won't take kindly to strangers turning up at Clash."

"I don't care what he might take kindly to," Tasker said. "I've spent the better part of three days on planes chasing people that were dead before I got there. I'd rather not add his name to that list."

Smail took that down without critique, clearly assessing the nature of the visit. Katryzna gave Tasker a pleased look, appreciating that irritable, get-things-done edge. The spy nodded and stood. "Okay then. I'll drive. Are you armed? Best leave your gun here. This city is really rather safe, compared to the rest of the country, and it's best we not send the wrong message."

"Are you not taking us into a literal fight club?" Tasker said.

"Trust me, we'll be fine talking, if you let me lead."

"And I will have my knife," Katryzna said.

"What? No. That's worse than a gun. There won't be any trouble, don't worry."

Katryzna's eyes met Tasker's, not convinced, but he said, "All right, no weapons."

Katryzna snorted disgust, but rather than complain she made a sharp comment to her invisible conscience, in Polish. Then she rolled her eyes, presumably at Rurik encouraging caution. She threw up her hands in concession.

They squeezed into Smail's cheap Citroen and drove with the windows down to circulate smoggy air. After twenty minutes bumping over hole-riddled roads, Tasker was starting to feel queasy. Smail's commentary of landmarks provided only scant distraction, as did his breezy account of how the Congo civil war was raging in the eastern reaches of the country. Smail rattled off names of militias and generals that meant nothing to Tasker, movements that had developed over the past months or years that the spy clearly enjoyed discussing but had no one to share the news with. More interesting here – Smail changed tack – was that an election was due but not yet scheduled and people were getting uneasy.

Before they could delve into that, they came upon Club Clash. It sat in a lower-lying district of Kinshasa, surrounded by desolate blocks. A two-storey windowless structure with an external iron stair going to the first-floor entrance. The name was painted above in block capitals, and alongside the door was a black-and-white decal of a man about to smash a guitar – the figure out of proportion.

"Paul Simonon," Smail said. "*London Calling*, you know? Not a bad likeness."

"The Clash?" Tasker raised an eyebrow. The last place he expected to see a reference to an English rock band.

"Used to be a music venue, way back when. I guess there was better money in fights. Now, can I suggest you let me make an introduction?"

Smail led them up the stairs to the entrance. He gave them one last warning with a smile, then entered. Inside was a wide room littered with training equipment, tinted green by filthy skylights and scented with sweat and old metal. The room encircled a central square cage, which cut through down to the ground floor – this area doubling as a viewing platform for a fighting ring on the ground floor. Electronic music blared from numerous speakers as one Congolese man heaved on a weights machine and another whipped large ropes off the floor. Both were hugely muscular, accompanied by similar big spotters, and once they completed a few final reps all four stopped to stare at the newcomers. The closest one addressed Smail in French, a threatening greeting. Smail responded chirpily and, after a second's consideration, the man shouted, "Monsieur Lopaz! Visitors."

Various shouts in French came from below, one voice rising above the others. Their host nodded to an opening, a spiral staircase going down, and Smail thanked him before continuing. Tasker followed with Katryzna, down the rickety stairs, as the men above converged on the stairwell too. On the ground floor, another half-dozen brutes had gathered, all ripped with muscle, every contour visible even under vests and sweatshirts, eyes following the newcomers. Amid the Black locals one man stood out: though not quite white, with leathery skin a shade of cork, Miguel Lopaz was patently not African. He was older and smaller, despite thickset limbs, with mean sunken eyes, thinning black hair and a tatty linen shirt.

Smail spread his arms in friendly greeting as Tasker kept an eye on the decidedly unfriendly men surrounding them. Katryzna shifted close, shoulder brushing his. Not for security, but to confide in a thrilled whisper, "You wish I had my knife now?"

"Lopaz!" Smail said, cheerily. "My friend here just got into town, hoping for an introduction. I left messages for you?"

Lopaz's expression was hostile as he wobbled slightly aside from the group, right leg unsteady. "Friend out of England?" His voice was thickly Latino, and his sneer revealed a gold tooth. "Don't belong here, does he?"

"No, sir, I expect not," Smail said lightly. "Could we step outside? I'll spot you a beer. They've travelled a long way to meet you."

Lopaz's eyes worked over to Katryzna in a way Tasker already knew meant trouble. "No way she's your friend, too."

Katryzna didn't speak, but returned the look with worrying enthusiasm.

One of the tallest men shifted close to Lopaz, leaner than the others, with a thin moustache and a thoughtful expression. He muttered in French, and Lopaz answered in a grave tone, using the man's name, Henri. Tasker's French wasn't up to much, but he got that Lopaz made particular reference to Katryzna as someone they had discussed before. *I told you, didn't I?* Henri regarded her carefully, then chuckled. The others joined in, before he spoke loudly in English, "Excuse me, but Miguel here thinks –"

"I *know*," Lopaz spat. "I know who *she* is." He said it with such venom that the audience went quiet again, though Henri wore his scepticism on his face.

Smail happily continued with no regard for the tension. "So what do you say to a private chat out back?"

"I say no," Lopaz answered. "I say you better walk out of here now and take her with you – *if* you can control her."

Smail turned an uncertain look back to Tasker and Katryzna; she still wasn't talking, eyes shimmering with anticipation. Tasker said, "Whoever you're expecting, we're not them. I'm from the Ministry of Environmental Energy. You've heard of us?"

"Yeah," Lopaz replied flatly. He spoke in French, too quick for Tasker to catch, but with an irritable *I-told-you-so* quality. His companions weren't joking, now – eyes going to the nearest weights and tools, expecting trouble.

"We're just here to talk," Tasker said. "A guy called Simon Parris sent us."

Lopaz's lips tightened, confirming the connection.

"You spoken to him recently?" Tasker asked.

"Why would I have spoken to him," Lopaz said, "recently or not?"

"He died before he could explain that part," Katryzna said helpfully.

Lopaz glared at her. "You've brought wolves to our door, Charles. But I'm ready, aren't I? These boys are ready."

"Great." Katryzna stepped around Tasker, but paused. A glance to her shoulder. "No, they had their chance." Another pause, spreading her hands to reason with her conscience. "It's *boring* and he is *asking* for it." The crowd of men were momentarily thrown. Tasker wondered if it was a trick of hers, like his arsenal of smiles – the imaginary conscience wrong-footing her enemies. She said, "Bla, bla bla, no one cares!"

"*Elle folle?*" Henri wondered aloud, calling her crazy.

"Katryzna –" Tasker said. She gave him a wicked look.

Lopaz stepped back, speaking harshly. "Yes, *Katryzna*. Who else. Charles, you –"

"Ah ah!" Katryzna waved a finger. "He asked you nicely. Sean did too. Now, it's my turn." She paused and swiped an irritated hand over her shoulder, making the nearest two men flinch. She shouted to where Rurik was flung: "You watch me!"

"Stop her," Lopaz instructed, quickly back-stepping. "Before she kills us all."

He turned away. Henri asked if he was serious, on the verge of laughter at the fear this woman inspired, and Katryzna jumped two feet off the ground, her right elbow cocked sharply ahead of her. Henri's head snapped back with a crack and Katryzna rolled off him to clamp both hands onto the next man's face. She slammed her head into his before breaking through the circle, after Lopaz.

Tasker moved after her but a heavy grip landed on his upper arm. He twisted the hand around and caught a wrist, pivoting to use the attacker's own weight to trip him – but another guy slammed into him from the side. He tripped on the first man and pulled his attacker down, all three tangling in grappling limbs. A blow glanced off Tasker's head and his glasses went flying. He got an arm up to protect himself, as Lopaz lunged for a kit-bag across the room. Katryzna was right behind him, another fighter just behind her. Smail shouted, hustled back by two others, as someone swept in to kick Tasker.

Struck again, Tasker writhed, trying to get clear, but they were pressing on him and he reached ahead in vain. Between lashing legs he saw Lopaz reach his bag, but Katryzna dived ahead of him. She pulled back with a bounce in her step, holding his gun. She turned and fired a single shot, clipping the leg of the man bearing down on her. As he crumpled with a cry and everyone froze around Tasker, Katryzna grinned. "Shall we start again?"

11

Zip stopped before the cowboy, arms at her sides. The man stood away from his vehicle, regarding her with a strangely distant look. He teased his hat with one hand, the other loose, gun forgotten. Reece crept up behind, his own pistol held behind his back. Something about the stillness of the encounter warned him against any sudden moves. The guy with the bolo tie was sat in the car, now, focusing hard on the dashboard like he was trying to remember something. Reece shot a look back to the truck; Stomatt was standing out the passenger side, his shotgun down out of view. Caleb and Leigh-Ann were all but leaning into the windscreen to watch.

Hat turned to the car, then back to Zip, and between the two showed no interest at all in Reece behind her, much less the truck. He scratched his chin and looked up at the sky. Zip could've been a statue, now, merely watching him. It was all Reece could do not to say something – come in with friendly banter now everyone was quiet. But the cowboy laughed heartily, a smile filling his face, then he turned away. He drew out a cigarette and lit it. The guy in the car reclined in his seat, turning his head to the roof like he was planning to get in a quick nap. Hat sauntered off the road, smoking. Not looking back.

It was like they were both brainwashed, lost in their thoughts and oblivious to the child and her criminal escort right before their eyes. Reece mouthed disbelief. "What in hell?"

Zip looked over her shoulder to him, a doll returned to life. She gave a little thumbs up and whispered, "I think it's okay now?" Not sounding sure herself what was going on.

Reece didn't need telling twice, though: whatever shade of weird this was, it was an opening. He spun to the truck and gave a quick wolf-whistle, gesturing to the gas stop. It took Caleb a second to get in gear. As the truck pulled over the verge to pass the Cadillac, Reece watched the guy in the car, still the least interested in the world beyond his quiet little space. Keeping his voice in a low hiss, Reece instructed, "Fill up before the wind changes. Quick as you can."

Caleb swung in quickly and Reece patted Zip to direct her towards the pumps. She trotted ahead as he threw the Steers one last look. Eerily damn disengaged. The moment the truck stopped, Stomatt was out, pump in hand and feeding the tank.

"What the hell you say to them?" Leigh-Ann asked, opening a rear door to invite Zip in. The child clambered in with her help, and answered happily.

"I didn't *say* it, exactly. But suggested they wouldn't notice us."

"This is freaky," Caleb said.

Reece moved round the front of the truck, looking in the shop. A man stood behind the counter, pole stiff and looking straight forward, hypnotised like the other two. Moving back to cover the Cadillac, Reece said, "Someone get in there and pay real fast – don't need them reporting gas theft."

"With him standing there?" Leigh-Ann exclaimed. "Ain't we already pushing –"

"Dammit Leigh move your ass!"

Grumbling, Leigh-Ann hustled over to the shop. This slight woman with crazy frizzy hair in her over-sized shirt and farmer's slacks, looking around every which way like she might get attacked by bees, it was sure to raise the clerk's eyebrows. She slowed at the door, braced herself then pushed on in, and all the while neither the Steers nor the clerk reacted in the slightest. Leigh-Ann went straight for the counter and reached it as the pump pinged, full.

"He ain't moved a muscle," Caleb commented, not sounding too happy about it.

"You a secret Voodoo queen, girl?" Stomatt said.

The clerk did move, though, engaging distantly with Leigh-Ann as she smiled her way through paying, making quick small talk before leaving. Not looking back. She bared her teeth at Reece as she passed him. "Next time you're braving the zombie."

Reece didn't reply, instead watching the motionless Steer in the car. He gave one more look over to the absent cowboy, now equally still, cigarette hanging down by his side. Zombie was right; this was some hoodoo shit. They all climbed back in and he bid Caleb go, no one else daring a word in case the spell was broken. In a minute, they were well down the road, Cadillac a distant silhouette, and still no sign that the Steers had moved. Finally, Stomatt roared with laughter. "That was some Grade A *freakshow* shit."

Zip smiled proudly in the middle seat, but the others weren't joining in. Caleb was tense at the wheel and Leigh-Ann gave Reece a dirty look. Reece kept an eye behind them, waiting for the moment the Steers realised what'd gone down. He said, "When's it gonna wear off?" Zip's smile disappeared. "*Is* it gonna wear off?"

"I – I don't know," she admitted.

"How'd you do that, Zip?" Reece asked. "Put an actual gris-gris on them."

"Um." She had that guilty face again, the one that said Daddy would be mad. "I'm not sure. I just knew I could. And that – that – no one would get hurt?"

"You never done that before?" Leigh-Ann said.

"I had to!" Zip insisted, like she'd just been caught lying. "To get on the plane – and – and – I was only trying to find my daddy – and they wouldn't have let us past, would they?"

"It's okay," Reece said. "Nothing to be sorry about. That was impressive, Zip – if we're quiet it's because we ain't never seen anything like it. Think your daddy might have been holding out on you."

"I'm telling you she's straight out a lab," Stomatt laughed again, not so bothered about the idea now. "We got some kinda experimental human weapon on our hands. Kid, *welcome* to the gang. But don't you ever try that shit on me." At Leigh-Ann's look, he corrected, "Sheep. Don't ever try that sheep on me."

"You try that on him all you like," Leigh-Ann said, signalling her own softening. "I'd give an arm to make men pay me no mind like that."

Caleb alone remained stiff up front, silent. Reece said, "Caleb? We good now, right?"

"We got gas," Caleb said, implying that, at least, wasn't a worry.

Reece and Leigh-Ann huddled by Zip and eased back into the journey. He let himself wonder, now, what all this was about – and more important where it might lead them. The job on the

Steer Trust had set them up, but a kid who could do things like that? Forget a reward from a rich father, they could walk right into a bank. Hell, could get music critics singing their praises!

It was smooth sailing for a couple of quiet, empty miles, before the signs started showing: state line. Welcome to Louisiana. They cheered crossing over and even Caleb finally split a smile.

"Not two hours out of Stilt Town, now," Reece said. Hell, only that long until they were clear. Fallon wouldn't chase them into Arcadia; his Steers didn't have enough sway to pick up their scent here. Plenty bent cops, but not bent his way. Reece drummed a quick beat on Stomatt's headrest. "*Damn,* I can't wait to get back on the horn. Zip, you're gonna hear us *play*. We got magic, too, you wait and see."

It cheered Zip, he could see; them relaxing around her, letting her in. And she turned to Leigh-Ann, thoughtfully, to ask, "What do you play, Leigh?"

"Didn't I say?" Reece laughed. "*She* has the voice of an angel."

"Yeah, Lucifer," Stomatt joked.

"Fuck your eye!" Leigh-Ann snapped, and shot a hand over her mouth. "Shit, kid, I mean –"

"My daddy swears," Zip said. Then she added, "I don't give a fuck."

It took a second of disbelieving silence before they all erupted in laughter. Reece ruffled Zip's hair. "You're gonna fit right in. Start you on a tambourine. We could go far together."

She knotted her brow. "What's a tambourine?"

"A tambourine, sweetie," Leigh-Ann fielded this, quick, "is a lot like Sto there. You gotta beat it hard to make it work, and the harder you work it the more noise it makes."

As Stomatt hooted protest, Zip giggled without quite knowing why, and Caleb turned them down an avenue of Southern oaks. The landscape wasn't all that different from one mile to the next, but this was their territory now. Reece hummed a scatty little tune of triumph. Caleb came over it, improvising a baritone, "Oh take me back – take me down deep – deep *deeper* down – show me Stilt Town!"

Stomatt thumped a paradiddle on the dash, and Reece nodded along.

"Oh I said take me – take me down –"

The truck jolted and the drumming abruptly stopped as Caleb

took a better grip on the wheel, a moment's panic. "Ah hell." His eyes were fixed on the rear-view. They all twisted round and saw a shape way up the road behind them. Gaining fast.

"Is that –" Leigh-Ann didn't bother finishing. They all knew what it was.

Zip gave Reece one of her apologetic looks and he quickly shook his head to tell her it wasn't her fault. None of them understood what she'd done back there, so no way she could be accountable for the Steers coming out of their trance.

"Sons of bitches got their guns out," Leigh-Ann said.

"Down, stay down!" Reece ordered. "Get us gone, Caleb!"

Caleb slammed his foot down and they lurched as the truck lumbered on. Weighed down with five bodies, this old farm-tech was already pushing the limits of its speed.

"Shift, shift," Reece told Leigh-Ann, keeping his eyes on the car as he climbed over her. She fumbled under him and came out the other side whispering at Zip not to worry. Reece drew his pistol. The car was tearing ferociously up to them, and behind the windscreen the cowboy driver was grimacing determination, the passenger itching to move in his seat, checking the ammo in a big revolver.

"Coming up on your side!" Stomatt warned, watching in the mirror. He held up his shotgun. "You want the Tonnerre?"

"Keep cool," Reece told him. "Hold us steady, Caleb."

The Cadillac swung out suddenly, over the centre of the road, and shot forward with a new burst of speed to get alongside them. The passenger was pulling himself up out the window, revolver first. Reece whipped up his own gun and fired into the Cadillac door. Enough to rattle the driver and make the passenger fumble, but the guy didn't drop his gun and the car kept coming.

Zip screamed.

"Hands on your ears, like this!" Leigh-Ann said.

The Cadillac pulled up again, the passenger yelling curses. He popped a shot that glanced the truck roof, making Reece duck. Stomatt bucked in his seat with shouts of his own, wanting to shoot over all of them. Reece rested in cover for a moment, steadying his breathing. More shots followed, slamming into the side of the truck and making Zip scream again.

"Reece!" Caleb shouted, warning that one came too close for comfort.

One more steadying breath and Reece rose, angled his arm and fired. Two shots – the first hit home and the Cadillac veered so suddenly the second shot hit the asphalt. He twisted out the window, keeping aim, but the car bounced as its front wheel burst to shreds. The passenger was thrown down in the window, doubled over the door, but somehow kept clinging to that gun. The wheel scraped sparks off the road over him, and the driver swung from side to side trying to keep control. They were losing speed rapidly, no matter what.

"Hell yeah!" Leigh-Ann cried, taking Zip in a tight embrace. "What'd I tell you!"

Reece slipped back down as the others cheered. It was a damn good shot, and they'd surely make Stilt Town now, but the damage was done. It'd been an idiot dream hoping they'd make it there unseen. Sure, Gray could still offer shelter and protection, but it made life more complicated for everyone, having Fallon able to figure out who hit him. Especially with this damn green hair – how hard was that gonna be to follow? No way those Steers hadn't already figured it, chasing the gang out here.

As the others calmed, Caleb picked up on that vibe first. Gray being his uncle and all, he'd always been most wary of taking trouble back there. Talking over Stomatt's happy comments, he said, "You think they know where we're going, Reece?"

It wouldn't take a genius. A gang of thieves cutting right towards Fallon's most outspoken critic in Louisiana. But rather than admit it fully, Reece said, "I guess we'll see."

12

"I didn't agree to this," Smail hissed, as Tasker finished tying off the last of the men's hands, all of them now bound to a pipe, sat shoulder-to-shoulder on the floor. "I thought she was your assistant or something."

"Respectfully," Tasker told him, "that was your assumption to make."

He hadn't agreed to this, either, though. Lopaz's fears about Katryzna were clearly justified. But Tasker found there was something refreshing in seeing his "assistant" punch Lopaz to the floor with his own gun. And she'd shown restraint, the moment everything was under control – it's not like she'd gone on a rampage. Lopaz, who doubtless would've otherwise evaded answers or run, at best, was now cowed on a small wooden chair, the opposite side of the room to everyone else, while Katryzna tapped the pistol contemplatively against her chin.

"She's lucky she didn't kill him," Smail said, indicating the younger man who she had shot. Tasker gave the wound a lazy look – a clean shot that missed the bone, now bandaged. The victim had cried up a storm about never fighting again, but it wasn't much more than a flesh wound, and as Tasker's head and most of his torso was throbbing, he was okay with it. Thank Christ his glasses hadn't been smashed. Smail continued, "We're not in the war zone, Tasker – there are rules in Kinshasa. And Duvcorp take care of their own, you know? They've got as much power as a nation state!"

"Relax," Katryzna said. "Lopey will not talk about this, or us, to anyone."

Lopaz looked his age, frail on his chair with all his energy channelled into a hateful stare. She had left him unbound. From the way he regarded her, he wasn't going to try anything else.

"Miguel," Smail said, "understand that I had no idea the MEE would condone this behaviour."

Lopaz's face told him to stop embarrassing himself.

"Notice he does not beg or bargain or threaten?" Katryzna said. It was true – Lopaz had known how dangerous she was, the moment he saw her. The assumption was they were here to kill him. Smail went quiet as he finally accepted that himself.

Tasker pushed his glasses up his nose and said, "We're here to talk."

"Obviously," Lopaz snorted. "*They* wouldn't let me live this long."

"*They* being Duvcorp? Your own people want to silence you like they did Parris?"

Lopaz regarded him carefully, then checked his gym friends before looking back to Katryzna. "You came here with this wrecking ball, why don't *you* explain?"

Katryzna shifted closer to Tasker and whispered loudly, "I don't think he likes me."

"No one likes you!" Lopaz snapped. "Should've been food for worms right out of puberty!"

"Worms don't have puberty," she deliberately misinterpreted. Then asked Smail, "Do they?"

"Mr Lopaz," Tasker continued calmly, as Smail flustered at the attention. "This isn't what you think. Parris was murdered, but not by us. He tipped us off to a massacre in Norway. No explanations, no other clues but your name. And 'Ikiri'. Something Duvcorp definitely didn't want to discuss. So how about we start with exactly who you think would want you dead?"

Lopaz had gone still at the name Ikiri, and it took him a second to regroup. "If you're not here to kill me, you've given them a reason to. Get the hell out of here."

"Oh I do *not* have patience for this," Katryzna announced and walked away. The bound men stirred as she approached them, pistol raised. "Six men. You have six chances to talk." Smail looked to Tasker, but both waited to see where this was going. Katryzna raised her voice: "Three seconds, tick tock!" She pressed the gun to Henri's blood-smeared head. He froze as the others shouted and tugged at their restraints. "Three, two –"

"Stop, goddammit, stop!" Lopaz roared, out of the chair with his hands raised. He was shaking, looking at terrified Henri. "I'm sorry boys, I'm so sorry –"

"Talk!" Katryzna screamed with such ferocity that Tasker almost ducked himself. "You were part of it! What did Eyes die for? Talk!"

"Okay, okay!" Lopaz raised his hands higher, keeping his eyes on Henri. "Don't hurt them, for Christ's sake – whatever I deserve, these are good kids."

Nothing in Katryzna's expression said she cared. Her finger rested heavy on the trigger. Tasker said, "You've got our word, *no one* gets hurt if you talk."

"Your word's not what I need."

"Now, Miguel," Smail chipped in, "our friend from the British government here –"

Lopaz cut him off with pitying laughter. "Charles, you are *in* intelligence, aren't you? And you let Katryzna Tkacz into this city?"

Smail frowned, then studied Katryzna anew. She shrugged with a smile, light and merry again. He echoed, "Tkacz?"

"Autographs later," Katryzna said. "Talk, Lopey."

"Promise you won't hurt them."

"I promise I *will* if you test me –"

"All right, stop!" Lopaz said. "What do you want to know?" He looked to Tasker. "She, I understand. What's drawn the Ministry into this? You've finally discovered the Source?"

"The what?" Tasker asked.

Lopaz paused. "No?" He gave Katryzna another look and his face twisted to an ugly smile. "Oh. Katryzna, is this all you? Did you trick the Ministry into coming here so they'd pay for your airfare?"

"You think this is funny?" She stepped towards him. Tasker put a hand on her chest to stop her. Her eyes widened and nostrils flared, fingers tight on the pistol, as her anger shifted to Tasker.

"No, it's not funny," Lopaz said. "Tragic, is what it is. Charles? I am so sorry you're mixed up in this. And you, if you really are Ministry. She's a lovesick child, still, isn't she? Coming for long overdue revenge for Eyes. Why *now*, Katryzna?"

"I did not –" Katryzna rose on her toes as Tasker held her in place. She slapped his hand away and snarled, "Touch me again and I will end you."

"Eyes was the best," Lopaz said quickly. "The best I've ever seen, maybe the best the world's ever seen – until he met her. She made him sloppy. Sentimental." She shifted around Tasker but Lopaz threw up his hands. "Hold on, I'm talking! It doesn't matter now – they will come, for whatever reason she put this in motion. Eyes came here, yes. Him and thirty of the hardest bastards I've ever put together. They went out into the jungle never to return. That trail ends here." He addressed Tasker and Smail. "And it's got nothing to do with *Norway*."

Katryzna took long enough to process this for Tasker to say, "Not good enough. These were Parris's dying words. How was he connected?"

"You're sure about that?" Lopaz said. "You heard him say that yourself?"

"I'm no *liar*," Katryzna spat, stepping closer as Lopaz took a frightened step back. "You think I invented your name and some African mountain?"

"You might've beaten information out of Parris – that doesn't mean it had anything to do with why he contacted the Ministry." He paused, reconsidering the man in question. "I remember now, Simon Parris – that snotty brat was MEE once, wasn't he? Jesus. He could've had any number of historical ties to you guys, couldn't he?"

Tasker hesitated. True enough, he'd taken details for granted here. But Parris had flagged Katryzna through this long-dormant Eyes connection. Tasker said, "Are you saying Parris wasn't connected to you? And this place?"

"Oh no, he was involved. Part of the research team back in London."

"Not Ordshaw?"

"Whatever. Honestly I'm surprised he was still alive. Everyone else involved must be dead by now. Or 'missing'. But that was eight years ago, and like I said, the trail ended here."

"If it ended then why are you still here?" Katryzna demanded.

"I was their handler," Lopaz said. "After Eyes and the rest of them went into the jungle and their comms went down, I was told to hang tight in case anyone returned. I've been hanging tight ever since. Expecting someone to tie up loose ends. But Hank Duvalier went off on some other tangent while heads rolled for the failure. The head of the project killed himself two weeks before it was cancelled, one of the lead techs was found *headless* in a river. Superstitious types wanted someone left out here in case it wasn't coincidence. As if those thirty lost souls were coming back for revenge. My assumption was that Duvcorp were tidying up after themselves. I guess Parris wasn't important enough to be considered a threat. Like me."

Tasker said, "What needed tidying up? Why not send everyone home with a severance package? You suggested the Ministry might have discovered this ourselves."

"Ah." Lopaz weighed it up for a second. "Those mercenaries made a hell of a mess getting to Ikiri. I don't even know how many they killed on the way." He sent a subtle, guilty look Henri's way. Some connection there. "We didn't get full reports, but after they went missing rumours came back of all sorts. Not just that they had abused people along the way, but that they left such a mess out there. The region was unsettled for a year or more before a militia took over, and people still talk about it like it's cursed. To go there is to die and die badly. That was *our* legacy – we sent in a small army who slaughtered locals for Duvcorp's gain, what do you think the bosses would do to keep a story like that quiet? They might've killed hundreds. Unchecked atrocities that tell you nothing had changed since the Belgians came."

"But what *for*?" Tasker pressed. "That couldn't have all been on them – the stories that continued after they disappeared? What's at Ikiri that was worth so much?"

Lopaz nodded along. "Yeah, that. Probably nothing. If there was any truth in what they were looking for, someone like the MEE or the American government would've come to find it, too. The researchers made jokes, when setting this thing up. Laughing as they promised, 'We're going to find the Source.'" A worried expression crossed his face as the word slipped out. Like he'd not dared say it in years. Then he smiled in sick satisfaction at how it sounded. "That's what it was they were after. The Source."

"Of the river?" Smail probed weakly. "A mineral deposit?"

"No," Lopaz said. "The source of *life*. All life. Everything."

"What are you talking about?" Katryzna said. "Make sense!"

"Eyes must've blabbed to you about the shit Hank Duvalier had him doing. Investigating supposedly haunted locations, anyone claiming to have paranormal connections. He travelled the world looking for proof of the supernatural, and something in all that pointed them out here. Duvalier was hoping to find some clue to ever-lasting life, what else?"

No one answered, waiting for a punchline. But Tasker saw Katryzna putting those pieces together. There was truth in the stories Eyes had told her; Duvcorp really did have him chasing ghosts, and the trail led him here. Their goal was to find evidence of the afterlife? He'd never heard the Ministry give anything like that credence. But he could imagine the justification, as they delved into a study of novisan. It was an energy little understood even by the Ministry, particularly notable around the many unnatural creatures and phenomenon they sought to conceal. It was measurable, fluctuating in line with connections to living creatures, human and monster – but he'd never heard it associated with the afterlife. Or any source. Though with Duvcorp's resources, who knew what they might turn up? Tasker asked, "So what exactly led them to Mount Ikiri?"

"Energy scans," Lopaz said. "They faffed about with big electronic boxes that turned up all sorts of numbers supposedly showing patterns in the air. One of them tried to explain it to me once – sounded like magic nonsense. Chinese medicine shit. They recognised a *pull*, in a lot of places they were scanning, pointing here. To Ikiri."

"Their scans pointed . . ." Tasker didn't finish the thought. It meant Duvcorp were capable of monitoring novisan patterns over massive distances, where the Ministry only ever picked up things locally. Parris might have picked up on something in Norway without having direct interests there – it could be part of the same monitoring. An ability to flag whatever monstrous force had killed those people.

"They never reported what they found," Lopaz continued. "A handful of researchers, twenty-eight mercenaries and your friend Eyes, and all they achieved was a lot of bloodshed. Of course they didn't report *that*, either – those stories came down the river later. Insane, entitled white maniacs freaking out on their way towards Ikiri. They were cut off right before reaching the mountain. Chances are one of the militias got the better of them. It put the Ikiri region into turmoil, with small bands of soldiers fighting over the scraps, and it wasn't until a year or so later that General Solomon, from out east, took charge of the region for himself. Nothing and no one goes in or out now. Duvcorp had given up on it by then anyway. Probably accepted that it was a fairy tale that needn't have got so many people killed."

"So no one actually knows what they found?" Katryzna said. "I guess we need to see for ourselves." Tasker turned with alarm. "There's *obviously* something there, isn't there?"

Lopaz barked a laugh. "This is the DRC. It's not a walk in the woods."

"I didn't ask your opinion."

Tasker locked gazes with Smail, his own uncertainty mirrored there. It was an unthinkable extra step. Lopaz continued, "Maybe you should, you fool. You aren't listening. The Congo alone is dangerous, but Ikiri is beyond reproach. Thirty well-armed men never returned – people continue to die there. Horror stories float down the river. Henri, tell them."

"Ikiri is cursed," Henri agreed, muffled by his bloody nose. "The creatures are wrong."

"The creatures are wrong?" Tasker said. "What does that mean?"

"They aren't normal. Their unnatural cries stop people going close. No one has seen them to say what they are – not seen them and lived. But bits of people have been found. They are horror stories, as Miguel says. Whole villages of people have disappeared – women, children, all gone. Each year, maybe, another village lost. No one knows why, but it is expanding. Those that dare go –"

"Do not come back, yes," Katryzna said. "We got that."

"The point," Lopaz said, "is that whatever our idiot men did, they made it a place best forgotten. The problem is still out here, and you want no part of it."

Tasker met Katryzna's eye. She was beaming, as though her claims had been confirmed. With what they were saying, Tasker didn't doubt a connection to Laukstad, now. Whole villages, Henri said. Dead children in Laukstad, dead children out here. He had to go out there, to know what ungodly force Duvcorp had unleashed. To stop it happening again.

A few minutes into the journey back to the hotel, Smail said, "This isn't what you came out here for, is it, Tasker?" He avoided looking in the mirror, as though ignoring Katryzna's presence in the back would make her less threatening. She was quiet, watching for Tasker's take.

He said, "Parris had a reason to connect Ikiri to the Laukstad massacre. Entire villages dead or missing seems close enough to me."

"Except that out here," Smail said, "millions have died without being accounted for. I could give you a hundred village massacres here that would look similar to your Norwegian town. Scores, *thousands* dead. You're aware the civil war is the second most deadly conflict in history? Globally?"

"If it was that simple, why wouldn't they connect that to Ikiri?" Tasker said. "Did that sound like men accounting for war atrocities? Creatures no one's seen, a region no one comes back from? Is that how people usually explain the war zone? Mount Ikiri isn't even *in* the war zone, is it?"

Smail went quiet, confirming Tasker's suspicion. This was different.

"Duvcorp traced something from halfway across the world," Tasker continued. "It frightened them enough to leave someone behind to make sure it was contained. Trust me, Agent Smail, this is precisely my area."

"Being from the Ministry," Smail clarified, in a tone that said the rest of the intelligence community had a few choice thoughts about the MEE. Somewhere between sceptical and distrusting. "Answer me this, then – if it's that unusual, why did Duvcorp give up on it?"

"Presumably," Tasker drew out the answer, not liking its implications, "it was deemed too dangerous to pursue. Which would be precisely why we have to pursue it."

"And will London put up an expedition for you?"

Tasker hummed. The Ministry were tight-fisted at the best of times, requiring a thousand forms before you could so much as requisition toilet paper, but if Caffery could run that gamut he might get some funding for transport and a guide. Little beyond that. He certainly wasn't getting support from Ward's people this time. But it jogged his mind back to Ordshaw and the numbers Ward had turned up. One of the columns appearing to indicate 360 degrees, a direction. He took out his phone and put through a call. Not to Caffery but to Ward. She answered prim and polite, and after quick pleasantries he got straight to the point: "Those numbers off Parris's laptop, have you got anywhere with them?"

"Yes," she said, lowering her voice to a whisper. "Actually.

The third column *are* co-ordinates. We've found Laukstad on there. Five rows relate to it, with marginally different co-ordinates and the final column all quite similar numbers."

"Have you tested them on a map yet? As angles?"

"As if the energy reading pointed somewhere else?" Ward skipped a beat. "What have you found out there? Did you speak to Miguel Lopaz?"

"Better we keep it quiet for now," Tasker advised. "Can you just do me a favour and look into that?"

Ward paused again, wanting to know exactly what was going on, but restraining herself. She said, "I'll see what we can do."

Tasker put the phone away, confident even without results that he now understood what Parris had been up to. The research that had pointed Duvcorp out here might have ended or not, but Parris had kept monitoring the patterns that guided them, either way. He had spotted something in those readings that raised alarms over Laukstad, and if the expedition out here wasn't somehow responsible, it at least contained answers.

"You are genuinely thinking to go out there?" Smail said uneasily.

"Relax," Katryzna said, with a laugh. "Me and Sean will be fine."

Tasker went quiet again, her cheery tone drawing another concern to mind. He was riding with a human onion; beneath her layer of dirt and grime sat a disarming liveliness, and that in turn hid a savage, dangerous nature. She might have killed in there. Lopaz, the others, even him. Out of convenience.

Tasker checked himself. He'd been so quick to join with her, and he realised even now it was her infectious, unflinching energy pushing him forwards. It wasn't an attraction; Tasker didn't get attracted to people often. With Helen at home, why would he? She was all he'd ever needed, and they shared a low-burning libido energy that needed satisfying only a few times a year. She didn't ever suspect him of cheating on his long trips away; she knew him too well. No. As always, there was logic in his interest in this young woman. Someone as volatile as Katryzna could be a key to progress, willing to do what he himself could not . . .

At the hotel, he walked her up to her rooms, offering noncommittal responses to her remarks about the hotel awnings and light fixtures and whatever else impressed her. Thankfully, she seemed to be delving into her own thoughts, her enthusiasm gone. Tiring, at last.

They stopped at her door and there he paused to clear his throat. She cracked a weak smile and gave his shoulder a light push. "Save your breath, Sean. I've already had it from Rurik. People like Lopaz are *slime*."

Tasker forced a smile but said, "Parris, the attack –"

"I would *never* lie to you," Katryzna said. "We are friends, aren't we?"

He hesitated and saw some of the liveliness fading in her eyes.

"Right. I'm not what he said, okay?" she went on. "I came from a slum, my uncle was a gangster, I stabbed a policeman through the throat when I was twelve years old – I was *raised* bad. And I've done plenty of bad things since. But I'm honest. *Always*. This does affect us both, it's not just about Eyes. You believe me?"

"Yeah," Tasker replied slowly. "I believe you. We'll talk later. Get some rest."

Katryzna nodded but looked worried. He gave her one more limp smile before turning away.

13

Caleb barely let his foot off the gas for the final leg of the journey to Stilt Town. He was driving so fast they almost missed the turn – a gap in trees that flanked the main road, with a mud-track winding into shadow. A wooden board with a painted name read: *Graystown.* Everyone shifted to look back out the windows, scarcely believing they had made it this far without the Steers catching up again. Then it was all eyes forward, passing through the thicket of trees to reach the perimeter wall. Twenty feet of old steel rose in either direction, with a truck-sized gap in the middle blocked by a huge metal grid, where another name sign hung. Through the bars sat an open plain of long grass with buildings beyond.

Leaning way forward in her seat, Zip cooed. What Arlo Gray had built in this small patch of swampland *was* impressive. Wood and metal huts of various sizes stood two metres or more above the ground, supported by thick pillars. From here they could see the long hall, a glass-topped grow-house and a couple of smaller units, raised even higher, connected by swing bridges, all made up of scrap salvaged from shipwrecks and derelict buildings. A scattering of concrete pillboxes were just visible in the field, behind sandbags. On the other side of the gate, a man in jeans, a dark t-shirt and a bandanna ran up, an M16 rifle slung across his waist.

"What is this place?" Zip asked with awe.

"Stilt Town," Leigh-Ann said. "Paranoia capital of the US of A, and a rodeo of truly special people to boot."

"Behave," Caleb said. "They're gonna keep us alive, after all."

Reece leant out the window, waving to the guard. "Teddy? It is Teddy, right? Open up, would you?"

"Was expecting you last night," the guard replied. "Where you been?"

"Open on up and we'll spill all." Reece hid his urgency behind a friendly smile.

"Drive straight through, Caleb," Stomatt suggested. "This thing can handle it."

"Not sure it could," Caleb answered. "And then we'd have no gate to hold off the Steers, wouldn't we?"

Teddy took out his radio, relaying instructions; beyond him, people were stirring from the stilted huts, coming onto balconies to watch. "You got the money, Reece?"

"Yes we got the damn money!" Stomatt shouted. "The hell you think we are, bunch of amateurs?"

"Sto," Reece said. "Yes, Teddy, but we mightn't have shaken the Steers yet."

"You haven't –" Teddy fumbled at his radio again and told someone to hurry up. With a big whir and great squeaking gears, the gate slowly screeched open. Teddy skipped aside, watching through the bars as if to spot their pursuers. "Go on to the guard house, boys, Mr Gray himself will be there."

Caleb drove through the moment there was enough space, and took them over uneven ground around the building cluster, aiming for a space on the near edge. Zip made more appreciative noises as the rest of the township was revealed: the guard house was a squat structure with barred windows and a watch-nest up top; behind that was a tower with a clock on one side and windmill sails rotating on the another. And in the middle of the community of raised buildings stood a huge marble cross, on a stone mound a metre high. Beyond the buildings, the metal walls surrounded the clearing in a vast circle that encompassed large patches of land dotted with fenced animals and crops. People in the fields were pausing their work to watch the newcomers, while three more men with guns hurried over to join Teddy in looking out after their entrance.

"You see," Leigh-Ann whispered an explanation, "Caleb's uncle, he got messages from God, so he thinks, to build this place where his people could be free from the tyranny of men and the rising waters. A flood gonna come, he says – wipe out all the sinners. But not Stilt Town – *Graystown* as they call it – because they ready. Ready to fight off the sinners *and* the flood. Only problem is, they done penned themselves in with a whole community of crazy. Looks nice, though, don't it?"

Zip nodded appreciatively, and asked, "What's a tyranny?"

"There they are, there they are!" a shaky voice called from the guard house as they pulled up. Leigh-Ann winked to let Zip know it was time to keep quiet. The gang got out the truck, looking up at Alban Gray, a bottom-heavy older man leaning heavily on a brass cane. He was dressed in suit trousers and a straw hat, with a mane of white hair and a big, ruddy nose. He came down a short flight of steps, every movement making his body shudder. "Dear Caleb, Reece – you're well! God clearly rode with you. But Maximilian – your neck –"

"Ain't nothing, Alban," Stomatt scoffed at the wound.

Reece got a jab in his ribs and turned to Leigh-Ann's scolding face. He'd noticed the old man leave her out, too. Never mind they were practically family, literally in Caleb's case; Gray's sympathies didn't stretch too far when it came to women in general, and cussing unwed women in particular. Wasn't that she was Black, he kept telling her – Stilt Town had its share of Black folk. Not a debate for this minute, anyway. Reece said, "Got some worrying news, Mr Gray – some Steers picked up our scent crossing the state line –"

"And who's *this*, my dear, what an angel," Gray said, ignoring him to hobble closer to Zip. He came up short, seeing her eyes. She offered a sweet curtsy and a how'd-ye-do. Gray forced his smile again – "Yes, yes" – but looked to Reece for an explanation.

"This is Zip, we came upon her in need of assistance," Reece said. "But that's another thing –"

"How much you get?" a rough voice interrupted him. Noah, Alban's strapping, moustached eldest son, marched around the guard house stilts, in a too-tight t-shirt with a pistol swinging at his hip.

"Got it all, cousin," Caleb told him. "Though not without a fight."

"All of it?" Noah demanded confirmation from Reece. Unlike his father, he was wildly sceptical of the gang's ability to achieve anything, considering their demonstrable lack of faith.

"Take a look for yourself" – Reece gestured to the truck – "but we got company. We shot up a Steer car a ways back on the highway."

"You're safe here," Gray said lightly, as Noah approached the truck. He leant over the bed and rifled through the bags, before nodding reluctant confirmation to his dad. Gray slapped his hands together. "Splendid! Now you must be exhausted –"

The growl of rapidly approaching engines got his attention where Reece's warnings hadn't, with multiple vehicles coming up the path. Hell, they must've been right behind. Probably holding back to be sure the gang came into Stilt Town.

Teddy shouted useless warnings that someone was coming, and a young man popped his head out the guard house to confirm it. Three cars on their way. Noah glared accusation at Reece and went into action-mode, drawing his gun and shouting orders. In seconds, the people in windows or on balconies disappeared inside, and those in the fields came running in. The guards by the gate moved into the cover of the walls and gun barrels appeared from the pillboxes.

"Up here, up here." Gray led the way unsteadily up the steps into the guard house. The gang hustled after him. Tyres screeched near the entrance as Gray ushered them through and shut the door. In the guard house, they were greeted with a wall of monitors, some showing the compound itself, others incongruous blocks of trees, and two showing the entrance: a pair of Cadillacs and a dark Hummer parked outside, with half a dozen Steers piling out, carrying rifles and shotguns.

Noah stepped into view, reaching the gate and shouting almost loud enough to be heard in the guard house. The Steers shouted back.

"Jesus," Leigh-Ann muttered. "This gonna get bloody."

It got her the first look of recognition from Gray, a deeply judgemental one nicely framed by a big cross on the wall behind him. Reece moved in front of Leigh-Ann and said, "Sorry about this, Mr Gray, but it was always a possibility they'd know it was us."

"A slim one, didn't you say?" Gray said. The bumbling friendly act was gone, now that they'd brought actual trouble. "Dressed up in that getup with masks and all, *two* getaway rides, wasn't the point that this wouldn't happen?"

Reece didn't have an answer, so Caleb came in: "Uncle, we've got the goods, all the same."

Gray snorted dissatisfaction and approached the monitoring desk, where a freestanding steel microphone sat. He pressed a button and said, "Teddy, hand me to Noah." They watched Noah take the guard's radio on the monitor. "What're they saying?"

"You might guess, Pa," Noah answered. "Say to hand them over or there'll be trouble."

"Can't the kid make them forget they saw anything?" Stomatt asked, in what passed for a whisper from him. Zip cuddled closer to Reece, and he sensed that no, this was outside her remit.

On screen, one of the Steers broke from the crowd, taking out a phone.

"Jam them," Gray instructed, and their operator threw switches. "Remind them our property extends to the road, Noah, and they're trespassing. Count them down from five."

The Steer making a call looked irritated, clearly not getting through, and he demanded someone else's phone. Noah relayed Gray's message and started counting.

"Get in cover, boy," Gray advised, and Noah did so, ducking around the wall and raising his voice for *three*. The Steers moved closer, flustering at the countdown, their shouts coming through the radio.

"– break your goddamned doors in!"

"– know who the fuck you messing with!"

"Two!" Noah shouted louder.

The Steer on the phone gave up calling to assess the situation. Likely their leader, from the way he carried himself. A big round jaw, eyes close together, a flat-top, black hat.

"One!"

The Steer pushed forward, waving at his men to stand down and yelling loud enough to be heard through the radio: "Big mistake, Gray. We know who y'all are – all y'all – and when we come back it won't be to talk!"

"Time's up," Gray decided and pressed another button. "Tower, put one in a windscreen for me."

A gunshot sounded like thunder in the sky, making Zip jump, and on screen the Hummer's windscreen shattered as though hit by an enormous hammer. The Steers dived for cover, yelling and holding guns above their heads.

"Tell them get back in the cars, Noah," Gray instructed calmly, and Noah relayed the order. "Leave now or next shot's taking a head."

As Noah shouted, the black-hat Steer instructed his men to pile back in, all of them keeping low and watching the gates. He lingered himself, the last to get in, and the radio picked up his shouts again: "Tell your pop he'll be hearing from Dustin Fallon himself – we'll have that green-haired freak's head!"

With that, the Steers retreated, wheels throwing up mud as they disappeared through the trees. They appeared again on another monitor, down the path, then were gone.

"Whatever you're toting up in that tower," Stomatt said, "I *want* it." Reece shot him a warning look and Gray gave one much nastier. But both glares only egged him on. "Seriously, Alban, I'll climb up that tower and take a watch myself. Free. Of. Charge."

"That's enough, Maximilian," Gray told him icily, and turned on Reece. "Get the cash in here. We'll talk over lunch."

14

Tasker drank stiff drinks at the bar while waiting for Caffery to get back to him. His handler had said a flight into the Congolese interior was unlikely: only two planes a week connected Kinshasa to Kisangani, and the latter city wasn't much closer to Ikiri, anyway. Together with the civil war out there, and the need to use airports where Lopaz's mystery assassins might spot Tasker, Caffery was veering towards this trip being too dangerous to pursue a dead case that the Ministry didn't necessarily have a stake in. Never mind Tasker's insistence that people were most definitely *dying*, that things were most definitely *fucked up* out here. Along with the initial arguments about their flights, Caffery was being particularly obstructive, and Tasker's mind couldn't help but go back to Parris. Killed after he contacted the Ministry. They were thoughts he almost didn't dare think, let alone speak, but given Duvcorp's reach, could this be big enough that someone on his own team was trying to block him from going further? Tasker sat hoping to pitch the idea to Katryzna, but two hours after they checked in she had not come down.

"Do you mind?" Smail announced his presence. The spy looked no less harassed than in Club Clash, checking over his shoulder. "She's not here?"

"In her room, freshening up," Tasker said, unsure if Katryzna could get "fresh".

Smail looked relieved. He took the stool next to Tasker and gestured to the barman for a beer. "I've been on the phone. Are you blown?"

"Huh?"

"You're not here on strictly Ministry business. You can't have told your people everything, I'm sure. You are aware of who she is?"

Tasker paused, Smail confirming his instinct that the MEE wouldn't have handled Katryzna's overt involvement well. He said, "I've got an impression."

"Do you? Because we have a file on Tkacz thick as six eggs, back in Vauxhall. An awful lot that *looks* like her doing, little proved. Chaotic, unaccountable cases of violence – victims relating to the Russian mafia or the same corporations you're chasing."

"You're not surprising me yet."

"And that troubles me," Smail said. "You must be aware of the possibility that she killed Simon Parris herself? And rather than bring her in, you got her a hotel room in the DRC and want to travel into the rainforest together?"

Tasker looked into his whisky and realised his mind was already made up on this. Katryzna was bold, direct and unafraid. He couldn't see her as a liar, and said, "That's my plan, yes."

"Tell me you know what you're looking for, at least," Smail implored.

"I couldn't say, that's the point. My gut – and a dead man who predicted a *massacre* – says it's worth finding out."

"Well I can't speak for the dead man," Smail moved closer, expression hardening. Tasker could imagine him wielding a knife in a windowless room. "But your *gut* needs educating. No one gets this close to Tkacz and lives, Tasker. She is legend. Charmed, somehow – the things she's said to have got away with. Your energy would be better spent taking her down."

It only made Tasker dig in his heels. "That sounds like your job, not mine. I'm not here for her."

"And what does your Ministry think about you going upriver?"

Tasker said nothing.

"Yeah, I didn't think so. But you intend to do it anyway." Smail took a big breath. "You need to rethink your friendships, at the very least."

"Did you come here to put me down, or do you have some other proposal?" Tasker prompted.

Smail paused. Yes, this was all a preamble to his own ploy; else he would've done as he suggested and gone after Katryzna himself. "As it happens, I do. So long as you know where you stand with her." A pause, pure theatre: he knew exactly where he was going. "I have eyes all over Kinshasa, all the way along the river. Mount Ikiri, however, sits in a region we're not well-informed on. Perhaps I was a little misleading before. I believe

Lopaz when he says there are people that would kill to protect the area, and considering it's a long way from the fighting or any resources we know of, these are not atrocities we'd associate with the war, as you rightly assumed. I don't think it's safe, or that you should go, but if you insist, I wouldn't mind knowing what's going on. There's a barge, I can get you passage on it. It's slower than a private hire, but safer. I can get you kit, a guide, whatever you need. But you'll report back to me when you return. If you return."

"And?" Tasker said.

"And as you're fool enough to go with her, I'll turn a blind eye to Tkacz until you get back. If anyone can survive out there, she's likely to, after all. But you'll bring her to me, afterwards, of course. *If* you get back."

"Ah. We get you the dirt on Duvcorp and Ikiri and you also bag a notorious assassin? Earn yourself a promotion and finally get to go home?"

Smail wore a faint smile. "Promotion, perhaps. As for home, like Lopaz, I'm quite happy here. I could take a step back from fieldwork, though."

Tasker's first instinct was to tell Smail and SIS to jog off a cliff. But if Katryzna's reputation was enough to get him moving, he could address the consequences later. In the meantime, whoever Lopaz was afraid of might get wise to their plans any day, so once again, Caffery's resistance was pushing him. With Smail all but confirming Ikiri was a force that warranted investigation, what choice did he have? He said, "You help me get to the bottom of what Duvcorp were up to, and you'll be the first to know about it. But you'll leave Katryzna to me, one way or another."

Smail backed off, studying his face. "We can work with that."

"You saw the way he was looking at you," Rurik goaded from the balcony table. Gripping the banister tightly, Katryzna tried to breathe in fresh air but got nothing but humid yuk. It wasn't peaceful here, with car horns honking and the loud discussion of street vendors and revellers audible, what, five storeys below? "You showed your true colours and now he's scared, like everyone else."

"He is not scared," Katryzna muttered. "He would do something if he was."

"He probably has. Phoned his bosses, asked for backup, ready to trap you. He's not just going to come and cut your throat – that's *your* style."

"I have cut no one's throat," she hissed. "I'm doing good."

"Yeah?" her conscience laughed, nastily. "Then why am I here?"

She screwed her eyes closed. She could feel it creeping over her. A dread shadow. Her skin tightening. Mind racing with a thousand unresolved thoughts. He hates you. They all hate you. You killed him, betrayed him – *distracted*, Lopaz said – oh! Eyes talked about you? Mocked you, probably. Or worse, believed in you – got sloppy. He could survive anything. What was a forest? What did she do to him? Why was she *she*?

Katryzna gritted her teeth. Remember one happy moment, one real memory. Eyes sitting on a rock by a lake after they left that Belorussian prison. Smoking, like always, staring into the water. He interrupted her teasing to say, "This is good."

This meant the calm – their companionship, their moment.

Those shark-dead eyes – like he had seen too much for anything to interest him again – they had a little light looking at her. Hope. Real emotion. Same when she bit his face, the first time they met, when Eyes was meant to kill her. This ancient source of unlimited cool had discovered he *could* still be surprised.

"You're thinking of when you savaged him," Rurik guessed. "That's your happy thought?"

Katryzna turned on him, looming over the table. But her conscience hadn't flinched from her since she was a teenager, and he didn't now. She deflated again. Had Eyes died distracted by this lunatic girl he had vaguely taken under his wing? Ah. The dread crept up through her veins. Sean *should* fear you. She fell onto the chair and said, "I need food."

"Indeed, why not go downstairs and ruin someone else's night," Rurik said.

She had no energy to argue. He was right. Better not to move or be seen – she'd been visible enough on the way. Prancing about the airport, letting herself *enjoy* it. No. Stay in the shadows – turn out the lights for a week. A year. Disappear into this feeling.

A knock at the door drew her back. She frowned at Rurik.

"Probably come to ask you to leave," her conscience said.

Katryzna dragged herself inside, lazily taking the old Hungarian pistol from the bed.

"Leave the gun!" Rurik shouted. "Listen!"

"I'm mad with listening!" Katryzna spat back. "I've been told! Told and told, how terrible I am!" In her anger she swept the door open. "What!"

Sean stood frozen for a moment, then raised his eyebrows. Katryzna bit her tension down and showed him her teeth. Not really a smile. He returned an empty one of his own. Pitying. "Everything okay, Katryzna?" Whisky on his breath. "I thought you'd come downstairs."

Oh. A little alcohol had made him bold, and ding ding! Activate creep mode. Katryzna rolled her eyes. "Not interested."

"I hoped you'd come down to *talk*." Swinging back to serious, *did* he want to scold her?

Katryzna took a step back. "Not now, okay?" He looked over her shoulder. She mumbled an explanation for the crumpled sheets: "I jumped on the bed." Another stupid thing. As if hurting people wasn't bad enough, she was idiot enough to –

"My people in London aren't happy with where this has gone," Tasker said.

Great. Boo hoo and damn. "Because you think I made it all up?"

"No." He looked even more serious. "They just don't see it the same way I do. But I think you and I are on the same side in uncovering this. Even if our methods differ."

"Okay. Thanks." Katryzna started closing the door. He put himself in the way.

"Without their help," Tasker quickly went on, "it'll take a few days to arrange passage. Can you wait? You'll have access to the full facilities here."

She put a hand over her face, massaging both temples. "Yes, I can wait."

"He's trying to connect," Rurik shouted. "Give him something."

"I will give *you* something in a minute," Katryzna snarled, half-spun towards the balcony. She turned very slowly back to Sean. The man hid his alarm well. Stupid Rurik's stupid idea spiralled behind her eyes. They always wanted to connect, then they got hurt. She said, "Eyes believed in me. I was bad for him. Lopaz was right about that."

"Forgive me," Tasker replied, oozing horrible calm, "but from what I've heard, I don't see that you were the most dangerous thing in Eyes' life."

Katryzna glowered. This was worse than his dislike: pity. "What do you know?"

"Come down for a drink –"

"I don't *drink*, Sean," she said, raising her voice. Then slumped again, suddenly spent. "I cannot. I'm about to get low. Just make your plans and leave me with your" – she flapped a hand – "full facilities. Don't *worry* about me, don't think we have . . . something."

He nodded carefully. "Yeah. So you know, I've got a wife and daughter back home." A brief pause. "They're everything to me, they're why I do this. When I saw those dead in Laukstad – they were the *same* – I couldn't let this go. I'd do anything for them."

Katryzna gave him a well-earned look of disgust. "Then why are you going after *me*?"

"What? I am *not*." A fluster in his cool – how could she *possibly* think that? Ha. "I'm –" He looked into the room, reassessing. "I'm only trying to make sure you're okay. Are you?"

"Always," Katryzna sighed, closing the door without a farewell. "And never."

"I'm not sure when I'll be back," Tasker told Helen, finally calling after breakfast. Even having slept off a long day and a lot of whisky, he was sure he sounded haggard, forlorn. "But once this is through, I'll be home first thing, no compromises."

"You're staying safe, aren't you?" Helen asked. She wouldn't ask why he was delayed or what exactly he was doing, but she did insist: "Just make sure you do *come* back."

That was always the bottom line: guarantee there was a return journey and a chance to reset. She had held him when he came home haunted by the memory of parasitic worms in Kuala Lumpur. She'd made him a hot drink and run him a bath after he'd tracked a blood drinker in Berlin. Then a week or more's respite, which he could dedicate fully to her and Rebecca. Tasker never told Helen exactly what he'd seen or why he woke up in terrified sweats, and she never asked. She knew how important the Ministry's work was, and how important *he* was to them. She was an expert at focusing on the positives, letting go of the negatives.

His silence stretched out, as he thought of home comforts. He could picture Helen leaning against the kitchen counter, talking while putting away dishes. Then he imagined their French windows shattering, smashed from the outside. An invasion of feral people clawing at his family. Suits like Marge Cosgrove would shrug it off and say *oh well*, as they did for Laukstad and had done for the villages of Ikiri for so many years. He imagined taking Katryzna into Duvcorp's palatial offices, unleashed as she'd been in Club Clash –

"Hold up," Helen said. "Here she is."

Rebecca's cheery voice came on: "Daddy? Did Mummy tell you about rehearsals?"

Tasker smiled. Of course, the school was preparing a Christmas play, more than a month in advance. Rebecca had a lead role and quickly rattled out a short account of how hard she was working and how she hadn't made nearly as many mistakes as *Robert*, who didn't even have many lines. Tasker said, "Our little superstar. I promise I'll be back for the performance."

"You will?" Rebecca cried, and bounced away from the phone, relaying that to Helen.

Helen warned, without malice, "Don't if you can't."

Rebecca's delighted squeal made Tasker wince. A flash of that body in Laukstad. He said, "I'll take care of this fast. I have to. I've even got a partner to help."

"Oh my days." Helen's tone lightened. "Agent Tasker with a partner? He must be very impressive."

Of the words he might use to describe Katryzna, Tasker was not sure *impressive* was one of them. Considering their uneven conversation last night, he might go towards confusing, unstable – mysterious if he was generous. He said, "Effective. I'm confident *she* will be effective."

"She'd better be," Helen said. "We can't wait for you to get back."

"Likewise."

Tasker made his farewells, and paused for only a second to switch from home-life back to work mode. He called Ward and immediately said, "I'm confident there's something out here. Tell me you can support that?"

"Yes," she replied, almost excitedly. "We absolutely can."

She confirmed what he expected: Parris's files showed Laukstad's energy pointed in this directions. Other co-ordinates on the list followed the pattern – locations on different continents, roughly pointing to central Africa. He was exactly where he needed to be. Ward said, "This is big. Support might find a dozen applications for a way to trace such large-scale novisan patterns."

"I'm not sure we want to dive into that yet," Tasker said. "This got Parris killed."

It gave her pause, but Ward said, "It's not something we can ignore, is it? We have to analyse the rest of this information, see what else he was onto. If I make the importance of this clear to London, we'll have all the support we need."

"Slow down," Tasker said, recalling the ill-feeling Caffery's reluctance had given him. "Deputy Director. I'm hesitant over who exactly we involve in this. Can you give me some time before passing this up the ladder? And whatever you do, make sure you do it quietly."

Though a little deflated, she agreed to his terms.

While Smail started making preparations for their trip, Tasker took advantage of the lull to rest, drinking in Le Cockpit Bar again. Katryzna had not emerged all day, and he was considering going to her when Lopaz's man, Henri, entered the bar. His nose had been stitched since Katryzna's attack, and he wore the wound well; it somehow matched his moustache. He was beaming – something to offer. "I come to make amends."

"For Katryzna breaking your nose?" Tasker said.

"Not broken, just split," Henri corrected. "And yes, for putting you in that position. Miguel's always been –" He mugged a face to mimic "not-quite-there". "He's like a crazy uncle, always worrying about who's out to get him. We mostly take it lightly. But seeing you come in? We only wanted to protect him."

"All right," Tasker replied, noting he was surprisingly well-spoken, that chiselled body now businesslike in a linen shirt and shorts.

Henri pulled up the adjacent stool, settling in for a heart-to-heart. "You really are planning on going up the river, to Ikiri? I thought you'd be going home by now."

"Unlike Lopaz, I tend to believe in confronting our fears."

"Ha, very good." Henri signalled for a beer, checking to Tasker in case he wanted one. Apparently they were drinking buddies now. "Well. He's gone into hiding again, we might not see him for months. But me, I want to go with you."

Tasker frowned. It was an about-turn after Henri's previous talk of jungle horrors.

"You don't know who I am, do you?" Henri asked. "My sister was Sara Ngoi."

"Yeah. I don't know who she is, either."

Henri's smile stretched, pleased to make the reveal. "She's how I met Miguel. We grew up in Binga, north of the river from Ikiri. We came to the city together, my big sister and me, seeking our fortune. Working in translation, tours, education. This white man, he brought the biggest opportunity. Help organise this trip, guide them out there, come back rich. Sara, she could speak a dozen languages, and she was so smart, so beautiful. Exactly who they needed."

Tasker noted that past tense *was*. "Your sister joined the Duvcorp expedition?"

"She was their guide – their translator. Made bookings on the boats, led the way."

"Never came back."

Henri's smile fell. "I wanted to go, too, but I was young. Miguel said no. I was only good for odd jobs here, not meant for their work out there. The men they gathered, you should have seen them. I've faced many militias, but never men quite as scary as them."

Tasker took a drink. This, he could use. "Did you meet this guy Eyes?"

"I'm sure I did," Henri said. "Most of the crew used made-up names, animals or activities. Moose. Bruiser. I remember the leader – they called him *Boss* – he looked like he'd never laughed a day in his life. Even the nastiest ones were scared of him. There was also a tall, thin white guy who watched over the scientists. He wore a long dark coat, even here, and smoked like an exhaust pipe. My sister, she joked that he was too spooky to die, so she'd stick close to him."

That sounded like Eyes, all right. Shame Sara's plan hadn't worked out.

Henri continued, "I kept working with Miguel, waiting for them to come back. Instead – well, he gave you the idea. You know, a hundred years ago, King Leopold's men hacked off hands for rubber, controlling the Congo with weapons we could not fight against. These people were the same. They had scanners to see rebels coming, guns that kill dozens in seconds, from a mile away. Unstoppable. They left rebel heads on spikes – then dismembered farmers and fishermen, for reasons we don't know. Maybe just because they could. I was terrified for what had become of my sister in their company. And then" – he made a *poof!* gesture – "they were gone. A plague that vanished after running its course. They're spoken of like a myth, up the river. Maybe they became the monsters people are afraid of. Maybe they angered the nature spirits enough to release something worse than them?

"When no one came back, and Duvcorp sent no one else, Miguel insisted it was something to be forgotten – perhaps even by force. I got other work while he got paranoid, but we stuck together, he with his guilt and fear, me with my regrets for Sara."

"So what do you think happened?"

"*No one* knows. Everyone in this country has lost people without knowing how or why. But this time, there *is* something to be done. If you'll have me, I will come to learn the truth. You'll need a guide and a translator. A *bodyguard*, even." This tickled him to laughter, lightening again. "Well, your friend might be able to take care of herself. But I can help with navigating the land; I know you're no better informed than Lopaz was, back then. You think it's a mountain you're looking for?"

Tasker gave him a look. "Kind of implied in the name?"

"We do not call it Mount Ikiri," Henri replied with amusement. "Ikiri sits in the Central Lowlands, there are no true mountains. It's tall, yes, but a range of hills at best."

"You've been there?"

Henri shrugged. "I know of it. An unremarkable area in the heart of dense forest. But I know how to survive the forest. How to avoid men like General Solomon."

Tasker hummed. If anyone was alive in the Ikiri region, they were under Solomon's command. Smail had given Tasker a brief introduction to the general and his Popular Liberation Union. Otherwise known as the Cursed Union. He had been murdering Rwandans in the eastern conflict before he migrated to fill the power vacuum Duvcorp's advance created, and he butchered all who crossed his territory. Tasker said, "You think he can be reasoned with?"

"Ah, no," Henri said. "I think he can be *avoided*. Some believe General Solomon to be a spirit himself, taking orders from the dead, commanding the *zimwi*, monsters that feed on human flesh. But I am a good Christian. I am not afraid of zimwi."

"That's not what you were saying yesterday," Tasker said, warily. "What is it, are there monsters out there or not?"

Henri eyed him with interest, impressed that Tasker took the stories seriously. "There are terrible rumours and things to be afraid of, perhaps. But I believe another reason no one sees Solomon and his beasts is because the Cursed Union is very small. Their brutality is to give them a bigger image. We can hide with just three people. I can find the paths we need."

Tasker sipped his drink, eyeing Henri over that presumptive *we*.

"Do we have a deal, Mr Tasker? Or do you prefer to trust only in Ms Tkacz?" Henri laughed. "Miguel says she is terrifying. He says ask her about Istanbul. And Croatia. And Vultuk, in Kazakhstan – he says that was the worst. Be *scared*. Of someone that looks like her?" He sounded a little too happy about all that, especially considering she'd already floored him. But clearly he had already expressed fondness to Lopaz about Katryzna. A seasoned fighter fascinated by the grubby little lunatic that felled him with one blow. Sure enough, he continued, "Is she coming down? I would like to buy her a drink."

If this journey was going to happen, Tasker had to dampen *that* affection. He said, "We might work together, but don't get any ideas. She doesn't drink. And I'm pretty sure she's gay."

Henri startled, but the surprise passed quickly. "We might work together?"

Katryzna hopped out of bed, stretched, threw open the balcony door and breathed in thick, hot air. Ugh. Whatever – to food! She bounced down to the restaurant to be told breakfast stopped half an hour ago, but they could send something to her by the pool. She wandered out into scorching sunlight. In the pool was a broad, muscular man who spent a lot of time in gyms, swimming to the edge with dignified grace that *screamed* Sean. He slowed into her shadow and looked up. Expression souring as he noticed her new shirt and trousers were frayed and stained. Well, she had spent three days in a stuffy room with no change of clothes.

"About time you got some vitamin D," Tasker said. He went to push himself up from the pool, but she placed a shoe on his shoulder. The tatty white trainer also displeased him. "We really need to take you shopping."

Katryzna pushed him back into the water and Tasker took a step back to avoid stumbling. She smiled cheekily, to stay his irritation.

"Good to see your humour's back. Everything's under control, so you know. We've got a guide and we're almost ready to go."

"Did you whisper that through my door last night?"

"It wasn't a whisper. Are you feeling better now?"

"Rested like a baby." Katryzna stretched her arms up with a yawn. She surveyed the pool area, with its sun loungers and one other guest, an older lady with sun-leathered skin. "We can go as soon as you finish floating like a duck."

"That look on his face," Rurik advised, "is because you've been lazing about while he's done all this work. It's been days, Katryzna –"

"I *know*," Katryzna said. "I told him I was taking a break, what's the problem?"

As Rurik cited a half-dozen problems, Tasker said, "We've got the public barge leaving tomorrow. On a schedule, so we can't leave any sooner than that. Enjoy one more night here – you can eat in the restaurant for once. If you tidy up."

"A barge? Not a plane or a helicopter?"

"We need to go unnoticed," Tasker said.

"Please," Rurik groaned, "he's obviously done what he can."

"I'll *try*," Katryzna said, feeling generous. She scratched her nose, looking across to the dormant sunbather, then crouched and gestured for Tasker to come closer. He stayed where he was. "I want to talk privately." He still didn't move. She rolled her eyes. "Okay. I expect Charlie wanted you to turn me in? From him and Lopaz, you must know I am a monster now? Did they talk about Kazakhstan? They always complain about that, but only because there were children involved. It wasn't the *worst*; I completed the job they wanted. Five kids dead instead of two, that's not exactly a massacre."

"That is a massacre," Tasker said, "exactly."

It made Katryzna smile. He spoke frankly, not with Rurik's snideness. He probably killed people for work, too. She said, "No, I suppose it *was* a massacre. But it would have happened anyway, is my point – it only went a little wrong. And Gomer – my handler – he deserved to die. *He* is why people like Lopaz get so upset about that case."

That got Tasker's attention better than the murder of children. Ah, he had a useless handler, too – he was definitely jealous. This was bonding.

"So that's out there," Katryzna continued. "I just want to say, I know I'm not always . . . good for people. And I can go on alone if you want. However crap your life is, I will make it worse."

"This isn't all about you," Tasker said. "And I can happily return the offer. You don't have to come, if you'd rather wait here."

Katryzna stood, squinting at him. "Well that's definitely not happening. Great. Good. We are on the same page, then – if you need me, I will be *gorging*." She turned, waving a hand behind her. "And cover yourself up. No one's impressed."

15

Antonio stumbled drunkenly off the pavement, hand against a cool earth bank to support himself. Piss powerful as a hose and a loud, satisfied groan. Answered by the frightened bray of a donkey. He turned, spraying urine across the road, and looked up the hill, past Raúl's half-finished house. Pockets of darkness between tatty brick, support planks sticking out here and there. Daft donkey got loose out someone's lot, trapped itself?

It brayed again, afraid.

Antonio grunted and shouted at it, be quiet, coming, coming, struggling with his fly. He tripped on rubble, steadied himself on a pile of bricks. Hooves scuffed back in the shadows, the animal kicking up a fuss. Antonio's buzz was fading as he absorbed the animal's fear. He slowed down, feeling his way through the building site. "Where you at, dumb mule?"

The braying got worse, the creature about screaming itself to death.

A disruption of rubble just behind made Antonio spring. A guy was standing there, silhouetted against the road behind. Antonio lurched, slurring a comment and pointing through the building site. Got a stuck donkey back there, hear it? The guy didn't move. Upset, maybe angry?

"Not trespassing or nothing," Antonio said. "Trying to help. Raúl? Is you, right? Say something."

The donkey stomped up a fury like Santa Muerte herself had come calling, and Antonio twisted to the sound, sobering fast. His back to the man, Antonio heard Raúl jump – and added his screams to the donkey's.

Leigh-Ann stepped out the steaming shower a new woman, clean and free of the smell of cordite; ready to suit up in defiance of the drab dresses of Gray's women. She padded out into the dorm in just a towel, leaving wet footprints between the coarse-linen bunks and their footlockers. Past Zip, curled on her side on a cot, twitching against a bad dream, to her own bed where her suit lay on the mattress. Amazing they hadn't replaced it with a nun's frock or something while the gang were away. She lifted the indigo jacket, tapered about the hip, black patches over the shoulders. Damn sight better than the potato sack of a dress the commune provided Zip. And the first step in getting back to *normal*. Dress to impress, Reece always said.

Zip made a little whimpering noise. Leigh-Ann set the jacket aside to perch on the bunk next to her and gingerly stroked her arm. "Just a dream, sweetie."

"Madero," Zip uttered. "The donkey . . . they're gone."

"Dreaming of donkeys doesn't sound so bad," Leigh-Ann said.

"All dead." Zip sat up suddenly, frightened red eyes seeing something else. "Villa Madero – all dead."

"A dream," Leigh-Ann reminded her, slower now, with how serious the kid took it. Zip calmed with big breaths. "We ain't nowhere as fancy as a villa. But I saw a couple boys playing on a jungle gym outside – you wanna put the bad dream to bed, go have some fun?"

Zip's face twisted with confusion. Not letting go yet. "Something bad happened."

"It was a dream, that's all."

"But . . . I'm scared Leigh. I get them a lot now. It *feels* real."

Leigh-Ann wondered at the best response. Did you invite a traumatised kid to share and relive their imagined shit, or just dismiss it? A sharp knock saved her deciding – Reece followed right on into the room. "How my amazing ladies doing?"

"Jesus, Reece," Leigh-Ann snapped, tightening her towel, "you can't come storming in the ladies' dorm, they'll cut off your damn balls."

"Forgive me, I got bored waiting all day." Reece bowed low, extravagantly, grinning. Asshole. He was dressed already in the same style suit as Leigh-Ann's. The Crewe's tailored uniform, handmade by Brittany back in Cutjaw, each perfect fitting with little flourishes to make them unique. His had lapels that curved out with a little kink halfway up; Leigh-Ann's had a double-stripe of black piping. All deep indigo, worn with crisp black shirts and shining shoes. With his trumpet in hand, as elegant as the pistol at his hip, he could've belonged to some kind of prince's guard, if not for that greenish hair. Some was back to his usual brown, but damn there was a lot he couldn't wash out.

Leigh-Ann informed him, "Your hair looks like clown vomit."

"Yeah." He ran an awkward hand through it but kept up his smile. "New style, here to stay, I guess?"

"I saw something bad," Zip interrupted worriedly.

"In a dream," Leigh-Ann clarified. "She was napping."

"Don't sweat it sweetie, Leigh here's a *lioness*, she'll protect you." Reece winked. "And we're just across the way."

"But why can't we all stay *together*?" Zip asked innocently.

"Because Alban Gray is a cu –" Leigh-Ann stopped herself with a cough. "Are we agreed that the kid's cool now – can we swear?"

"Between you and your God, you wanna live with that," Reece said. "Now there's fierce scents coming from the mess hall, if you would *kindly* join me."

"Look remotely ready to you yet?" Leigh-Ann sneered jokingly.

"Sorry." Reece lifted his trumpet. "You must be waiting on your fanfare." He played a little trill, short and sharp, surprising Zip. She laughed. "Nah, that's not it – here, something I been working on." He played again, a heavy sound followed by quick descending notes, then another bold toot. Zip giggled again. He gave her a cock-eyed look. "Not quite there, is it?" Reece checked with Leigh-Ann. "Not sure this one's for the horn."

"Again!" Zip demanded, then remembered her manners. "Please."

Reece drew it out, then nodded. "Okay." He repeated the same little riff and added a flourish. Pulled his head back to make a show of it. Zip clapped, forgetting the nightmare at last. "Now hold on. I'm getting irresponsible, putting music in a kid when she ain't ready."

"I'm ready!" Zip turned a worried look to Leigh-Ann. "Tell him, Leigh!"

"Sure?" Reece said. "Because I had an inkling we might need your daddy's permission, before we do something like make music. And how we gonna ask him, not knowing where he is?"

Oh, he was smooth. Leigh-Ann imagined him sitting back in

his bunk plotting a way to get the kid to talk without pressing her. But Zip's eyes narrowed, recognising a ploy. She said, "He's not here. I can listen to music."

"He might get wind of it, though," Reece said. "Especially if we're close to this river with a pyramid. This Grithin guy? Think they might be nearby, now?"

Zip considered it. "Closer."

She sounded a little too sure, making Leigh-Ann shift. The playfulness was leaving Reece's expression. Hell. Zip had hypnotised those Steers, why shouldn't she have psychic tracking skills. Reece said, "You see him in your head? Know where –"

"No!" Zip suddenly winced, screwing her eyes closed. "I *can't*. It's not safe!"

"Jesus if someone didn't do a number on her," Leigh-Ann muttered. "Sweetie, thinking about a thing ain't gonna do no harm."

Zip considered it carefully, at length, and looked genuinely unsure. Leigh-Ann wasn't so sure herself, now.

"Cher," Reece said, "I got another proposal, for me to think on while you get ready for more music and the *best* food. Can you tell us your daddy's name, at least?"

Another pause, but she accepted this one: "We're Masons. Seph Mason, that's my daddy . . . but they call him something else. Not nice."

"I been called plenty not nice things myself," Leigh-Ann said, imaging the racial shit this half-Black kid might've endured. The slurs might point them in the direction of her father's ethnicity, at least. But Zip's answer caught her breath.

"Headhunter. They call him Headhunter."

Leigh-Ann exchanged a look with Reece, acknowledging the same thing. This was getting more fucked by the moment. She clarified, quietly, "On account of him hunting them monsters?"

Zip nodded, then brightly changed the subject: "Can you play another tune? Please."

"For sure, cher," Reece said. "But after you get some food. If Leigh has the decency to put on some clothes."

In the mess hall, busy with Gray's people eating at long tables, the counter was spread with thick gumbo, spiced rice and beans, crispy bacon and butter-soaked baked potatoes. Reece and Caleb filled their plates while Reece made small talk as scant distraction for his concerns over that kid and the Steers. Gray was right that it *shouldn't* have been like this – he'd planned things carefully, used disguises, found camera blind spots. But the delay, and that gas stop encounter, had cost them all that grace.

The head chef asked Reece, "Y'all dressed for a parade? After missing the welcome dinner last night?"

At Reece's side, Caleb squirmed, resenting the attention garnered by their fine suits. But Reece replied warmly, "My apologies, Chef, you know we wouldn't have missed it but for the gravest circumstances. Sto's still being stitched up as we speak. Though this looks mighty fine – can't imagine how you topped it for last night."

He smiled all the way, no one knowing he was aching with concern underneath.

When they reached a table separate from the crowd, Caleb said, "Don't all seem too happy to have us here, do they? Probably have some idea the people we hurt – they got *thou shalt not kill* engraved big somewhere round here."

"Quoting scripture now?" Reece said. "They all knew there might be casualties."

Caleb tried to keep his next complaint down, but couldn't. "And the kid. Pretty sure they know, Reece. I seen them looking at her."

"Know what? That she's lost and afraid and we're all she's got? Till she's safe, she's part of the Crewe. That sit okay with you?"

Caleb's pause said no, not really, but he said, "Course it do."

"You're more hero than any of us, know that, Caleb? But now's time to quit worrying and start planning how to spend our rewards."

It tweaked a smile. "Not too early to jinx it?"

"Leave worrying about that shit to Leigh. Come on, impress me."

"Figure I might get a ring."

Reece cocked an eyebrow. "You ain't worn jewellery since you gave up that cross your momma gave you. Remember that thing? Heavy enough to bend a horse's neck."

Caleb shook his head. "Nah, not for me. Thought maybe I'd try something – big gesture style. You know? Gotta spend four figures, to make it worth it, I read that online. I found a shop in Lake Charles, they do them special to order."

"Special . . ." Reece should've seen this coming: the consequences of making his boys rich. Wouldn't all be touring the States drinking, playing nightclubs and sprucing up their trailers. But marriage? When Caleb wasn't even *dating*? He had to mean Leigh-Ann, one hundred fifty per cent not interested, which was the epitome of how fools got parted from their money.

Reece smiled uncomfortably, looking for the right way to tell Caleb to absolutely not do that, but Gray entered before he found it. The upset was written on Gray's face and in the postures of the three men behind him. Noah and two Stilt Town soldiers. Gray hobbled up to the table, cane tapping all the way. He pulled a leg over Reece's bench to sit next to him and Noah took the opposite seat, while the soldiers stood, stony-faced.

"Let me guess," Reece said, "you got riled up counting that cash, not knowing where you'd store it all?"

"The money's good, Reece," Gray admitted. "No complaints there."

"How much we talking? With all that escaping we never got a chance to count."

"Money can wait," Noah said. "You said it'd come without strings. Practically guaranteed. Weren't those your words? Practically guarantee the Steer Trust won't know who hit them."

Reece dug a fork into his rice and took a small mouthful. Chewed contemplatively, then said, "Does sound like something I would say. But there was always the possibility you'd need to do more than simply wash that cash for us."

Gray exhaled through his teeth. "Dustin Fallon done wrong, and they've been deserving of righteous punishment – and your contribution to Stilt Town and the church is greatly appreciated." His pale eyes listed to the side.

"But?" Reece prompted.

"But, Reece," Gray said. "You gotta tell me what happened on that farm."

"What –" Reece began, but Gray held up a shaking hand.

"I know you boys," he said. "Basically good, deep down in there. Better than most that come outta Cutjaw, and I oughta know. The memory of those evils I saw growing up out there, they're the mortar that makes our church *strong*. And Caleb –

when you reached out, after all them years with your mother twisting in the wind, that gave me so much hope. But it's hard, it is, purging ourselves of the poison Cutjaw sows."

"Mr Gray…" Reece interrupted the trip down memory lane. Another minute and they'd get a lecture on how each of their families wronged the righteous Grays a hundred years ago. "How'd you know about the farm? It make the news?"

"You were there, then?"

"We came upon a place looking for help. Found a girl bound to a chair. Things got out of hand and people got hurt, but it was all in protecting Zip."

Gray's expression shifted. "They had that little girl bound up?"

"You know I was gonna tell you all about it, right now. Your people pick it up on the police scanner?"

"Not my people," Gray said. "Fallon."

Reece straightened up. "You spoken to him?"

"Think I shouldn't have? He's got three cars outside camp and another two in a motel up on the 28. Gearing up for a fight. He reached out, Reece, and I didn't like what he had to say."

"Showed us some things we didn't like," Noah added.

"You can't trust a damn word –" Reece started.

Gray held up a hand. "I know. That one's more snake than man. So let's hear your side of things. You found this girl on a farm, broke her free, carried on your way?"

"A man got shot," Reece said. "And we got attacked on the way out. There was an animal. Tore up a truck, the farmer's daughter. I was gonna ask your boys to help explain it."

"How about this?" Noah placed his phone on the table, showing a photo. Caleb jumped up with a curse. Reece swallowed. "You explain this, at least?" The face on the screen was contorted and drooping in waxy horror, skin pale and eyes vaguely empty. Donny. His severed head on a wooden pole.

"How did – no way – not –" Caleb paced away, then back.

Donny hadn't made it, after all, cut down by the same guy that got Nina. Vile? With dark echoes of that other name Zip used. Headhunter. Reece said, "Fallon sent you this?"

"You recognise him," Noah said.

"Yes I fucking recognise him," Reece bit back. "He ran out on us and we never found him. You seriously think we could do a thing like that?"

"No," Gray said, eyeing Noah to be clear on his stance. "We do not. Fallon said his people found the man like that. Found your car. You know what he said? Keep the money, for all he cares, he only wants the monsters capable of this brought to justice. No harm to Stilt Town if he gets *your* head." Reece watched the old man's face. No way he would do it, with Caleb being family and the Steer Trust being their sworn enemies. But Gray's expression was severe – at least believing Fallon's suggestion that this wasn't the work of the Steers. He continued, "I reminded him that for your imperfections you've got the Lord's light in you. That he ought to worry about his own judgement before the Lord. And if he outstays his welcome in Louisiana, that'll come sooner than later. But I need to know, Reece. You boys ain't all of the same cloth. And with the woman you travel with –"

"We did not do that," Reece said firmly. "Don't ask me again."

Noah got hot at his tone, but Gray held Reece's gaze steadily. It was all Reece could do not to slam a plate in his face for suggesting such a thing. Gray tilted his head. "We to believe the Steers set you up? Like this?"

"No. We just might have an enemy beside them, right now. Telling you, someone wanted that girl. A guy in black with some kinda gorilla."

Gray glowered hard enough that Noah stifled an instinctive insult. "A gorilla? This a game to you, Reece?"

"I ain't laughing, am I? It was a creature big as a truck. And it don't make any more sense to us than it does to you, but we're working on it, Alban. Trust me on that, and don't for a minute take to Fallon's thinking."

Noah snorted. "Listen to them talking mystery men and gorillas, you gonna allow this, Pop?"

His son's aggravation only worked to make Gray take it more coolly, though. He stood, nodding. He put a fatherly hand on Reece's shoulder. "Frankly, I pray whatever evil you touched out there *does* find itself here. Anyone that could do a thing like that – they will face the Lord's judgement." There was an edge of threat to his voice; still considering one of Reece's friends responsible. With that, he ambled away towards the counter. Noah lingered, to let his hostility be known, then fell into line behind his dad.

Caleb deflated onto the bench, gasping, "Holy hell, Reece. I mean, holy hell. That thing – these monsters – what is this?"

"I don't rightly know," Reece admitted. "But it don't exactly feel like we're safe yet."

16

The Congo River barge was a vast platform with multiple staged tiers at its front, crowded with people. Right from when they arrived at the ramp, up onto the boat, everyone was suspiciously friendly, with smiles and handshakes too enthusiastic to be genuine. Strangers wanted to know where Katryzna was from, who she knew *out there*, what she did. She answered with curt snarls and they laughed. Presumably, the locals regarded crazy white tourists as an amusing oddity rather than threatening. It reminded her of Eyes' disarming responses: their second meeting, when she tried to kick his groin and he merely stepped out of the way, showed her his gun and said, cool as a cucumber, "I don't want to use this. I just want to talk."

And they had talked. He asked about her upbringing, listened to her stories of moving to grotty Rostov without judgement or calling her a liar. When she told him how her night-club-owning uncle had first given her a break, a courier job that turned bad, Eyes smiled like it was no surprise. When she explained that she'd finally had to kill poor Uncle Nikodem himself – that creep – Eyes nodded and said he'd been there, too. He never explained that. But more often than sympathising, he looked amused by her. The same way these Congolese were – not afraid. They didn't know they should be.

On board the boat, traders ran small market stalls and the people packed shoulder-to-shoulder were scrambling to get higher up, to where the living conditions were less reminiscent of a landfill. Henri pushed a path through to the highest passenger tier, just one ledge down from the captain's cabin. He offered Katryzna a hand with a leery smile. She sneered. This guy was too eager to please and all – probably wanted her guard down so he could stab her in her sleep for being shamed in the fight club. What was Tasker thinking?

Even on the desirable upper level, there was barely room to move, and the wooden floor was wet with excrement. A caged alligator snapped furiously at its bars on the edge of the deck. Henri muscled on to the small interior, where a handful of rooms lined a narrow corridor. The best rooms the barge could offer were little more than sheds, containing soiled mattresses and buckets for toilets. Katryzna was almost too hot to complain, but managed: "I've stayed in better prison cells."

"I've slept on better streets," Tasker replied, flatly. Joke or fact?

But Henri said, "You prefer to sleep on the lower decks?"

Katryzna threw her heavy canvas bag down with a bang, surprised it didn't go straight through the floorboards. As the men went to their rooms, she tossed through the spare clothing and supplies Tasker had found her, to focus on her fancy new rifle. Yes. He had delivered guns, at least – this and an upgraded pistol. With the barge packed as it was, she could kill a hundred people in a matter of seconds. Her smile returned.

Rurik complained, questioning the judgement of someone who'd give her any weapon at all, and she said, "In a fight, we all know who's going to be saving who." Pause. "Whom?"

There was a knock at the door and she answered, "Go away."

A white man poked his head in: fat, chinless, red from the heat and wearing a vast floral shirt. He spoke in a cheery American Midwestern accent: "Well met young lady. Howard, that's me – bunking down the end of the row and I must say it's a pleasure to make –"

"My God, why are you talking?" Katryzna cut in. "This is a private room."

Fat Howard stood stricken, struggling to maintain a crooked-toothed smile.

Katryzna pulled the pistol from her bag and laid it on the mattress. "Go. Away."

He left, face slack and pale. As Rurik piped up, Henri appeared with a sickly amused smile on his face. "These walls are thin, Ms Tkacz. You might get used to the idea there's not much privacy on this barge. And that" – he nodded to the gun – "won't make you special here."

"It's not what made me special in your gym, either. You want to keep the peace, keep all these idiots away from me." Henri lingered, waiting for more. Katryzna rolled her eyes. "Want me to break your nose back the other way?"

"We dance again, I'll be ready to show you some of *my* moves."

"Your *moves* will involve flying off this boat," Katryzna shot back. Rurik perked up with irritated shouts, and she said, "Seriously? You are defending this sleaze?"

"Hey, not me!" Henri raised his hands innocently, and backed off, grinning. "I'm here to help. You want me gone, I go. You want me to come, I come. Welcome to the barge, Ms Tkacz."

He slunk away and started up another conversation in French. Rurik said, "It wouldn't hurt to make more friends. Especially one willing to forgive you threatening to kill him."

Katryzna didn't answer, glaring at the open doorway, expecting some other irritation to creep in. Sean should be saying she needed to keep calm. But he didn't appear. Good. She wouldn't want to hurt him.

Waiting for her irritability to settle, Tasker kept his distance from Katryzna, difficult as the overcrowding made it. He set Henri to warning others to keep their distance. She prowled the floating market, where excitable men approached her to offer fetishes and bowls of indiscernible food, and the novelty kept her amiable until dusk, when she punched a vendor who stood too close. The press of the crowd kept the fight tight and Henri intervened fast. She restrained herself, to stalk off to her room.

On the second day, Katryzna hung her legs over the edge of the barge as they drifted in and out of ramshackle ports, while Tasker got the measure of the other foreign passengers: a pair of mining consultants, a retired Swedish couple on an adventure, a weaselly French arms dealer and a teacher. All quickly took his hints not to ask about him.

At twilight, Katryzna came to Tasker as he sipped a noxious homemade spirit on the upper deck. She had an armful of skewered meats and offered him one. When he declined she shoved them messily into her mouth. Henri remained in the middle of the lower deck, chatting with one of the captain's lieutenants, one eye on Katryzna. He winked Tasker's way, and by way of dismissing him Tasker turned full on to Katryzna and offered up his bottle.

She suppressed a momentary look of irritation, working through a full mouth, to say, "I was told, Sean, that the mind is a terrible thing to waste."

That made him smirk. "You do hurt people for a living, don't you? I'm not mistaken about that."

"And? I protect *my* mind." She tapped her temple. "My life. Other people's are their own problem. Do you actually know what you are drinking?"

Tasker looked at the unmarked bottle. It smelt like an acid that had been strained through old socks. But it had taken some of the edge off, and he'd seen a bunch of the locals swilling it before accepting any himself. He shrugged and Katryzna rolled her eyes with exaggerated disappointment.

"Well, rot your senses if you want, but do not suggest *I* do so, okay?" She turned away, looking down at the bustle. "I guess you need it, doing this sort of thing all the time. Is your job always this *weird*?"

"It varies," he said, happy to move on. "I once visited a mountaintop village where they wove feathers into their flesh and communicated in bird trills. I was following rumours of vampires. That was nonsense, but the village was strange as hell."

Katryzna's full mouth was partly open. She tried to speak, spitting food.

Tasker grimaced. "Finish chewing, for God's sake."

She winked and swallowed. "Think we're chasing rumours, now?"

"No. I've got a pretty awful feeling about this, actually. If you'd seen the state of that village in Norway, you would too. Women, children, torn apart, no sign of exactly how or why." He trailed off, mind going back to that girl. Rebecca. He took a breath. "Everything about this – with Parris's numbers pointing here, these fears of the monsters in the jungle – this is Ministry material and it's bad. Really bad."

Katryzna eyed him like she was trying to weigh up exactly how serious he was. "Eyes would say do not believe it until you see it yourself. Even then he might not be sure."

"I'm guessing Eyes didn't have quite the same background as me," Tasker said. Screw it, with what they might be up against, she needed to hear it. "Monsters exist, Katryzna. I've seen creatures that can drain people dry, animals that leave you paralysed while they peel off your skin. Things too terrible to reveal to the general public. I don't know what's in Ikiri, but I believe it's something up there with those horrors. The difference being, whatever's going on out here somehow managed to affect people in the Arctic Circle. And if it can reach Norway, it can reach anywhere, including my own home."

She paused. "You're actually serious?"

Tasker nodded.

"Sounds like you should have got us more support, Sean." Katryzna gave a light laugh, betraying just a tiny hint of concern. "Well, supernatural or not, I'm good at making things stop."

"Never said anything about supernatural," Tasker said. "We have people researching these anomalies, explaining them. They're often wholly natural, just better off unknown. But by all means, I look forward to seeing how you destroy whatever this is."

"*Now* you sound like Eyes," Katryzna replied fondly. "He said I could break anything. Often without trying."

"Did he try to get you to wash and eat with your mouth closed, too?"

"He actually did!" Katryzna pushed him playfully. "But he could defend himself against me. You have a death wish."

Tasker smirked, knowing it was the opposite, befriending one dark force to stop another.

"So, Sean. Can your Ministry explain this?" Katryzna pointed at the railing. Tasker frowned, not following, and she picked something out of the air. In her mind, holding up her conscience between thumb and forefinger. "You know how big a headache this guy gives me? And I have to put up with it *alone*."

Voices and imaginary companions weren't something new to Tasker or the Ministry. He answered honestly, "We've come across certain things. Dreavers plant ideas in people's minds. Whisper Casts take over part of the brain, and manifest in split personalities. But they're insidious parasites, they don't directly communicate with the host. The mundane truth, true of most of what I pursue, is that it's likely your own mind's responsible."

"I'm imagining it, right," Katryzna said, placing the conscience back down. "Created my own miniature enemy, always nagging." The miniature was an interesting detail; he might believe she'd encountered a Fae, if she wasn't so clearly indicating an empty space. She frowned as her invisible companion said something disagreeable. "Want me to feed you to a crocodile?"

"You ever seen anyone about it?" Tasker asked.

"Like a doctor? Take pills?" Katryzna twirled a hand around her temple. "This is delicate enough already. And he has his uses. Sees round corners I can't. Pushed a box under my feet when I was strung up by my neck, once."

Tasker looked at the empty space where Rurik supposedly was. The Fae certainly could pull tricks like that, but his instinct said no, the voice was in her mind, and to his knowledge, the Ministry had encountered no proven cases of the ability to move things with the mind. Most likely she imagined those results, too. All sparked by some long-buried trauma. He said, "You remember when you started seeing him?"

"When I was a kid," Katryzna said. "Maybe as a teenager. He's got worse. Back before, he didn't just appear wherever, whenever." Her face clouded over, remembering, considering, but she didn't share, only sighed to let it go.

"I can ask my people to investigate it," Tasker said. "If you like."

"Eh" – Katryzna flapped a hand – "forget it." He followed her gaze down into the sprawl of the noisy barge, adrift in murky waters between the jungle thicket, lanterns glowing yellow. "Kind of romantic, isn't it?"

A group of men were wrestling another alligator into a cage, with onlookers yelling advice or waving sticks. Katryzna edged slightly closer and Tasker's body tensed. She said, "You're really not planning to make a move on me, are you?"

He looked down at the top of her scraggily shaved head. "I've got a wife."

"Not what I asked."

"No," Tasker answered honestly, leaning on the railing, letting it out. "That kind of affection doesn't come easy to me, and definitely not for a girl that can't even keep herself clean." Her eyes danced happily at the blunt assessment. He added, "You've got me curious, that's all. I like knowing things. It's how I protect people."

"Makes you feel important? Behaving like a dad to all the mixed-up girls out there."

He stalled. No, it wasn't *that*. But she smiled crookedly,

childlike again, and he thought of home, and Rebecca, and he wondered if maybe it was.

Katryzna accepted an invitation to the captain's dinner on Tasker's insistence that it would be a banquet. A table was decked with steaming plates of meat and vegetables, with all the barge's foreign guests present, but Henri was not invited. The captain sat in the middle, a large man with an old cloth draped over one eye; a temporary eye-patch that had become permanent. He spoke of the area south of Bokema, where they would be alighting.

"People's Free Resistance territory," he said. "Not a good place to be, unless you are hunting Jean-Baptiste Matka. Even then, it is not a good place to be."

"We hear the mountains are nice," Katryzna said. "Mount Ikiri, especially."

The captain's face got more severe. "You plan to cross the Cursed Union?"

"We don't intend to cross anyone," Tasker said.

The French arms dealer said, "They say those that travel to Ikiri never come back."

Howard scoffed. "They say that of most of the interior. Often truthfully."

"General Solomon's head would make you a lot of money," the captain noted.

Katryzna pricked up her ears. "Who's paying?"

"Matka would, I am sure – their territories border. The government might, too. Take enough body parts and you could get paid many times." The captain's shoulders shook with flat laughter.

"Maybe I will," Katryzna responded brightly. They took it as a joke.

Once dinner was over and they moved into relative privacy outside their rooms with Henri, Tasker said, "You know we're planning to lie low, not join in their war?"

"So?" Katryzna leant against the flimsy wall. "We can get paid."

"What's this?" Henri asked carefully.

"Hell," Tasker huffed, his fears that she was serious confirmed. "They were putting ideas in her head about going after Solomon himself."

Henri's face fell. "Why would you do that?"

"I thought you would be pleased," Katryzna snorted. "Didn't men like this get your sister? The rest of your family?" Henri looked shocked – probably as surprised that she'd paid attention as at her plain speaking. "Don't *worry*, claiming bounties on untouchable people is how I maintain this luxury lifestyle."

"No." Tasker's hand was suddenly on her elbow, his face next to hers. Her eyes burned back at him. "Our intention is to avoid them. Henri's here to guide us through without incident. That's the plan."

"*Your* plan." Katryzna placed her other hand on top of his, gently. "Plans go wrong. I improvise." Her fingers tightened and she twisted suddenly, too quick for him to react before his face was pressed into wood, the wall squeaking like it might break. His wrist was pinned between his shoulders, and when he moved his other hand she slammed it against the wall. Henri made the slightest move but her eyes burned a warning at him to freeze. Her lips were at Tasker's ear, body pressed into his back. "You've been doing well, Sean, but you are *not* my dad, understand?"

She backed off abruptly and gave him a companionable slap on the back. He straightened out his glasses, turning slowly back to her. Rurik kicked up a storm on her shoulder, snapping about what the hell had she done – apologise, for God's sake apologise – but she held his eyes. Tasker stared for what felt like a very long time, and, at last, Katryzna couldn't suppress an uncomfortable smile. She glanced at Henri, still watching in mute alarm, and said, "You can plot my murder together, now."

Henri's shock became confusion and Tasker's eyes softened. He said, "We're not going to do that, Katryzna. And neither of us want to be *anything* to you. We'd just like to survive."

She watched him for a lie. Watched Henri, too, and found him nodding insistently. She said, "Then follow my lead. Surviving is what I do best." A light wink and she turned away, problem solved.

17

At the centre of Stilt Town sat a three-tier communications hub packed with radio equipment and snaking cables. On the peaked roof was a score of satellite dishes, transmitters and masts to ensure Gray could send and receive broadcasts all over the world. Mostly, he preached messages of the impending flood, and scoured the internet for signs of the coming apocalypse. Occasionally his people could be put to more specific uses, such as searching for Zip's father.

The gang waited for Reece in the widest tier of the hub, a storage space for old electronics, where Zip touched a hand to the old machines with wonder, like she'd never seen radios before. Leigh-Ann kept everyone distracted with made-up shit: "First wired radio in Beauregard came courtesy of this man Arthur McGee, flew cabling over hills, spooling it out like a crop duster – those old cable planes, they were marvels."

Zip's delight was too bright to be real, watching Leigh-Ann's eyes.

"Think my grandpa used to fly one of them," Stomatt said, probably serious.

"We got something," Reece interrupted, returning down the creaking stairs. "Any of you know there was a giant blue pyramid by the Memphis harbour?"

"Oh yeah, right across from their acropolis?" Leigh-Ann whipped back.

"They got an acropolis too?" Caleb fell for it. "What for?"

"You even know what one of them is, Leigh?" Reece said. "Don't answer. But this pyramid *does* exist, in Memphis, and as it happens there was some trouble there not two days ago. Dockworker out with his pals got set upon by some maniac with a sword, hid up his sleeve. But the guy fought back, somehow – got hold of a rebar to fight him off."

"How you hide a sword up a sleeve?" Leigh-Ann asked, and Reece watched Zip like she oughta know. The child shifted uncomfortably, and he continued.

"We can get back to that. So, they chased one another off into the shadows, to God-knows-where. Two friends on the scene said they didn't know what it was about but haven't seen their pal since – stood 6'5", bald, went by *Gus*. Been working the docks two months and no one knew much else about him. Except he had one eye. News article appealed for anyone to share more if they knew it."

"One eye?" Stomatt said. "How in hell this guy fight off someone with a sword?"

"Your guess as good as mine," Reece said. "But it sounds like a lead. Right, Zip?"

The child nodded. "Grithin. He has one eye, no hair. And Daddy . . ."

"He's got a sword hand," Reece said. Zip nodded again, another guilty admission.

"The hell's a sword hand?" Stomatt demanded.

"It extends," Zip said, voice only getting quieter.

"Right," Caleb spoke up. "I'll say it if none of y'all will. This is giving me the damn creeps – heads on poles and sword hands and monsters. We done wrong back in Waco – we done wrong and none of y'all can tell me this don't sound like judgement."

"The crosses round here got you thinking messy, Caleb," Leigh-Ann said. "Nothing religious about us tripping up on some wackos attacking one another."

"We find this Grithin," Reece said, "assuming he survived, we might get some better answers. If not find Zip's father himself. Gray's boys will keep looking long as we're here."

"How long will it take?" Zip said, voice pitching a little high. "We shouldn't stay."

"This place stinks but it's safe, sweetie," Leigh-Ann said. "Those Steers ain't getting in. Even your gorilla would have a hard time with those walls."

"It's *not* safe," Zip insisted. "They'll come for me."

"Ah, let them come," Stomatt said. "Gray's boys up the tower could tear them in two with that elephant rifle."

"Please," Zip said, "Vile is different. We need my daddy, we shouldn't stop."

"I'm in broad agreement, actually," Reece said, turning his gaze to Caleb now. "Makes me a little uncomfortable relying on Alban right now, given he's already got his doubts about all this. Maybe should've kept some of that cash back for ourselves."

"So we could ditch this place?" Leigh-Ann said. "For where?"

"I dunno, I'm spitballing. Not to her dad yet, at least. Gray's people found no word of any Seph Mason, anywhere to do with Memphis nor nearby, and these guys" – he screwed a thumb towards the ceiling – "are scary with what they can turn up. Your daddy got another name, Zip?"

"Other than Headhunter," Leigh-Ann added.

Zip shook her head. "Mostly, he doesn't use a name."

"When he took that flight? Books in a hotel? What's he tell them?"

She shook her head again, as though he didn't give names ever. It recalled the weird trance of the Steers at the gas stop. Leigh-Ann said, "You guys travelling hypnotists or something?"

"Mortal enemies with a one-eyed bandit and a mutant gorilla," Stomatt said.

"It's the power," Zip said uncomfortably.

"These other bastards got this weird power too?" Stomatt asked.

"It's not *weird*," Zip replied defensively. "It's *dangerous*."

"All right," Reece asked. "I gotta ask, Zip. You ready yet to tell us where's home?"

Zip's expression got stonier. Still a no.

"You sure we even want to be taking her back?" Caleb said. "Her dad don't sound like good people, I'm gonna say it. It ain't normal hiding away from the world, having her scared of her own feelings."

"Not exactly our place to say," Reece said, holding Zip's eyes, "but Caleb's right, cher. Some of the things your daddy's told you, I wouldn't necessarily trust them. Specially when he's saying trust no one else. We're here for you, see? You can talk to us."

Zip stared, locked in conflict, before lowering her eyes. She said, "There's a stream. And from the upstairs window, you can see the city, on a clear day. We're on a hill. I've seen the sea in the other direction. Daddy says it's not possible but I have. There's a big oak for climbing, next to the tower, and I went to the post office on my own, once."

"City got a name?" Reece said.

She gave a blank expression. Maybe didn't actually know.

"Australia, right?" Stomatt said. "With that accent. Not got many cities, do they?"

"Australia?" Leigh-Ann exclaimed. "Dammit, Sto, kid talks like Mary-fucking-Poppins. You ever even met someone that wasn't Arcadian?"

"I can't," Zip said. She cringed and closed her eyes. "He'll come, he'll come and we'll never be safe!" She was trembling, the emotion taking over her again, and Reece met Leigh-Ann's eyes with worry. Her responsibility somehow, now they were on the verge of making the kid bawl.

She put a hand on Zip's shoulder and said, "Enough for now, huh? How about you and me take a walk, Zip? See the goats."

Zip peeked, straightening up. "Goats?"

"You like that? And the sheep, cows. Might even spot a rabbit or two."

"I like rabbits!" The girl's eyes were bigger than ever.

Leigh-Ann guided her away from the others, all watching uncertainly. She mouthed at Reece, *Figure this out.*

Reece left the comms tower to head back to their room, with Caleb and Stomatt dogging his heels. He told them, "You might be right yet, Caleb – she might not belong back with her dad, but we got a responsibility to see that through. I do, anyway, I got us into all this. And you all seen what she can do. Won't necessarily come without reward, one way or another."

"You ain't got the feeling, though," Caleb said carefully, "we might not wanna cross these people?"

"We just took on Steer Trust," Reece smiled. "Who's gonna stop us now?"

Stomatt jumped to ruffle Caleb's hair, shoving his head. "Yeah, cheer up – we rich as all saints and you're crying cause some fairy with a sword got a beef!"

Caleb pushed back. "Get your dirty paws off me!"

"Go on and make me, you morose motherfucker." Stomatt lunged, trying to get him in a headlock. "Where's your muscle?"

Stomatt pushed too far and Caleb shoved him hard. "Said back the hell off, Sto!"

Reece skipped ahead, up the steps to the private little room. The instruments were laid out between their beds. La Belle Vérité chief among them. The matte black nickel and brass trumpet, his world in a twist of metal. As he picked it up and tested a note, Stomatt and Caleb tussled in behind him. Another note. Ran his fingers over the buttons for a little flourish. There was the sound. *That* was the truth, and it calmed the boys.

"Damn swords and gorillas," Reece said quietly. "And red eyes and psychic powers. Leave that to the breeze, we got this."

He gave it a blast as Caleb plugged in the electric bass and Stomatt squatted for a tom tom. The big trombone lay between them, a violin to one side – ready for later. Reece picked up a tune, blended it into the Stilt Town Serenade, that little light number he produced just for this place. Community looking out for each other, like the gang did. Except he'd seen Gray was unsettled and Zip was even more so. Didn't like those odds.

As they relaxed into the music, letting all that go, he let the truth run through him.

Sure enough, their journey didn't end here.

Come the calls for dinner, the gang joined the packed mess hall. Gray sat at the centre, with Noah and the same few hulking guards, watching as Reece made small talk with his people. Leigh-Ann watched the old man herself. A man capable of drawing all these people away from society, just for him. You couldn't trust that. Reece slowly led them over to him, and as they got close Leigh-Ann hung back with Zip.

"Heard the Serenade earlier, unless I'm mistaken," Gray said kindly, and regarded Zip. "And that dress is very becoming, young lady."

It looked like shit, Leigh-Ann didn't say. She'd get Zip back in the old clothes as soon as they dried. Zip mumbled thanks.

"Any more word from Fallon?" Reece asked. "Or on that other thing?"

"I had, you know I'd have come to you," Gray said. "Don't worry, Reece, it's all in hand. We've doubled the guard, got everyone recalled and the perimeter locked tight, but Fallon's not making a push. He'll back down once he accepts we're ready to fight back."

"Think that bullet in their window got them scared?" Caleb said.

"Plain as day Stilt Town's no pushover," Gray said. "Likely they'll wait till we're sleeping and try and sneak in. We're ready for it, long as everyone keeps their heads." He directed this at Stomatt, and Leigh-Ann too, for good measure. "Y'all just get yourselves some fine crayfish stew, bless us with sweet melodies, keep the faith."

"Always do," Reece winked, damn charmer. Leigh-Ann couldn't muster an ounce of that suck-up. And despite his and Gray's fronts there was something stifling in the air, with the Steers so close. Noah had an even harder face than usual, quietly eyeballing her around a fried chicken wing. Zip's continued tension didn't help – seeing the animals eased her a little, but the kid looked like she thought a ghost might jump out the ground. As they left Gray to head for the counter she squeezed Leigh-Ann's hand.

Leigh-Ann shifted closer to Reece and whispered, "Get the feeling Zip's right to be worried?"

Reece didn't play down the concerns, now. Something in his set said he'd been thinking along the same lines. He gave the commune's miller a quick how'd-ye-do before continuing towards the food, and waited until the rich aromas welcomed them forward before answering: "We'll get through dinner, think about our exit after."

18

When they disembarked at a rickety riverside town, Tasker found leaving the confined barge for the ominous forest a strange relief. Between the ups and downs of navigating Katryzna himself, he had spent days afraid he'd turn a corner and find someone with his throat slit for irking her. At least out here he needed only worry about himself and Henri, and Henri had sensibly backed off trying to flirt with her. He had discovered a new tactic for winning her friendship, by expressing wild shared enthusiasm for food. Katryzna was utterly oblivious to the bubble of tension she'd created, bouncing off the gangplank with an eager smile.

They took a small ferry across from Bokema to the southern riverbank and rode on motorbikes over narrow, bumpy tracks into the trees. Katryzna frequently peeled ahead, jumping the vehicle over bumps, either very skilled or enjoying the luck of the recklessly brave. When the mud-road and foliage became impassable, and they needed to walk the bikes, she swung her machete like a child's baton.

With her lost in that assault, Tasker quietly reiterated to Henri that they travel via the quietest route. At all costs, don't get noticed by the militia. Henri needed no persuasion there, never mind how much longer such diversions would take them. Then he swung the subject back to Katryzna and asked if Tasker had any luck with her on the boat. As if he could have escaped such details. Tasker didn't answer and Henri made his own conclusions, smiling happily. "She's softening, don't you see? You only need to treat a woman right – she'll give you her heart."

Tasker kept quiet, fairly sure no part of that was true.

Katryzna wasn't sure what had woken her, but she was out of her tent with her rifle in the pitch black before she'd stopped to think about it. In just her pants and top, she trod noisily through the undergrowth, expecting swarms of flies to descend. The way everyone talked about it, this forest was full of bugs ready to eat you alive or impregnate your flesh with worms, but she had seen little evidence so far. Made all their pills and repellent sprays seem a waste of time. But there was *something* out here, she knew that.

Between the trees, in the shadows.

Despite blinking hard, her sight wasn't improving; the darkness was absolute. She turned back to the tent and a tiny yawn drew her attention to the entrance, Rurik stretching as he exited. "What's going on?"

"Don't know. Pass me the torch."

He looked up, unamused, and she gave him a quick sneer before leaning past to get it herself. Never any help. She turned the high strength beam to the trees, casting jagged shapes all around. They had set up camp in a tight spot, three tents with no real perimeter. Katryzna scanned one way then another, tramping about. Could be anything out there.

Something, far off, made an ungodly noise. She spun to it. The sound came again, further away, moving. Had *that* come close enough to wake her? She turned back and went rigid, finger on the trigger.

Fifty metres away or more, a man was standing between the trees. The torchlight didn't quite illuminate him, even as Katryzna moved from side to side – obstructing trees cast heavy shadows over his features. He was just standing there.

"See that?" Katryzna asked Rurik, as he wandered up alongside her.

"No," he answered.

Hardly surprising considering the useless idiot didn't reach her ankle. Katryzna turned the torch away, checking around, then back to the man, still motionless. Then out to the side. There was another one. And another further back. She growled, picking out at least half a dozen silhouettes, staggered through the trees, all in shadow despite the torchlight. If she got closer, she sensed, they wouldn't be any clearer. Not the first time she'd seen spectres. Though they didn't usually haunt her in groups. She backed off, crunching twigs, and finally roused Tasker. He groaned sleepily, then saw the beam of torchlight and bolted upright.

"Katryzna – what is it?" he hissed, emerging in a half-crouch with a pistol. She gave him a bored look and checked the trees again. They were still there. Swinging the torch around – *all* still there – she realised they might not be in her imagination.

"Okay," she said. "Tell me if you see them, Sean."

Her nonchalance threw him for a second, then he stood, followed her torch beam and suddenly pulled her down into cover.

"What are you –"

"Henri, we got company!" Tasker shouted, moving in a crouch to the nearest tree. "Katryzna, stay down! You see who they are?"

Katryzna moved off to a different tree, clutching the rifle and giving him a scolding look for the stupid question. But he saw them. They were real. She hissed, "Why are they standing out there like ghosts?"

With Henri scrambling out of his tent, hurriedly preparing a rifle, Tasker slowly stood, and the edge of Katryzna's torchlight cast deep worry lines on his face. She stood for another look herself, aiming the torch at one of the creeps. Still not moving, a bunch of scarecrows, trying to freak them out?

"Who are you?" Katryzna shouted. "You can't see we're trying to sleep?"

Tasker made an upset sound, but waited for a response. None come. Henri was out now, his own torch ready and searching the trees. He said, "Matka's PFR shouldn't be out this far."

"Try your clicky tongue language or whatever," Katryzna suggested, and Henri nodded. Except he called out in French. *She* could've done that. Still the men didn't move, ominously waiting for something, so Henri tried another language, one she didn't recognise. Still nothing.

"How about –" Katryzna started, and Rurik cut in.

"You can't just shoot random people!"

"Out here?" Katryzna told him, "I'm pretty sure I can."

On the other side of Rurik, still low, Tasker scowled. Didn't follow her chain of thought but didn't approve anyway.

She leant around the tree. "Last chance. Explain yourself or it's ba –"

The man in her torch beam ducked to the side, down into the thicket. Leaves moved around him as he crawled closer. Behind him, the other silhouettes dropped out of sight, quickly.

Katryzna fired. The shot was met by the cries of nearby birds and animals. Tasker shouted, but he saw the movement and backed off, raising his pistol. Torch clamped to the side of the rifle, Katryzna picked out one of the men and fired again. With an eruption of leaves, a black arm flapped up and fell down.

She swung the gun the other way, picking out another movement, but a sound drew her back to the first man. Shadows shifting where he'd fallen – not dead. She fired a burst, until he was still.

Tasker fired, too, at another approacher. Then Henri, on her other side, the pair accepting this was an attack. She glanced to the other shapes scrambling through the trees as the boys fired and tree trunks burst around them. Lots of shapes moving now, all coming from that general side of camp. She swung back to the sound of movement from her first victim. No, closer – her torch swung to light up the shredded face of a Congolese man on his belly, propelling himself out of the thicket on elbows, shattered teeth bared and bloody. Katryzna fired right between the eyes, bursting his head open. He flopped still, at last.

She stared. The earlier shots had torn through his torso. One had taken off half his jaw. And his clothes were already in tatters. As she stared, his fingers twitched, and she yelled and unloaded a half-dozen more shots into the back of his already-exploded head.

"Grab the stuff!" she shouted. "Whatever you can!"

"What?" Tasker turned as she skipped through the tents.

"I hit one, he keeps coming!" Henri shouted, reaching the same panicked conclusion as her.

Katryzna grabbed her boots and shouted over her shoulder as she hopped into them, "Stay if you want – I'm not!" The men stopped firing, to fall back and snatch their own gear. Their dark attackers were making horrible scuttling noises, circling closer. Katryzna fired a warning shot at one, knocking him back through the shadows. She jammed her clothes into the backpack and swung it over a shoulder, then pulled back, watching for where the strangers were. Picking a direction that looked quiet, she ran between the trees. A few paces in, it became a tangle of vines and leaves, and she angrily fumbled the rifle strap over a shoulder and pulled free the machete.

"Katryzna!" Tasker shouted from behind. Unclear if he was in trouble or wanted her to stop or just wanted to cry her name. No time to care; she hacked out a path through the weeds.

"On your left, on your left!" Henri said, bouncing up alongside her. He had his pack on, too, and a machete swinging much more efficiently.

She fell in behind him and held out her blade. "You cut, I'll cover!"

Without another word, Henri pressed on with a storm of two spinning machetes, while Katryzna kept pace moving backwards, aiming the torch and rifle. She fired, pulling up at the last second, as Tasker tumbled into their path. He raised a hand, the other down with his pistol. No pack on him. Tasker half-ran and half-tripped his way to join them as they kept moving. Katryzna watched the shadows, waiting for one of these things to jump at them. Her torchlight caught the peaks of the tents, far back now, and the shapes of men descending on them. Arms ripped into the clearing where they'd been moments before, material shredding.

19

Following dinner, Reece figured a performance was exactly what everyone gathered in Stilt Town needed, all still bustling in the mess hall, eating, talking and praying. They started out with the Ain't You Someone gambit. Stomatt's voice gradually rose as he loudly questioned Reece over exactly what music he played.

Ain't no bebop, dixieland or jive. Can't be swing nor big band with what you got. What do you call it? Show me. A few examples on the horn. Rougher than Creole, that some kind of street jazz? But we don't have streets in Cutjaw, LA. By this point Stomatt's up slapping hands against the table giving a back and forth tempo and they hit the high point together as Reece reels out something longer. The whole room can agree this is nothing less than raw, righteous Cutjaw Caravan Jazz.

Those that could keep up clapped along and all the rest smiled with daft glee.

While Caleb and Leigh-Ann slipped out unnoticed.

Reece could play all night. Feel the eyes of a hundred people loving every second, alive in it. The raw language of music brought them peace and calm – from the overworked kitchen staff down to little Zip, cheering and clapping along. She looked younger than she'd been since they first picked her up, like she hadn't heard real music before. A little more of this and she might even forget all the fears her daddy put in here. And Reece held everyone with his own kind of hypnosis, letting Leigh-Ann and Caleb do their thing. Making ready, just in case. No need to actually flee, no one harmed, no plans unsettled – just opening doors and making options.

With another tune down, Gray nodded along from across the way. Even Noah gave a concessionary shrug to say it wasn't half bad; by his standards that was practically an orgasm. Reece held up the horn for attention, turning on the spot.

"Alright now, who's got a request?"

They started shouting out hymns – a bit of gospel would definitely stir this lot up.

"Go Down Moses?" Reece threw to Stomatt, who nodded and thumped up another beat. Give it a minute before bringing in the trumpet, work them up first. Stomatt started a throaty chant, and however much they hung on wanting the horn, they couldn't resist the words, some of them joining straight in.

Reece felt a little tug on his elbow and found Zip looking up. "Got a request, cher?"

"Reece," she said. Some of the joy went out of him. Hadn't taken long for her to regain her fear. "They're coming."

He frowned and scanned the room. Not a soul looked bothered about the dangers outside, right now. He leant close and whispered, "They're ready for it. Enjoy the music."

She glanced to the exit as Stomatt boomed: "Way down in Egypt's land!"

"They're not," Zip said restlessly. "They're not ready."

"Well," Reece said, lifting the trumpet. "We will be."

But he faltered before playing, seeing Noah's expression shifting. He looked unhappy now, as if stewing on similar concerns, of a sudden. Not a fan of the song? Stomatt belted, "Let my people go!"

Leigh-Ann rubbed her hands together to get some blood flowing, the temperature dropping fast now the sun was down. Her breath made clouds before her face as she watched Stilt Town's shadows. Outside the ruckus of the mess hall, the rest of camp was dark and she had some ominous feeling borrowed from Zip; guards were walking the perimeter wall and keeping watch in the towers, but Leigh-Ann couldn't help feeling it wasn't enough. And she didn't like getting stuck on lookout while Reece and Stomatt kept the party going.

"I can't get in," Caleb said in a hushed whisper, drawing her attention up. He leant out of a dark doorway, crouched so as not to be seen. "Need proper tools to crack the safe. And time."

"So what you got?" Leigh-Ann said. He held up a small packet.

"Might be five thousand, I reckon? Had it in a locker."

"Five thousand? We didn't go through all this for five fucking thousand."

"Didn't go through all this to steal from my uncle, neither, did we?"

"I told you this ain't *stealing* – he's got *our* cash, owed us." She took a breath to keep her voice down. "Sure you can't crack it?"

"You feel like tryin'?"

"Shit. So we come back for the rest another time. Once this all blows over."

Caleb crept down the stairs, every step creaking and making him wince. He whispered, "Maybe we shouldn't be doing this, Leigh? My uncle's done right by us. Even if we're square on the money, it don't feel right sneaking off."

"We're not sneaking off, Caleb," Leigh-Ann said. "Just giving ourselves the option to. Told Reece we shouldn't trust them with all that cash outright, should've kept our hands on it until we were sure to be safe here. Now we can't be sure of nothing, not even our money. You got a back door key at least?"

"Got that." Caleb patted a pocket. "But that's another thing – how far we gonna get on foot, going out the back?"

"Further than if we open the main gates and start up an engine. Fuck it, we're not making life easier yakking about it. Swing by the room and drop it off, I'll go back tell the others we're ready. And *don't worry* – it's only a precaution."

Caleb turned to leave. But he hesitated, looking into the dark. "Leigh, I ask you something? Being out here alone and all."

"You gonna propose in this romantic forest of building foundations?" Leigh-Ann joked. Then she couldn't hold down a laugh. "With a backdrop of holy wackos."

But Caleb's hurt expression stilled her amusement. "No. No, I wasn't gonna do that." He said it too seriously, leaving Leigh-Ann open-mouthed. Damn if he hadn't been thinking somewhere along those lines though. Just what she needed.

Leigh-Ann forced an awkward smile. "Joking, Caleb. Come on now, let's get moving." She went to punch his arm in a friendly way but he was too far off and the stretch made it more of a push. He frowned like this added to the insult. Turned away with a ponderous look, needing some time to think now.

She watched him amble off, then cursed under her breath and turned the other way. That boy with his notions, never getting the concept of I Don't Like You Like That. She was gonna have to have Reece play go-between again. Don't shit where you eat, dammit – how was the gang supposed to enjoy a carefree life on the road if she had to keep worrying about any of them getting hung up on her?

Those uncomfortable thoughts brought her back to the mess hall, but reaching the last gap before the yellow glow, she saw the way blocked. Two bulky guys standing before the door to the hall. Dammit, had to be Noah, with one of his cronies, and they'd seen her the same time she saw them, gospel jazz blaring behind them.

Neither moved. She put on a smile to approach the steps, saying, "No privacy in those latrines. And I *needed* my privacy."

That should've been enough to get Noah's usual look of disgust at her general existence, but he stared blankly. The guy next to him was no better, silent. Leigh-Ann stopped on the steps before them.

"Shouldn't be out here," Noah said. Something off with his voice. Hadn't Gray said no drinking?

"Didn't realise there was a curfew?" Leigh-Ann tried to laugh it off, going to pass him, but Noah stepped in the way. Here it was: calls of immodesty, no real lady, posturing because he couldn't get in her pants as easy as a Stilt Town girl's. Leigh-Ann waited. He said nothing, only looked a bit sweaty. "Well if you're not gonna give me shit, you wanna step aside?"

"Shouldn't be out here," he repeated, voice cracking.

"You on something? You guys –"

"Shouldn't be out here," his friend agreed, voice equally weird. She looked in their eyes. Wasn't booze – did they have something homegrown? The sort of thing might make them act on their general base misogyny.

Trying to keep cool, Leigh-Ann said, "I'm heading back inside, ain't I?" She tried to pass again, and this time Noah put a hand on her chest.

"Down," Noah instructed. He tilted his head the way she'd come.

"Yeah, no thanks –" Leigh-Ann started, but he pushed her, throwing her balance enough to send her skipping back onto the grass. She took a quick couple steps and balled her fists. "I ain't going nowhere with you."

"You're going." Noah quickly advanced. It took Leigh-Ann a second to react, surprised at his sudden approach. He didn't look angry, not crazed exactly – weirdly vacant. Leigh-Ann sidestepped but he matched her pace. With the mess hall's music rising, she'd need to scream loud to be heard. But Caleb would be back any moment. Noah took a quick step closer – Leigh-Ann shouted, "Hey, Ree –"

Noah suddenly had a hand on her mouth, and Leigh-Ann was dragged down as she kicked. Her arms were pinned by the goon, her shouts totally muffled. She was lifted, struggling – no use – and hustled under the nearest building, into deep shadow. She took a gutshot punch that pushed the wind out of her. Noah hissed, "Stop. Stop and be saved."

Wheezing to catch her breath, Leigh-Ann tried again to shout, but Noah clamped his hand tighter over her face. The men went rigid, watching something. Leigh-Ann searched the shadows – *Caleb!* He was jogging between the buildings looking one way and another, suspicious as a man could be. Leigh-Ann bit down hard on Noah's hand and he hardly reacted, giving her a lazy look. She screamed into the palm as he pushed harder on her mouth, totally muffling it. Caleb's eyes tracked their way. Ran right over them.

Didn't see. Didn't hear.

He kept on, briskly, up the steps and into the mess hall. The doors let out a second of hopeful light that swept over the surrounds, and Caleb gave one last look. Then he was gone. The doors closed behind him.

Noah squeezed Leigh-Ann's face and said, "Shouldn't be out here."

Reece took Caleb's return as an excuse for a break, putting down the trumpet and catching his breath. Sweaty from the fun. A couple people booed mock disappointment at the music pausing, but mostly they clapped and celebrated as he cut through the crowd, and Stomatt picked up another beat, encouraging Zip to join in. She was dancing, enjoying herself as if she had no worries left, finally. The kid did a twirl, eyes closed, lost in the moment.

Reece smiled as he took Caleb aside. "All good?"

"Not great," Caleb confided. "Got a small cut – real small, comparative – but got the key to the back. No signs of trouble, anyhow, might be that we can wait it out."

"Might be, only pays to be cautious." Reece met Caleb's eye, hit by a realisation. "Leigh-Ann not with you?" Caleb scanned the room. She should've been here first. Reece noticed another absence. "See Noah out there?"

"No. Could be checking on the guards?"

Rather than watching the band with general disapproval? This didn't feel right. Reece looked over to Stomatt and Zip, the pair drumming together now, with a little audience. Good. He moved away, out onto the steps, and checked the shadows. Quiet outside. Caleb caught up, with an urgent whisper bound to draw attention: "What you thinking?"

Reece narrowed his eyes at the dark. No way Leigh-Ann would linger out on her own in Stilt Town, not in the middle of the task she'd had. He said, "Thinking we'll spread out, find her fast."

"What's up?" someone called, the worry noticed inside.

"It Steers?" another man asked, and a mix of hushed questions and concerned silence swept the hall. Stomatt made a noise, shouldering his way through.

Zip came bouncing out with him and Reece fixed on her. "You sense something?"

She focused, all those fears flooding back in. And she definitely did sense it. "It's bad."

"Fuck." Reece jumped down the steps, scanning the shadows ahead. Shouldn't have sent Leigh-Ann out here. Of all people.

"What's going on, Reece?" Stomatt called from the top of the steps.

"Get the guns, Caleb. Keep Zip safe!" Reece cut away at a jog, crouching to see under the buildings. He could hear the crowd moving behind him, commotion building. No movement ahead, though. He ran faster, dodging between stilts, until he'd passed half the commune and reached an outer perimeter. A goat bleating made him slow down. Another. The worried cry of animals in distress. Sort of shit Zip kept hearing in her dreams. Scanning their low wooden pens, he couldn't see anything wrong. But the noises got louder.

Back through the buildings, Gray's people questioned, "What's got them spooked?"

"We got company? Report!"

"Steers still out on the road!" a guard shouted from high up. "Not moving. What's going on down there?"

The chickens were clucking, flapping their wings against the hutch, loud at some hundred yards off. Reece moved out from the buildings, watching the fields. He saw a silhouette of a man. A guard, halfway between the camp and the perimeter wall. Reece shouted, "You seen Noah or Leigh-Ann?" The man was motionless. Oddly stiff. Reece raised his voice: "You hear me?"

Wasn't some scarecrow, was it?

Voices were rising behind him, Stomatt's the loudest: "Leigh? The hell are you?"

"Hold up now, Steers on the move!" the elevated watchman shouted, and panic followed. Shouts for order, the thumping of feet up stairs and across walkways. Reece glanced back out to the man in the field and reached for his pistol. Wasn't there – left in the bunk – he only had his trumpet in hand, and tightened his grip on that.

"Reece where you at!" Stomatt boomed.

"They coming on the gate!" the watchman cried.

"Everyone keep calm now!" Gray's voice. Louder even than Stomatt. "We're prepared for this! They won't get in – but get to arms. Marie, you move along. Marie, you listening?"

Reece turned to the strange exchange and started back under a building.

"Get moving, Ruben, dammit!" another man shouted just ahead.

"Marie!" Someone else.

This wasn't about the Steers, this was weirder, Zip's domain. Picking up his pace, Reece threw a last look back to the field. He stopped. The guard was still standing there, and there was another shape now, further off. Another motionless man.

"The fuck is this?" Reece hissed, and a terrified woman matched his confusion with a shout of her own: "Why aren't you moving?"

Far across the camp, a gun went off. In the centre, Stomatt shouted, and near him Caleb joined in. Another gunshot followed, off in another direction, and the shouting and movement clamoured into a din. Reece spun, seeing people running between the stilts as more shots went off near the perimeter. But the chaos was *inside* the walls. Reece gave a final look to the field.

The silhouettes were finally moving.

Ambling towards him.

20

Following a long night of evasive movement, Henri finally guided Tasker and Katryzna into a village of wooden huts. He moved ahead while they waited in the trees, neither talking. No one had said much since the ambush, if that's what it was. In their flight, Tasker hadn't been able to make sense of it. Ghostly figures in the dark, watching them without striking. Not quite surrounding them, failing to catch up again, like they weren't within their wits. Definitely not the co-ordinated attack he'd expect from a militia. Were they even armed?

While they waited for Henri, who had dived into chatter with a stout villager as if they were old friends, Katryzna rested against a tree, staring at Tasker. He couldn't read her look. Weary in posture, but eyes bright, partly invigorated by the escape. If it could be called an escape. They had been driven further into the forest, and without half their gear. Tasker had proved their weakest link, failing to grab his bag in their flight. He couldn't even talk to the locals. Katryzna might've guessed his thoughts – she gave him a slight, knowing smile and a wink. Like she'd take care of him.

It didn't help.

Henri returned and explained, "This village has no love for the PFR and they have food. But they warn that five men went missing in the night – gone from their huts without a trace. Others have gone looking for them, but not returned. They are confused – there have been no rumours of militia activity near here, not for many weeks."

"Do they normally see them coming?" Katryzna asked.

"Rebels might strike quietly," Henri said, "but they are brash. They do not move unseen. And the men who are missing are not who you'd expect. Older, weaker. There are children here, untouched."

"Children," Tasker echoed. They might be abducted for soldiers, but who would take old men?

"There were six out there, around our camp," Katryzna said. "I think."

Tasker frowned, following her chain of thought. "Why would these villagers get up in the dead of night to stalk us?"

"A better question," Katryzna said, "is why they didn't stay down when I shot them."

"In that dark, with all that cover," Tasker said, "I'd say you missed."

"I do not miss," she snapped. "It's some kind of jungle mystics."

"There's no mystics here," Henri said, slowly. "These villagers are Kimbanguists."

"That *sounds* mystic?"

"Kimbanguist Christians," Henri explained. "They follow Christ, and the teachings of Simon Kimbangu, a Congolese man who they believe came down from Mount Zion –"

"Near Ikiri?"

"No," Henri got even slower, unsure if Katryzna was messing with him. Rather than face that head on, he said, "The point is they are puritans. They and the other villages nearby – they reject ideas of magic and witchcraft, even alcohol and dancing."

Now it was Katryzna's turn to regard Henri with a look of disbelief. She glanced from him over to the village, perhaps considering this muddy, low-tech village had at least some common ground with her. But she uttered, a little hurt, "They don't *dance*?"

"They're not our problem, are they?" Tasker said, hearing himself sound tired, irritable. "We're getting close to Ikiri, correct?"

"Closer. Mr Tasker, Ms Tkacz," Henri ventured, "if I may. We have lost our bikes. Much of our supplies. On foot, it will take us three days, at least, to reach Ikiri, moving safely. Not knowing what threats we face, I humbly suggest making a decision here."

"Can we retrace our steps?" Tasker said. "Get back to the camp?"

"I'm not sure it is worth the risk," Henri said. "But the villagers talk of a good road that will take us towards the river. Seeing as we are already in danger –"

"Turn back?" Katryzna said. "This weirdness proves we're on the right track."

Henri shifted anxiously, not a comforting sight from their muscle-bound escort. Tasker shared his concern, but Katryzna was right. He said, "If those were the people from this village, something or someone had control of them. None of us are in doubt they *would* have attacked us, right? In Laukstad, there wasn't anything to suggest outsiders, or other creatures – and here's some kind of answer to that. What if it was people from within their own community who were responsible? Something might've gripped them, too. We have to figure out what this is. We can't take bikes from the village?"

"They have none."

"And if we forget caution and take the better roads?"

"Yes," Henri said unhappily. "Taking better paths could halve the time to Ikiri."

"So what's the problem?" Katryzna said.

He gave her a grave look but didn't bother spelling it out. Tasker brushed right over it to say, "A day there and a day back, we can do that? Alone if necessary, as long as you can point us in the right direction. You've done your bit."

Henri stalled, wanting to take the offer, but couldn't. He said, "My bit ends with finding answers, the same as you."

Katryzna put a hand on his shoulder. "That's the spirit. We will not let zombies stop us." She beamed, and Henri managed to look even more uncomfortable.

The stout villager named Ade did his best to welcome the trio, and insisted they join him for an earthy tea and dried meats. He spoke in a local language which Henri translated, explaining the villagers were effectively hunter-gatherers with loose ties to three or four other settlements nearby. This village, Igota, was the closest anyone lived to General Solomon's territory, and the base of the Ikiri hills, as Henri referred to them. Igota used to trade with villages further east, but such contact was cut off after Duvcorp arrived, many years ago. The stories of that time had faded in detail, and the best man to ask, Mbu, was one who had gone missing in the night, but the broad strokes were local legend. The mercenaries had come through the rainforest with the brutal entitlement of an imperial expedition. For the most part, heavily armed, violent men, though their number included some who tried to befriend the locals, including a beautiful Congolese woman. Henri took this detail with sad hope: confirmation his sister had made it this far, practically to Ikiri.

The expedition had stayed in a neighbouring village before reaching Ikiri, where one of their number mutilated a local woman over some minor dispute. The Westerners fought amongst themselves over this – the man was ultimately taken away in restraints, to be punished by the Westerners themselves. There was violence in the forest shortly after – two other mercenaries were found dead from sword-wounds, and local trackers found evidence that another man had been chased through the trees. Perhaps the mutilator escaped from the group. Some in Igota still used his example to scare their children into behaving, Ade said. Watch out, or the outsider who roams the forest will get you . . .

After that, the Duvcorp expedition was never seen or heard from again. Contact was also lost with the closest eastern village; days later, Igota villagers travelled there and found the people savagely massacred. Not by men with guns but as if by animals. Brutal, horrifying scenes. The search party kept going, looking for answers, but retreated after hearing strange sounds at night. Since that time, as Henri first reported in Club Clash, many more villages in the area had similarly gone quiet – one as recently as a year ago.

Ikiri itself was now avoided like a graveyard, a site of some inexplicable evil. Not for the first time, Ade said: those hills had an old reputation. People had gone missing before Duvcorp's time, and no one lived directly on Ikiri. But after their arrival, the taboo area expanded. It all but confirmed Tasker's assumption that it wasn't Duvcorp's advance itself that was responsible for the deaths and disappearances, but something long concealed that they had unsettled. They weren't good people, no doubt, but their abuses up to this point were not unnatural, nor well hidden. The savage massacres, without explanation, happened *after* the mercenaries reached Ikiri.

The mystery was cemented by the arrival of Solomon a year or so later. His reputation had reached the surrounding territories, and the locals' superstitious habit of keeping clear of Ikiri now became a matter of survival. Villages were raided. People who ventured too close were hung from trees as warnings, to mark a perimeter. But Ade reflected the same doubts Smail had harboured: it was unclear *why* Solomon had settled in this area – there was nothing of value. Perhaps he merely desired land to call his own?

With the legends exhausted, and the trio rested, Ade and his friends offered supplies and wished them luck. The sort of luck offered to people you don't expect to make it.

On leaving, Tasker and Henri took a bag each, while Katryzna shouldered the canvas and poles of a makeshift tent. They followed a scrappy map and compass, wary that within an hour they would enter General Solomon's territory, where things might get even worse. The "good road" was ribbed uncomfortably by tyre tracks, and before long they had to veer off onto a path that required a lot of hacking. Katryzna volunteered – cathartic, she said, with a smile. Henri tried to share an appreciative look with Tasker, watching her push on ahead, but his prior enthusiasm had been sapped.

The ground grew steeper as they reached the base of the hills. Keep climbing up, that was the key. They discussed the previous day's events only once, when Katryzna asked, "Could the rebels have drugged those villagers? Turned them psycho?"

"Whatever happened to them," Tasker said, "its source is somewhere up here."

And on they walked.

By nightfall, the incline had become a climb, tiring but encouragingly mountain-like, even if Henri still insisted it was just a hill. What was the difference; it felt high. They kept going by torchlight, looking for a gap in the trees clear and flat enough to pitch a tent, which proved hard to find. The search took them an hour further than Tasker intended to walk, but it was progress. Finally, they raised the tent, and stood side by side studying their handiwork.

Katryzna burst out laughing.

"Oh, we're all far from home," Henri said, cheered slightly by their pitiful shelter.

Tasker merely smiled, too tired now to care. It was cover, at least. Just wide enough for all of them, though they were going to take shifts keeping watch. Katryzna insisted on going first, feigning energy, and as the men settled to sleep she began quietly chattering to her conscience. Tasker caught Henri's eyes alight in the dark, watching the tent opening. He had probably wanted to ask about her since the barge, but he kept quiet.

Outside, Rurik somehow made her laugh.

She was cut off by a faraway sound, the rolling cry of an animal. They were all silent for a long, chill moment, recalling the noises Ade claimed drove his people back, the rumours of horrors out here. Nothing more came. Finally, Katryzna whispered, "Do you get lions on mountains?" Tasker considered answering in the dark, but she continued, apparently replying to Rurik. "You know everything about how I should act, why shouldn't you know about African wildlife."

Her voice got quieter, the one-sided conversation dwindling. Tasker rolled over, expecting nervous energy would make sleep hard to come by. It did not.

Tasker blearily blinked his eyes open onto Katryzna's face. He reeled back with surprise, but froze at the weight of her leg pinning his. It was already stiflingly hot, and light was peeking through the canvas. Morning, and she'd crept in to practically sleep on top of him without waking him for his shift. On his other side, Henri snored. All packed in together – they could have been damn killed.

But they hadn't been.

Tasker pushed down his annoyance and disentangled himself. Katryzna stirred. Eyes half-open and groaning, she asked, "What time is it?"

"You didn't wake us."

"No? Thought I did. Rurik was keeping an eye out, anyway."

"Hm." Tasker climbed out of the tent and stretched, squinting against brighter sun than the day before. The trees were sparser here – the ledge they'd climbed gave something of a vantage point over treetops below. Wild, exotic and vast.

"You better not have tried anything funny at night," Katryzna warned, sleepily emerging behind him. Henri grumbled, slowly wakening. "Either of you."

"Back at you," Tasker said.

She looked out at the forest, too. "Did you hear those things out there? Your monsters."

"Gorillas, possibly," Henri said, not entirely convinced. "None came close?"

"Yeah, actually," Katryzna said. "We played cards while you slept." She looked to Tasker. "Is he serious? What are we *actually* dealing with out here?"

Not liking that doubt creeping in, Tasker said, "You said you could stop anything, didn't you?" Then he looked to Henri. "Besides, that was probably perfectly normal for a rainforest. Right?"

Henri offered a weak smile to say he hoped so. But doubted it.

Tasker turned, to where the slope rose and the trees became thick again. They had a day of hiking ahead, but they were close. He took out the map and checked it against the compass. If they left the camp and their belongings here, only took the weapons, they could reach the cut-off point by early afternoon. The last known signal from Duvcorp's team. Today they'd get an insight into exactly what they were chasing. Maybe get away before nightfall and whatever was out there came back.

With the burgeoning heat, a small breakfast and a lot of water were all they needed to keep going. Trekking higher, higher. The sun blazed even through the canopy, sapping anyone's desire to talk. Tasker checked the compass every few minutes, as the terrain got steeper. Roots climbed over jagged rock.

Then, with no clear difference in their surroundings, the compass needle started spinning uncontrollably. Tasker backtracked, down the slope, and it slowed down as he crossed some threshold – stopped turning entirely. Cursing, he continued back up the slope to where Katryzna and Henri were waiting. She had her arms folded in impatience, he looked exhausted. All three of them were wet with sweat.

"We're here," Tasker said. "Guess we follow a straight line and hope for the best."

"Fingers on triggers," Katryzna said. She already had her rifle ready, and Henri uneasily readied his. Maybe a bad idea; in Ministry work, combustible weapons were often more trouble than they were worth. Tasker was hot and tired, though, so he followed their lead. They walked on with tall steps, over rocks, scanning the trees, the earth, whatever they could. Katryzna said, "It doesn't *feel* special."

The forest answered with a feral cry, a long way away. It *did* almost sound like a lion. They exchanged uncertain glances but pressed on. This was only where the expedition lost the ability to communicate; the real danger lay ahead. It raised a question. The scientists must have realised their technology was failing them – why didn't they retreat to get a signal again? Tasker kept a hopeful eye out for discarded weapons or clothes, human technology of any kind. But the forest was thick and overgrown; no one had been here in years.

There were bigger gaps between the trees as they progressed, and larger rocks. And Tasker started to feel something. A wariness, chasing over his skin, hard to pin down. It was directional, pulling him towards something. He stopped and Katryzna stopped with him, shoulder brushing his back.

"What do you think it is?" she asked, no question that they were both feeling something unreal. Henri slowed down a few metres back and made an uncertain noise.

Tasker said, "I don't think it's in the right direction."

"How would you know? We could've got spun in a circle."

"But we've been going *up*. That way takes us down."

"So?" Katryzna didn't wait for an answer. "Doesn't matter. We're going to check it out, aren't we?"

"If it's not the destination?" Henri blurted out, all the nervousness of their night ambush and the animal sounds rattling him again. This weird feeling might break him. "Why should we investigate this – this thing – when we are so close?"

"If it scares you, don't come," Katryzna said, and pressed on, downhill, towards the strange feeling. Tasker followed, gesturing at Henri to join them. He jogged to catch up, afraid to be left behind. Katryzna moved faster as they got closer. She tore her way through some vines and skipped to a stop with a gasp. Surprise from her sounded as unnatural as this pull felt, making Tasker hurry. He froze at the sight of what she'd found.

A gnarled tree stood before them, at least two arm-spans wide. It rose into a dense, crooked canopy. At around head height was a woman's torso, hanging head-first out of the bark as though halfway swallowed by the tree, impossibly long hair draping down to the ground.

"What do you make of that?" Katryzna asked, as casually as if she'd noticed a light left on. Before she could answer, the woman lurched upwards, and Henri cried her name: "Sara!"

21

Noah's goon dragged Leigh-Ann through the double doors to the chapel as he punched the lights on. She kept kicking, for the little it was worth, as they heaved her between the pews, to the lectern. She tripped, pulling the goon down with her. The man kept his grip, kept a hand over her mouth. Noah grabbed a polished brass cross off the altar and growled, "Cleansed. Time you were cleansed."

The lights cast demonic shadows across his face, and Leigh-Ann saw mania in his eyes – worse than intoxicated. The man had snapped. Leigh-Ann screamed into his goon's fist, watching the hefty metal cross. Noah approached slowly, savouring what was coming. Then gunfire sounded. He looked up with confusion.

There was shouting. The others looking for her? Then more gunshots. Panicked cries. The goon slackened his grip at the sounds, and Leigh-Ann burst free. The man was too slow, this time, and she shot out of his reach to plough into the nearest pew. Noah took a desperate swing at her, missed and shattered an armrest with the cross. She was away, yelling, "In here boys – these motherfuckers want to kill me!"

Leigh-Ann skidded through the doors. In the darkness, people were running between buildings, under them, some fleeing and others chasing. All Gray's people, near as she could tell in their drab garbs. A man shrieked as he was struck from behind and rolled across the grass – another man on top of him, check shirt flapping as he brought both fists down on the guy's face.

Thumping footsteps drew Leigh-Ann's attention back – just in time to duck another swing from Noah, using the cross like a bat. It smashed into the chapel's doorframe, jarring him long enough for her to half-jump, half-fall down the steps. She landed on her knees and pushed up to keep running. A woman came screaming from under a nearby building. Aimed at *her*. Leigh-Ann dropped on instinct as the woman reached murderously over her – she shouldered her into the air with a cry, letting her own momentum fling her. Then Leigh-Ann was up and running, with glances one way and another. As chaotic as when that monster struck the farm. Only more people were shouting here, and firing off guns. *What the fuck was going on?*

"Reece!" Leigh-Ann shouted. "Where are you?"

"Leigh!" Not Reece – Caleb. He stumbled out between stilts, frightened for her, pistol in one hand, little Zip's hand in the other. "What's happening? Where you been?"

"Noah –" Leigh-Ann half-twisted back – the big guy was lumbering across the grass, waving the cross as he looked one way and another but was somehow unable to focus. His goon was just behind him. "Fuck, keep moving."

They moved into the shadow of another building, out of view. Caleb panted as he went, "Lost the others, looking for you." Another burst of gunfire. "Who's shooting? They're – hell, they're going at each other!"

"Someone spike the damn punch?" Leigh-Ann said, watching another pair of Gray's people grappling on the raised ledge of a building, one throttling the other.

"What punch?" Caleb asked desperately. "They were all normal a minute ago. We left the hall looking for you, all of us, and this started up behind us – you ain't seen Reece?"

A roar made them leap back as another pair of fighters rolled in front of them: Stomatt with one hand on a man's neck, the other punching his face. Zip shrieked and clung onto Leigh-Ann's leg as they tumbled across the grass. Caleb kicked Stomatt's attacker in the side and knocked him aside. He sprang onto hands and knees like a cat, eyes flashing in reflected light.

"Stay down, man, this –"

But the man jumped, baring his teeth, and Caleb fired. The chest-shot sent him rolling, wheezing. Likely fatal, but not right away. Leigh-Ann covered Zip's face with a hand, turning her away, as Caleb helped Stomatt to his feet. The big guy shouted, "Lost their fucking minds!"

"Breach!" the guard Teddy cried, somewhere on high, so shrill he was barely recognisable. "We've got a breach!"

"You think!"

"Come on," Leigh-Ann instructed. "Let's get eyes on whatever this is."

They ran for the nearest stairs, up onto a ledge. Kept going as more people grappled beneath them, up another set of steps to one of the town's second-storey tiers. Another gunshot met a flash of light in the field. Two men were backing towards the buildings, firing in the opposite direction, towards the walls. A dozen or more shapes were out there – hell, the Steers were through the entrance gate. A vehicle was wedged in the bars, but it'd created a gap and a gang of pricks were advancing, shooting. One of Gray's men in the field went down.

"The Lord is with us!" Gray yelled somewhere towards the centre of the compound. Gone mad like Noah? "Look to the light, stop turning on your brothers!" No, just his usual self.

"How they doing this," Caleb said, uncomprehending. The Steers were panning out into a line, shooting randomly at the buildings. But one twisted to shoot the other way – tore down his nearest friend with a burst of bullets. The others staggered and slowed, their confused yells echoing across the plain.

"Hell, it's got them, too," Leigh-Ann said. "Whatever *it* is."

She pressed on, dragging Zip by the hand, round the corner of the building. Stomatt let out a small laugh to say he was trying to enjoy this. Struggling. They ran over a short walkway. A woman made horrible violent noises, straddling someone on the ground.

"Juliette, no!" Gray roared, off to one side. He hobbled out with two large men and the three of them advanced on feral Juliette as Leigh-Ann kept running. Across the bridge and around another corner and there was Reece, sprinting across the grass below, armed only with his trumpet and trying to avoid someone grasping at him.

"Up here, Reece!" Leigh-Ann shouted.

He skipped but didn't stop, flashing them a glance then picking out a staircase ahead. He dodged through more scrambling people. They ran to the top of the stairs to meet him as the cries and gunshots grew unbearable.

"The fuck is going on," Caleb demanded again, almost whimpering it.

As Reece bounded for the steps, Noah and his goon leapt out the shadows to block the way. Noah swung the cross and missed by an inch as Reece bounced back and swung the horn. The trumpet's bell caught Noah on the jaw with a heavy clang, dropping him. He flapped about snarling, thrown but still coming, and Reece smacked him on the other side of the head, bending the instrument out of shape. The goon jumped over Noah to slam Reece to the ground, trumpet rolling off, and at the same time Stomatt shoved past Leigh-Ann and threw himself off their ledge, arms spread. The lunatic landed bodily on Reece's attacker and rained punches on him as the pair spun off to the side. Leigh-Ann cursed Stomatt's recklessness, barely better than the people gone mad, but damn he had his uses. In seconds, Stomatt had beat the man until he was motionless then backed off, panting. Leigh-Ann and Caleb ran down to reach Reece and pulled him up as Noah twitched on the grass.

"Back to our bunks," Reece said. "Get our shit and get out of here."

"What about the – what about –" Caleb stuttered, trying to make sense of it. What about the town. Gray's people, driven into murderous frenzy.

Leigh-Ann said what they were all thinking: "The hell can we do about it?"

"This way," Reece instructed. "I think."

Another shrieking attacker ran out of the shadows a short distance ahead and Reece pushed himself in front of the others, fists up – but a blade flashed along the madman's path. The scream was cut short and the man crumpled before a short, dark figure, arms and legs spread, long sword out to the side. Zip shrieked and squeezed into Leigh-Ann, again, both arms wrapped around her legs as Stomatt lurched in front of them.

"I got this little prick," Stomatt announced loudly. A head taller and twice as wide as this guy, he somehow managed to look feeble before the swordsman. Encased in shadow, Vile stepped to the side, big paces for a small man, a lion preparing to pounce.

"Leigh, take her – Caleb" – Reece gave them a push – "we'll catch you up."

Someone screamed a death-cry across the commune.

"Reece!" Gray again, coming into view with one man left. Their shirts were ripped, faces bloody. The old guy looked crushed, ready to collapse and leaning heavily on his cane, but his companion at least had a shotgun ready. Spotting Vile, Gray said, "What devilry have you brought upon us . . ."

An answer came from further afield, with a terrific scream of raw animal power that shook the buildings on their stilts. They all froze, under the swordsman's knowing watch. It had to be Giza, as alive as this bastard.

"Don't let them get me!" Zip cried, loud enough to move them all. Leigh-Ann shoved her ahead, running for a gap in the buildings. Caleb whipped up the kid and took the lead.

"Fuck this, go, Sto!" Reece shouted, following. Stomatt fell in too. "Shoot him!"

Leigh-Ann shot a look back over her shoulder as Vile gave chase, blade drawn to one side, and Gray's man fired. The blast clipped the swordsman, throwing him aside. The same time, there was another flurry of gunfire, higher up – Teddy or some other raised sentry? – cut off with an agonised scream and the crash of shattering wood. The ground shook with a heavy impact and another roar. Definitely the mutant gorilla.

The gang ran to the boys' bunk, where Caleb dropped Zip to leap up the steps. Leigh-Ann bolted after him and they snatched a bag each then jumped back down. Stomatt hauled Zip up onto his back, assuring her, "I got you," as Reece took his pistol and kept cover. Everyone ready, he pointed out over the dark field behind them. "Rear exit. Over there."

Caleb hurriedly tried to distribute weapons from the gun bag as they moved – a pistol for Stomatt, Leigh-Ann's Mac-10.

"Wait!" Gray wheezed, far behind them, hobbling to catch up while his guardian fearfully scanned all around. Vile had disappeared back into shadow. "What is this!"

A massive shape tore through one of the stilts beside him. The structure split apart around the huge emerging form of the beast Giza.

"Alban, run!" Reece yelled. He turned side on, one arm up in a marksman pose, and fired into the mass of darkness. Giza's long arms stretched out, propelling it in great leaps as Gray's man abandoned him and fled. Gray tripped over his own feet. One of Reece's shots knocked the beast off course – but not by much. With unreal agility for something so large, the gorilla rolled and kicked off another stilt to jump onto Gray. Leigh-Ann gagged as its huge fists beat Gray into the ground, the town leader barely able to scream. Reece pulled her away. "Nothing we can do!"

They ran on with all the energy they had left, Caleb and Stomatt already close to the perimeter wall. The guys pulled the rear bulkhead open, creaking on its hinges. They piled out into pitch dark on the other side, and went to heaving the door shut. Through the gap, Leigh-Ann saw the dual shapes of Vile and Giza stalking through the field. A casual pace – like the fuckers were toying with them.

Caleb got the bulkhead locked, for a second's breather, but none of them were fooling with the idea they were safe. Reece pushed on. "We make the river, lose them there!"

No fucking sense in it, Leigh-Ann knew, but didn't have the breath to say so – she was running too, all of them racing down a path they could barely see, between trees and weeds. Stilt Town's wall shuddered with a bang behind them. If that gorilla couldn't climb the thing, it'd smash its way through.

They ran on, Zip bouncing on Stomatt's back, big bags bouncing on Caleb and Leigh-Ann's. Bags of what? Leigh-Ann caught herself thinking. All that money was left behind – what'd they have now? Clothes and ammo? What now, what now. Minutes of mad running and none of them even knew what direction.

Sounds came through the trees, on both sides. Big thumping beats of the giant gorilla, crashing through the undergrowth. Flanking them on one side then going quiet. Reappearing on the other. Hounding them or herding them or something – not moving in for the kill. Leigh-Ann's heartbeat got hot and furious and unsustainable. Her foot hooked in something and she went down – Reece at her side a second later, arm through hers, hauling her up. The monster tore through the trees behind them, jagged teeth gnashing through shadow, and Leigh-Ann unloaded the Mac-10 with a defiant scream. With flash and fury the gun buried every bullet in the beast's bulk, sending it tumbling back into shadows with a whine, hurt but dammit how could it not be dead?

No time to consider it – the pair were up and running again, chasing the escaping sounds of the others up ahead. Giza roared, far off again, angrier than ever.

"Water, I see water!" Caleb shouted hopefully ahead. "Gonna be okay!"

They pushed for all they were worth, but as they caught up Stomatt shouted a curse. Reece and Leigh-Ann bowled into his back together, and the whole gang stopped before the stream. A motorboat was sitting there, ready to go. But a figure stood between them and it. Vile.

The parting clouds let some moonlight on his features. He was concealed head to toe in some kind of combat armour, like what special ops might wear, except tattered by age, ripped in places but revealing nothing but shadow underneath. Remnants of a balaclava covered his head, missing chunks as though it had been hacked at. The precious little flesh visible in the gaps was sickly pale, crossed with deep scarring, and his eyes stared reptilian from the mess. And down at his side, there was the long sword, flat along one edge, unadorned but unmistakably sleek, unblemished by the battle.

"Behind me," Reece whispered, stepping in front of the others, gun down at his side. He raised his voice. "The hell you want?"

Vile said nothing.

"You can't have her, hear me? One step closer, you're dirt."

The MAC-10 felt slick in Leigh-Ann's sweaty hand. Empty, she knew. Stomatt lowered Zip, flexing his fists, and Caleb stepped forward too. Vile merely waited. Cockily self-assured.

Reece took a breath. There was nothing he could say to this zombie-ninja motherfucker. He moved in a flash, gun up and firing in the same motion. He almost hit the bastard – but Vile moved impossibly fast, predicting the shot, down to the side. The swordsman spun across the ground, low, legs at spider-like angles. Caleb fired too, not even close, and the shadow spun between them. They dropped away as one, a flower of bodies falling to the sides, as Vile spiralled up in a shimmer of whispering steel. Reece rolled and fired again and Vile avoided the shots with unnatural speed, springing into the trees. Leigh-Ann scrambled to her feet, grabbing for terrified Zip, as Stomatt and Reece watched for the next attack.

Caleb stayed down, gasping.

A gash ran from his waist right up to his throat, blood seeping from every inch of it in thick black gushes. Leigh-Ann screamed, "Caleb!" as Reece stepped towards him – but the swordsman reappeared, sword raised.

"No!" Zip screeched, a pulse that shuddered through the trees. Leigh-Ann felt it pass through her bones, and flinched as Vile was thrown back. He hit a tree with a hard crack, and kept going, tossed into darkness. Zip kept screaming, marching between their group with her fists balled, rage directed into the shadows where Vile had fallen.

The gang froze as Zip went quiet. She breathed in heavy, tearful whimpers. Leigh-Ann looked down at Caleb; his blood had already stopped flowing, his eyes looking lifeless to the sky. Past her face. Reece grabbed at him uselessly, saying, "Caleb, no – no no –"

"You got him?" Stomatt asked Zip, fists raised as if to punch the swordsman.

Zip sniffed hard and admitted, "He'll be back. Soon."

Leigh-Ann searched the shadows. No sign of movement now. But the kid knew, didn't she? Reece was clutching at their friend. Stomatt turned and stared, impotent, waiting to be told what to do.

"We gotta go," Leigh-Ann said quietly. Too quietly, as Reece dipped into a low, anguished sound. "Reece, we gotta go!"

"I ain't leaving –" He turned to bite back, but Leigh-Ann grabbed him, pulled him up by the shoulder. Took one last look down at their friend. Sweet, gentle Caleb, dammit.

She gritted her teeth and shoved Reece. "Sto, get the kid – *Reece*, the boat – we gotta go!"

22

"*Pas plus*," the woman in the tree pleaded in broken fragments. She added something in one of the Congolese languages, then switched to English: "No more."

Her voice was raspy and unused, her face hollow. Her hair hung down to the ground in cordlike greasy black curls. Her faded clothes looked like the remnants of an eaten-away shirt, with many pockets, partly concealing a frail body. Her eyes were dark, too dark to see the irises. She lurched up, clawing at the air to try and drag herself free, towards them. Henri took quick, frightened steps towards her, hands raised but too shocked to get closer. There he froze, stunned.

At Tasker's side, Katryzna raised her rifle and said, "Stand clear, Henri –"

"Wait," Tasker said. "Just wait."

The woman slumped and sobbed. "No more . . . *sans elle*."

Tasker moved around Henri, studying the point where her body met the tree. She wasn't stuck, she was *fused* with it, bark growing into the bare skin where the shirt was torn. Henri whispered, hoarsely, "What's happened to her?"

Tasker twisted back. "Your sister?"

Henri struggled to pull himself out of the shock. He took another step towards her but backed off, repulsed. "We have to help her – how can she be here? Like that?"

"Let's pull her out?" Katryzna suggested.

The woman swung her way, bobbing like a bird. "*Non*! No more – *pas plus loin*."

Katryzna stared. "She's crazy."

Tasker couldn't blink either, no idea now what he'd imagined they'd find but sure he couldn't have predicted this. Were the others like her, somehow trapped by the rainforest itself? The tree-woman, Sara, *Henri's sister*, rasped again. "Henri, give her some water?"

Henri looked closer to bolting than helping her. But Sara swayed his way, focusing on him, and his deep, frightened breaths slowed. She whispered, "Henri. Henri." His arms drooped, face relaxing, as he looked sadly into her eyes. Then he hurriedly tore through his pack for the water. He approached and offered the bottle, offering rapid reassurances in French. He poured water that Sara lapped at thirstily. Then he took a step back, watching her. He spoke in French, the meaning clear: *how do we get you out?*

But when she stopped and looked him in the eye, he slumped back, muttering something in quiet resignation. Something had shifted in him, and it didn't look natural. Tasker checked with Katryzna to see if she saw it, too. Her brow was knotted and her hands tightened on her gun, so that was a yes.

"Is she . . ." Tasker began. But he didn't know what to ask, exactly.

Henri half-raised a hand to her, reaching for a connection. An understanding gripped him and he said, almost dreamily, "She cannot be moved . . ."

"*S'il vous plaît.*" Sara dragged the last word out at length. "*Please.*"

"We can end her misery," Katryzna said.

Henri met her eye, with an expression that said he didn't entirely disagree.

Sara hissed again, "No more. *Pas plus loin.* Without her."

"We can't continue," Henri somehow inferred. He was studying Sara as though reading her mind. "Not to where her team went. It's too dangerous. Not without . . . help."

"Help from who?" Tasker pressed, but Sara turned her gaze to him and he felt something swelling in him. A peace. Understanding of his own. She had drawn them here, generated that feeling that they followed. Saved them from continuing to certain death. He said, "We shouldn't continue."

Katryzna snapped: "I'm not letting some half-tree psycho tell me when to stop."

"Find her," Sara said, further trembling with emotion. "Katryzna."

Katryzna's face went taut. "How does this thing know my name?"

"You don't feel it?" Tasker said, calmly.

She glared at him – then Henri. Then around the clearing, as though checking the air itself. "Enough. You two need to focus, and this thing is –"

"Eyes loved you," Sara interrupted with an awe-filled realisation.

Katryzna fixed a deadly look on her. "What do you know about Eyes?"

It was a threat, not a question. Tasker stepped between them, slowly. "Don't." His voice came out mellow. "She's right. We can't go on. We need to find –"

Pain lanced through his face as he reeled from a slap, the crack of Katryzna's palm on his cheek echoing through the trees. Her face close to his, she clutched his shirt in a fist and said, "Get a grip – I'm not going on alone."

Tasker blinked, hard, and shook his head to refocus. She released him and he took quick steps away from the tree, holding up his hands. His senses came back sharper, the strangeness freshly apparent – a swaying woman hanging out of a tree, Henri standing in a trance. Sara looked surprised, even frightened, as Katryzna bore down on her. "What about Eyes? You tell me he's stuck like this, I will *scream*."

The tree-woman pushed back into the tree, but laughed. "*C'est toi* – waited, I've waited –" Katryzna raised a fist but the woman slumped, laughter turning to tears. "Bring her. *Arrête ça*."

"Yeah? I can stop it right now." Katryzna braced her gun but held back in the face of the woman's erratic nature. She glanced at Henri, the man vacant, not even seeming to watch. Tasker saw what he'd gone through himself – whatever Sara had become, she had entranced him and Henri. Subtly, merely to accept and believe her. Katryzna stepped to Henri and jammed a fist into his gut before he could react. He keeled over, wheezing, as Tasker opened his mouth to protest. But Rurik got there first, and Katryzna spun a circle, shouting, "What do you know? I'm the only one with any sense right now!"

"What – what –" Henri struggled to ask, on his hands and knees, tears in his eyes. He took in Sara again and fell to the side with a cry. "What's happening?"

"Stay down!" Katryzna ordered, then turned on Sara. "Explain or I put a hole through your skull."

Sara breathed deeply, gritting her teeth with the effort of holding her torso up. She hissed, "All are gone now. Only me. And . . . *it*."

"Sara," Tasker said. "That's your name? Sara –" He clicked at Henri.

"Ngoi," Henri said weakly.

"See your brother?" Tasker said. "We've come to help – talk to us – you remember coming here? Duvcorp?"

Sara nodded, heavy hair swaying. "Gone, all gone. *Pas sécurisé – hateful –*" She turned madly to Katryzna. "No further – *sans elle.*"

"This again," Katryzna said. "Who is she talking about?"

She directed the question at Henri, but he was staring with teary eyes, at a loss.

"Find her," Sara's voice wavered. "*Tu.*"

Letting out a little noise of deep frustration, Katryzna raised the rifle. "Make sense."

"She doesn't," a new voice advised. Low, thick Congolese accent with a French tint. "Your gun won't change that."

Sara cried shrilly as Tasker turned to find men in military fatigues dotted through the trees behind them. Around them, appeared as though ghosts. All armed with old assault rifles, many wearing dusty cloth masks. At their head was a man in a cap and aviator sunglasses, no weapon in hand. His face was just recognisable from the pictures Smail had shared, but gaunter, dark skin strangely ashen. General Solomon's once proud uniform was ragged, metal buttons hanging on loose threads, rank insignia peeling off his shoulder, his pistol holster cracked. They had the shabby collective appearance of soldiers who had dragged themselves out of a grave.

Henri raised his hands in surrender. "General Solomon – we mean no disrespect – this woman is my sister –"

"Save your breath," Katryzna said, eyeballing the soldiers. Hell, she was prepared to attack them. And given her reputation, she might survive, but Tasker and Henri certainly wouldn't. "You men want to die today?"

"No one needs die," Solomon said, with calm, measured authority, though his voice was dry. "The Popular Liberation Union welcome you. You are Katryzna, correct? I only ask you lower the gun."

"I'd rather not," Katryzna said. "People who know me are not normally friendly."

Solomon spread his hands to the sides. "We could have killed you before you saw us. And I only know your name" – he pointed at Sara, the tree-woman watching with horrified fascination – "through her."

Katryzna glowered from him to Sara. Wanting to bite back, but thrown again by the strangeness. She made an angry noise.

"We've been expecting you," Solomon said. "Though not your companions?"

"Agent Sean Tasker," Tasker said, quickly taking the opening for diplomacy. "UK government. And as he said, this is her brother. Henri."

Solomon regarded Henri with slow, sad curiosity. "Yes. I see it now. I invite you to talk, but not here. It is not safe out here. We have food, lodgings, at the camp."

"My sister –" Henri protested, half-rising.

"Has been there a long time," Solomon said. "And will remain there. *She* is safer than any of us. I wanted you to meet her, though. If you would please come."

"We're not done here," Katryzna said.

"Trust me, you have heard all she will say."

"Trust you," Katryzna echoed with a leer.

Tasker frowned at her. Sara had manipulated him and Henri, planting her message of danger, but that didn't make it untrue. The fact that she'd demonstrated such power fired all sorts of warnings. He said, "Katryzna, slow down. We don't know what we're dealing with."

"Isn't that why we are climbing this mountain?"

"I can tell you," Solomon said. "What lies up Ikiri will kill you if you continue. It would kill you now, if Sara wasn't protecting us. We will share all we know with you."

"Before or after you cut off our ears and boil our bones?" Katryzna shot back, only getting more agitated. "Thanks but I'll take my chances –"

"You asked her about the one called Eyes," Solomon said. Katryzna froze. "We know about him. We are not the monsters you might believe us. Our *curse* is not what we do, but what was done to us." She narrowed her eyes. "I guarantee your safety and your answers. If you wish to continue after we talk, I will take you on myself."

Katryzna gave Sara another look in her tree, and Tasker saw Henri doing the same, at pains to see what his sister had become.

The woman was slumped forward again, chest moving with breaths but otherwise spent. If Solomon wanted to talk, this was their best hope. The man sounded tired, but vaguely hopeful. Katryzna met Tasker's eye, as close as she'd get to asking his opinion, and he tried to suggest consideration with his expression. She lowered her gun, unhappily. "Tell me about Eyes right now. Right here."

Solomon watched her, wearily, and said, "He was one of the named ones. The few people she has spoken of. He died to save her – so she has assured us. What more there is to tell, you'll have to come with me to hear."

23

As the gang sped down the river, the hazy dawn peeked through bald cypress trees either side of them. All they had in the world now was their dirtied suits, a big bag of guns and a pile of regrets heavy enough to sink the boat. Leigh-Ann sat on the middle bench beside Zip, thoughts racing. Caleb was gone. All he ever wanted was to do good by his family, including them. He *really* wanted that to include Leigh-Ann. Now he was dead? Just like that? Never gonna hear his goofy laugh again. For what?

Reece had his head down, at the front of the boat in a kind of misery coma. He'd taken them all out of the Cutjaw Shitheap for a better life, and where'd it got them? Stomatt sat at the back, manning the throaty outboard engine, tetchy. Not even space for his angry, irritable smile or malicious laugh now. Best friend dead. And Zip. Little Zip down at Leigh-Ann's side. Stiff as a board, hadn't even blinked since their escape. What *was* she? Did the kid even know?

No one had said much. All thinking the same shit.

Why Caleb, when all of them got to live. Plenty worse people deserved death more.

And what the hell, Stilt Town? People tearing each other's faces off – that monster gorilla – the swordsman that ignored fucking bullets? The kid who threw him through the air with a scream?

The last thing Leigh-Ann had said to Caleb was another *No*. He deserved better.

"What *are* you?" Stomatt finally broke their silence, addressing Zip. They all should've been comforting the kid but so far no one had the guts, and now this.

Zip flinched as he let up on the motor to lean closer. His suit, fresh before dinner, was now torn and bloodstained, as bad as the boiler suit had been. Reece looked up, in no better shape. One knee was torn, his jacket ripped near a tail.

"I'm serious," Stomatt said. "What *are* you?"

"Leave off, Sto," Leigh-Ann said, quietly.

"I been leaving off. She's been left plenty, and now Caleb's *dead*. Dead, Leigh, opened like a fucking piñata –"

"Sto –" Reece said, but Stomatt half-rose, not about to be told.

"You can fuck off all to hell. He died and we left him there all because of this kid." Stomatt laughed with nerves, throwing his hands up. Almost tripped out the boat, and scrambled for balance. "How we gonna leave him back there like that? When she coulda done that shit all along? Zap people with her *mind*. Oughta call you Zap, shouldn't we, not fucking Zip. Zap."

"Seriously Sto," Leigh-Ann growled. "You need to shut up before I gut you."

"Seriously? Caleb would be alive right now if it wasn't for this brat. Correct me if I'm wrong – I ain't wrong, am I?"

Reece half-rose, too, something fearsome stirring in his reddened eyes. "Caleb would've been the first of us wanting to help her – you think we had any damn choice?" His voice was cracking.

Stomatt shifted his weight and the boat rocked. Leigh-Ann snapped, "The pair of you stop before we all flip in the slosh!" The men held gazes. "We all loved him and we're all hurting but it ain't Zip's fault what happened – she's a damn victim too."

Leigh-Ann put an arm around the child, pulling her close. Zip remained hard with tension, worried eyes resting on Reece, not Stomatt. Shit, she saw it too. Reece had frozen back there and had to be a hair's breadth from snapping now. Their damn leader.

"Sit your ass down, Sto," Reece said tiredly, creakily lowering himself back onto the gunwale. Stomatt huffed but did as he was told, still angrily glaring at Zip.

"Question remains. What *are* you? Why didn't you do that with your mind before?"

"I'm just a girl," Zip whimpered. "I don't know – it only happened because – because Vile hurt him – I had to – I had to –"

"It's okay," Leigh-Ann said. "It was a good thing. You got us all out of there."

"This that power your daddy spoke of," Reece said, hoarsely. "Things you can do no one else can. Same power that makes Vile special?"

Zip nodded. Reece sniffed aggravation and rubbed his forearm.

From weary to angry again. Thinking up a plan that wasn't gonna rest on logic, for sure.

"What else can you do?" Stomatt said. "Freeze time? We know you read minds."

"I can't do anything," Zip said. "It's *all* bad. Daddy said –"

"Daddy was scared," Leigh-Ann said. "And he obviously wasn't the only one. Vile and that beast back there didn't come at us head on, did they? They know about you? Scared of you?"

"Scared," Reece murmured, "like those farmers were scared."

Zip regarded him guiltily, fearful of his judgement.

"Not us," Leigh-Ann assured, eyeing Reece to support her here. "We ain't scared of nothing, Zip, and definitely not you. But we gotta know what's going on. You can sense feelings, danger? Put those Steers in a trance, threw Vile back. You got any idea how?"

"And what about them going psycho in Stilt Town," Stomatt said. "That wasn't the Steers. Gray's own people, biting each other up. That her, too? Spread some mind plague."

"No!" Zip cried. "It was *him* that made them act strange!"

"Vile?" Leigh-Ann said.

Zip didn't hear, racing on: "He makes people mad. Wants them to hurt each other!"

"But not us?" Leigh-Ann said. "How come not us? Gray? Half the camp –"

Zip shook her head quickly, the memories, the thoughts, mounting in her upset. "He can't – can't control everything, and especially not when you can notice it. When *I* can notice it." She frowned as though realising it herself. "That's why he does it when I'm sleeping."

Leigh-Ann tried to check in with Reece for that, and found him listening warily. More than bad dreams, wasn't it? Leigh-Ann ventured, "You weren't sleeping then, though."

"I was listening to the music," Zip whispered.

"Shit," Stomatt scoffed. "You want me to believe she protected us, rather than corrupted them?"

"Gave us a break, didn't she?" Leigh-Ann said. "You saw that monster – question to ask isn't what she is, it's what the hell is *he*. Like no one I've seen before, the way Vile moved – his skin. *That* bastard killed Caleb. Killed all those people, one way or another. Right, Reece?"

Reece's jaw was locked in grim acceptance. He nodded.

"Damn right." His mind was going somewhere now.

"What you thinking?"

"What you think I'm thinking? This motherfucker came for her, cut down Caleb. Let him come again. Whatever tricks he's got, he's just a man. Next time we make ourselves ready."

"We can't!" Zip said, urgently. "Can't use my powers, signal them –"

"We're past that," Reece said. "They're coming, one way or another. Vile killed Caleb, Zip. And Leigh's right – he's gotta answer for everyone else. Everything Gray built, all *we* did – up in flames because of that bastard. But next time, when he comes – you do what you do, we'll do what we do. No more putting music first, we embrace who the hell we are and take him down."

He looked heavily up to Stomatt and Leigh-Ann. She said, "We ain't killers . . ."

"Good as." Reece shrugged.

"You ain't thinking straight, Reece," Stomatt said, for once not diving straight into a plan of reckless chaos. "Let me play devil's avocado and say it – those *things* were near on unstoppable. God rest Caleb and all those people but he wouldn't want us dying too. Can't tell me it's all on us, this thing."

"Then who's it on?" Reece spat back. "I didn't see anyone else out there about to stop them."

"We could drop her by a cop shop –"

"Cops? You hear yourself? When they ever done shit for us beside make things worse? You wanna crawl back in your hole in Cutjaw, Sto, no one's gonna hold it against you. But I ain't running off to hide after seeing my best friend *killed*. Can't bring him back but I can make that bastard pay."

"You can't," Zip said. Reece looked about ready to blow his top, but she sped on. "You can't stop him. He's not normal – not a real person –"

"Then what the hell is he?" Reece demanded.

"A monster," Zip insisted, more firmly. "The sort my daddy knows about. The sort my daddy knows how to *stop*." She was almost up out the seat, now, a fire in her almost as strong as his. "Only he knows how."

Reece kept staring, not needing to hear that, already feeling impotent, but told all the same. They'd all seen that maniac, all knew it was beyond them.

"You ready to tell us where Daddy is? Where's home?" Leigh-Ann came in, softly.

Zip relaxed again. "I already said. A mill, near a city. In England. I've never . . ." She went quiet again, shame weakening her resolve. "I've never been in the city. I don't *know* our address."

"Bullshit, she –" Stomatt started.

Reece cut him off, finding a new place to direct his fire: "We got another place to start. We pin down this Grithin in Memphis. He'll have answers, won't he?" He said it like he hoped not. Like going after this Grithin might give them someone else to hurt. And that's exactly what he intended to do.

A couple miles up Red River, the motor ran out of fuel. When it started struggling, the gang moored by a rickety riverside diner. A single-storey wooden shack whose stilts cut an unpleasant reminder of where they'd just been. Inside, it smelt of old fish and burnt fat. Three burly white men in swamp gear sat eating grits, watching them suspiciously. A big waitress wiped her hands on a greasy apron and asked if they were lost. The gang looked a sight, true enough, in their dishevelled suits, with a kid in a thick, formless dress. At least they'd washed off the blood in the river.

Reece tried to turn on his usual charm but it wasn't coming easy. His account of them being a band of travelling musicians, jumped nearby and lost their instruments, their ride and their money, sounded flat and empty. Leigh-Ann chipped in with colourful descriptions of fat, redneck assailants, right down to the boils on one guy's nose. Not happy being painted a victim, Stomatt said he'd knocked one of their teeth out. The pair of them gave a better account than Reece, claiming they were penniless and drifting with an aim to reach Memphis. A kid to feed between them. Why not – Zip was pretty enough, just the right shade if Reece and Leigh-Ann ever did bump uglies.

The waitress took it in with a dose of scepticism, but after lingering on Zip she insisted they have breakfast on the house. Offering up tin plates of dirty-smelling food, she explained they had a mighty long way to go just to get to the Mississippi, let alone Memphis. But might be she had some trucker friends who could help, if they waited round.

They settled into a corner, where Reece quietly took stock again. By now they should've been planning youthful retirement. Thinking of clubs they might play in New Orleans. Not mourning a friend, on the run. Shit, he'd shamed Stomatt with the idea but they *would* be better off heading back to Cutjaw.

Leigh-Ann ordered up a round of early-morning bourbon, which the waitress didn't blink at, and once the drinks arrived Reece stared into his glass in silence. They were waiting for him to say something. He cleared his throat. Best thing he could say now was that they oughta clear out.

Reece took his drink in hand and met the others' eyes. Leigh-Ann puffed her lips like she had things to say, too, but was waiting for him to go first. Stomatt, damn his eyes, gave his usual gummy smile. Gotta laugh, he'd say, now he was getting over the night's tension. Reece said, "Caleb was always with me. Long as I remember. We fought off the Howie twins together before we could even reach a cupboard door. Stuck by me for every hare-brained scheme I had – sold Harlan Jenson his own aluminium siding back, and took a whooping for that. Stuck by me when I lifted my first trumpet from that store in Leesville – swore on his life it couldn't have been me. Did all this because I wanted it. Loyal as a hound. Same as y'all. He never didn't do right by me, and now . . . now I gotta say –"

"It's time to do right by him," Leigh-Ann cut in, eyes warning Reece not to disagree. "You show us how, Reece. To Memphis and beyond. Cutjaw Kids gonna see justice done." She raised her glass and Reece did too, cautiously. "To Caleb."

"To Caleb," Stomatt agreed, "and to taking down the bastards that got him."

Reece hesitated. They'd go home if he said so, he knew it. Or into hiding, someplace better. But Leigh-Ann's expression said he better not dare. He forced a smile, at last. "To Caleb."

They clinked glasses and drank.

Stomatt let out a big breath as they thumped the glasses down. As if the panic and tension on the boat belonged to someone else entirely, long forgotten. That was how it had to be, wasn't it? Shit happened, you moved on . . .

As they finished their breakfasts, the waitress came and dropped a little metal dish in front of Reece. He expected a bill but instead saw a pile of cash. The waitress said with dreamy eyes that they needn't wait for the truckers. Folks down on their luck, with a kid in tow, deserved a hand. One of the boys there could take them to the interstate, where they could hop on a bus. Reece thanked her, but watched Zip. The way she avoided his eyes told him he was right to wonder. Hell. Their secret weapon and none of them knew how it worked. But they could figure that out on the way, Lord help them.

24

General Solomon led the trio down to a grass clearing populated by wooden shacks, decorated with macabre carved statues hanging off wires or standing on posts. Blocky, barely human forms sporting old blades and bullet shells like jewellery. Battle-scarred men lurked around the huts, wearing the same fatigues as their escort, carrying antique Soviet rifles or dirty, nicked blades, all harrowed and haunted. Tasker took note of one man leaning against a wall wearing a shirt long enough to be a tunic, a short axe on his thigh and heavy gold chains around his neck. His frame bulged, the best fed in camp.

Meat cooked in a bubbling pot over a central fire with a welcoming smoky scent. Solomon said, "Please, fill a bowl, rest your legs."

"What's in the stew? Human meat?" Katryzna said. She'd been eyeballing Solomon all through the journey, always a second away from knifing him.

"It's boar," Solomon said, plainly.

Katryzna sniffed at the broth. She dipped a finger in as Henri let out half a warning – she flicked the heat away and sampled it, all the while watching the general. She nodded satisfaction, then took up a tin bowl and started spooning chunky liquid in. "Suppose you save people for special occasions."

"There are no cannibals in this forest." Solomon paused. "Though, if you believe those rumours, there is the Blood Doctor, in Virguna."

Katryzna grunted dismissal, dropping onto an overturned barrel to start ravenously spooning stew into her mouth. Tasker and Henri took smaller, more cautious portions for themselves. It did smell good; robustly earthy. They joined Katryzna, Tasker perching on a crate, as Solomon sat on a fur-padded throne of a racing car seat supported by an old car wheel.

The general gestured to the man in gold chains, who peeled himself upright and ambled over. "I appreciate your concerns," Solomon said. "Ikiri is a dark place, and the last the world knew of us, we were bad people. We murdered and raided without cause. This is Jonah – he was my fiercest lieutenant, before we came here. Most feared him. Now, he is a priest of Ikiri. He understands Sara better than any of us." With that suspicious scowl, his axe and all that gold, Jonah looked like no priest. Following Tasker's thoughts, Solomon added, "A warrior priest. We are changed men, but must remain militant. Every day we survive here is a triumph. Sara's protection stretches only so far."

Henri cleared his throat, filled with concerns but too nervous to speak. Solomon waited, so he asked weakly, "How long has she been there?"

Solomon gave a sympathetic nod. "It must be unpleasant to see your sister so. She is no longer the person you knew. She cannot be saved – will not be saved."

"Does not need to be," Jonah added, in a deep, angry tone. "She has power."

"Jonah fears sharing that power," Solomon explained. "We all do, in truth. Ikiri is something to be protected, concealed and hidden. Its spread would damn others as it has damned us." Solomon arched his fingers together. "Though we do not fully understand it. Sara speaks to us only as she spoke to you. Not in sentences, sometimes not even in words. But she told us you would come, Katryzna. She repeated your name."

Katryzna paused, mouth full. She swallowed and said, "She knew Eyes, I guess he mentioned me."

"But she only used your name recently," Solomon replied. "Please, let me start from the beginning. I founded the Popular Liberation Union twenty years ago, and we were a *terrible* force. I killed my own uncle at the age of fifteen."

Katryzna made a noise to interrupt. "I killed *mine* at twelve."

Solomon raised his eyebrows. "Indeed? But look at us now." Tasker shared the feeling he saw reflected in Katryzna and Henri's slowly scanning eyes. Surrounding them like ashen scarecrows, the Cursed Union looked weathered, worn, and darkly frightening. Yet Solomon saw something else in them. "We came here to claim a fortune, but the mountain instead tried to claim *us*. We survive only through protecting one another – no man could stand here alone. This is Sara's influence. We are good people now – or we try to be. It is all we can do."

"The stories have it," Tasker came in carefully, not wanting to provoke the man but seeing there was room for a dialogue, "that you kill to keep Ikiri to yourselves."

"We warn off outsiders," Solomon said. "So they don't fall into the same trap as us. The outsiders themselves bring violence to us, when they are corrupted. And Ikiri has its own defences. The Westerners were gone long before we arrived. The nearby villages long dead or abandoned. But we found Sara Ngoi – trapped as she is today. Sustained by the tree itself. No longer truly human" – Henri winced, and Solomon's tone became consolatory – "but her mind is free – she feels the world. She knew my name, as she knew yours, Katryzna. She felt our natures and softened them. She tried to warn us about the darkness, but we touched it all the same."

"What –" Katryzna started, but spat food. Tasker could guess she might demand *what are you talking about?* She wiped her mouth and reconsidered. "Be specific."

"I will try," Solomon said. "But Ikiri is greater and stranger than anything of religion and false gods. The power itself is unclear – though its origin is clear. There is a chasm in the side of the mountain, large enough to walk into. It gave Sara the power she has now, long ago, though it trapped her. We cannot go inside ourselves. Two of my men tried. Only bits of them came out."

Katryzna snorted. "Bits – what kind of bits?"

"Blood, mostly," Solomon answered readily. "They were inside for three minutes, then an explosion of what *was* them came out."

"What's it look like, this place?" Tasker said. "How do you feel near it?"

"Jonah," Solomon said. "Describe it."

"A hole in the world," Jonah said, with gravity. "A gate to hell. To see it is to suffer."

"Be real," Katryzna said. "Is there a bear in there or something?"

"A bear?" Solomon said. "There are no *bears* –"

"A gorilla or a monkey or whatever," Katryzna said. "An *animal*. Or" – she clicked her fingers – "a trap! Duvcorp left mines, to stop anyone following them?"

"This was no mine. The mountain hums, there. The air shimmers. It feels *wrong*."

Tasker had encountered pockets of energy before. There was one beneath a lake in Russia that affected boat engines, but did little else. He couldn't recall any that made people explode. He said, "I'd still like to see it for myself."

"Getting close carries a risk of its own," Solomon said. "After we discovered it, we found we could not leave the area. If any of us travel beyond three miles of Ikiri, our minds decay. My men have turned on one another, as savage as the monsters in the hills."

This was it. The effect that had touched Igota. Laukstad. Not an outsider manipulating them or a monster they couldn't trace. They had attacked *each other*. Locked, somehow, in Ikiri's spreading darkness. He said, "It drives them mad?"

Solomon regarded him for a moment. "You know it, don't you? The corruption."

"We were attacked last night, before coming here, by men out of their minds."

"Who couldn't be killed," Katryzna added.

"I'm here because the same thing happened a long way away. In Norway."

The general was momentarily thrown. "Sara senses movement abroad. Could Ikiri reach that far?" He looked to Jonah for an answer, and the other man's grumpy expression suggested he had no idea. Solomon continued, "Ikiri is a jealous, violent power. And as we retreated, to here, we learnt our area of safety was only thanks to Sara's protection. She keeps the minds around her safe. But while we were safe from each other, the creatures began to emerge. You heard them, last night. Great, monstrous beasts stalk these hills. Almost impossible to kill. So. We are hunted by Ikiri for staying, yet unable to leave."

"Not much use to us, by the sounds of it," Katryzna said.

Solomon shared another look with Jonah, then said, "We have gathered some information that might interest you. About what became of Sara's companions."

"Everyone who came with her is gone," Jonah took over. "Four were buried in these hills. Five men have been named. Of the named ones, there was Moose, who died in Sarajevo –"

"In *Sarajevo*?" Katryzna cut in. "You seriously expect us to believe you know that?"

Jonah stared impassively, insulted by the question, so Solomon answered, "We have no reason not to believe Sara. She speaks, very rarely, of specific locations, very far away. You have come here, after all, talking of Norway – you know these links are possible." He addressed this more to Tasker, who had to agree, grim as it was to consider the implications. A force that could reach anywhere, as he had feared. "Jonah, go on."

Jonah grumbled but continued. "There is Fender, who *did not understand*. Shearjoy, who is to be feared – whose dangers Sara has identified in many places. And there is Eyes, who died to protect her. These are the lessons we have learnt." He puffed up his chest with importance and Katryzna stared with her mouth open.

"Where's his body?" she said. "What happened?"

"We don't know," Solomon answered. "This is what she has told us, and she cries for him. She connects him to a nameless *he*, a friend who left them behind. The rift between her, Eyes and this man, we believe, is what trapped her. It is also when we think the nameless girl was taken from here."

"The *she* Sara mentioned?" Tasker came in before Katryzna could heat up again.

"Yes," Jonah said. "*She* is our hope. One person who can calm Ikiri's dark heart. We could do nothing ourselves, to find her, trapped here, and so have waited, and waited, for help to come."

"Me?" Katryzna asked brightly, sitting back on her barrel.

"Not *you*," Jonah spat, taking offence. "*You* are a link. You can bring the girl to us. That is what Sara has promised us." He looked to Solomon as though he had doubts, now.

"You resisted Sara's influence," Solomon clarified. "I believe you could resist Ikiri's, too. If you can leave here and bring us this girl, we can end this curse. We know where the girl is – just over a week ago, the shroud that hid her was somehow lifted, and Sara saw her, at last. She has given us co-ordinates. If you can –"

"You discovered her location just now?" Katryzna said. "How brilliantly convenient."

"Around the time Laukstad got wiped out," Tasker said. Exactly as he had feared and Simon Parris must have suspected; something had changed with the threat out here. It was branching out, able to cause harm anywhere – and if they couldn't answer why Laukstad, they might as least answer why *then*. "There's a connection, isn't there? This power gets used, the girl comes out of hiding."

"Are you serious?" Katryzna said. "You believe this?"

"You saw Sara yourself, Katryzna. You felt her power –"

"I *felt* annoyed. As I do now. Annoyed and bored and thinking these guys are nuts." She made an irritated noise at a space down near the barrel, dismissing Rurik. "No, no – they don't know a thing and they're wasting our time."

Solomon was stony behind his dark glasses, some hint of his calm fading. However amiably he'd welcomed them, they were still in a rebel camp a long way from civilisation. Tasker quickly turned to Henri. "You know the expedition. Were those names familiar? Moose? Shearjoy?"

Henri startled, happy to have been dwelling in his own bubble. He stuttered a few non-words before making sense of what he'd heard, then nodded. "Yeah. Yes – Fender was the lead scientist. He was officially in charge. There was a man called Moose, too. Shearjoy, I'm not sure . . . maybe? As to the girl, I don't know. There was one female scientist, the rest were men. Certainly no children, if it's a girl –"

"It is a girl," Solomon said. "We're quite sure. And we believe she has been into Ikiri itself. It is possible that Ikiri only became corrupted because these people entered. The understanding we have is that Sara, Eyes and their allies fought to contain that corruption. Some survivors escaped to bring it back to your world."

Katryzna set her jaw and looked away, closing her fists tight. Tasker ran it back through his mind, trying to compare it to Ministry lore. Particularly combinations of anything that could warp a woman into a tree and control minds. There was a predator in Guatemala that could travel through shadows. Animals in Siberia that exerted a kind of hypnosis to distract prey. But there was usually a physical creature attached to energy manipulation. Not a doorway in a mountain.

"You are different," Solomon said, watching Katryzna. "Most feel Sara's pure heart in their own. Accept the truth as it is spoken."

"Most idiots?" Katryzna said. "Maybe you are just too scared to go in – too *explody*. So you make things up about people you don't know. You say Eyes is dead when you've got no idea. Sean, it's time we see for ourselves –"

"He is dead," Solomon insisted calmly. "Sara deeply regrets his loss. And you will die too, without the girl's help, if you don't bring her here. We will all fall to Ikiri. It is spreading, isn't it?"

"I'm not an international kid courier," Katryzna said, standing. "If Eyes was last seen entering some hole in the ground, that's where I'm going."

"Even after all I've told you?" Solomon said, flatly. "It was after discovering the power of Ikiri that we were trapped here. Once the force is aware of you, it will do all it can to destroy you. If you leave now, find the girl, there's hope."

Katryzna glowered with venom as if to say she wouldn't be so easily persuaded. But Tasker's mind ticked faster, seeing a fault in Solomon's thinking. He said, "The force is already aware of us. It took hold of nearby villagers – it already tried to kill us. It knows we're here. Just like Sara knew. But for whatever reason, it couldn't get directly at us." He looked from Katryzna to Solomon, both waiting for a conclusion that, while it made sense, he didn't really want to draw. "If it couldn't get us there, it won't make any difference now. I'm with Katryzna: I think we should see this place."

25

Night, again, and people running, screaming.

This town perched on rocky outcrops, buildings flush with terrifying drops. Shadows moving between the houses, scurrying across sheer slopes like spiders, some fleeing while others chased. Men and women searching for knives and tools to fight the mad press of charging attackers.

A man slipped in his desperate attempt to draw a kitchen knife – a feverish woman snatched it off the cobbled floor. Jammed it deep into his side and screamed bloody fever in his ear.

A bell rang, men shouting from the top of a tower, calling for help – calling merely to be heard in their terror. Awful shrieks as people fell over the edge. Tripped, pushed, thrown into oblivion. At the town's periphery, a fire rose. No one to stop it. The bell rang more furiously, the screaming getting worse.

Leigh-Ann perused her phone outside their motel room. Rest hadn't come easy, trying to sleep on the stiff bed with Zip twitching against bad dreams and Stomatt's snores shaking the dividing wall. At least the air was relatively fresh on the balcony, compared to the stale muskiness inside, parking lot fumes notwithstanding. A few miles south of Memphis, a little respite before honing in on this Grithin character.

The phone was a necessary distraction against Leigh-Ann's thoughts. Crazy fantasies about mutants and ghosts and psychic kids. Paranoia about what Zip might be capable of, stacked against what her dad and co might do. But the phone wasn't helping: Leigh-Ann's research said the phenomenon of creeps attacking each other with swords wasn't exactly uncommon.

Reece came strolling up and asked, "Couldn't sleep?"

"Got enough. You?"

He shrugged. "Save it for when I'm dead. I've been checking the news on their computer down there. No word about Stilt Town." His voice was dry, cheeks and eyes puffy, not in a good place. Leigh-Ann held in her sympathy. She didn't reckon they had the luxury to give in and cry quite yet. She held up her phone.

"Well, you wanna know how many results you get searching for sword attacks? Two days ago in Toronto, a week ago in Finland, one in the Big Easy itself just last month. There's people all over the world stabbing each other. Angry spouse, a psycho vet – two best buddies who fell out, just happened to like swords. Whole subculture of dudes solving problems with swords that no one knows about."

"One of many I bet," Reece said, distractedly leaning against the rail. "Probably the same for axe attacks. Rat poison. Socket wrenches, whatever."

"Yeah," Leigh-Ann said. "But I *did* get the report on this Memphis attack. Nothing new, except a photo of where it happened. Load of empty concrete." Reece nodded. "Something else up, Reece?"

Reece paused, which meant yes but he didn't want to say so. "I didn't find anything about the farm or Stilt Town."

"What, then?"

He took her phone and tapped in a search to show her.

There was a bad photo of Reece – his mugshot from five years back when he got picked up for fighting in Lake Charles. Bruised face, hair a mess, but still with a glint of mischief in his eye. Under it, a story. Reece Coburn, wanted in connection with a shooting in Waco, a crazed young thug out of Beauregard, LA, along with at least two friends. Call themselves the "Coburn gang" and are presumed armed and dangerous. No mention of Steer Trust, made it sound like a drugs turf war or something.

It was on a Louisiana state news site. Posted just this morning.

"Shit," Leigh-Ann said. "Fallon figured out who we are – widened the net without getting his own hands dirty?"

"Looks like," Reece said. "Either they found a trace of us in what was left of Stilt Town or someone survived to talk. On the positive, looks like it'll mean Fallon's handing us off to the authorities rather than come at us himself."

"After last night," Leigh-Ann said, "I guess he might. At least until someone slaps cuffs on us. Probably got his money back, even. Meaning all we managed to do was get our faces on a good old-fashioned Wanted poster while a ton of innocent people died." Reece nodded glum acknowledgement, like he needed telling. "Shit, Reece. It's not all on us – we stumbled in on something bigger than ourselves. Who knows how many others have been hurt because of this thing? But damned if I know what we do now. That's your area." Reece raised an eyebrow, so she prodded his chest. "I bring the cheer, motherfucker, you bring the plans." It made him smile at least.

"Just wish they could've got the name right at least," he said. "It's Cutjaw Kids, I *always* said that. Calling us a gang, putting my name up like it's all on me."

There was the old him coming out. The bit that cared most for how they carried themselves and everyone got due credit. She wanted to say welcome back – but a shriek rang out. Zip. They shared a quick look then both burst through Leigh-Ann's door. Leigh-Ann ran to Zip's side. The child sat upright in bed, sweating and panting, staring terror through the wall.

"Bad dream, sweetie, that's all –"

"No!" Zip locked fierce eyes on them. "It's real! I know it is! Svet. The bells!"

"Sweating bells?" Leigh-Ann joked, making Zip angrier.

"Svet's a town! The same happened to them – the same as in Stilt Town!"

That stilled Leigh-Ann, making her step back. Reece's face made it worse. Hell, after the nightmare of last night, he believed it and she was having a hard time not. Reece said, "You saw it? This town, Svet?"

Zip nodded.

"Just like the other one? In the rainforest? You remember that?"

"Igota. And Villa Madero. There were more, before. Danvale. Laukstad. They're getting worse. It's *him*, I can feel it."

"Vile?" Reece asked. "How's he doing it?"

Zip shook her head, not privy to that. She continued quietly, "Poor . . . poor town. On a mountain. They had fur hats. They didn't want to hurt each other – they weren't thinking anymore." Zip screwed up her face. "Svet. Not in America, nowhere near here."

Leigh-Ann quickly started searching for the names on her phone. Igota? How did you even spell that? Random results about corporates or song lyrics, no use. Svet? A handful of different ideas, something in Prague, a resort in the Crimea. Not a mountain town. Villa Madero – that worked – a town in Mexico. News stories, in Spanish, with pictures. Leigh-Ann showed Reece.

"Hell," he said.

Bodies in the streets. What was left of bodies. Cheap homes ripped down. Viciously rent animal carcasses. Leigh-Ann said, "Reported yesterday." She hit the translate button. "Suspected drug gang? No witnesses. Doesn't look like they were shot to me." She turned to Zip. "What happened in Villa Madero?"

"Do you believe me?" Zip answered with fearful hope.

"We believe you. But what's going on, Zip? Why's this happening?"

"Because he *made* it happen, that's why."

"Got in their heads, the same way you did with those Steers?"

Zip swallowed. Shit, Stomatt was right. The kid herself might be capable of what they saw in Stilt Town.

"Why?" Reece pressed. "What's it to Vile, hurting these people – coming after you – our friends in Stilt Town –" He stopped as Zip's lip trembled. She didn't know any better than them, and all this was only getting her more scared. "Cher, you said your daddy hunted people. Did he . . . this sort of thing, is it familiar?"

"I told you," she said. "It's because I followed Daddy – I used my senses – that's why people are dying. But you can take me home, can't you? If we go back, it'll be safe again, he won't see us anymore. It'll stop!"

"Doesn't make any damn sense," Leigh-Ann whispered.

But Reece was firming up again. Seeing how big this really was, and the monster they were dealing with. Stilt Town was bad enough, losing Caleb a nightmare – but this went way beyond that. Getting his determination back, Reece said, "We're gonna make it add up, right?"

The gang reached the Memphis Harbor Town at mid-afternoon, on the trail of the men from the news story the boys in Stilt Town had turned up. Not hard, once you started asking around – they'd enjoyed having their names in the paper and were happy to talk up their part in the incident. A short, overweight slob and his younger, pock-marked colleague; Reece had Leigh-Ann lure them off the riverfront under the charade of another interview. They were all too happy to oblige, and even when they rejoined Reece they chose leering at Leigh-Ann over questioning the tatty suits or Reece's mad green hair.

Shorty pointed out over an empty stretch of asphalt. "Happened about here. We were on a break, middle of the night shift, sitting over there." Warehouses flanked them to one side, the river to the other, and the blue pyramid Zip spoke of was visible just over some rooftops to the north. "The guy came outta nowhere, you know? Appeared right next to us – Rudy damn near shit himself."

"He put a real fright on me," the other one, Rudy, admitted.

"Tall as Gus, he was, if not taller," Shorty continued. "And that's saying something – Gus is a *big* boy. Only this guy weren't as broad." Not Vile, then; hopefully Zip's father himself, Seph Mason. "He didn't say nothing, just stood there in this long coat, hood up, expecting Gus to recognise him. It was me, spoke first, wasn't it? Said, 'Can we help you, pal?' Then Gus got up growling."

"Always the quiet ones," Rudy said. "Came out of nowhere, didn't drink."

"Anyway," Shorty said, "this shady guy, he pulls out this sword from God-knows-where. Suddenly sticking out his sleeve. Must've been the length of my leg, what do you think?"

"*Your* leg, maybe. Length of a forearm at least."

"Watch it." Shorty forced a smile for Leigh-Ann. Probably took height jokes with less humour when there weren't ladies present. But the point stuck: a sword hid up his sleeve, that idea of Zip's, the *sword hand*. "Neither of them spoke – they just stared each other down. Then – BAM!" Shorty punched a hand into his opposite palm. "Gus whipped up this rebar from down there and they just start *going* at each other, springing about like Spiderman. By the time we got into cover it was over, they fought each other off into the shadows there. Disappeared. Then they were gone – all she wrote."

"Damn craziest thing I ever saw," Rudy said.

"The guy smelt funny too," Shorty added. "Hard kind of smell. I dunno how to describe it. Like something big. A bull. Interesting detail for your story?"

"Sure," Reece said, liking the sound of Seph Mason about as much as he liked Vile. "But we don't have a story if we can't pin these two down. Gus hasn't been back to work?"

"Nuh-uh. Dropped by his place a couple days ago. No answer at the door. You guys know what it was about?"

"The mystery's what's got us interested," Leigh-Ann said. "Got an address?"

"Certainly do." Shorty wrote it down on her phone, along with his number in case she needed anything else – anything at all. The pair had little else to share: Gus never spoke about his past, or plans for the future, or anything much else. He stared out into space a lot, they said, and must've been on the lam from something dark. One eye and an ugly scar over the other. Flinched at sudden sounds like a paranoid vet. That's what they figured him for – someone back from the wars, struggling with civilian life. Or a gangster thug or something? *Yakuza* specifically. Had to be, with those swords.

When Reece and Leigh-Ann parted from the men, he told her, "You watch over Zip and I'll take Sto to go knock on this guy's door."

"Forget that, let's go straight there," Leigh-Ann said. "I can handle myself."

"Don't doubt you can." He gave her a smile. "But there's no doubt Gus is really Grithin, right? Part of a whole community of nasty supercharged nuts? With all Zip's told us, and all we've seen, *I* might need more protection than you can give."

With that kind of cheek, and a mission to follow, yeah. He was on his way back, and Leigh-Ann gave him a punch on the shoulder to show she appreciated it.

Stomatt was busy changing TV channels every twenty to thirty seconds. Antiques show. Someone selling necklaces. Televised court case. News about a forest fire. The antiques show again. Vintage crime show. More news. Yadda ya. Better than looking the kid's way, with her weird eyes that searched inside him. Picking out the worst of him. No one needed that.

A cartoon came up, some moron cat chasing a bird, which Stomatt lingered on. Dumb cat ran into a plank, flattened his face, pretty funny. Stomatt clicked the changer, back to the crime show, and Zip sighed disappointment. He gave her a glance. "Liked that one, huh?"

Zip fixed her face blank. Didn't wanna talk.

Stomatt changed back to the cartoon. He sensed Zip smiling. The cat was propelling itself up off the ground with a hose now, like some kind of jet pack – but damn if he didn't miss the bird and fly head-first into a beehive. Zip laughed and Stomatt joined in. Stupid cat.

The kid shifted closer, then, watching properly. Stomatt took a tense breath, but got distracted as the cat started setting out bear traps. They laughed together as one snapped on his face. Funny music, too. He could lay out a beat like that, punctuate little animals chasing one another. Probably good money in it. One to throw Reece's way . . .

The cartoon ended with the cat trapped in a barrel, with another bird pecking at his head, and Zip swooned happily. Stomatt said, "Like seeing that nasty cat get whooped, huh?"

She looked uncertain. He'd made it an accusation, hadn't he? Shit. He tapped the changer, things getting awkward again. How was anyone supposed to deal with kids? Fuck, the others were straight with her, might as well go for it himself. "With your mind reading? How much you know?"

"I can't read minds."

"You know what people think, right? Knew about my mom. That's reading minds."

Zip shook her head. "Not in words. Like . . . I know feelings. They give me ideas. I know when you're unhappy?"

Stomatt paused. "I'm unhappy?"

"*You're* worried," she said. "You don't want anyone to know."

He straightened up. "I'm an open book, kid. Secrets are for cowards."

She didn't answer that, only looked a little ashamed. Yeah. What'd he have to hide? Always spoke his mind, always did what he wanted. Scared of a kid thinking him unhappy, pah. Stomatt flicked channels again. A news show had switched to game highlights.

"I keep secrets," Zip said, quietly.

"Like about where you live?" Stomatt huffed, making her flinch. Shit, she suddenly looked close to tears. "Ah. Look, everyone tells stuff to their friends, don't they? That's why we're upset about it – don't you think we're friends?" Zip sniffed. Stomatt put a big arm around her, gave her a squeeze. Anything better than risking bawling. Damn those two for leaving him babysitting. "And you *know* we'll find a place in the gang for you and those freaky powers." Something hit him, then. "Say. You ever played cards?"

The door clicked open and Stomatt half-jumped off the bed, reaching for the shotgun by the pillow. Reece froze in the doorway. "Hell, Sto, it's only us – and I definitely would've had the drop on you there. Everything cool?"

Stomatt found Zip nodding happily. Where was his mind a second ago? On the verge of a genius idea, wasn't he?

"Great. You and me are gonna knock on this Grithin's door."

26

Katryzna marched ahead of Tasker and Henri, behind Solomon and a couple of soldiers. She had little idea where they were now, having taken a truck part of the way up the hill, and the day's waning light wasn't helping. But so what – they weren't far off now. Eyes might be there. If that freak woman could live eight years in a tree, he could've survived in a cave. If anyone could, Eyes could.

He'd bring some normalcy to this whole thing, seeing as no one else was able to. They were all under some spell from that Sara woman, believing this crap about psychic energies and miracle children. Henri and Tasker were buying into it, she could hear them discussing it – Tasker asking if he was alright, Henri admitting that it was a shock, but he wanted to help. To end her suffering. *It wasn't her, was it?* he mumbled, regretful. *But what about her new skills?* Really buying into this mystic crap.

Rurik suggested, from Katryzna's shoulder, "You can't deny there's something wrong with this place. It gives me the creeps."

"You do not get to have creeps," Katryzna said, getting a backwards glance from the soldier ahead. She showed him her teeth and he looked ahead again. She turned to Henri. "If any of this *was* real, why didn't your sister send you psychic brainwaves already?"

"How?" Henri frowned. He turned to Tasker. "Could she have – somehow – what if she *did* contact me, and I never knew?"

"Her mind is elsewhere," Tasker said. "Locked in resolving whatever mess they created. Surely you feel it's not right up here, Katryzna?"

"What's *right*?" she shot back. "Doesn't feel right locked in prison or jumping out an airplane, but I don't blame that on living mountains or whatever. Sean. In your expert opinion, isn't this nonsense?"

"In my expert opinion," Tasker echoed, "it's not like anything I've come across. They've talked about things that sound like teleportation, but a naturally occurring displacement device wouldn't explain the massacres or how Sara works. And psychic energy wouldn't explain how she got in that tree – or how anyone got out of this place alive, unseen. Or why Duvcorp would kill to cover it up, but never came back here."

"They didn't know there were survivors," Henri said. "Or if they knew, Miguel didn't. He would never have hid my sister's survival, I'm sure."

"None of it makes sense," Katryzna grumbled. "Including your willingness to believe any of this." She stomped on ahead in disdain.

Rurik urged her, softly, "Give it a chance. *Try* and feel it."

She growled but resisted the urge to attack. Fine. She studied her feelings and felt nothing but the growing cold. Besides, who *wouldn't* get uneasy on some darkening mountainside about a million miles from the nearest telephone? She shook that idea off.

A sound whistled through the trees. The screech of some horrendous bird.

They all slowed down to listen for it, but it didn't come again. Katryzna said, "Why's Africa so *weird*."

"That's not a call I recognise," Henri said, worriedly.

"Now you are an expert?"

"We should move quicker," Solomon said. "It's not far now."

They continued at speed, without talking, until the soldiers stopped ahead, waving hands and calling for stillness. Clear of the trees was a great rock-face veined with roots and vines. At its centre, a jagged crack, filled with darkness. Katryzna stared wide-eyed. *Now* she felt something. This was exactly where it all led. This was where Eyes had gone. She took a tentative step closer, past Solomon, and the feeling strengthened in her. Air thick as water. She tensed and asked of the world, "What is this?"

Tasker shuddered behind her, with an involuntary noise. She shot him a look and saw Henri was edging fearfully towards a tree, for cover. The soldiers didn't look much better – all these tough guys glaring with thinly hidden worry. Solomon said, "You don't deny it now?"

"Don't tell me what I feel." Katryzna turned back to the dark hole. She gritted her teeth and took another step closer. Something pushed back. Like it was blowing out air, resisting her. Even if the air was still, the forest quiet.

"You can't go in there," Rurik said, full of fear.

"I can do what I want," Katryzna replied, strained. She took another step forward, and it got harder.

"Don't!" Rurik cried. More emotion than she'd ever heard from him, shouting into her ear. She swatted him off her shoulder and he fell shouting. Another step. The resistance came with noise now, a throb of unformed sound repelling her.

"Katryzna, that's enough!" Tasker called, from far away.

Then another sound – something like that monster from the night before. Closer than Tasker. Katryzna blinked against it, ignoring whatever comment Solomon made. She could do anything. Face anything. A dark crack of rock wasn't going to stop her. Another step and her vision blurred. Foot on the threshold of the entrance, hand on the rock to support her. Struggling to take that final step – feelings flooded into her. Pain, happiness, laughter, fear – visions, a thousand faces at once, fires burning and waves crashing – she heard her own sound of defiance rising up against the flood. Pressing slowly into the shadow, vision growing brighter, stranger – a cacophony of human sounds –

She was pulled back, suddenly, with panicked shouts surrounding her. She tried to break free but her arms were weak, mind unfocused as the faces and voices dispersed from her unclear vision. Tasker's voice in one ear: "Move – it's coming!" Henri's voice in the other: "My God what is it?"

And another animal scream, drawing closer.

Katryzna pushed them both off her, steadying herself to find her feet as they stumbled into the tree line. Her senses were returning, the world refocusing, and she heard a new savage noise. She was breathing heavily. There were tears on her cheeks. She hated it but she knew it then, that they were right. This place was unnatural and deadly. They could not stay. It had killed Eyes and it would kill them all, too.

"Hurry, hurry!" Solomon shouted, pushing them on. They were running through the trees, dodging branches, watching footfalls, as the animals closed in, sounding at once right near them and also very far away. One of the soldiers started shooting, but Katryzna couldn't see what at. The men were shouting in their native tongue now, panicked, firing at shadows. When Katryzna tried to slow and join in, she was pushed on by Henri, urging her not to stop.

Suddenly they broke out onto the truck, piling in. The wild sounds pressed ever closer, soldiers firing at them as someone started the engine. Then, with final panicked shouts, they were all in and driving away.

Katryzna rested her head back against a window, recovering her breath, trying to understand what she'd felt. Tasker and Henri were both watching her, terrified, confused, but looking to her for something. Hoping that she'd reflect the same belief they'd already got from that tree freak. Katryzna closed her eyes, listening to the sounds of the unholy beasts, just audible now behind the truck engine. She said, quietly, "If this thing killed Eyes, I will burn it all down." She opened her eyes, and found the guys looked no less worried. "We will get this child."

Tasker barely slept, hearing the noises of the monsters of Ikiri hunting for them. During the evening, Katryzna had retreated into the same miserable quiet that caught her in the hotel, revisiting the truth that Eyes was dead over and over, not knowing what to do with it. Once they'd settled into a private hut, she barely reacted to the sounds outside or Tasker's attempts to spark conversation. Henri, too, had lost his carefree manner after their previous night's encounter, seeing his sister, and now this. He wasn't all there. Leaving Tasker alone to consider the possibilities: that Ikiri's corrupted power was capable of lashing out to cause such harm as he'd seen in Laukstad. That the people thought to have gone missing here might still be out there, guarding this secret. Somehow, deep down, he knew that this child Sara spoke of, this girl, was necessary. And with the possibility of Ikiri striking anywhere, at any time, they had to cure this haunted land as quickly as possible.

The wretched things never got close, but those sounds had all the screeching, death-hungry hallmarks of the preternatural creatures the Ministry investigated. The likes of which were culled in most places but carefully contained around such cities as Guidalezam in Mexico, Istanbul in Turkey. Under Ordshaw in England. He couldn't imagine the lives of Solomon and his men, evading such creatures every night.

Thankfully, the gentle dawn saw the creatures silenced, and Solomon roused a beanpole soldier to drive them to the edge of his territory, as eager to see them on their way as they were. He said they could take the Jeep further themselves, as his man would use a bike to ride back. He wished them the best of luck, and warned, "If you start to feel strange, come back."

Henri lingered at the edge of the camp, looking up towards the slopes of the hills as though he could see his sister stuck there. Sadness and shock behind his eyes, at a loss. Tasker asked if he wanted to say goodbye, but he shook his head.

"There's no hope," Henri said, "until we do what she asks."

He turned away, arms folded, rather than discuss it further.

Katryzna, on the other hand, approached the Jeep with something like disinterest, calling, "Are we going or what?"

Despite having accepted Ikiri had some illicit power, she scorned the idea of the PLU's curse, and insisted they wouldn't lose their minds because *she* wasn't a coward. Tasker sensed there was some truth in it, given they had been safe from whatever gripped those men from Igota, but it was no comfort for their driver, who watched the forest with mounting fear as he drove. He kept an AK-47 across his lap, impractical but inseparable from him. After a little over an hour of bumpy travel, he pulled the Jeep up where the dirt track split in two, disembarked with the bike and pointed down the left fork. "Two miles to Igota, then join the road to the river."

He rode away as quick as he could, almost falling off the bike in his urgency. Katryzna looked ready to mock his fear but held off, for some reason regarding whatever Rurik said with more generosity this morning. However cool she played it, Tasker had seen her fear before that cave. As they drove on, though, apparently now outside Sara's influence, Tasker started to feel more at ease himself. The further they got from Ikiri the better, as far as he was concerned.

When they came upon Igota, Henri pulled the Jeep to a stop with a worried sound. He stood from his seat to get a better view over the dirtied window. "Oh no. No no."

Tasker leant out to see. The village was destroyed. The closest hut had collapsed like something had been driven through it. There were bodies on the ground, limbs twisted at impossible angles, dry earth and wooden walls painted with blood. Near the entrance to the village sat stout Ade, their kind host, too much gore on his flesh to identify a single wound, lifeless eyes open with terror. There would be more, worse, if they looked closer. More children, brutally killed.

"Henri," Tasker said. "We should go."

"These people . . ." Henri said. "They were good people, they helped us."

"There's nothing we can do."

"At least we don't have to worry about those freaks' intentions the other night," Katryzna said, lightly. It didn't help Henri's trance, as he started to make a low keening noise.

Tasker leaned forward to tap him. "Let's go." Henri snapped out of it and nodded, dropping back into his seat. He started the engine again. Movement flashed out of the trees – more from between the huts – people, suddenly emerging. Tasker twisted in his seat. "Hell."

"Survivors?" Henri said with empty hope, quickly looking around them.

"Drive," Katryzna advised. "Straight through them."

Three people shuffled into the path ahead, standing at crooked angles as though held up by some force other than their own. All focused on the Jeep.

"Drive!" Katryzna shouted, loud enough to force Henri's foot down on the pedal. They surged forward, Henri shouting, and the villagers screamed and charged.

27

By the time they reached Grithin's address, Reece had heard Stomatt's rambling assessment of Zip's prowess a dozen times over. It essentially amounted to "the kid's alright" and "we should take her to a casino". Never mind casinos didn't let children in – he repeated the sentiments each time sounding like he'd just come up with the idea. It was the conversational equivalent of fitful, irritating scat music, with a predictable refrain, teasing progression then looping right back . . .

But then they were at the apartment: a two-storey red-brick block opposite a pair of desolate parking lots. It had big square windows and a set of steps that led up to a black-iron entrance gate. They worked out which were the windows for Grithin's place – ground floor, to the left of the entrance, curtains drawn, no sign of life. Stomatt leant heavily on the buzzer, but no one answered. Reece went back out to the street, checking their options: a balcony stuck out of the landing above with no way to climb up. Round the side, the block went back a way – different apartments forming the rear side. Reece came back to find Stomatt had his hands on the window, the lower sill about chest height, looking in.

"Can probably get onto the super," Reece suggested. "Say we're friends."

"Thin glass," Stomatt said, scanning the road. There were another couple of small blocks in sight, but this was a dead little pocket of squalor with few cars and no pedestrians. "We can be in and out real quick."

"Depending on what's inside," Reece said. "If anything."

"Your call, boss."

Reece bit his lip. Every second they wasted, that ninja freak and his gorilla were likely getting closer. "Fuck it." He drew his pistol and bunched up his jacket under it, gave the street one last glance and tapped the handle hard into the base of the window. The pane cracked straight across with a sound that split across the street. Reece gave it another tap and the lower pane split out, four or five segments falling inside and crashing with tinkles. He winced. But still no sign of movement on the street.

"This place is dead, man," Stomatt assured. "We're good."

"Keep watch," Reece said. He reached under the dangling sharp blade of the upper pane and unhooked the window, then pulled the sash up. With Stomatt's help, he wriggled inside. Glass crunched underfoot as he steadied himself in a dark living room. Not much to see bar a moth-eaten sofa and an old TV. Lot of dust.

Pistol in hand, Reece moved through darkness, curling his nose at a stagnant, heady smell. He passed through a corridor, checking a kitchen yellowed with age before coming to a bedroom-cum-office. A rickety wooden desk flanked a sunken camp bed which bowed under the weight of a man too tall to fit on it. Ripped with muscle, lean, he would've been in great shape if not for the gash running up his side, and the other crossing from his left ear down to his sternum. Both had been partly cleaned but were almost black from dried blood – he hadn't lasted long enough to properly dress them. Bandages and needles scattered the floor next to him. Reece took a step closer, covering his nose – Grithin, and the one eye hidden by scarring confirmed it was him, had been dead a while. He was in work overalls, likely came back here after that fight and hadn't done much more. Besides those two big cuts, his clothes were ripped in a half-dozen other places.

Reece checked the desk to the side, madly strewn with papers, some spread across the floor. Someone had gone through Grithin's files in a hapless way. And there were a *lot* of files.

Hell.

Newspaper clippings, photos of faces, police reports, all with big, frantic writing scrawled over them. Reece shifted closer, pushing a couple printed maps aside to reveal a set of photos. Men's faces. Some had been circled then crossed out, with big feverish markings. Hard-looking men, some in uniform, sitting next to news articles with daunting headlines: *Maniac Swordsmen Slays Ten. Unexplained Murders in Albuquerque. CEO of Fenk Co. Found Dismembered.* Reece turned over one of the photos, a shovel-faced man, and found a word written on the back. *Ruin.* He turned over a couple more: Mad Moose, Shearjoy, Flay.

"Scorecard" looked the least offensive, with a skinny, bespectacled mathematician look. Shit, these were guys with abstract monikers fitting to Vile. Many dead, going by the crosses. No sign of Vile himself, though.

Then, another one caught Reece's attention. Headhunter.

A square-headed, cold son of a bitch – this one with a smaller photo attached by a paper clip. Half the age she was now, but recognisable all the same, with the name jaggedly scrawled on the back. Zipporah. Underlined multiple times, like it'd been repeated excitedly. So Grithin was a hunter just like her father. It wasn't one man against the monsters – they considered each other monsters?

Reece noticed the stains on some of the papers on the floor, then. Finger smears of blood. A big boot print on one, next to something that'd been screwed up. Reece crouched to pick it up and unfolded another map – an area he didn't immediately recognise, with a bunch of towns named and an X marking a spot. A conclusion had been written in big triumphant letters: *Mason*. Reece looked from the map over to Grithin's body. Well, hell, the guy had located the Headhunter. Might've been just about to pay him a visit when Zip's dad caught up to him first.

The news came up on the TV half an hour after the boys left. Leigh-Ann's instinct was to tell Zip to look away, but, hell, the kid had been there. Close shots, aerial shots, body bags, gathered law enforcement vehicles – none of that looked as bad as it had on the ground, with lunatics ripping each other's throats out. It was the idea of becoming a celebrity that troubled Leigh-Ann more. Her face was on CNN – *her* rough-freckled features looking ugly out the TV like some kind of reprobate. National news. Could be international, even, couldn't it?

The unexplained massacre of almost a hundred people, that was something likely to spread everywhere. There were no survivors, they said, bar a handful of Gray's followers who'd been out of town at the time. The dead Steer Trust employees raised questions, with about two dozen found, but the reports chased that fact with Dustin Fallon sat sombre at a desk insisting his men were assisting with the pursuit of the Coburn gang, who Gray was harbouring. They were victims themselves, Fallon told the cameras – the Coburn gang *must* be stopped. Cue more flattering mugshots of the four of them. No mention of the fact that Caleb had bought it, like they hadn't even found his body yet.

The FBI were launching a manhunt, with the anchors warning everyone to be on the lookout, as if these psychos might creep in your bedroom window and cut your throat for no damn reason. Journalists would be swarming on Cutjaw to get dirt from families and friends. There'd be double-barrelled shotguns waved from porches.

If they got caught and avoided a deadly shootout, Leigh-Ann considered, she might get a book deal or go on a reality TV show. One of the Coburn gang, straight out of jail to eat bugs in the jungle for Saturday night thrills? It'd be a living.

When Reece got back with Stomatt, she showed them the news and Stomatt whistled and laughed. "They gonna make a movie outta us?"

"I know, right?" Leigh-Ann said. "Assuming we're not murdered by vigilantes."

"Whole of the South's gonna be gunning for us," Reece said. "And we got no story to tell that'll turn them off, short of 'track down this one's dad and let him explain'. Hell, we wanna be gone yesterday."

"No luck with Grithin?"

"Dead as roadkill," Reece said. "But not a total bust." He turned from the TV to Zip. "Got a thought, cher. The way you made them Steers look the other way, out on the highway? Just how well can you do that?"

"Um." Zip considered it. "It's not safe –"

"Never mind safe, nothing we're doing is safe. If you can get people to look the other way, that's all we can hope for. You flew here, didn't you? Got a plane all on your own? That's some amazing ingenuity and I'm sorry I didn't proper respect it sooner. Especially sorry your daddy's never respected it." He crouched in front of her, smiling. "Think you could do that again? Maybe walk us all right out of the States."

"Like through an airport?" Leigh-Ann said. "We'll walk right into cuffs."

"He's fixing on us going to England," Stomatt said.

"England?" Leigh-Ann exclaimed. "Just the other side of the damn pond, slide on over for a tea and cake? You serious, Reece?

You think we can get on a plane now –"

"Not much further than DC, is it?" Stomatt said, defensively. "I had a friend flew Charleston to there, took him a couple hours. Bus from Cutjaw to Alexandria's four hours – ten, twenty dollars on the bus."

Leigh-Ann gawked. "Think England's an island just off Savannah or what?"

"No, 'course not, just saying it's not like trying to get into China or something."

"It might as well be! You got any idea how an airport works? Reece. Come on – we don't even know for sure Zip's *from* England."

Reece took a piece of crumpled paper from his pocket and held it up for her. A map, with the name "Mason" scrawled by a cross. Leigh-Ann checked the printed place names near it, one bigger than the others. "Ordshaw? What is . . ." She slowed down and looked to Zip. The child had been watching them all in chill silence. "That your home, sweetie?"

Zip swallowed, and admitted quietly, "Maybe."

Leigh-Ann bit her lip. "All right. So what, no one's gonna notice us prancing onto flights with stolen cash and no passports?"

"That's the dream." Reece winked, the cocky bastard, and locked on Zip again. "But I wanna test the waters first. Zip – this is for all our sakes. To get justice for them people in Stilt Town and Caleb – and to make sure all that never happens to no one else. Least of all *us*. I gotta say I'm scared of your daddy too, okay, and he must've had some reason for keeping you sheltered – but he's the best hope we got, and he wouldn't want you out here stranded when using your powers might help, don't you think? So how about we start small. See what you've got?"

Zip quickly nodded.

"Right. Let's start by looking the part."

Reece had them all undress and put Zip to the test by taking her with him down to the motel's cleaning service. Wrapped in a bedsheet, Leigh-Ann shared an unpleasantly tense twenty minutes with Stomatt waiting on Reece's return, or for police sirens or whatever, before he burst back in elated: even with their faces shining up on the news in the foyer, and that *unmistakable* ridiculous green hair, the receptionist hadn't given him a second look, only took the clothes and told him they'd be dropped by later.

For the next test, while they were lingering in their underwear, Reece got on the phone to a travel agency and coupled his chatty charm with Zip listening in, focusing hard, to swindle flight tickets to Ordshaw. The woman on the line agreed to every damn thing Reece asked – business class tickets, payment deferred, no question of names or passport numbers – just pick them up at the counter. Intensely staring at something they couldn't see, Zip warped that admin's mind at a distance of God-knows-how-far. Forget celebrity TV, there were a million and one scams they could run with this. Leigh-Ann said, "What if we put in a call to Quantico or some shit? Tell the FBI to back off."

"After those TV broadcasts?" Reece said, seeing Zip's rising panic at the suggestion. "We'd have to get a hell of a lot of folks to forget."

"But she's got something there, don't she?" Stomatt chipped in, lingering by the door. He kept checking out the window, past the curtains, as if he'd wrestle any coming threat to the ground in just his vest and trunks. "FBI says we're off the hook, everyone else can damn accept it."

"But *they* will notice," Zip insisted. "They're everywhere."

"What *they*?"

Reece sniffed at that, his easy smile fading. "The rest of them. The others like Vile." For Leigh-Ann, he said, "There were pictures at Grithin's. A whole heap of these bastards out there. No, Zip's right, we can't put up any flags that'd point them our way. Hell, even now, Vile's likely to pick up on what we've done, isn't he?"

Zip nodded guiltily.

"It's fine." Reece rubbed her head. "Soon as we're suited, we'll jump across town, hunker down by the airport. Then hope Vile can't fly." It came out like a joke, but after his smile lasted a second, he looked to Zip for confirmation.

She said, "Um. I don't know how he travels. Fast."

"Screw it, that creepy son of a bitch *better* keep following us," Stomatt said. "Can't wait to punch his damn teeth out."

"I'd pay to see that," Leigh-Ann said, picturing joy at the end of this road. Some madman hero waiting on Zip to come home, able to stand up to this bastard and explain away what happened in Stilt Town. Maybe a bigger book deal out of it – idiot fools playing their part in resolving a mass-murder plot. Provided Zip's daddy wasn't just as bad as Vile. He had a kid, though, didn't he? Stirring at that thought, Leigh-Ann asked, "Zip. Can you get our guns on that flight, too?"

28

The Jeep was making unhealthy noises all the way through the forest, and Henri was leaning into the dash as though he could push it on himself. One of the bodies had gone under the wheels, making the vehicle jump, and another had bashed its head against the windscreen, obscuring visibility with a web of cracks. Tasker suspected a couple of enraged people jumping out of the trees might've jammed something in the right rear tyre, but they were still bouncing along so he didn't raise the doubt. No way they were stopping to check any time soon.

It'd been the familiar, previously friendly villagers who were driven to mindless rage, hurling themselves towards a moving vehicle, bloody teeth bared. If Tasker had any doubts left over the Laukstad connection, they were gone. This is what had cost those fishermen their lives. Some inexplicable mania, apparently generated by Ikiri itself. The Ministry would throw resources at this, at last, but he couldn't tell all yet. Still couldn't be sure who to trust, or where the people wanting to silence this had got to; did they *want* this force to get worse? Better to keep a low profile until they secured the girl.

When they reached the next village, Henri sped up rather than slowed down, in case the people there were corrupted, too. They came upon a patrol post shortly after, though, and had to stop. Another Jeep, and three armed men – too late to turn back by the time Henri saw them. Besides, there were no other roads to choose from.

As Henri pulled up, Katryzna reached for her rifle, hidden under their bags in the foot well. Tasker shook his head – she didn't look impressed. The men levelled guns at Henri, regarding the bloodstained vehicle. Tasker rolled down his window and leant out, hoping a white face would be enough to warrant consideration. He gave the briefest introduction, using one of his many covers – Preston Pullwick, imports and exports – and asked who they worked for. The men sneered him off, speaking rapidly in unimpressed French. Henri answered in a forced happy tone. They looked from the driver back to Tasker, sceptically, as Tasker tried to interpret. Katryzna picked up something herself and laughed when the guards did. The way they looked back at Tasker, the joke was on him. The soldiers nodded satisfaction and invited Henri on with smiles. They went back to their vehicle and pulled out ahead.

"What'd you say?" Tasker asked, as Henri drove behind them.

"They're from the rebel force that controls the area the rest of the way to the river –Matka's men," Henri explained. "I told them you're lost. Basically."

"Just me?" Tasker said.

"The way he said it was funnier," Katryzna said. "And saved their lives. Well *done*, Henri."

Henri's smile turned more uncomfortable. "Well. They'll take us all the way to the river. You'll wire them whatever money they ask for. Don't worry, their ambitions won't run too high." He was finally relaxing, now they had an escort and a clear path out of the rainforest. Even if they were armed rebels, the mere fact that the men weren't out of their minds was a blessing. After a few minutes of driving, Henri said, "We are free of Ikiri's influence, aren't we? This is proof – people we can reason with – our minds safe."

"Sure," Tasker replied. All bets were off there, though. Whatever warped those villagers had also hit a village in the Arctic circle. He looked to Katryzna, expecting her take, but she was back to looking out the window, in her own grim thoughts.

By dusk they reached the river and crossed to Bokema, where the soldiers hammered on a squat hut for a moustached man in glasses. He had computers inside, satellite dishes up top, and evidently ran some kind of electronic wire service. Under the rebels' eye, he set up a satellite phone link so Tasker could call through to London. He arranged for Caffery to wire the rebels' asking fee of £3,000 to their chosen account, apparently making the three men the happiest people in the DRC and Tasker's new best friends. It wasn't insignificant – Caffery would complain about this for months – but the gift kept giving, as the rebels insisted on arranging a private boat to leave that evening to take them back to Kinshasa. The barge, after all, wouldn't be back for days. It meant Tasker could also arrange for Caffery to set up his flights as soon as possible. His handler demanded answers, of course, but had to settle for Tasker hedging with a promise that he'd have some real results soon.

Tasker settled with relief onto the boat, once they were cruising into the night, the well-compensated captain and his second not the sort to fraternise. The vessel was just big enough to give their trio a private compartment below deck, with a corner of thinly-cushioned benches. Henri brought down a bottle of clear liquid which he handed to Tasker. It smelt flammable; Tasker gave it a sip and gasped at the fiery pain. He said, hoarsely, "That'll do," and absently held the bottle across the small space to Katryzna.

She curled her nose and folded her arms. "Do you actually want me to hurt you?"

"Huh?"

She scoffed at her conscience, apparently down on the bench by her knee: "Shut up, *he*'s the rude one."

"Sorry," Tasker said. "I figure it's always polite to ask." He took the bottle back and drank deeper. Hell, he hadn't realised how tense he'd been, venturing into the interior. He almost wanted to laugh, at the relief of getting away. But Katryzna's past words came back to him, *the mind is a terrible thing to waste*, and he stayed his hand on the bottle. She was staring at him as though to see what he'd do next. He passed it back to Henri, saying, "Your mind, in particular, Katryzna, might've saved us. Able to resist Ikiri, apparently. Henri and me were jelly before Sara, without you. And we got clear of Solomon's supposed curse. How about you, Henri, did you feel anything in that village?"

"Like I could've died there," Henri said. When Tasker's gaze rested more steadily on him he gave it proper thought. "Yes. I felt lost. Or that I was getting lost. I've been . . . dizzy. Since we found Sara." He forced a smile, shaking his head at himself. "I have fought ferocious men, three on one, with weapons. I do *not* scare easily. But that – I was afraid. I was losing control."

"But you didn't," Tasker said. "And neither did I. Possibly because you" – he pointed to Katryzna – "never would have."

"Hear that?" Katryzna laughed at the space on the seat near her knee. "Yes – oh, jump in a toilet." She looked up. "Rurik says I shouldn't take credit. Apparently I am too *mad* to be manipulated." Her eyes rested on Tasker like she knew that was where his mind was going.

"I don't think you're mad," Tasker said. "Besides your imaginary friend, you've proved pretty sane to me. I do think you're special, though. Your openness, perhaps –"

"Open?" Katryzna laughed, harshly. "Idiot. Look at carefree Katryzna, best friend until she cuts your throat out." She grinned wickedly, challenging. "Exciting until she crawls into a hole, too sad to move. You know what I did after Eyes disappeared? Why I came here *now*? I was about to –" she dragged a finger across her throat – "finish a job, and then I just could not do it. I *broke*. Ended up in a jail. It was two years before I got out, and most of that time I didn't feel any better."

"Broke?"

"*Cried*," Katryzna spat. "Sat on the floor in darkness. I am miserable, Sean. What'd you think I was doing in the hotel, masturbating?" She looked away, disgusted at herself. "Were you paying attention? It was a year before Solomon came to Ikiri. There was infighting, there was a child, some of these people got away – Eyes might have been *alive* some of that time. I could have helped. Instead, I was stewing in a cell feeling sorry for myself."

Her words hung heavy in the air. Henri quietly said, "How? If you were imprisoned, how could you do anything?"

Katryzna's expression darkened. "I could've found a way. I live a *charmed* life, Eyes told me. Not the only person to say so." Hadn't Smail used a similar word? "I'm everything that shouldn't work in this world, an anomaly like those men Lopaz hired." She swung an arm. "Violent, horrible people, who somehow survived Ikiri the same as me. People that the world throws up to disrupt things – just as it threw us together. Look at you, partnering with someone crazy enough to get you out of there. They spoke about Ikiri like some terrible force of nature – well, so am *I*. My kind, we live to do damage. Systems glitch and set us free – ultra-powerful men decide we're too useful to let die. We're kept alive and we're kept from cages, and I could've used that to *save him*."

Her voice had become manic, almost desperate. Wanting to confess, to be believed and forgiven. She stared madly into Tasker's eyes and he stared back, at a loss. The very things she was beating herself up over, he realised, might be the very inconsistencies that kept her alive. He said, weakly, "Well, you weren't there then, but you're here now. And I'm thankful you're able to help get to the bottom of this."

"Don't you listen?" she hissed through gritted teeth, leaning closer. "Eyes trusted me and he died in a crack in a rock. I'm not a witch, I'm not supernatural, okay, Sean? I *am* mad."

Henri came in, softly, "Ms Tkacz, if I may?"

She gave him a sideways look.

"Your friend Eyes – I don't believe he was waiting on anyone to help him. If that's true, about people the world preserves – well, none of those men would rely on friends. It was not your responsibility." It calmed her, momentarily. Well done Henri. But he moved on, some of his past smile creeping back in: "And I agree with Agent Tasker that you are definitely *not* mad. He might be too stuffy to make his proposal directly, but I will. I would like to invite you to dinner when we get back to Kinshasa. No funny business."

She stared with momentary disbelief, then barked a mean laugh. "Inviting me to dinner *is* funny business. You've paid less attention than Sean."

"You like to eat, don't you?"

"We can't go back to the city," Tasker came in, then. They both gave him questioning looks. "At least, not us two. We might be the first people in years to get away from Ikiri alive – there's a dozen survivors from the expedition that might be watching. They were a step behind Parris, letting him talk – probably a step behind us when we got to Africa. But they'll have caught up now, I'd bet. We'll get off the boat early, head straight to the airport."

"Did you get Henri a plane ticket too?" Katryzna asked with sudden concern.

Henri shook his head. "I am not coming with you, no, I'm sorry. This thing affects my world too. If they mean to silence people, they might come for my family, my friends. I have to make sure they're safe."

"So I can return to find you dead too?" Katryzna's eyes burned.

Henri tried to smile. "I will be fine, this is where I belong. And I'll make preparations for when you come back with the child."

Katryzna didn't look happy, but Tasker saw the spark of something in her that he needed. She'd become protective, looking for ways to make right on whatever ills she was piling on herself from the past. He said, “We’ll be back quick as we can. With a way to end this.”

She nodded and exhaled loudly to get past this tension. A clear goal obviously helped. “Yeah. I am going to make it right, isn’t it? Once we kidnap a child.”

29

As the gang walked through Memphis International Airport, they kept scanning every face around them. But Zip's trick was working. They existed in a bubble where no one looked at them, no one spoke to them. The woman at check-in entered their details and smiled at Reece but asked no questions, merely wished them a good day. No one asked for their bags and when they got to the security checks, a guard gestured for them to go right on through with a friendly wink to Zip. Three guns in their single holdall bag, no x-rays.

Reece hummed a tune as they waited at the gate. That new composition growing stronger in his mind. Dramatic like theatre, not club music. He tapped it on the armrest, watching people not watching them. Eerie as those Steers at the gas stop, no one noticing these finely suited criminals and a kid in a burlap sack of a dress. Reece wished he had his trumpet, to make more of a scene. Lead the terminal in a parade of music. He hummed a little louder and caught Leigh-Ann watching him. Her expression was blank, nowhere near as relaxed, so he shot her a smile. She scarcely returned it. Then they were called to board, and the gang went on to the front of the line, welcomed through without a second glance. Caleb would've got a kick out of this.

"This what you did before?" Leigh-Ann asked quietly, checking over her shoulder as they walked onto the plane. "Just waltz on through and catch a flight?"

Zip nodded, innocently.

Imagine that. This kid was something else.

Leigh-Ann set about picking something to watch with Zip while Stomatt squeezed hard into his chair, jaw clenched against the idea of them flying. Reece said it'd be okay, safer than riding a bull, which the big guy had done a couple of times. That didn't help. Then the engines were whirring and they were rolling out for lift-off, and Stomatt bucked like he might freak out and hit someone. Zip took his hand. Stomatt regarded it like an alien gesture, then softened like he'd been drugged. Breathed out his worries. They banked up, Reece grinning, Leigh-Ann staring wide-eyed out the window, and once they cleared the clouds Stomatt shouted for a whisky. Soon, he was loudly annotating the crap on the entertainment service, and Reece had to tell him to keep it down. But the other passengers still didn't notice a thing. Just gave them dumb, creepily pleasant looks.

It was dark in England when they touched down, so they made their way to another hotel, all delighted by the accent of their chatty taxi driver. He noticed them better than anyone else had in the previous two days: asked if they were some kind of jazz band. He insisted he'd come see them play, but never asked where or when he could. At the hotel, Reece tried to sit up and keep vigil when the others hunkered down for the night, but weariness got the better of him and he had to turn in himself.

Come dawn, Leigh-Ann stirred him, looking rested herself. Wearing something of her old smile. She said, "Gonna sleep all day or you ready to grill this psycho father?"

After a hearty breakfast with sausages that touched Stomatt between wonder and disgust, they got a rental car and followed Grithin's map. Zip started to recognise the territory, excited that they were definitely going home. To her place on a hill, looking down on the city, where on a good day you saw the sea. As they got closer, Zip sat forward excitedly, guiding them. Pointing, as the crow flew, in the direction they needed. Reece drove along narrow, winding roads, past greenery lighter than Louisiana's. Up hills, through what passed for a small town – a single row of tiny, moss-swept stone houses settled in like they'd been there forever. Stomatt and Leigh-Ann pressed themselves to the windows to take it all in. Fairytale landscape, didn't look big enough for full-sized people.

Out of the village, the road curved again and again, gradually climbing, till they reached an old mill, stood at the hill's peak. Dark windows dotted the curved walls, and a ruined annexe flanked the right side of the building. The mill itself could've been abandoned, if not for the car out front. Zip was itching to burst out, announcing this was it, they were home! Leigh-Ann held her back, asking, "That your daddy's car?"

As Reece pulled up, the kid's brow knitted, searching whatever psychic wavelengths she could. She said, "Yes. He's there. Daddy's inside."

But in a second, he was outside.

The mill door was open and filled by a man with a massive frame, half-cloaked by a draping duster coat. He stepped into daylight, revealing his hard-worn face, features deep-set, angularly rugged and humourless. A blade stuck out of his right sleeve instead of a hand, and the set of his shoulders said he was ready to fight.

"You took a wrong –" Mason began, voice booming. He stopped abruptly. Noticing Zip. Her face lit up, as he said with deep, surprised, relief, "Zipporah."

"Daddy!" Zip cried, going for the door. "I'm so –"

"Release the child," Mason ordered, raising his blade-arm. The sleeve fell back, showing not a hand holding the weapon but a brass contraption; the "sword hand" was a metal box with cog mechanics around it, fused with his forearm.

Stomatt said, "The hell is that thing?"

"We're friends!" Reece called out, raising a hand out the window. "Bringing her back to you!"

"Here, Zipporah," Mason said, ignoring him. He stood as a pillar of defiance, even as he lowered his arm. Something whirred within the sleeve and the blade extended, two foot long, dark and nicked, like something salvaged from wreckage. He rolled his head to one side, upper lip curled back.

"Jesus," Leigh-Ann said. "He ain't happy to see us."

"They're my friends!" Zip cried, voice high with tension. She scooted back into hugging Leigh-Ann, demonstrating, which only make Dad madder.

"You should have killed her when you had the chance!" Mason took a step closer. His bone-shaking voice didn't sound capable of an ordinary tone. Hard to imagine a conversation where his every other word didn't make you flinch. And that accent was rough – nothing like Zip's educated tone.

Leigh-Ann opened the holdall on the backseat, picking through their guns as she muttered curses, but Reece said, "Hold up, give me a chance."

"Can't you mind-trick him or something?" Stomatt suggested, but Zip looked ready to wet herself. As shit-scared of her father as everyone else. Hell, they did *not* think this through properly.

"We rescued her," Reece hurried to explain, "and kept *Vile* off her back. Lost a friend doing it. You know who I'm talking about, right?"

The name made Mason stop. "Impossible."

"Yeah, we had the same idea seeing him in action. Look, I'm getting out, let's have ourselves a little talk, okay?" Reece slowly opened the door and stood, hands up. He felt a million miles from his pistol sitting on Leigh-Ann's lap, and half his usual height before Mason. The guy had to be pushing seven feet, broad as a doorway. Something told Reece he could clear their ten-metre gap in an instant.

"Who are you with?" Mason demanded. "Shearjoy? Ruin?"

Reece flashed a smile. "We're with you, if you'll let us talk. I'm telling you little Zip here was being chased by Vile –"

"Vile is dead," Mason cut in.

Reece laughed, light as he could muster. "He didn't look mighty healthy, but I promise you he's running around stabbing people. We come all the way from Louisiana to be here, my friend. To help her – and you."

Mason's madly trembling eyes ran from Reece to the car again, fixing on Zip. "Louisiana. You foolish child. Do you have any idea –" He pushed the frustration back. "Get inside. We will talk once I deal with these people."

"No!" Zip jumped out, past Leigh-Ann's snatching arms. She balled her fists at her side and said, "They're *good*! We need their help!"

Mason glared at her audacity. "I taught you better than this. Get inside."

"No!"

Stomatt rose slowly from the other side, as Leigh-Ann hurried after Zip. He looked the least comfortable with a pistol that Reece had ever seen him. Spotting the gun, Mason slid a foot back and his coat fell away to the side, revealing plates of dirty hammered metal over his chest and exposed leg – the duster covering fragments of armour. His blade-arm was cocked down at the side, ready to strike. "Get *inside*."

Reece raised his hands higher. "You want us gone, we'll go. But Vile is coming for her and we've seen how he moves. Figure it might take all of us to stop him, don't you?"

"Whatever trickery you're attempting –"

"It's not a trick!" Zip cried. "I'm sorry, Daddy, but I didn't know – Vile came from nowhere –"

"Stop saying that name! Vile is dead!" Mason roared so loudly that the trees themselves rustled nearby. So loud, in fact, he gave himself pause, unable to deny the height of his emotions. He reconsidered Zip, hesitant, but continued. "I broke his skull myself. A long time ago and a long way away."

"Well," Reece replied very carefully, "I shot him, more than once, and that didn't work. And given he killed my best friend and was after your daughter, I'd say we have a common interest. Less you think you're better off alone?"

There was the smallest shift in Mason's posture. Zip stared with silent pleading. Slowly, he lowered his arm and the brass contraption whirred, the blade retreating. He looked past them, seeming to scent the air. "Come inside."

30

For the two days they drifted along the river, making only brief stops to refuel and restock, Katryzna was pleased to find everyone basically pretended they hadn't talked to a tree-woman and been chased by zombies. Tasker and Henri started to get a little more chatty, asking about her past, but she threw them off with dismissive remarks. What else was there to tell, anyway? She was content instead to watch the trees glide past, the high rocky banks, the snout of an alligator. Henri blabbered at her about what was out there but she barely listened. Didn't bother to jump off with the others when the captain made his pit stops, either, just waited things out. Not despairing, not miserable. Content.

The boys were right. She might've failed Eyes, but this was a way to make good. She was better suited than anyone to bringing all this down.

Kinshasa came into view as a procession of low, miserable buildings gradually blossoming into the dirty dense metropolis. Tasker had the captain stop before the city proper, and he chose a jetty as rickety as those out in the forest, before a cluster of little huts and people busying themselves with nets. It would've been an unremarkable stop, except as they came to a halt a white man came ambling out onto the boards.

Smail was smiling, like they were supposed to be expecting him. The boat captain was already off the side, tying the boat in place, and he steadied himself as though expecting this encounter. Traitorous scum. Katryzna unzipped her bag on the deck, going for the rifle, but Tasker put a hand on hers. "Wait. He's British government, for Christ's sake."

"And he's not supposed to be here," she snarled back.

Smail strolled closer, hands in his pockets, jacket barely concealing his shoulder holster. He hadn't felt the need to wear that around them before. "Tasker! Delighted you made it back. All of you?"

Henri's footsteps sounded on the steps up from the cabin, and Tasker tilted a low hand to indicate he stay hidden. As Henri discreetly moved back into cover, Tasker put on one of his false smiles. "Surprised to see you here, Charles."

"Indeed? The river does talk, and I thought you'd appreciate a friendly face." He definitely didn't look friendly; the judgement on his face screamed *you were going to cut me out?* "We've a secure ride waiting, back to the hotel. Can I take your bag, Ms Tkacz?"

"You may not," Katryzna said, holding the bag closer. British government, who cared? He'd bleed like anyone else. Rurik hissed from her shoulder, "Yes, you moron, and his blood will be on all of you."

"So?" Katryzna said.

Tasker said, "We're going straight to the airport."

"Without so much as a goodbye?" Smail sounded strangely sure of himself. Up the jetty, the fishermen had cleared out already, and the huts beyond were still, everyone getting the hint and shifting off to shelter. Save two big Africans loitering at the bank, probably with pistols stuffed in their belts. "What did you find out there? Won't you come for a drink and share?"

Tasker followed Katryzna's assessment of the jetty, to the boat captain off the bow and back to his second, on the deck, behind Katryzna. The boatman had a hand behind a barrel, *definitely* hiding a pistol, scared about using it. Tasker said, "How'd you –"

Katryzna didn't care for the explanations – she dropped the bag, holding onto the rifle, and spun to the boatman. He whipped up his pistol and the captain fumbled aside, drawing a pistol of his own. Tasker shouted but she pulled the trigger. The gun clicked empty. She pulled again, same – and the boatman ordered, "Don't move – don't!"

The pigs had emptied their guns at some point? That's where a complacent journey got you, dammit. Had the boatmen been bought before they left Bokema, or on one of the stops? Didn't matter. Katryzna weighed up her rifle, considering simply clubbing the man down.

"I got him!" the captain announced, his pistol aimed at Tasker, who had his hands out to his sides. Up the jetty, the two locals covering them as well. One had a pistol, but the other had a miniature machine gun of some sort. He'd probably kill everyone by accident if he started spraying.

Smail stood proud as the pair moved down past him. "Very well, this is where we are. I can't simply let you leave without a report."

"I'll report on what I find in your guts," Katryzna promised.

"One more, below," the captain told Smail.

It didn't surprise the spy. "Outside, Henri, or we hurt them!"

"I think you hurt them anyway!" Henri shouted from below. "No, thank you." Good on him, Katryzna would have done the same.

"Get him for God's sake." Smail gestured to the boatman covering her. The captain shifted his aim to her as the man moved. "Tasker, didn't I warn you people lose perspective around this woman. Or was it the secrets of Mount Ikiri that inspired this subterfuge?"

"You knew we'd be on this nothing wharf," Tasker said. "You don't already know everything else?"

Smail smiled modestly. The captain shifted uneasily as the boatman reached the cabin steps, both of them super cautious. Neither was quite close enough for Katryzna to jump on, and with this soggy deck she might slip anyway, but they were definitely both dead men. Rurik whispered, "He's willing to talk, you don't –"

"Shut. Up."

The steps creaked as the boatman entered the cabin and warned Henri in French.

"There is something out there, isn't there?" Smail continued, addressing Tasker. "Share freely, and I'll make this painless. Otherwise . . ."

"You want those answers, have SIS run their own investigation," Tasker replied.

Below deck, there was a shout and a crash. The boat swayed, a gun went off – the captain was distracted and Katryzna pounced. Her boot skidded over the slick deck and she cartwheeled over the side as the captain fired up – the bullet going where her chest would've been. She flapped her arms, lost her grip on the rifle, and hit the jetty hard. But didn't stop. She swept her foot as she rolled, kicking the captain's leg from under him. Before he hit the deck, she had her hunting knife out and stuck it in him. Two quick jabs in the neck, before she rolled off, ripping his pistol from limp fingers and firing without aiming, flat on the boards.

Smail ran like a terrified penguin, his two goons covering him with shots peppering the boat. Katryzna clipped the nearest man with a shot to the arm, spiralling him off onto the muddy verge, and the other dived for cover as he let the little machine gun rip. Too rattled to aim properly, his spray went high and messy. Both he and Smail ducked around the huts as Katryzna kept firing until the pistol ran empty. She screamed an animal noise and tossed the useless thing in their direction, then pushed herself up and jumped in the boat, down into cover.

"Tasker!" Smail cried shrilly. "See sense! Finish her and I'll let you walk!"

"Come aboard and we'll talk about it," Tasker shouted back. He was crouched by the low wall himself. Watching the cabin, unsure if it was safe.

Katryzna called, "Henri, are you okay?" By way of answer, Henri poked his head up the steps, keeping quiet. He raised a hand for attention, then slid the boatman's pistol out, over to Katryzna. Quieter, she instructed, "Start the engine. Let them think we're leaving."

Keeping low, Henri moved for the controls. There was movement by the huts, Smail or the other guy rushing to another position. Smail fired a hopeful shot, nowhere near.

"Tasker!" Smail tried again. "There's nowhere to go!"

"There's a whole river, idiot!" Katryzna yelled back, then started to quickly slide across to the back of the boat.

"Who are you doing this for?" Tasker shouted. "Sloppy as hell for SIS!" Smail was quiet. "Someone else got you keeping watch? Duvcorp, since Lopaz lost his edge?"

"Duvcorp are nothing, Tasker," Smail called out. "The smartest thing they did was give up on Ikiri. Lopaz's a loose end no one bothered to trim, that's all."

The boat engine coughed, then spluttered, then settled on a noisy hum. Katryzna peered into the river. Even close to the bank it was as welcoming as a thick rotten soup. Probably full of snapping jaws and tetanus or whatever.

"You're moored, you fools!" Smail reminded them, almost amused. "Tasker. There's no running from this. You have no idea what you're dealing with."

"No? I'm guessing it's the ones that got away," Tasker shouted. "What leverage have they got? Money, threats? How'd they get you onside?"

"Leverage? You saw Ikiri, didn't you? You tell me about their leverage."

Katryzna twisted herself with great care over the side of the boat, to Tasker's alarmed look from the opposite side. He mouthed something that Rurik mimicked: "Be careful!"

"What *did* you see?" Smail pressed, voice giving Katryzna pause.

She smiled and mouthed to Tasker, "He doesn't know."

Tasker considered it as she lowered herself down, then shouted, "You'd cross your own government to figure this out?"

"Please," Smail snorted, oblivious to Katryzna half in the water. "To keep this quiet, and keep *them* happy, I would cross anyone. To figure it out? I'd keep you alive a little longer."

Katryzna let go and sank into chill water. The flow immediately pushed her on. Dark, thick water. She powered down, underwater breast-stroke towards the nearby edge, moving faster than she'd expected. Crap, bad idea. But she drove on for all she was worth – hit the bank and surfaced suppressing a splutter. She snatched at land, tearing up clumps of grass and mud to stop the river's push, then pulled herself up, out, and rolled with a breath of relief. Suddenly expecting gunfire, she jumped into a crouch – but found herself hidden by tall grass.

A way upriver, the two men were still shouting. Perfect.

Katryzna stalked through the grass, drawing the pistol from her belt and flicking it aside to clear the water. She ran in a half-crouch onto a dusty road, where any remaining civilians had already run for cover at the sound of shooting. Smail's irritating voice came clearer: "– powerful enough to resist governments!"

She panned along the closest hut wall and peered out, putting the jetty back in view. The chump with the little machine gun was the next building over, pressed to a wall, almost by the boat. Katryzna stepped out and fired twice, throwing the man into the wall and down to the ground. Smail shut up. She paced quickly the other way, out into the road, as the spy moved away from his own wall, pistol in two hands by his waist. His mouth formed a surprised O, but she fired too fast for him to lift the gun – a bullet right through the face threw him back into a door.

Katryzna ran past him, scanning the area. There was a little drinking stall across the road, where a couple of men were cowering behind barrels and a counter. No one else about. She jogged onto the jetty, shouting, "All clear, boys, time to go!"

Tasker and Henri hesitantly rose from cover. Henri looked impressed, relieved, but Tasker wasn't so happy. "You killed him?"

"Yeah. He tell you who sent him?"

"No."

"We'll figure it out next time they catch up to us." Katryzna beamed. How could he resist that smile? He tried to, unhappy that nonsense conversation had been cut short, as he slowly climbed down from the boat.

"It was never Duvcorp," he said, looking from the dead captain up towards the hut where Smail's legs poked out into the road. "The survivors from Ikiri have a hold over some powerful people. Smail was working for them and he didn't even know *why*."

As Henri jumped down, Katryzna gave him a friendly, appreciative pat, before turning back to Tasker. "It's not just tree-woman who can bend people to her will, is it?"

Tasker nodded agreement, eyes still on Smail. Rurik interpreted, "He's upset you killed the British spy, Katryzna."

"In case I did not notice," she snorted. Tasker frowned, so she moved on: "Let's find his car and get out of here. Henri – I owe you one. Next time we're in town I'll get you a lemonade or something."

He regarded the bodies. Surely, finally, not interested in going on a date now. But he said, "I pray the rest of your journey is safer than this, and Godspeed to you both. Indeed, Ms Tkacz, when you come back, and we have saved the world, I will let you take *me* out."

31

Mason dropped heavily into an old armchair that barely took his weight. Zip ran to his side for a hug that he ignored, staring dead at the gang as they entered more slowly. The mill was as dilapidated on the inside as out, a dark open-plan space with a chipped wooden table covered with scrappy paper, dirty dishes piled in a sink and – one simple marvel – a rickety old piano tucked behind a rotten central staircase leading up to, presumably, the bedrooms.

As the others hovered near the entrance, Zip rattled out apologies, saying she'd never leave home again, she was sorry, so sorry. Mason scarcely seemed to listen, staring at Reece. The man seemed intent on killing him with his eyes. Zip hurriedly explained she had followed him to America, then been chased by Vile, captured on the farm, rescued – attacked again! Giza! Then there were Steers on the road, and – wow, Stilt Town! – before the madness and poor Caleb. Poor Caleb. Zip slowed, sniffing. Mason continued watching Reece with nothing less than accusation.

"It's okay now, though, isn't it?" Zip said. "We're back and you can stop Vile, can't you?"

"It's not okay," Mason grunted. He finally looked at her, neck-deep in disappointment, and she shrank under his gaze. "You left the circle of my protection, Zipporah. They will all come, now." He breathed a deep, angry breath. "But perhaps it is time. I am ready." He looked at Reece again. "You have my gratitude for returning her."

"As shown by the joyous reunion," Leigh-Ann whispered. Not really quiet enough.

"You claim you fought Vile yourselves?" he continued, ignoring her.

"That's right," Reece said. "Short, dressed all in black, carried a sword. Looked like he'd crawled out a grave."

Mason considered Zip as she stared, imploring him to believe. "Very well. I shall see the truth of it myself. You may go now. Forget any of this happened." He nodded to the door. Zip flicked the gang a concerned look.

"Yeah," Reece replied slowly. "I don't think so."

Mason paused, with genuine surprise that they were still there. "I said you may go. Why are you . . ." He went quiet. Expecting something to happen? Then back to Zip. "You foolish child, what have you been doing?"

"I . . . I told you," she answered meekly. Her father huffed loudly and kicked up from the seat, back to his full height. Looming – he was a sure loomer. He scanned each of the gang in turn, face folding with aggravation. Leigh-Ann caught Reece's eye, to ask what was going on.

Reece said it for them all: "He's fixing to mess with our minds the same way Zip can. But he can't. Zip's shielding us, ain't she?"

"Not knowingly," Mason said. "Then we do this the old-fashioned way. I suppose it would break her heart for me to harm you. So how much do you want, to go away and speak nothing of this?"

Reece checked quickly with Leigh-Ann and Stomatt – both looked as thrown by the suggestion of monetary reward as he was. "We don't want your *money*. You remember our damn friend was killed?"

"So. You wish to stay and fight?"

"You gotta appreciate you need help. Holing up in here leaving a kid all on her own while you go on murder rampages, you ain't exactly well equipped for this."

Mason stared hard. "Is that so. Well, perhaps you can slow them down. There are spare rooms in the annexe. Until we see if any of you survives, further talk would be wasted breath."

Damn but he had mastered the art of speaking down to people. Could've been an English Lord if not for this ruinous shack of a home. Zip avoided looking at any of them, cowed. Leigh-Ann said, "Can we at least discuss her powers? Seeing as we might need them."

Mason answered, harshly, "This will *not* involve Zipporah."

"No one wants to involve her," Reece said, "but you got to admit –"

"The plan is established," Mason cut in, as if he'd just laid out some masterstroke of strategy. "You may rest. Make yourselves ready."

"It'd make us a hell of a lot readier," Stomatt said, "if you told us what's going on. You all freaks out a lab? Magicians? What is it?"

"There are powers in this world that you cannot understand," Mason rumbled, his hostility simmering back up. "Powers people cannot be *allowed* to understand. I am the shield, I am the sword that keeps this world safe. You will leave us. Wait. Prove yourselves when they come, *then* we can talk."

"When *who* comes, dammit?" Leigh-Ann said.

"The Legion of Ikiri," Mason replied as though it were obvious. "Whoever's left to find us. Now go."

Reece tensed, about ready to smack this guy, arm made of sword or not. Zip quickly shook her head at him and said, "Please. Rest. It's comfortable out there."

Leigh-Ann touched his elbow and quietly added, "Yeah, another minute with Chuckles here and I'm gonna flip." He gave her a sideways look, and she nodded to the side door. Back to Mason. The man looked ready to go to war. Reece raised his hands in submission and turned away. Hell, at least they were close to the answers, even if this brute wasn't talking.

As they made their way out, Mason lowered his gaze to his daughter and studied her. Zip said, "I missed you, Daddy." He stiffened, and it took all Reece's will not to scream at the bastard.

The side door led out to a stone corridor as dimly lit and run-down as the mill, with three doorways off to the left. The first opened onto a bedroom that barely looked liveable, with crates stacked to one side and a single bed lying under a mountain of dust. A small window let in the barest daylight. Reece tossed their bag into Room One and continued on.

"Don't like him?" Leigh-Ann said.

"Not much less than I expected to," Reece said, checking the second bedroom, then continuing to the third door. He stopped before a cluttered office space, a central desk covered with scattered papers, photos and maps plastering one wall and a rack of swords and bludgeoning weapons on another.

At his shoulder, Leigh-Ann gasped, "Holy serial killer mess."

"Grithin times fifty," Reece said. He walked in to scan the photo wall. Some of the same faces he'd seen in Memphis, some new ones. He checked back over a shoulder in case Mason was coming after them. The man must've known they'd snoop – didn't care what they pieced together for themselves?

No. He expected them to die when the trouble caught up to them . . .

"Here." Leigh-Ann pointed to a group shot in the middle of the wall; tons of mean-looking men in combat fatigues, with the sort of guns you could use to suppress armies. Mason was at the centre, the most miserable of a pretty miserable bunch. About half of the faces had been crossed out.

"That's Grithin," Reece pointed. The big bald guy had two eyes, back then. Running his eyes over the others, Reece picked out the shortest of the group, also crossed out, standing apart, with a little ratty face that said he knew he wasn't popular. "From the size, I'd venture that was Vile."

"Right?" Leigh-Ann said. "With the cross suggesting *deceased* again?"

"Guess they were mistaken," Reece said. The photo's background offered no convenient landmarks, just a cracked wall. He studied the other pictures: tons of faces, more than Grithin had collected, along with CCTV shots and other clippings that picked them out around the world. That ratty-faced man didn't feature in any of them. "He's not here. Vile. He wasn't in Grithin's collection, either. But there's more here than he had. Basilisk. Loan. Look, these are younger." He checked the main photo again. "They weren't part of the original crew. Shit . . ."

"They're people that got recruited or figured something out later?" Leigh-Ann voiced his rising concern. "Meaning we hang around and keep asking questions, we get up there too?"

Interrupting that thought, Stomatt said, "What's with the medieval weaponry?"

He was running a hand over the rack of tools. Swords, axes, hammers suited for breaking things. Up-close-and-dirty tools, nicked and grimy from frequent use.

"Along with that armour he's wearing," Leigh-Ann said, "this is only getting weirder."

"Yeah." Reece looked over some of the papers on the desk.

There wasn't much to indicate the group's origins, only where they'd dispersed to after whatever happened. Rap-sheets of dates and locations accompanied some of the names, where Mason had traced the men over the years. Some had past job roles, ex-military and security companies. And even after a quick scan Reece noticed a pattern in the dates. Almost all showed no professional positions in 2009 and randomly dispersed locations afterwards. These men had done something together in 2009, and Mason had spent the eight years since tracing them. Paris, 2014, Makassar, 2016, Santa Marta, 2017. Grithin was seen in Croatia, Russia and Colombia. "Ruin" was shown in news-clippings of violence in Cairo. "Shearjoy" had his name over a list of companies and names: Raystaten, Warlowe, Duvcorp, DGSE, Audrey Flan. The connected companies, men and women had profiles of their own, with addresses. Some names were crossed out.

For it all, nothing jumped out about Louisiana – no sign of Fallon, the Steers or Stilt Town. This was a world apart: a plague that'd spread everywhere but didn't need to hit them. But it had, and it might just as well have been Caleb up on one of those lists. Damn all these people – Reece would be ready when Mason's trouble came.

After his frosty welcome and wall-like conversational prowess, Mason provided hospitality in the form of crusty towels for cold showers and, a little later, a dinner of baked beans in steel bowls. While Reece occasionally tried to engage him, Leigh-Ann tried to reconnect with Zip, smiling at the child and asking if she'd rested and commenting on how *interesting* her home was. Interesting like a broken toilet.

Zip smiled back but had lost her tongue in Mason's presence. Leigh-Ann felt awkward talking near him, too, and it was a wonder to see Stomatt all but silent as he struggled to keep up his defiant leering smile. The place had an aura like a graveyard.

But once Mason finished his meal, he leant back on his bench and finally opened up: "When she was not here, and I could not feel her, I believed Zip dead. One of the others must have blocked me, knowing that we were separated. But I have meditated, carefully, and understand we are easily found, now. Grithin located us. Others must have, too. At least four are on their way."

It silenced the room.

"You, uh," Leigh-Ann ventured, "saying you guys can sense each other?"

Mason's unblinking eyes told her that was surely obvious.

"Like ants?" Stomatt suggested. "They share a hive mind and that, don't they?"

"Okay," Reece moved on, "four *what* are on their way? Because Vile, he wasn't natural – and that ape –"

"Giza," Zip put in.

"Yeah that. Where'd *that* come from?"

"Ikiri," Mason said. "And yes, I admit that those coming are not what I expected. They are not of the Legion's ranks; someone has unleashed them from Ikiri itself. I was a fool to think such a thing could be contained. Shearjoy, at least, should've been watching. Though it's possible he himself unleashed this horror."

"He's another one like you?" Reece said.

"With a dumbass name," Stomatt offered.

"He is one of the Legion, yes," Mason said. "You've seen photos of the others." The gang averted guilty gazes, but he sounded like he'd expected them to study the office. "Zipporah's powers are both a threat and a beacon to them. I kept her hidden, all this time, to face them on my own terms. But when she left . . . she was exposed. Now, they will not stop coming." He looked up as though contemplating what else to share, then decided merely on immediate plans: "Tonight, we will run two watches. Four-hour intervals."

"Fine," Reece said. "We've got guns, bit of ammo. Got any yourself?"

Mason snorted at his apparent ignorance.

"Got something against guns?" Reece said. "We saw your stock. Vile's running around with a sword, you've got that arm of yours – what's with the blades?"

"Bullets are too uncertain," Mason said.

That hung there for a second before Stomatt guffawed. "Typical fucking Brit, you don't *get* guns here, do you?"

Mason's glare silenced him. Given the photos of these soldiers, he definitely got guns. "When I kill one of the Legion, I want to be sure of it. If Vile has truly returned, I will take his head off, close and personal enough to remove any doubt."

Leigh-Ann choked on the comment. "Jesus, pal – there's a kid here."

"She understands," Mason replied coldly. Zip's little face was down-turned as she stirred her beans. Used to this mountain of weirdness. "All you need worry about is slowing them down. I don't care how."

"Best method we seen," Stomatt said, fork pointed down the table, "was when Zip zapped the motherfucker with her mind."

Mason arched an eyebrow, then turned on his daughter. Zip cringed.

Stomatt blundered on, "Can you all do that? What's the deal?"

"No," Mason said, not removing his gaze from Zip. "Ikiri granted heightened senses, powers of distraction, but not . . . that."

That word again. Leigh-Ann said, "What the hell is this Ikiri? How'd she get mixed up in it? Any of you?" That got her a healthy dose of mind-your-own-business from Mason's scowl. With a side order of we're-done-discussing-this silence. She tried to smile it off, and added, "We all think she's real special. Be nice to know exactly why."

Without explaining further, Mason got up and threw his bowl in the already-full sink, then stomped across to the central stairs, with thumps like the steps might break. No goodbye. Leigh-Ann exchanged a *seriously?* look with the boys, and they both mugged. This guy was intense.

If his general demeanour, tone and room of dungeon weapons weren't indicators enough, a night of split-shifts outside the murder-mill gave Leigh-Ann all the confirmation she needed that Mason was a creep-ass of the lowest degree. The cold English night was bad enough, which required a mountain of blankets to fight off, but worse was watching the sinister shadows of the mill with its irregular edges. It could've been haunted, but nothing supernatural could be grimmer than the hulking master of the house dragging his blade-arm about. What kind of psycho replaces a missing hand with an extending knife? And who raises a child here? To that point, how'd Zip turn out so *normal*?

The sun crept up after hours of Leigh-Ann jumping at shadows and generally reassuring herself she was never complaining about her trailer in Cutjaw again. A different impression came in daylight. The mill stood high on its hill, the fields below twinkling with the glitter of wet dawn. The blocks of a city were just visible in the distant haze. She hadn't appreciated where they sat, the evening before. Made England look soft. Safe.

Maybe that's what did it – Zip being exposed to this beautiful nature. This view and that cute village they'd driven through on the way up might've kept her sane.

Mason interrupted Leigh-Ann's thoughts, appearing a foot from her shoulder. "Go in, there's food."

"Jesus!" Leigh-Ann barked. "You can't –" She stopped. He actually *could*, with his size, that face and hands that could crush bricks. She swallowed and went inside, leaving him standing glaring at the hills like they personally offended him. Where she saw soft, he no doubt saw *weak*.

In the kitchen area, Zip was up on a stool stirring a pot, sweet cinnamon filling the room. Leigh-Ann grinned. "Whatever that is, I *love* it."

Zip wrinkled her nose. "It's only porridge."

But it was the best damn breakfast Leigh-Ann ever tasted, coming off a night like that. And it helped that Reece joined them in good spirits, throwing Zip compliments and getting smiles from her. Stomatt was starting to relax, too, getting brave enough to insult Mason's upholstery. When the swordsman was out of earshot. The morning was theirs and they were gonna enjoy it, scarcely tensing again when Mason rejoined them to skulk in a shady nook.

"I got designs on that." Reece pointed at the piano.

"You'll need a hammer and nails," Leigh-Ann said. "It's ready to collapse."

"I'm game." Reece beamed, standing and flexing his fingers. "If Mr Mason approves?"

Mason was nursing his murder-stump with the other hand, like stroking a pet. He grunted wordless assent and Reece bounced over to the piano. He knocked out a few bum notes – the thing worked, but not well. He opened it up and tweaked a few strings – who knew he had that talent – then he sat back and produced something that was, well, not great, passable. Then, after a little warm-up, he dropped into something he'd apparently been planning a while. Heavy chords and a steady descent. Simple, but powerful. He played a few bars and shot a look over his shoulder for approval. Leigh-Ann gave a thumbs up. It was borderline classical. Then he let rip, skipping over faulty notes to throw in improvised riffs, teasing out the tune. Back where he belonged, only sounding darker. Leigh-Ann breathed it in. Music the opposite of light and smooth. Powerful. Damn if it wasn't powerful. Even Mason was listening, absorbed.

Reece sat back, smiling his most honest grin. "How'd you like that?"

"Fresh, my man!" Stomatt answered loudly. "Damn fresh sound."

Zip looked excitedly to her father for approval. Mason dragged a hand over his face as though pulling himself from a daze, and his general disapproval sank back in. He said, "Exactly the sort of distraction we don't need. Can't sense them if your head's elsewhere."

"Can't – what?" Reece could scarcely believe it. "Morale mean nothing to you?"

"Can't *sense* them," Mason snapped, stomping over to the stairs. Angry enough that it was clear it wasn't *their* distraction he was worried about. Gritting his teeth, he shook his head and clambered noisily up. Stomatt caught Leigh-Ann's eye and mouthed, "The fuck's his problem?"

She had an idea that the answer was long and complicated and painful.

32

The overnight flight out of Kinshasa was a world apart from the journey in, with Tasker on the phone trying to shore up provisions for once they touched down. All he needed, really, was a car and maybe a hotel, but Caffery kept pressing for answers – what had he seen? How were they justifying the spend out there? What had happened in the forest? What was back in England? Tasker batted off one question after another. Finally, the threat that was bound to come: "We can't keep writing you blank cheques. You'll have to report in in London."

"I don't need your cheques," Tasker replied hotly. "Not now. When I touch down, I'll make my own arrangements."

He turned off his phone and reflected it might be a good thing to stay out of touch. If the leak that had got Parris killed originated with the Ministry, the less he said the better. He still balked at reporting that they'd killed a British spy – with luck, whoever was running Smail would at least temporarily assume he had succeeded in stopping them. Bigger things weighed on his mind, though, such as how grim it felt to be right about this. With the girl back in England, the threat was right on his doorstep. He avoided calling home to keep it from becoming too real.

After landing, Tasker ushered Katryzna through the airport, while looking out for threats. She got distracted by a gift shop, fixing on a postcard of a sketched dog, and he hissed, "Not now."

She batted him off with happy smiles, the gunfight on the jetty having lightened her mood back to increasing irresponsibility. She was used to being chased by the most powerful men in the world, she confided; it was the opportunities she got to defend herself that made it fun. Tasker urged her on, through customs, out to a car rental office, where he had to wait an impossibly long time for someone to process the papers. The news cycled silently on a flat-screen behind the rental counter, something about an earthquake in India. Tasker leant back against the counter and studied Katryzna again. She'd slumped back into a plastic chair, yawning far too broadly.

"Shall we take a day?" Tasker suggested. "Get a hotel room, continue tomorrow."

Katryzna narrowed her eyes. "You scared?"

"Cautious. You got any idea what we might come up against?"

"Ah. Like that?" She pointed a finger over his shoulder. Tasker frowned before looking, as if it might be a trick. She was pointing at the news, though; the story had changed. An aerial shot of a field filled with cabins, surrounded by police and medics. The headline ran: CONFIRMED NINETY-THREE DEAD IN GRAYSTOWN. It cut to a closer image: investigators mulling over body bags. Lots of body bags.

"What is this?" Tasker said. The young man behind the counter looked up.

"You didn't see? Some religious cult in America, went nuts and killed each other."

A sinking feeling that this personally affected him was confirmed as Tasker found Katryzna's eyebrows raised in agreement. Tasker took out his phone but hesitated. Wait until they were on the road. He hurried the rental guy on. With the keys in hand, he whisked Katryzna out to their car and pulled onto the motorway. Forty-minute drive, soon pulling into country lanes. After ten minutes he found a news broadcast on the radio and got more details of Graystown. Almost a hundred people brutally murdered by *each other*. A handful of roaming criminals who'd been in the area were now unaccounted for. But who'd believe a handful of criminals could pull off this madness?

It had the same bloody hallmarks of Laukstad.

He pulled up in a lay-by canopied by trees, short of their destination by a half mile. Katryzna trotted off to piss, while Tasker turned his phone back on. Multiple missed calls from Caffery and, oddly, Deputy Director Sam Ward. Well, they were here now, he might as well face the music. He returned Ward's call.

"Agent Tasker, you're back in town?"

"They told you?" he replied, imagining Caffery trying to head him off in frustration.

"Yes," Ward said. "About an hour ago, I was asked to look out for you. I wanted to talk anyway –"

"About Graystown? I just saw it on the news."

"Then we're on the same page. They've kept some of the details from the reports, but it's the same, isn't it? Halfway across the world, on a much bigger scale."

"You found a connection between them? Laukstad and Graystown?"

"Not yet, but our American friends were running novisan scans in the area, this time. There was a big surge. But if Duvcorp have scans for Graystown, too –"

"I don't think they're behind it," Tasker said. "They pulled out of the Congo. It was the people they left behind that are the problem. Parris must've been moonlighting on it all this time; I'm guessing his superiors were pressured into dropping it, but he never did himself. The people who stuck at this, who were still killing to protect it, they might have people in Duvcorp but . . . well, they definitely have influence in the government."

Ward was quiet for another moment. "I was afraid you might say that."

"What?" Tasker frowned. Katryzna came bounding back out of the trees, sighing with loud satisfaction. He waved a hand for quiet, and she stuck her tongue out. "Why'd you say that, Deputy Director Ward?"

"I've found – that is, my people have found – three other massacres that fit the same pattern as Laukstad. Following the numbers on Parris's list. There was mass hysteria, unexplained deaths, *savage* murders, all with no discernible connection. A small Canadian town called Danvale, two weeks ago – a village in Argentina a month ago. All bite marks and other wounds seemingly coming from people, but no sign of anyone new in town. These weren't ever flagged by Ministry Support, despite their unexplained nature. I'm worried they've been *purposefully* ignored. And again, the angles all point in the same direction. What did you find in the Congo, Agent Tasker?"

Tasker could've predicted it but it made it no easier to hear. As Solomon suggested, the corruption was spreading. Ikiri was lashing out across the world – with no clear indication how or why, only that the threat originated in that cave and it was getting worse. It'd been paranoia before; now he knew how easily those corpses *could* be people he knew. He said, "If I tell you, I'm pretty sure it'll make you a target. But I'm honing in on some answers. Once I'm done, we can talk. But can you do me a favour, Deputy Director? If anyone comes looking for me, friend or not, throw them off, for now."

Ward hesitated. "I'll do what I can. Agent."

"Thanks." He hung up, and found Katryzna staring expectantly. He said, "There's a chance this is even bigger than we feared."

"Oh, that," Katryzna replied, blandly. "I mean. I hope so?"

Tasker looked up through the trees. Hard to believe beyond this thicket there might be a child that could help them make sense of this. He said, "Let me go first. Try not to do anything rash."

"Only what's necessary," Katryzna replied brightly, enjoying this.

He tried to ignore it, tense enough already. He moved as quietly as possible, off the road through the woods and up a steep bank of grass, with her ambling more casually behind. The track took them onto the road's end, where it expanded onto the plot of a rotten mill, exactly where Solomon's maps said it would be. Two cars outside.

Tasker signalled Katryzna to wait, and moved closer to listen at the oaken front entrance. Piano music came from inside. He crept under one of the high windows and peered in. A group of people – a murky green-haired guy in a fancy suit at the piano, a big man and a woman at a table in similar suits, and an even bigger guy by the wall in a duster. And at the table – there was a young girl, and in the instant of seeing her Tasker knew she was the one. Though she was lighter-skinned than her mother, he saw some of Sara in her. Innocent face focused happily on the music. She was the key. But – shit – the pianist rolled his head to the side and Tasker ducked with alarm. The man from the news report. The fucker they were looking for in America. Graystown, sure enough, was part of this, and the kid was with those responsible.

Crunching gravel announced Katryzna sauntering up with her pistol ready, other hand resting on the hilt of her sheathed knife. He waved for her to stop and whispered, "Back to the car."

"Is the kid there?" she asked, callously loud. Tasker checked the mill for movement, but the music had everyone's full attention.

Tasker said, "There's at least four people in there."

Katryzna shrugged. "Four is nothing."

"We have no idea what they're capable of."

"And what? You want to *ask*?"

"I want to act smart," Tasker insisted. He had flashes of the reckless Clash Club and Smail gunned down. The mess they might make if Katryzna waded in. "We'll lay low, wait for nightfall. Make a move when they're asleep." Katryzna considered it, then continued, past him. He hissed, "You hear me? We're not just walking in there."

"I can look, can't I?" she answered with irritation, then went to the window and looked in. She whispered to her shoulder, "Yes, he already made that clear." She turned back with a heavy frown. Another glance to the window said she wanted to go in right away and confront whatever concerned her. But she shook her head with a sharp Polish word to her conscience, then moved away again, still frowning.

"What is it?" Tasker said.

She raised a finger for quiet, deep in thought, and continued past him. He hurried after her, back into the trees, heading towards the car. Pulling slightly ahead, she muttered to her shoulder.

"It's not the odds, is it?" Tasker asked, drawing up next to her.

She sniffed at that, something beneath her consideration. "No. That kid."

"What about her?"

Katryzna stopped, frown intensifying, unable to quite figure out a puzzle. Her face had been similar after seeing that messed-up cave. "There is something about her . . ."

"That's the idea, after everything."

"Not that. Something . . ." She trailed off. Unable to put it together in her thoughts, much less to say it. She fought it down, at last, and laughed at herself. "Sean. I think I know how you felt now. Around that tree-woman. You think it's the kid's doing?"

Tasker looked from her back to the mill, dread mounting. Hadn't even considered the sort of defences the kid might have. Had she had some impact on him, too, which he hadn't even realised?

"I think she's even messed with Rurik." Katryzna laughed. "He tells me don't hurt them, any of them. I mean, he always says that, but he says they are her people. They should not be hurt either." She scowled at her shoulder, but couldn't keep up the disdain. "I have a similar feeling. I do not trust it."

"Are you up to this?" Tasker asked.

Katryzna locked eyes with him, face steeling serious again. "Am I –"

There was a slap of sound in the branches above and Tasker tensed as they looked up. The leaves rustled, a patter building through the trees, and he relaxed as large raindrops started breaking through. Only rain. Getting heavier, quickly. Might be a good thing, for extra cover; Tasker was starting to feel they were going to need all the help they could get.

33

"I knew this place was rainy," Stomatt said, watching through the kitchenette window, "but thought it was supposed to be dreary, pathetic rain?"

Reece watched through another window. The deluge had made the already gloomy mill even darker, with Mason's weak lamps doing little to help. Lightning struck and thunder followed seconds after, dangerously close with them in the only building at the top of this hill. He said, "Often get storms like this up here?"

"Sometimes," Zip replied, standing on a chair to watch too, Leigh-Ann behind her. It was a simple pleasure, and if Mason stayed out of their way meditating upstairs, or whatever, they could enjoy it all night. But Zip yawned broadly, and someone had to be responsible here. Reece said, "How about you turn in, Zip? Leigh can read you a story."

"Leigh can *read*?" Stomatt jumped in quick as the lightning.

"Comes easy to some of us," Leigh-Ann shot back just as quick. But patted Zip's back, rolling with the idea. "Shall we?" The child gave Reece a hug, eyes drooping.

"I'll set us up some cards," Reece told Leigh-Ann as she passed. "Seeing as music's not welcome." She nodded and took the kid up the stairs.

Stomatt pulled himself away from rain-watching to join Reece at the big table, and Reece dealt them in for a game of Cutjaw Slam. Falling into weak banter, tired themselves. Stomatt asked, "You think that bastard's tugging himself off up there?"

Reece winced at the thought, and was about to joke back when a crash made them jerk their heads to the door to the annexe. Rain howled in somewhere – the rear door blown open? Reece shot up, whipped his pistol off the table and moved to the doorway. Stomatt fumbled, catching himself on the bench and cursing loudly. Reece leant into the annexe as wind blew streams of rain through the corridor, the rear door knocking against the wall. Nothing there. He threw a look back – no sounds of movement above. Mason and the others must not have heard it. Stomatt hung back in the mill door, clutching his own pistol in two hands. Reece nodded for him to stay put as he moved into the corridor. Carefully, he passed the first bedroom – no movement there. Not in the next one either. He pushed the outer door closed against the wind and rain and reset the latch. Then he hit the light switch for the office, aiming in.

Nothing there.

He turned back to Stomatt. "Just the damn storm –"

Lightning flashed with a crack of thunder and the lights cut out. Another crash came from back in the mill, the front door swinging open. Stomatt spun back into the room with a shout and Reece ran. Stomatt fired and moved out of sight as a dark shape flashed across the doorway. "Sto!"

The shape flashed again, skirted right past the opening – Reece got off a useless shot before bowling out of the annexe – just in time to see Stomatt thrown back against a wall, yelling as he grabbed his gut and slumped down. Somewhere above, Mason roared and Zip shrieked. Reece shot as the shadowy intruder sprang across the middle of the room, blade flashing to the side, and the bullet hit stairs between them. The attacker slid down past the piano and Reece panned out into the room. Mason jumped onto the stairs, steps cracking under his furious weight. The dark attacker flashed out of cover again. The blade hissed behind the stairs, catching Mason as he came down. The big man fell, snapping the banister in two and booming like an injured beast as he swung his blade-arm out to one side. Reece fell back, towards the wall, to Stomatt's side, as Mason smashed into the floor. The intruder launched out of darkness for the kill. Mason rolled and Reece fired, the big guy looking up as his assassin was thrown back by the shot. Clenching down his pain, Mason jumped upright and swung the blade-arm out to one side, fully extended.

Lightning struck again – a flash illuminating Mason hulking towards the table, the intruder in a half-crouch on the other side of it. Mason heaved the table out the way, but it was too big and caught on the ceiling, tumbling past him. The attacker shot down behind it for cover and Mason grunted with the effort of following. He tripped on the fallen table and the intruder kept going, straight outside as Reece fired another shot, clipping the entrance. Mason kicked through the table with blind rage. The smaller attacker was leading him into the rain. Reece shouted, "Wait!"

But Mason stepped into the trap of the doorway as the mill entrance exploded in. Brick and wood splintered around him, the big man tossed like nothing through the air, into the table. Huge punching arms reached through the shadows towards him, too big to be human, but the massive beast jammed into the doorway – couldn't squeeze in even as it tore chunks of building off around it and flung rainwater across the room. Reece unloaded every bullet he had into the struggling shape of Giza, pacing into the centre of the room. His gun clicked, and the gorilla was still raging violently, roaring and spitting, teeth flashing white in the darkness. Reece dropped his clip and slipped another out of his pocket as Mason groaned weakly up out of the wrecked table.

A smash in the annexe drew Reece's attention again – the door broken open once more. Lightning struck to cast the shadow of a man in the corridor; Vile had circled round to flank them for the kill.

Leigh-Ann just had Zip down when the crash made her sit upright. "Just thunder –"

"They're here," Zip gasped.

The rain was still beating down, lightning struck – no way of knowing what was near or far. But the kid was too sure to be wrong, and Leigh-Ann went for the door. "Wait here. I'll check, okay?"

She started down the stairs, hearing the floor creaking in Mason's room, next storey down. The big guy loomed massive out of his doorway, eyes accusing the very shadows. He fixed on Leigh-Ann, blaming her for disturbing him, before another crash drew their attention back downstairs. The entrance smashed open, definitely the entrance. Movement inside – Stomatt shouting – a gunshot.

"They're here!" Zip came running down the stairs.

Mason reeled on her monstrously and said, "Stay."

"Zip can help, you –" Leigh-Ann started, but he shoved her chest, a simple movement that slammed her into the wall and did for all the wind she had in her.

Zip came running to her side. "Leigh!"

"You will not interfere!" Mason boomed, voice filling the tight space like an explosion as Zip screamed surprise. Then he was away, launching himself down the stairs, into more gunfire below. Leigh-Ann pushed herself up on her hands and knees, impossible a little shove could hurt so bad – she couldn't breathe – gasped – looked over to Zip.

The child had backed right off again, shivering with fear. Leigh-Ann wheezed, trying to say her name at least, held out a weak hand her way. But Zip was terrified, as the crashing continued downstairs. "Zip . . ."

Leigh-Ann keeled forward, coughing, struggling just to inhale. Some tremendous force hit the building, shaking them all, and the noises below got worse. She pushed herself back up, slowly, weakly recovering. Christ. She said, barely audible, "Zip, you can help –"

But Zip only screwed her eyes closed and squeezed her arms tight around herself, dropping into frightened sobs. Damn her fucking father. Leigh-Ann turned from her to the stairs and listed over to them. The moment she reached the top step, Reece shouted, "Stay there, Leigh! Hold back and shoot all hell out of anything that comes up!" He twisted on the spot, near the middle of the room, and shot towards the entrance. Down to the side, Leigh-Ann saw a figure step into the annexe doorway. Vile.

Leigh-Ann took a quick breath and shrieked, "Throw me a gun, Reece!"

But Reece backed off towards the kitchenette, met on two sides with that monster Giza pulling back then pushing again with another hard smash – it'd take down half the building in a second. Vile was staring in, motionless, savouring the challenge ahead.

"Come on you bastard son of a bitch," Reece said, masked in shadow himself but unable to hide the fear in his voice. "You're not getting past me."

Leigh-Ann threw another look back to Zip, saying, "Kid – sweetie –"

But she was shaking her head quickly, balled up against the world. Leigh-Ann could only watch as Vile stepped in and the bricks cracked around Giza. Reece swung the pistol up to fire. The room lit up brilliantly with another flash of light and the walls exploded in.

*

Katryzna was staring at the gun in her hands, imagining that she'd be killing a fair number of people again and ignoring Rurik's comments that she should care more, when she noticed the big shadow move through the rain. She looked to Tasker to see if he'd noticed, but he was busy staring into la la land, hung up on his own insecurities. Without a word, Katryzna got out and moved to quickly pick out what had passed them. Too dark, too much water in her face. But there was something – going up the hill towards the mill. As quick as she picked it out, it was gone again, off over a hump in the ground.

Tasker's door slammed behind her and she shouted, "You didn't see that?"

"What?" He had a hand flat over his glasses, for all the good it did against the rain.

"Think it's time to go," she said, rather than bother explaining.

He nodded, grim-faced.

"Whatever happens up there –" Rurik started from Katryzna's shoulder.

She grabbed him in a fist and said, "Do not interfere." She shoved him in a pocket as Tasker gave her a worried look, but he said nothing. Then they started off, under the trees for limited cover. Lightning flashed, thunder right after. Katryzna picked up her pace, water soaking through to the bone. Tasker stalked ahead, gun low as he broke from the trees to race over the grass – another thunder crack. No lightning this time. Another crack. Tasker slowed down, turning Katryzna a look of concern. "Gunshots?"

"Yeah."

They ran together, sliding on the mud and almost falling, until they reached the mill in time for another shot, light flashing through the mill windows, and the great shape of something hunched before them, between the cars. Its torso heaved slow breaths as it perched like an immense gargoyle, its back to them, waiting. There was shouting inside, something happening.

"Piss," Tasker summarised.

"Get the car," Katryzna suggested. He gave her a look, but got it a second later. Whatever was happening, a quick escape was going to trump discretion, now. As Tasker turned, the shadowy monster lurched forward with a familiar animal roar. Something like the terrible sounds they'd heard around Ikiri. How did it get *here*? Tasker froze to watch as a man shot out of the mill entrance and the gorilla flew through the air into the door. Katryzna repeated, "*The car.*"

Tasker nodded and retreated back down the slope, half sliding. The man who'd escaped straightened up, ignoring the monster that was trying to smash its way into the building. He strode quickly towards the building annexe, a blade down by his side. Someone new in the equation – an assassin here to thwart them? Katryzna flicked rain off her face and moved after him, little need for caution for all the noise the beast was making. The short man kicked through the annexe door and entered, and she hurried after him, keeping low. Another gunshot inside and the gorilla thing screamed all sorts of anger.

Katryzna slowed on entering the annexe, seeing the little swordsman was taking his time, calmly approaching the connecting door. He wanted to be seen. She crept in behind him, but paused at the sound of the engine. Tasker had moved quicker than she would've credited him. As the swordsman entered the mill, Katryzna checked out the window to see the headlights approaching, bouncing through the rain. He wasn't slowing down.

Oh hell yes – he skidded towards the building. Deliberately, she hoped. And as he got closer, and someone shouted inside, she ran forward. With a tremendous crash, the car slammed into the gorilla from behind and the building shook like it might collapse. The swordsman staggered, and she came out of the corridor with her pistol raised. Surprise!

He sensed it – moved as the gun went off. A fraction too slow, the bullet tore through his cheek and made him twist and reel with a scream that wasn't quite human. He dropped through the shadows with unreal speed, sword flashing again, and Katryzna followed him into the room, firing.

The mill was lit by a single car headlight – the other smashed and buried in rubble. The gorilla was pinned between the crumpled mess of Tasker's car and the wall that had collapsed around it. It was still moving, one arm free and flapping dangerously. The bottom of the wooden stairs towards the room's centre had been caught by flying chunks of wall and shredded; a kitchenette was strewn as though hit by a bomb, and a man was coughing on dust, a pistol in the hand covering his mouth as he pushed himself to his feet. Another man was shaking off debris, the big guy in a now shredded long coat; he flicked an arm to one side, blade sticking out of it. Both guys saw the swordsman come in and reacted at the same time, as Katryzna sidestepped the wrecked stairs to get a better angle.

The guy with the pistol dropped, firing as the swordsman jumped over him, blade missing his face by an inch. Katryzna fired, their bullets slamming into the little ninja and throwing him off course. He crashed into the sink and rolled, somehow able to kick off again, blade out and swinging for a kill-shot.

It connected with a metal clang as the big guy blocked, and the swordsman rolled again, swinging the blade for another stroke. The big guy's weapon, sticking out of his forearm, flashed in quick movements to deflect the dark guy's rapid blows, but the smaller man was driving him back, wearing him down. The gunman kicked clear of the mess around him, and another shot caught the maniac's chest and threw him off – enough of an opening for the big guy to punch the guy's gut. But even as the swordsman folded forward he brought his blade up, clinking off the big guy's weapon and slipping through his defences to hit him with a slice that made him grunt and fall back. Momentarily stunned, the big guy was down and the ninja had an opening, spinning to bring up his sword for a death-stroke.

The perfect distraction for Katryzna, now mere feet away, to fire right into the swordsman's dark-clad face.

The shot threw him into the kitchen cupboards, then down to the floor. He was still for a second – then twitched, sword arm wanting to come up. Katryzna cocked her head to one side. Stepped forward and fired again. Again. Another twitch and she kept firing, each bullet jolting the dark figure, until the slide clunked back on the gun, empty. She stood over him, watching for more movement, half his head spread across the counter. But it was done.

Another gunshot made her flinch the other way, Tasker standing on the chaotic ruin of his car, over the gorilla. The beast twitched under him and he had to fire again. Only two bullets to finish that one.

They met each other's gaze with a shared conclusion: these things did not die the way things should. Tasker was caked in dust, one lens of his glasses cracked, and blood down the side of his face. Better than they could say for the others. Katryzna picked out the big guy, down on one knee, heaving. He watched her with unreasonable hate considering she'd saved his life. He was cut bad; a great gash down from his right shoulder across his chest, having parted a plate of metal that should've protected him. Probably had more wounds she couldn't see. And the guy with the pistol, he was down on his arse, staring at her with a different kind of alarm, breathless.

"Don't, don't!" Rurik started up shouting from somewhere.

Katryzna regarded her gun again. Couldn't simply clear up the stragglers with no bullets, anyway, so she tossed it aside and held out a hand, flashing a smile. "Hello. I'm Katryzna. I would like to meet the child."

The man stared dumbstruck up at her for the briefest, silent second, before the building creaked around them. Rather than settle, the groan got louder, and something massive started splitting. Tasker jumped down from the car and shouted, "It's going to collapse. Where is she?"

"Fucking Christ, who are you people?" a woman cried from high up, a thick Southern American accent. Katryzna spotted the thin Black lady with big hair halfway down the wrecked stairs. A small shape shied behind her. The walls shuddered, the light from the car flickering as broken brick fell around it.

"Throw her down, we've got to go!" Katryzna demanded, holding up a single hand to catch the child.

The man at her feet pushed himself up and backed off, wary of them. Rather than figure it out, he moved for the stairs. "Quick – Leigh – the mill's coming down."

Tasker moved quickly to the other side of the broken stairs, holding his hands up, too. The woman, Leigh, edged down, taking the child by the hand, and helped her into their arms. Tasker hurried her towards the annexe door as the man helped Leigh. Katryzna checked the others: the swordsman practically decapitated, he definitely wasn't going anywhere, and the gorilla a sure broken mess. But the big guy was struggling to his feet. And she spotted another man, down near the entrance rubble, watching her with pale-faced worry.

"Help him!" the pistol guy shouted. "We have to move!"

"Now!" Rurik frantically joined in.

Katryzna rolled her eyes as she rushed to the fallen man's side.

He was heavy to lift, and a mess all around his middle. They slipped on his blood as she got under his arm, but she hauled him up, and as the building quaked she limped with him to the doorway. Leigh ran to help, while the pistol guy raced for the big guy. In a slipping, staggering mob, they charged through into the annexe, as the mill creaked its last and the walls crumbled heavily in. Katryzna was thrown forward in a cloud of dust and an avalanche of bodies, tumbling against the walls and down to the floor with the building collapsing behind them.

The ground kept shaking for a moment longer, as people started coughing in the dusty dark. Katryzna shifted on bodies beneath her and twisted to find her face right next to Leigh's. She grinned into wide, frightened eyes. "And who are *you*?"

34

Time passed in a blur of necessity with no room for Reece to stop and ask questions. Leigh-Ann found an electric lantern in one of the bedrooms while he and the suited Brit tossed files off the office desk to lay Stomatt on. No room for Mason, so he slunk against a wall. Zip found a kit of medical supplies and ran around in circles, somehow everywhere and not getting in the way at the same time. There was arguing, shouting, as Mason refused to let anyone help him tie off the gashes across his chest and legs with steely determination. Something he had done before, from the looks of it. Reece and the Brit cleaned and bound Stomatt's middle, though the savagery of the wound demanded a hell of a lot more than a bit of gauze.

They spoke quickly as they worked together, Reece saying, "So who are y'all?"

"Agent Sean Tasker, Ministry of Environmental Energy. And you're the gang out of Graystown."

"Gang?" Reece kept the pressure tight as Tasker tied the bandaging. "We ain't whatever they been saying. Didn't get rated in *Two Shoots Magazine* to be called no gang. That bastard back there" – he huffed, the pair of them rotating Stomatt to finish the job – "he's the one got everyone killed. Coming after her."

Tasker glanced to Zip, standing by with Leigh-Ann by the door, then focused on finishing the job. They stepped off from Stomatt, regarding their handiwork. The bleeding was contained. Didn't mean he was gonna make it.

"We gotta get him proper help this time," Leigh-Ann said, hand rubbing Zip's shoulder. The child herself was eyeing the tatty woman with the shaved head. Outside, the rain kept beating down, hammering on the roof.

"I can get an ambulance," Tasker said, adjusting his broken glasses, "discreetly."

Mason tried to move, but his injuries held him in place. Clenching his teeth, he said, “No authorities. No calls.”

“Think we want to?” Leigh-Ann said. “Sto’s gonna die!”

“They’ll bring trouble,” Mason growled, eyeballing Tasker, then the woman. “If he’s Ministry, he belongs to Shearjoy.”

“I belong to no one,” Tasker said. He turned to Reece. “We’re not part of this – only interested in the child, to help.”

Mason released a caustic laugh. “So much as touch Zipporah.”

“We’ll take better care of her than you,” the woman said. Tasker as a government agent, Reece might buy, but she made no sense. Appeared as much a violent shadow as Vile, behind him, with a gun. That massive knife hanging from her belt. She moved with the same callous efficiency as the madman. These two were surely the others Mason warned were coming. And Reece’s gun was down by Stomatt’s head. Arm’s reach away, not something he could subtly ready. Had to at least give talking a chance.

“You’re not with them.” Reece indicated the faces on the walls. “Then who are you?”

The woman mugged confusion, and pointed out the door. “Katryzna. We met back there?”

Tasker started checking the photos himself. “This is them – the ones who went out to Ikiri?” It made Katryzna look, too, and she suddenly leapt to the pictures, frightening Zip closer to Leigh-Ann.

“This Ikiri again,” Reece asked. “About time someone explained exactly what it is. Some place they all went, you’re saying? And *they*, meaning not you?”

“Yes it’s a place,” Tasker said. “It’s dangerous, we’re not sure exactly how yet. We’ve been tracking these people –”

“Is he here?” Katryzna interrupted, flitting along the wall like a bird and finding the group photo. “Where is he?”

“Vile’s there,” Leigh-Ann said. “But they figured him dead.”

“Vile?” Katryzna said. “What Vile? Where’s *Eyes*?” Mason shifted with recognition, and she spun on him with such tension that his blade-arm came up. Bent and chipped but still a savage hunk of metal. She had her knife out, unafraid. “You know what happened to him?”

Mason regarded her flatly. “How do you know Eyes?”

“How the hell do you think?” Katryzna spat, inching towards him.

"Oh." Mason lowered his blade. "It's *you*." He spoke with disbelief and disgust. "His . . . friend?"

"Share it with the rest of the room?" Leigh-Ann said.

"Legion or not," Mason said, "if she was close to Eyes, she's a killer. He was our civilian security expert. The deadliest man on the team. Why are you here?"

"To do right by him" – Katryzna pointed her knife to Zip – "by taking that child."

Reece flashed his hand out and whipped the pistol off the table. Katryzna's wide-eyed surprise turned to delight at seeing the gun aimed her way. He said, "Say that again. Slower."

"All right, hero," Katryzna said, rolling her shoulder as though she might jump him anyway, knife against a gun. "I am here for her. To make sense of what killed my friend."

Reece stepped back, towards Zip and Leigh – this woman might've saved them in there, but Mason was right to be worried.

"Stop, stop." Tasker held up a hand. "Can we talk before we gut each other? You two are clearly too young to be connected to Ikiri." He tapped the wall of photos next to him, then looked at Mason. "Their *Legion*? You've got mixed up in something you shouldn't have? She's not your kid, is she?"

"Might as well be," Leigh-Ann said. "God knows she's got no one else rooting for her in this international murder cult. But no – we just found her in need in help."

"We're not part of this either," Tasker insisted. "Katryzna, please lower the knife. Listen – you lived through Graystown, you've seen what's at stake – but she holds answers. You're special, aren't you honey?"

"Don't," Mason warned.

"You ain't having her," Leigh-Ann said. "Wanna strap her to a table with needles or what? Fuck off."

"No, we will take her to Ikiri," Katryzna replied factually. "In the Congo."

"The Congo? *Africa*? You out of your minds? Reece –"

"Bear with us," Tasker said, before she could appeal to flee. "What happened in Graystown, that wasn't the first time. There's been a half-dozen similar cases, at least – entire villages, towns driven mad, killing each other for no reason. And it's coming out of a power they uncovered. No one needs to take anyone anywhere quite yet – we just have it on some authority that she's the key."

"No," Reece said quickly, "you're wrong. It was Vile, in there, that did it. Corrupted people as he went. And he's dead now. It's over. Right, Zip?"

Zip choked on an answer. She collected herself and whispered, "Maybe?"

Reece lowered his gun to his hip, still ready. He asked Mason, "What do you say? You believe it was Vile now? Does this end with him?"

Mason sneered. "Not even close. See for yourselves how many more of the Legion remain. But they aren't driving towns mad – yes, there is power in Ikiri, but not like that. Not for *us* and definitely not for Vile. I killed him myself – he never even made it to Ikiri."

"But that *was* him?" Reece pushed, and Mason didn't deny it.

Tasker frowned. "He was the traitor? Who hurt those Congolese villagers and escaped? Killed two of your men?"

Mason almost looked impressed, but covered it quickly. "He was a liability. He almost escaped us, but we punished him."

"So this half-dead freak," Reece spit-balled, "made it to this place – Ikiri – after all. Came back to get revenge on your daughter? Maybe picked up powers you didn't appreciate."

"A man could not do that," Mason rumbled. "Not alone. And he was *not* in control. What you fought in there, that was nothing like the powers of the Legion. An automaton at best; monsters sent out of Ikiri. And *I* will find whoever's responsible. These are exactly the abuses I work to prevent."

"Christ, that's all this is to you, ain't it?" Leigh-Ann said. "Bunch of boys got hold of some power they don't want anyone else to have. Thinking you know best and ain't no one else can get a handle on it? That's why you've kept Zip so repressed? In case she could do shit like that with her mind?"

"Leave Zipporah out of this."

"No, I'd say it's time we brought her right in" – Leigh-Ann got hotter – "seeing as she could've helped us back there!" She turned this to Tasker and Katryzna. "You know she's special? What she can do?"

Tasker started to reply, but Mason boomed over him, "No! She is *not* to touch Ikiri."

In the quiet left by his outburst, Katryzna cleared her throat. "Well. *Sara* claims this girl is the only one that can end Ikiri's corruption. And she lives in a tree out there – she should know. Sounds to me like this handless oaf is scared of the kid."

Without entirely knowing what all that meant, Reece flashed on an idea. "Could Zip take away your power? Nullify it, the same way she protected us from going nuts like the rest of Stilt Town? That scares you?"

"She could cause untold destruction," Mason snarled.

"Or she could *stop* it. That's why not everyone was losing it in Graystown, isn't it? It's how we resisted Vile while other folks all fell apart. She can protect against this here shit, she just doesn't know how because you never let her!"

Zip peeled away from Leigh-Ann's thigh with some similar realisations creeping in. She asked, hoarsely: "Could I have helped? In Stilt Town? Or Villa Madero? Svet, Danvale, Igota, Laukstad?"

Tasker startled. "You know everywhere it's struck?"

"I was there," Zip answered, emotionally. "I *was* there." To Leigh-Ann: "It *wasn't* a dream. I could've done *something*!"

"Not safely," Mason said, his own voice cracking slightly, finally accepting he might have done wrong by her. "Not safely. To use your powers at all would signal them. To effect *that* kind of change, you'd have to be –" He swallowed. "Have to use Ikiri itself. And if you touched that place, there's no telling the damage." He lowered his gaze. "I had to take her away."

"Away?" Reece frowned. "She's *from* there?"

Mason went quiet, deciding he'd said too much.

"You're saying the place itself is capable of this power," Tasker processed this. "That's where we're coming from. She can stop it if she's there. Because that's where she started out?" He paused. "How old is she? You had a year before Solomon came. Was she born there, is that why . . . ? Is she *Sara's* child? My God." Tasker turned to Reece, to share his rising shock. "They left her mother there. In the forest. Trapped by Ikiri. She's *still* there."

"And Eyes?" Katryzna said. "What did you do to him? Was he protecting Sara from you?"

"Absolutely not," Mason fired back, taking this one personally. "We were working together. Doing what we had to. It was the *boy* that was the problem. Her *twin*."

That shook the room quiet, and the rain itself pattered to a stop outside. Mason took a breath, and continued, "Yes, they were

Sara's, born of Ikiri. We stayed to stop the others from getting out – or returning. The children's power was immediately apparent. They had to be separated – from each other and from Ikiri. Eyes took the boy, I took the girl. But he made a mistake. He hesitated. Even at that young age, the boy resisted. I wasn't there but I sensed it all. Eyes was wounded, mortally. Near the mouth of Ikiri. Sara tried to drag him in, as if that would help. He died and she was damned. But the threat was contained."

"You contained the threat," Leigh-Ann said, weakly, "of two newborn kids? You're saying you people *murdered* –"

"They were more than children!" Mason cut in.

"They weren't even that!" Reece said. "You're talking about *babies*!"

"I have a brother?" A tiny whimper came from Zip. She was clutching closer to Leigh-Ann, more scared of her father now than ever. With good reason.

"No," Mason replied without apology. "You do not. It was necessary – the boy had power *far* beyond ours. He was capable of –"

"Destroying whole towns?" Tasker suggested. Simple as that. He shook his head, accepting a reluctant truth. "You never contained the threat. You're afraid of what she's capable of but it's already happening. The boy survived. *He* is in there – he's what corrupted Ikiri. These people going mad, this man and his monster coming after the child – they're coming from him, aren't they?"

"Impossible," Mason said. "I would have sensed his presence."

"You sure about that? You hid Zip and her powers, you think he couldn't have done the same? All these years, preparing for something."

"Waiting for his sister to come out of hiding first?" Reece suggested.

Mason's face was stone frozen. Something he'd never dared consider, but from the reaction, something that was very possibly true.

"God damn," Leigh-Ann whispered. "You're the worst father ever."

"So you're saying there's another one like her" – Katryzna pointed at Zip, working this through – "back there? We should have rolled a grenade in there."

"No!" Zip cried, pulling away from them. "He's my brother!"

"Cher –" Reece raised an impotent hand, but she wasn't running. She backed into the wall and screwed her eyes closed. Focusing, hard.

"Zipporah, don't –" Mason began, but Leigh-Ann snapped: "You don't tell her what to do no more!"

"It's true!" Zip flustered, finding it somewhere in her mind. "He is out there! I know it! He was in Svet – Madero – Igota! He didn't want me to know – did it while I was sleeping because –" She bit it down, shaking all over. "He's angry. He's really angry and he wants to hurt people. Everyone."

"We can stop this, can't we?" Tasker demanded.

"I'm happy to drag her back to that cave and make this boy pay," Katryzna said.

It took Mason a moment, staring grimly at his daughter, but he slowly shook his head. "No. If the boy survives, you won't be able to stop him. Don't you see? If he is truly corrupting people, it's because he knows he can find Zipporah. Vile and that monster, they're nothing against what may still come. To say nothing of what the Legion will do to stop you."

Zip regarded him with fearful pleading, willing it not to be true.

"Don't pay him no mind," Reece assured her. "Look at me, Zip. Caleb died for this, Sto's in no good shape either – that's never being for nothing. We're here for you. We'll do whatever it takes, find a way. Tap into those gifts of yours."

"She can't –" Mason started.

"I *can*," Zip snapped, then screwed her eyes closed again. "I can send thoughts to him – I can connect – we don't need to go anywhere. Daddy, I can do what you do, I can –" Zip gasped, suddenly, opening her eyes. "He knows. He knows I know – he knows I –" She winced, gritted her teeth and suddenly looked terrified. "No – oh no –"

"Easy, Zip –" Leigh-Ann started, but froze. "You hear that?"

Reece listened himself. Distant, but unmistakably a scream.

35

Reece ran out onto the drive, gun up and searching the dark. The rain had stopped, the gravel and nearby trees left glistening. All silent for a second, before another shout came, off to the left, past the trees. Reece threw a look back, finding the others hurrying out after him, Leigh-Ann with her hands on Zip, the child full of guilty fear. She'd triggered something, searching her mind for her brother?

"It's the village," Leigh-Ann said. "Down the road. How many people live there?"

"No," Zip said, breaking away across the drive. "No, not again!"

More screams came, closer. A sound of something big smashing.

"The evil is upon us," Mason rumbled, leaning up against the doorframe by Tasker and Katryzna. The British agent looked particularly pale at the thought – disbelieving the madness had caught up to them here. "She *brought* this. We must leave."

"No!" Zip reeled on him, fists balled at her sides. "Not this time!" She screwed her eyes closed again, fighting to focus her energy. She let out a pained sound.

"Zipporah!" Mason shouted, straightening up to his full height. "Can't you see you've done enough? *You* are the threat here –"

"I can stop it!" Zip cried.

"You're not to!" Mason roared, making Tasker and Katryzna step away from him. Zip's eyes shot open, old fear coming in. "That power is *never* to be touched."

Except this guy didn't know, did he? Thought Vile was dead, and that the boy was dead, and spent all Zip's life keeping her in the dark. Now they had more trouble coming, and she might be the only one of them with some clue towards fixing it. Reece said, "What I say, Zip? Don't listen to him. You better off without a father like that. You think you can do something? I wanna see you try."

The screams were rising, down the hill, more people joining in. Another crash. Still uncertain, Zip checked one face after another. Leigh-Ann put on an encouraging smile, using all her willpower not to freak out, and said, "Try, Zip."

"She's a weapon, you morons," Mason growled. "A bomb waiting to explode."

"Respectfully, sir" – Reece stood square to him with the pistol down at his side – "I disagree."

New screams echoed up the hill. Louder, nearer than before. Katryzna jumped onto the balls of her feet. Not frightened but readying herself. Grinning. "Do something fast if you're going to, or I'm taking over."

"She's already done too much," Mason said. "If she tries *anything* else, I will cut all of you down." His metal murder-stump whirred an unhealthy sound and the blade extended, just a tiny bit longer. "Zipporah, come here." He absolutely would try and attack four people carrying guns and knives. Given Vile's efforts, he might even succeed. Reece flexed his fingers on the pistol regardless. Surely he could get a bullet in this maniac before he cleared the distance.

Tasker slid a wary foot back, too, hand hovering towards his holster. He gave one lame attempt at final diplomacy: "Gentlemen . . ."

Zip stared dead at her dad, the strength of the four of them there bolstering her. She took a deep breath and said, "I'm going to stop him." She screwed her eyes closed again, and Mason rumbled an animal growl. He sprang forward.

Katryzna was suddenly on him, knife at his neck, her other hand slamming his blade-arm back into the wall so hard the stone cracked. He moved the other arm up fast in his stumble, but she deflected the punch with her elbow as she dug the knife in. Mason froze at the cut, blood cresting over the blade. More than a head shorter than him, she had the big guy pinned.

"You've done enough," she told him, with soft menace. "And you'd be dead already if not for the *howling* whine of my conscience." She cringed at her shoulder. "You want to help, tell the kid to look away!"

Zip wasn't looking, though, eyes closed, keening slightly as she shook. The screams down the hill were coming. Not people attacked or afraid, but the mad, murderous sounds of feral beasts, out for blood.

"Reece," Leigh-Ann whispered. "Think we oughta move –"

"Hold on," he hissed back, seeing Zip straining. Doing the Lord knows what but *something*, and something her hard-ass dad didn't approve of, that had to be good. The thump of feet approached up the road, a good number of people charging, together.

Tasker suggested, "Let's get to a car –"

He stopped as the first silhouettes ran up out of the dark. Katryzna dropped away from Mason, turning to face them. Twenty metres down – three, four, more people, eyes madly wide, mouths open in attack. Leigh-Ann and Reece spun away, taking quick steps back – and Zip exhaled loudly, falling down. Reece dropped into a quick crouch to catch her. Her eyes flitted, breath shook, and the gnashing, pattering charge of the people staggered into an uneven stumble, aggressive shrieks turning to quivering gasps of confusion.

The approaching people stopped not ten metres off from the mill, arms out to steady themselves, slung into deep, silent confusion. Their mouths moved wordlessly – slowly regaining their senses. The world beyond was quiet again.

"Holy hell," Leigh-Ann whispered.

Zip blinked up at Reece. A faint smile appeared on her face. "I did it?"

"Looks like." Reece grinned. He helped her up, as one of the people asked what was going on, terrified. They looked completely lost, exchanging frightened looks, worrying over the odd collection of people before them.

Tasker moved carefully past the others, giving Zip only a brief, questioning look, before raising an authoritative hand, "Stay calm. We think there's been fumes released from the ground. You're alright now? You know where you are?" He was quick. Good. As the people checked themselves and shook their heads, he went on. "You're experiencing shock. Don't worry, I'm with the government."

"What happened *there*?" One of them noticed the wrecked mill.

A new shout came from further off in the dark. More confusion – something similar to that written on these people's faces. Tasker directed them back towards the road. "Looks like it took the whole village, huh? Let's see what's going on."

They uncertainly followed his calm direction, and Tasker led them away. He threw a look back to the others saying figure this out, follow on, and moved down the road. Leigh-Ann uttered, "She did it. Stopped them dead in their tracks just like that. Didn't she?"

"Zip," Katryzna said, suddenly at their side. Her grin had spread in mad awe. "That was . . . *wild.* I would like to formally invite you to the Congo." Zip looked up uncertainly at the woman who would surely fit *wild* better than her, and Katryzna went right on, particularly focusing on Leigh-Ann: "You can come, too? We can have a whole party."

"Fools," Mason croaked, pushing off from the wall. He stared at Zip with new malice, like she'd utterly betrayed him. By peacefully damn resolving whatever hell had been about to descend on them. Even as the sounds down the hill quietened, Tasker swiftly getting ahead of it, Mason rumbled, "You'll all die."

Katryzna flipped back to an angry shout: "Last warning, handless – not another word like that about my friends!"

"If you're so sure of the danger," Reece said, coming in past Katryzna, "then join us. Do something right with your damn life, if you care one iota for Zip. Give her the best damn chance she can get."

Mason glared vehemently. Too proud to so much as consider it. He said, "You'll bring this world to ash. Her responsibility is yours now."

"You cold motherfu –" Leigh-Ann started.

Reece put a hand on her chest, holding her back. "Suits me just fine. She's a Cutjaw Kid now, and we take care of our own."

EPILOGUE

Blood and shattered glass mingled with the rivulets of rain as people darted about trying to help one another. A cloud of general confusion hung over the village – distraught, injured people sat on low walls or helped one another clear away debris. Windows had been smashed, cars dented, pots and pans scattered across the road. Two people were seriously injured, another dead. Cuts and bruises all round, at the least. Tasker assured everyone this was a natural anomaly – trapped gases driving people from their senses, that old Ministry staple. They didn't all believe it, but what other choice was there?

As he surveyed the scene, he tried to cling onto the relief that a worse disaster had been averted. But this was everything he had feared; the horror of Laukstad on British soil. If it could take a whole village then what next? Cities? The country? Rebecca's safety was the very tip of it. Tasker held that in, though. He had the means, and the allies, to stop this spreading. He watched the criminal Reece supporting an old lady as she crossed the road, whispering encouragingly. The big-haired Leigh-Ann was with Zip, handing out plasters, and an ambulance was on its way to see to their other friend. With a little respite, at last, Tasker returned to the car where Katryzna was leaning, watching like it was a show. She said, "Will your Ministry come through with memory wipes or something?"

"No need," Tasker said. "Give it a few days and no one's going to seriously question the cause. But it's something I can really take to the Ministry now." He took out his phone, but weighed it in his hand. What was it Mason had said? *If he's Ministry, he belongs to Shearjoy.* Fully aware the MEE was at least partly compromised.

"Worried you'll get in trouble for this mess?" Katryzna asked.

"Worried I don't know how big this mess is. I haven't known

who to trust for a while."

"That's *easy*," she grinned, pushing off from the car. She patted his cheek. "You trust me. No one else. Always worked for me."

He couldn't help but smile back. "And you're gonna get us safe passage to Ikiri?"

"I can." She shrugged. "I've got my ways. And I already convinced the Americans to come – they seem like fun. Want me to get us a private plane?"

He didn't doubt she could. It would likely involve people getting hurt and wouldn't keep them hidden. Her conscience apparently took the same view, as she irritably said, to the side, "It would be for a greater good! I cannot win with you!" She rolled her eyes back to Tasker. "Rurik might not get it, but you should, Sean; I can do whatever is necessary."

"Yeah." Tasker smiled, believing that, but equally happy he still had that invisible voice in her head to help him focus her dangerous potential. "Leave the plane to me." He'd call Ward. There was no keeping her away from the mess here, after all; they could talk in person and avoid a trail. Book on a few flights, straight from the airport to a private boat, and they'd be back in Ikiri before anyone knew it. Thwart the machinations of this wicked spirit living there, use Sara's help to identify and clear up whatever members of Mason's "Legion" remained. Save the world, as Henri had so blithely put it.

As Tasker pictured the end game, his phone buzzed. No caller ID. He answered.

"Agent Tasker," a man said, voice chocolate smooth with a nondescript accent. "Is the Headhunter there?"

Tasker said nothing for a moment, meeting Katryzna's eye again. As she sensed trouble, her hand hovered over her knife, like she could stab someone down the phone. Tasker finally replied, slowly, "Excuse me?"

"You know him as Mason, I suppose? He is alive, isn't he? And his loving daughter?"

"Who is this?"

"A friend, if you want one. Or an enemy, if you choose that path. Either way, this is a courtesy call, Agent Tasker, to let you know I'll be seeing you soon." He could practically hear the man smiling down the phone. "Oh, and one other thing. If you happen to kill the child before I get there? Then I'll let your daughter live."

Tasker went silent, his heart dropping through his stomach.

"Think about it," the man said brightly. "And do tell everyone Shearjoy says hi."

A NOTE FROM THE AUTHOR

Kept From Cages has roots deep in my young writer's psyche. I've lived with Reece Coburn, Seph Mason and the mystery of Ikiri since my teenage years, when I first wrote this novel. Over a decade or so, I rewrote the whole book about half a dozen times, with very little changing, and followed it with about seven other novels in the series, including two prequels and a spin-off "what happens when Katryzna and Eyes take a boating holiday near Fiji" (one of my favourites; it was at once perhaps the funniest, creepiest and least relevant book in the series).

When I started the Ordshaw series, it was always with an intention of reviving this story a few books down the line. Coming back to it has been no small task, though, requiring ruthlessness with things that had long been established as canon in my mind, though it has brought fresh new energy too. To draw a line and release this book into the world is a strange feeling to say the least. But it's a story whose time has come, and I only hope you've enjoyed reading it at least partway as much as I enjoyed writing it (again, and again, again).

To help this book find more readers, please take a moment to leave a rating online; even just a few words can really help. You can review *Kept From Cages* online on Amazon and GoodReads.

www.phil-williams.co.uk

You can connect with me through:
Facebook: **www.facebook.com/philwilliamsauthor**
Twitter: **www.twitter.com/fantasticphil**
Email: **phil@phil-williams.co.uk**

ACKNOWLEDGEMENTS

Kept From Cages has a long history, and as such owes its current state to a lot of people who probably don't even know they were involved. Back when I first got access to the internet I pitched a lot of nonsense that would one day inform the evolution of the Legion of Ikiri, so first a big thanks to everyone that ever encountered that misguided alter-ego Zeke and the Brotherhood of EWW. My childhood friend Phil Rich, I believe, was involved when we first came up with that name. Something we might've put into a school newspaper, but the details escape me. Anyway, it's all part of it and thanks to everyone involved!

To more specific thanks, in the recent iterations, as always the biggest praise goes to Carrie O'Grady for editing this book and holding the ropey details to task. Any errors outstanding are my own. And many thanks to all those who helped me develop the cover design; in particular Stuart Bache and his SPF Cover Design community, who helped question the original design, and my fellow authors who are always supportive, Travis Riddle, Josh Erikson and Carol Park. Thanks to to my fellow authors who keep supporting me on my journey, Phil Parker, Jon Auerbach, Dave Woolliscroft, Kayleigh Nichol, Devin Madson, Richard Buxton and Steven McKinnon, and my always essential advance readers, particularly Ami Agner, Sam Stokes, Adawia Asad and Heathyr Fields.

A growing group of book bloggers are also consistently pushing me on, some of whom offer me far more time than I deserve! Massive thanks to Justine Bergman of Whispers & Wonder, Lynn Williams of Lynn's Books, Jen and Timy on Rockstarlit Book Asylum, Mihir and the team on Fantasy Book Critic, Adam and Calvin and the Fantasy Book Review team, Maddalena of Space and Sorcery, and Sarah J. Higbee on Brainfluff. There are no doubt countless more that deserve thanks, and my humblest apologies to any I've missed out.

Finally, repeated thanks to my family. My siblings, Nick, Fran, Alex and Christen, who read my most pointless nonsense, and my parents for giving me the comfortable kind of life that let me slip away into this fancies. Above all, thanks to my wife, Marta, who makes it all make sense.

About the Author

Phil Williams is the author of the Ordshaw, Estalia and Faergrowe series. Living in Sussex, UK with his wife, he also writes educational books and spends a great deal of time walking his impossibly fluffy dog, Herbert.

Also by Phil Williams

ORDSHAW SERIES
The Sunken City Trilogy
UNDER ORDSHAW
BLUE ANGEL
THE VIOLENT FAE

THE CITY SCREAMS
THE ORDSHAW VIGNETTES VOL. 1

ESTALIA SERIES
WIXON'S DAY
BALFAIR'S CONFINEMENT
AFTAN WHISPERS

FAERGROWE SERIES
A MOST APOCALYPTIC CHRISTMAS